Automata

*The Imaginative Legacy
of Jacques de Vaucanson*

Automata

*The Imaginative Legacy
of Jacques de Vaucanson*

translated, annotated and introduced by
Brian Stableford

A Black Coat Press Book

ISBN 978-1-61227-934-3. First Printing. February 2020. Published by Black Coat Press, an imprint of Hollywood Comics.com, LLC, P.O. Box 17270, Encino, CA 91416. All rights reserved. Except for review purposes, no part of this book may be reproduced or transmitted in any form or by any means, electronic or mechanical, including photocopying, recording, or by any information storage and retrieval system, without permission in writing from the publisher. The stories and characters depicted in this novel are entirely fictional. Printed in the United States of America.

TABLE OF CONTENTS

Introduction

The artist and inventor Jacques Vaucanson (1709-1782) was born into a relatively poor family, but was educated by the Jesuits and then entered the monastic Ordo Minorum in Lyon, where his talent for construction attracted patronage to work on the development of machines mimicking the forms of living creatures—something of a fad at the time, continuing a long history of such endeavors going back to Classical times—although some members of the Order apparently thought his ambition to design automata in humanoid form blasphemous, and it probably led to his secession. In 1737, he constructed a life-sized automaton known as the Flute Player in imitation of an antique shepherd, which attracted attention in the French court and established him as a pioneer in the field. It was swiftly followed by a Tambourine Player and the most famous of all his automata, the Digesting Duck, which appeared to consume and excrete food, although the process was deceptive.

Vaucanson regarded his automata merely as a device for advertising his skills as a mechanician rather than as a serious endeavor, and he gave up that kind of work when Cardinal Fleury, Louis XV's chief minister, gave him a position as an inspector of silk manufacture. He redirected his efforts to the improvement of weaving looms. He attempted to develop an automated loom half a century before Jacquard produced final solutions to the technical problems his machine addressed, and the latter succeeded—belatedly, and not without great difficulty—in persuading a few silk-manufacturers to employ his machine industrially, eventually revolutionizing the trade. At the time of his pioneering efforts, however, Vaucanson's invention only assisted his election to the Académie des Sciences and did not have any influence on industrial endeavor. He was also successful in designing a new kind of lathe, described in detail in the *Encyclopédie*, but that too failed to attain any practical industrial application at the time. When he died, he bequeathed a collection of his machines to Louis XVI, but they were destroyed during the Revolution, perhaps because too many of the active Revolutionaries, unlike their progressive intellectual supporters, regarded automation as an aristocratic plot designed to deprive workers of employment.

The results of Vaucanson's enterprise were, therefore, somewhat ironic. His endeavors in matters of industrial automation were thwarted and largely forgotten, but the ingenious toys he had built in order to advertise his skills, by stimulating the imagination, became legendary. Instead of revolutionizing the weaving industry, as he had hoped, his name became notorious as the inventor of an artificial duck that appeared to defecate. Jacquard eventually reaped all the kudos for perfecting the weaving apparatus that Vaucanson had pioneered and for his heroic resistance to the disgruntled workers who initially smashed his machines, but it was Vaucanson's legend that inspired all dreamers fascinated by the idea of humanoid automata and their potential—a potential far more symbolic than utilitarian, and thus infinitely more attractive to litterateurs. The idea of machines that could successfully mimic human form, and perhaps human ambition, became a magnet for writers of speculative fiction.

Like some of the Minims from whose religious Order Vaucanson became a renegade, some of the speculative writers contemplating the idea of humanoid automata thought it intrinsically blasphemous, and hence horrific. The most widely-read and most widely-appreciated of all stories featuring an automaton capable of being mistaken for a human being, E. T. A. Hoffmann's hallucinatory fantasy "Der Sandmann" (1816; tr. as "The Sandman"), belonged to that school. Hoffmann became as influential in France as he was in his native Germany, although his story was reprocessed as black comedy in a number of *opéras bouffes*, most famously Offenbach's *Les*

Contes d'Hoffmann (1881), and was drastically stylized in Léo Delibes' ballet *Coppélia* (1870). That kind of transposition is typical of the French attitude to the inventions of German Romanticism, and French imaginative works drawn directly from the inspiration of Vaucanson—as illustrated in the present collection—are often less nightmarish than "Der Sandmann," frequently treating the notion with a more considered and even-handed approach to its moral implications. The most celebrated of French fantasies featuring a humanoid automaton, however, Auguste Villiers de l'Isle-Adam's *L'Ève future* (1886; tr. as *The Future Eve*), in which Thomas Edison is hired to create a mechanical bride for an aristocrat disillusioned by real women, is set firmly in the Hoffmannesque mold, and the melodramatic potential of murderous machines was inevitably exploited and extrapolated, albeit with as much glee as terror.

The general idea of automation, however, remained controversial in France for the reasons that inhibited Vaucanson's industrial endeavors, partly on sentimental grounds and partly on political grounds. Pragmatic automation was lauded by many utopian socialists, in the tradition of the Comte de Saint-Simon and Charles Fourier, who saw it an important instrument of liberation from the hardship of labor, and it was enthusiastically embraced by such pioneering Anarchists as Joseph Déjacque as an essential instrument of eventual social equality, but others at the same end of the political spectrum regarded mechanization as an instrument of oppression, not merely supplanting workers but dehumanizing them, by turning them into adjuncts of the machines they operated. That notion eventually reached a melodramatic apogee in the depiction of Stahlstadt in *Les Cinq cents millions de la Bégum* (1879), initially written by the Anarchist Paschal Grousset but rewritten and signed by Jules Verne at the insistence of the publisher, and was recycled thereafter in such political fantasies as Claude Farrère's *Les Condamnés à mort* (1920; tr. as *Useless Hands*). The idea that sophisticated machines, whatever their form, might eventually replace human labor com-

9

pletely, thus usurping key human privileges, became a nightmare on a much vaster scale than the intimate one envisaged by Hoffmann: the idea that the Industrial Revolution might be followed, in the example of the crucial watershed in French history, by an Industrial Terror.

By the time that many of the stories included in the present anthology were written, in the latter decades of the nineteenth century, Vaucanson's imaginative legacy was very evident in Paris, where small clockwork automata—especially the birds manufactured by Blaise Bontems and his sons—were mass-produced in numerous workshops. All of the French authors who produced stories of automata in the 1880s would have been familiar with them. However, it was almost invariably Vaucanson that they referenced in their work, and it was from the legend of Vaucanson, especially as it had been recycled by previous works of imaginative fiction, that their own flights of fancy took wing, rather than from contemporary amusements.

The prophets were half-right, as wise prophets often are. We now live in a world where sophisticated machinery has transformed industrial endeavor in every field, and in which "robots" equipped with "artificial intelligence" are achieving a remarkable sophistication. One of the most famous of the eighteenth-century automata, the chess-playing Turk, was a fake—a human in mechanical dress, as explained in a work of speculative fiction by Edgar Poe—but modern chess-playing machines can beat anyone but grandmasters with insulting ease, The nightmares that have not yet produced actual examples are on the brink of doing so—but like all nightmares from which we cannot awake, they have simply become circumstances in which we are learning to live, savoring the advantages they bring as well as the inconveniences they generate.

That does not mean, however, that the notions developed and extrapolated in these pioneering works of fiction have become redundant, or that the tale they tell as an unruly collective is devoid of interest. It is, in essence, a tale not told by idiots, whose sound and fury is not devoid of significance. It is a tale told by seers ahead of their time, to whom the modern world gives every right to say "I told you so," and who posed a host of subtle and oblique questions, in hypothetical form, that require answers far more urgently now than when they were written.

Brian Stableford

The Mirror of Present Events
or, Beauty to the Highest Bidder
by François-Félix Nogaret

*I. Aglaonice decides to marry
and offers her hand on the conditions to be seen.*

Is it a good or a bad thing for a woman to be her own
mistress at the age of fifteen? While awaiting the solution to
that question, which has its difficulties, by virtue, on the one
hand, of the shackles of dependency, and on the other, of the
abuses that a young person might make of her liberty, I shall
tell you, my brothers, a story of times past, which it is necessary not to regard as apocryphal, for I obtained it from a genu-
ine Traveler, whose great-grandfather heard it recounted by a
sage, who had it from his grandfather, who had read it in the
Serapeon before the books in that library were employed to
heat the baths of Alexandria.[1]

Syracuse, after the memorable siege that it endured on
the part of Marcellus, finally enjoyed, although included in the
number of lands conquered by the Romans, a liberty submissive to the laws and the benefits of a profound peace. Like the
birds of spring who recall verdure after the mortal breath of
winter, the arts that the tyrants had frightened away returned to
settle in that beautiful abode. The reputation that Archimedes
has left behind attracted lovers of the higher sciences from far
away, curious to see the debris of the instruments of war that

---

[1] The Serapeon, or, more usually, Serapion, was the temple of
Serapis in Alexandria. The spelling employed by Nogaret is
employed in Claude Guyon's *Histoire des empires et des
républiques* (1736), in a passage that records that the building
housed a library.

had repelled the enemy for three years in succession, sometimes astonished by such considerable losses.

That city had never seen so many inventors of genius in
its bosom, gathered from all the corners of the earth. They
were all in an admiration that verged on amazement, all saying
that there was no genius comparable with the celebrated Ge-
ometer who had defended Syracuse for so long; but that homage was accompanied by a certain discouragement, because
none of those men, so lauded elsewhere, took the trouble to
give the slightest idea of his talents here. Thus the brilliant
light of the torch of day causes the feeble light of the stars of
night to disappear.

Aglaonice, a young woman of seventeen, orphaned of
her father and mother, having no other relatives than an older
sister, whose only wealth was a beauty of which she might be
able to take advantage, took it into her head to make all those
handsome men of genius do something. All that was required,
in order to succeed in that, was the consent of Marius Cornelius,[2] a Roman praetor, a worthy man of sixty for whom a

---

[2] Author's note: "*Marcus Cornelius, Praetor peregrinus*. Foreign Praetors governed for two years, one in the quality of
Praetor, the other in the quality of Propraetor. They presided
over all judgments, but did not judge; judgments were rendered by a certain number of elected citizens drawn from various bodies of State. It was in the Roman year 418 that the Plebeians finally succeeded in winning a victory over the Patricians in also having themselves named to the Praetorate. As I
have found in Cornelius the excellent qualities of a good Plebeian, I was curious to know his extraction. Marcellus' expe-
dition, made in the Roman year 540, more than a hundred and
twenty years after that great conquest by the Plebeians, gave
me grounds to hope that I might find in him a man of the people. My research has verified my presumption. There are honest people everywhere." The praetor in Sicily in 211 B.C.,
which is presumably the year in which the story is set, was

pretty young woman was not yet indifferent, but of a probity so recognized that the Senate, interested in capturing the hearts of the Syracusans, were convinced, with reason, that no better choice could have been made.

Aglaonice had seen the Praetor sitting in his curule chair more than once, but his imposing gravity, the ceremony resulting from a large number of Judges placed around him and perhaps also the crowd of the audience, had frightened her a little. There is, however, no way of keeping the magistracy out of the matter of marriage. One morning, therefore, without consulting the pontiffs as to whether or not it was a good day,[3] Aglaonice went to see Cornelius, and, as she found him much less serious and dressed up than with his long robe fringed with purple, she asked him cheerfully whether he would not see with pleasure all those great makers of machines, so long inactive, finally taking flight and leaving some monument to their knowledge in Syracuse.

"Certainly," Cornelius replied. "I agree that, out of a hundred things imagined by those gentlemen, ninety-nine are almost useless, but in the end, since it's recognized that one good one might be found among the hundred, it's an acquisition that is not to be disdained. What are your means, though? It's not you, presumably, who proposes to set these skillful laborers to work?"

"Excuse me," said Aglaonice.

Marcus Cornelius Dolabella, about whom very little is known, thus leaving space for Nogaret to improvise.

[3] Author's note: "The knowledge of that difference of days when one might go to ask for justice was, for a time, a mysterious science, in which the Pontiffs, or 'makers of bridges,' makers of religions, had rendered themselves the master, and which they kept carefully hidden in order to appear necessary and oblige litigants to have recourse to them. Learned citizens ended up making fun of that charlatanism." The untranslatable wordplay derives from the fact that *pont* is French for bridge.

The good magistrate started to laugh. He thought he had divined her secret, but that was an error on his part. Aglaonice was virtuous without prudishness; knowing that youth and beauty are inappreciable treasures, she thought of putting them in the balance with lucrative talents, in a way that would enable her to escape criticism.

Whatever the idea was that passed through the Praetor's head, as it is rare for a man to refuse anything to beauty, he replied: "Do as you please," and did not forbid himself to kiss her hand amorously.

The following day, Aglaonice, taxed for a long time by a youth as fickle as it was hasty, tormented and persecuted by the choice of a lover, or at least of a husband, had it published by a herald in Epipoli, in Ortygia, in Achradina and Neapolis—in sum, in all the quarters of Syracuse—that she was disposed to listen to proposals of marriage that anyone cared to make to her, but that she would only give her hand to a Mechanician who had invented some machine that would prove not only his skill but that he knew the heart of women well. As for the birth of the individual, that was the least of her concerns. *Nobilitas sub amore jacet.*[4]

II. Two aspirants present themselves; one offers a mobile tripod; the other a little ivory chariot and ship.

The original proposition of the beauty spread throughout Sicily and passed into Italy and beyond. It was not long before Aglaonice was besieged by visits. All those who believed that they had enough talent to compete wanted, before anything else, to judge the prize that was offered to them. In addition, however, the same artist appeared ten times a day; the beauty was at risk of being stifled by the crowd of her admirers. She made the decision to go and see the Praetor again, convinced

---

[4] Nobility gives way to love; the quotation comes from Ovid's *Epistles*.

that she would obtain there a lodgment that would be infinitely more secure.

Cornelius did not see without chagrin a beginning that presaged that Aglaonice would soon find a husband, but in the end, rendering justice to the thought that he was past the age of pretentions, he consoled himself with the pleasure of serving as her protector.

"I consent," he said, "to lodge you in my house and I promise to treat you as my daughter. Have no fear of the influx of a society that I understand the difficulty of keep away from you. They will be able to see you to the extent that you permit, but I shall be present and you shall have guards."[5]

She did, indeed, and did not go out without being accompanied. It was a further motive for increasing urgency and curiosity. No one was any longer talking about anything but the joy of seeing, and above all of espousing, Aglaonice.

I would never finish if I went into detail about all the things imagined in order to reach that much-desired objective. I shall pass in silence over all those that do not merit a certain attention.

The first one who came, after two long months, to present his masterpiece of Aglaonice was a species of imitator, a native of Pystira, an isle neighboring Smyrna and Petgama, who had constructed, in accordance with known descriptions, a polished steel tripod that walked on its own, so to speak, although it was necessary, beforehand, to set up the mechanisms hidden in each of its three legs.

Aglaonice, who was aiming for the useful, refused the fine present flatly, on the grounds that a tripod that did not flinch when carrying a saucepan is preferable to one that can move away from the fire.

---

[5] Author's note: "This attention on the part of Cornelius was great; it does not, however, offer anything so extraordinary as to expose it to criticism. It is well-known that the Vestals walked preceded by a Lictor when they appeared in public. Agalonice also had her treasure to guard."

That man was succeeded by a certain Mymecide of Miletus,[6] who offered the beauty an ivory chariot, wrought with so much artistry and so small that a medium-sized fly could cover it entirely with its wings. That was only half of his tribute; he also presented a pretty ship with three rows of oars, also made of ivory, with all its rigging, every bit as dainty as the chariot.

Aglaonice took great pleasure in considering those two marvels, but when she harnessed the chariot one day to a fly that was a little too big, the insect flew away, transporting the vehicle, through the window.

The ship, for which a font full of water was no less vast than the Atlantic Ocean, could no longer be found one evening when Aglaonice had invited her sister and a few of her friends to come and see it. The Praetor and the ladies were at supper in a room softly lit, not by candles but by the light of the full moon. Aglaonice, asked to show her ship, asked for the vase in which it had been deposited; the surface of the water presented filaments of a greenish hue, which extended from the center to the edges of the bowl, but there was no more ship; it had disappeared.

Aglaonice showed a great deal of ill-humor to the slaves that Cornelius had placed with her to serve her; she accused them of theft with considerable vivacity, adding nevertheless that if they had not stolen the ship, it was probable that they had been clumsy enough to throw it away thoughtlessly, since it was obvious that she was not being presented with the same water.

The Praetor, who was something of a naturalist said to her: "My lady, do not put any of those who are here to serve you on trial. The water you see in the bowl is the same in which you set your pretty trireme afloat a fortnight ago. The

___

[6] The term Mymecide is featured in Guillaume de Saluste du Bartras' dictionary of arcane words, where it is defined in the 1641 English translation as "a cunning and curious carver in small works."

green filaments that cover the surface today are nothing but Polyps, a voracious animal species whose form is infinitely variable, which one tries to destroy but only multiply by chopping them up. It's a freshwater Polyp, an ogre in miniature, that has swallowed the ship."[7] He added, in a low voice: "Such a misfortune, could surely never happen to a large vessel of prudent Lutetia."

"Lutetia!" said Aglaonice. "That's a Gaulish city. Are there polyps in cities?"

Smiling, Cornelius took one of her plump little hands, which he squeezed in both of his, and only said, by way of reply: "Aglaonice, you are charming."

"I don't understand all this gibberish," she said. "At any rate, the Miletian has not found the secret of preventing me from remaining a virgin; let him know, I beg you, that a polyp has swallowed half his hopes and that a fly has flown away with the rest."

III. The story of Téréos-clouni-ca-law-bar-Cochébas; or, the telescope without lenses.

The slave charged with that commission set out for Mymecide's house. He was stopped on the way and retraced his steps, announcing a Necromancer whose name was a mixture of Greek and Hebrew. His name was Téréos-clouni-ca-law-bar-Cochébas;[8] he had arrived from Egypt, where he had been initiated into the mysteries of the Great Goddess, and he was asking to speak to Aglaonice.

"Send him in," said the Praetor.

---

[7] The particular freshwater polyp that Cornelius has in mind is presumably a hydra.

[8] Author's note: "Téraois-téréos-clouni-ca-law-bar-cochébas is equivalent to false prophet, speculator, pickpocket, etc., etc." The Greek *tereo* can mean "observer"; Bar-Cochebas is a Latinized form of the name of Simon bar Kokhba, the leader of a Judean revolt against the Roman Empire in 132 A.D.

Meanwhile, the taps on two fountains were turned, which poured an excellent Greek wine into the cups.

"What do you have to show us that is fine and beautiful?" asked Aglaonice.

"I could, my lady," Bar-Cochébas replied, "talk to you about the secret I have or making gold, but you would doubtless think more of a talent that serves to procure it deservedly and strike good coin. Such as you see me with my long beard and my rather modest accoutrement, I have the right to hope for an alliance to which others have aspired in vain before me. Metals follow me as the trees and rocks once followed the singer of Thrace. You see this long tube of beaten iron; it is my talisman. With the aid of this machine, I can make known to you a host of objects that escape your overly short sight, and of which neither you nor anyone else can have a perfect knowledge without my help. Take, for example, my lady, the moon, from which you are presently receiving such a soft light, which you prefer to the annoying light of a hundred resinous candles, simultaneously wounding to the senses of sight and smell. The moon can serve as proof of what I say. Do you believe it to be inhabited?"

"No, in truth," said Aglaonice.

"It's something that it's necessary to suspect," said the Praetor. "Pythagoras thought that the moon is a world similar to ours, where there ought to be animals, the nature of which he could not determine."

"That is true," replied Bar-Cochébas, "and the necessary instrument that he lacked, I have devised. I will render sensible to you things even less probably that what was suspected by Pythagoras."

"That may be," replied Cornelius, whom these magnificent promises did not fail to inspire some interest. "You doubtless intend to talk about the stars, considered as so many suns, and the planetary bodies that are liberally placed around them? I'm a descendant of Anaximenes, who heard it said by Thales, who got it from Heraclitus, who had read it in the verses of Orpheus, that the stars are masses of fire, around which certain terrestrial bodies, which we cannot perceive, carry out periodic revolutions..."

"It is charming to listen to Lord Cornelius!" exclaimed Bar-Cochébas. "No one is more learned in Memphis or Babylon, and I'm tempted to believe..."

"In fact," said Aglaonice, "those are compliments indeed, but many things have been announced, and we haven't seen anything. Let's stick to the moon, Sir Mechanician, and hurry up."

Then the Israelite was seen to aim his long tube, composed of three sections devoid of lenses, whose unique property was that of directing the sight and rendering it clearer by separating the considered object from the surrounding objects.

"If the moon is inhabited," said Bar-Cochébas, "the other planetary bodies are too; whoever proves one, proves the other. Such a discovery is of incontestable utility; in any case my lady, take note of one thing: that the parts of the moon that cast the brightest light toward our eyes are massive mountains of silver; so that if we succeed, as I hope, in convincing ourselves that the planet has inhabitants, it will only need a good loudhailer to inform them of our needs. Now, if that is so, and if my lady obtains some pleasure in convincing herself of it, my rivals have nothing more to expect; it is me who will triumph; it is me..."

"Well yes," said Aglaonice. "That follows. Let's see, then."

"See my lady."

Aglaonice then drew near to the rather broad aperture of the long tube, which hid more than a quarter of her lovely face. Her left hand provided support for the body of the telescope, while her right lowered the eyelid of the other eye; her attention was entirely focused on the object of her consideration.

The Praetor, who had heard talk of mountains of gold and silver, was almost sorry to have had a serious conversation with a man who was, in the final analysis, making mock of the company, or proffering errors in good faith, which has happened to more than one scholar to whom statues have nevertheless been erected. He regarded it as possible that Bar-Cochébas had fallen into delirium, without being entirely exempt from reason in consequence.

The members of the company, including Cornelius, therefore awaited their turn impatiently to see the seas, the forests, the shiny masses, the rocks and precipices that Bar-Cochébas had advertised, and which Aglaonice had not succeeded in discovering. When each of them, one after another, had become weary of looking, someone wanted to speak to send the promise-maker away and advise him to go see whether, in all those supposed worlds, he could find a jewel similar to the one that he had dared to aspire, but they looked to the left and right and all the corners of the apartment in vain; the supposed inventor of the tube had disappeared. Aglaonice and the ladies found themselves, to their great astonishment, relieved of their purses and some of their jewelry.

The Praetor tried to catch up with the clever rogue and make sure that he never saw the pyramids again, but as his beard and cassock were found at the bottom of the stairs, it was thought that it would be a waste of time running after him. Aglaonice was not the woman of the company who had suffered most from that accident; Cornelius was not a man to let it go unrepaired.

IV. Apparent neglect on the part of physicians. Serious conversation between the Praetor and old Cyaxare, former secretary of good King Hyeron.

Meanwhile, it seemed that the orphan beauty's project had failed complete, for I count for little an heir of Euclid who talked to her about dioptrics and catoptrics and made her a long serious of propositions, the last of which—the only one that was intelligible to Aglaonice—was no more welcome than all the rest.

The days succeeded one another without any mention being heard of anything, and the beauty's self-esteem was suffering a little therefrom. She had time to think that her charms had not put such a large number of artists to work, and that they had not had the effect that she had promised herself at all.

One consoles oneself as best one can. The windows of her apartment overlooked the flowery banks of the Arethuse;[9] she frequently cast her eyes upon that spring, whose good fortune made her hope for another Alpheus. Prosperity came to her while she slept, she told herself, and she tried to go to sleep to the amorous murmur of its waves, surrendering herself to sweet thoughts and the void in her heart. She did not know that the appearances of inaction hide labor, most of it undertaken by skillful individuals, and that all of it was about to appear at once one fine morning.

The Praetor, whose age and the sacred title of Protector had eliminated from the ranks, scarcely able to talk to Aglaonice about love, conversed with her about politics, and his grateful ward deigned to listen while waiting for something better.

The Senate had charged Cornelius with analyzing the character of the Syracusans in order to discover in what manner they could be managed without embittering minds so versatile and always less submissive than independent.

Cyaxare, a former secretary of the good King Hyeron[10] came to see the Praetor from time to time. That former servant

---

[9] Author's note: "A Sicilian spring that runs through Ortygia, the quarter of Syracuse in which Cornelius was lodged." It was named after the nymph Arethusa, the object of the lust of the river god Alpheus.

[10] Author's note: "Hyeron II. The historians who have mentioned that King, an honest man, have all praised his good taste for the science and his love for the public good. 'My subjects,' he said, 'are my children and the State is my family.' Remarkable words! He was mourned like a father. Time has

had displeased the young Hyeronimus, the unworthy son of the best of princes, an insolent dissipater of the treasure destined for the embellishment of the city and to pay the defenders of the fatherland, a violator of old treaties and, in sum, a declared enemy of public wellbeing. The young insensate had perished not long before under the vengeful swords of citizens in revolt one day when he had left Syracuse to go to the land of the Leontines.

Cyaxare was no more satisfied with Hippocrates and Epycides, enterprising Praetors,[11] usurpers of limitless power, maladroit politicians whose seditious maneuvers had been the cause of the siege, because both had openly declared themselves for the Carthaginians.

The old servant spoke as an eye-witness of everything that had happened for many years; he also knew by tradition the mind and heart of the Syracusans, and, in more than one conversation with Cornelius he put his mind to giving the Senate an accurate idea of it.

"The Syracusans need a King," he told him. "They're capable of an extreme fidelity and a limitless attachment. This city has, at all times, been exposed to strange scenes. It can be compared to a sea, more often agitated by stormy winds than refreshed by the breath of zephyrs. Exposed to the most terrible revolutions, it has passed from liberty to slavery. It has groaned under the iron scepter of Denis,[12] and had breathed easy under the mild reign of the immortal Hyeron. It has sometimes been seen surrendered to the caprices of an unbri-

---

not damaged his reputation." Hiero II ruled Syracuse from 270-215 B.C.

[11] Author's note: "Praetors of the Senate of Syracuse, in the fashion of the Carthaginians." The two were brothers educated in Carthage, who held off Marcellus' siege of Syracuse for some time before the Carthaginian fleet sent to relieve the siege turned back and left the city to its fate.

[12] Denis is the French form of the name of the Sicilian tyrant Dionysius I (432-367 B.C.)

dled populace and sometimes submissive to the authority of laws.

"Such opposite extremes could be attributed to the Syracusans themselves, whose levity was their dominant character, but the primary cause of so many evils is the form of government, composed of two ever-militant powers and deprived of a third whose counterweight might have established equilibrium; with the result that liberty, too often groaning under the hand of aristocrats, rose up more than once, and rendered Sicily witness to the bloodiest scenes.

"What also renders the government of the city less easy is that its citizens, bellicose although frivolous, have not forgotten the signal victories won in Africa by their ancestors and their advantages over the Athenians, too proud of a maritime power that our people successfully disputed more than once with those rivals jealous of their glory.

"Although one has the right to say that wealth has softened the heart of the Syracusans and given them a kind of distance from all that has no affinity with games and pleasures, it must be admitted that they are nevertheless resistant on occasions to the voice of their orators, and then become capable of the greatest enterprises. The same men who went to sleep in the bosom of confidence wake up terrible and threatening, with the most superb heads, and, in their frenetic transports, massacre everything that has contributed to harming them.

"I regard them, therefore, as men inappropriate to enjoy a complete liberty or to accustom themselves to an entire servitude. They need a King, and I want that; but it is also appropriate that they should always be the masters of their own revolutions, when the utility if it is generally recognized by the most sound minds. The Prince will then enjoy the fine advantage of facilitating its execution, and everyone will be happy; otherwise, Rome will probably not have in the Syracusans a people on whom they can reliably count."

That idea of Cyraxare, of giving them another King, did not please Cornelius; he tried to make that honest man, misled by the memory of the great virtues of Hyeron—as if such sovereigns were not phenomena, to whom nature took centuries to give birth!—abandon it.

"The Roman Senate does not think as you do," he told him. "I don't know who you would designate today to reign, but you, who scarcely think of it, would be on the throne now if Rome, which makes Kings, had judged it appropriate to its own interests and those of Syracuse that the constitution of the city should be other than that of a Republic.

"Sicily conserves its ancient rights and customs, as you know, and Rome does not extend that distinction to any of its conquered lands. You are more her friends and confederates than a submissive people, as you also know, since it is true that Rome does not levy and tribute from you by the entitlement of monument and the price of victory.[13]

Sicily is Italy's neighbor; you regard yourselves as being part of it. Kings, Cyaxare, too often affect an absolute power; their procedures, stripped of the forms of justice, then become violent actions rather than. Do you count for nothing the advantage of only obeying laws that you have made yourself, and of choosing your magistrates annually? No more judges henceforth that the parties cannot remove; and it is the ad-

---

[13] Author's note: "Sicily, in becoming a Roman province, conserved its ancient rights and customs. The Sicilians were not treated like the Spaniards and Carthaginians, on whom the Romans imposed a tribute as the price of victory. *Quasi victoriae praemium ac poena belli*. Let us say everything, for the best things only last for a time. So long as Rome was only dominant in Italy, the people were governed as confederates; the laws of each republic were followed; and Sicily, which added a great deal to the strength of Rome, of which it was the storehouse and granary, was to enjoy that privilege for a long time. As Montesquieu says, however; 'Afterwards, that liberty, so vaunted, only existed at the center, and tyranny at the extremities.'" The quotation, from Cicero, translates loosely as "as if it were a reward for victory and a penalty of defeat."

vantage of the Valerian law, which ought to have all its force here as it does among us, that the people now have the right to pronounce the death penalty against the enemies of the state."

Cyaxare was not without a reply to those observations.

"As all Kings," he said, "do not resemble Hyeron, all Praetors do not resemble Cornelius, and Rome will only leave you here for a short time...but I do not want to anticipate the evils that your successors might occasion here subsequently. Let us enjoy the present; I yield to your arguments."

Thus reasoned the good Cornelius and old Cyaxare, and at those moments the Praetor scarcely thought about the annoyances of the beautiful Aglaonice, which were increasing every day, by virtue of the silence of the mechanicians on whom she had founded her hopes, and by the nature of those grave conversation, by which she was somewhat embarrassed. But Cyaxare had no sooner left the apartment than the keenest interest in favor of the lovely orphan was reborn in Cornelius' heart. He begged her pardon so obligingly for having talked in her presence about anything other than what might please her that the most passionate of men would have seemed less expressive and less amiable.

V. The Flying Chariot and the Conspirators

Thirty days had gone by since the adroit thief who made people read the stars in order to rummage in their pockets had dared, in the magistrate's own house and before his very eyes, to obtain such a good result from his villainous métier. Amour and the arts seemed to be sleeping lethargically, and the good Praetor was secretly laughing at the thought that the beauty might perhaps not succeed in finding an abode other than his own house.

As he was yielding to the deceptive charms of that pleasant reverie, however, a great ardelion arrived, a hasty valet dressed up to the nines. He came on behalf of Lord Lycaon-agrios-kai tyrannos akeirotos-kai apenès-kai polémios-Brogli-

Lam-Beden-Mail-Aristos,[14] and begged Cornelius to permit that a machine be brought into the largest and most open of his gardens, the marvelous effect of which Aglaonice would see in a few days' time. The emissary added that the public might enjoy the spectacle, because the machine surpassed the clouds.

The lord in question was a direct descendant of a Spartan, one of those who, having acquired so much glory a hundred years before under the leadership of Gylippus, has ended up, like the miser Polemarchus,[15] by tarnishing the reputation of Sparta. A considerable number of those Lacedemonians, obliged to flee, had taken refuge in Sicily.

Aristos, born in the country, had no lack of castles and fine lands. He was one of those who could not bear the idea of a perfect equality, and had not yet despaired of the success of a tyrannical plot. It did not seem credible to him that nature had given the people the same organs as patricians; he could not imagine that they were capable of governing without their help, and even less of forcing themselves to obey.

That identity of constitution with the Roman Republic did not appear to him, in any case, to be so well-established or so strongly supported that the Syracusans could not be recalled to their former regime. A daughter of the people, a poor young woman like Aglaonice, would surely not refuse to accept a sum of money or some other advantageous proposition to favor the project he had formed of entering Ortygia by night and slaughtering the garrison. However, the dangers of the project

---

[14] Author's note: "Lycaon etc. In Latin, *lupus crudelis, praestantissimus*; in French, *cruel and powerful beast*. The whole is abridged." Lycaon was a king of Arcadia who unwisely put the omniscience of Zeus to the test and was transformed into a wolf

[15] Not the Athenian Polemarchus featured in Plato but a Spartan mentioned by Pausanias, although the word was a title rather than a name and thus appears somewhat promiscuously in Greek writings.

sometimes enfeebled his hope. Then his sad joy was that of the guilty; he only laughed bitterly.

It will be remembered that the Praetor had said to Aglaonice that no one would speak to her except in his presence. That mark of attention, which only had beneficence for its objective, did not worry Aristos to the extent that he regarded it as impossible to replace Cornelius by some woman in Aglaonice's confidence. As he excelled in the art of composing his exterior, and the perfection of his hypocrisy shielded him from all suspicion, it was not difficult for him to make Cornelius understand that it was very embarrassing for a man when he had to talk about love before his fellow; that the resultant constraint made the suitor seem so awkward that it was not astonishing that no one had succeeded thus far with Aglaonice; otherwise, it was more than probable that someone would even have made her forget the conditions she had imposed.

"Oh, let that not be an obstacle," said the Praetor. "I know that she has a sister to whom she's very attached. I'll cede my place to her. I don't intend to embarrass either you or Aglaonice. If you think it advantageous to talk to her before showing her your discoveries, come tomorrow; you can chat entirely at your ease."

Aristos did not fail. The machine followed, guided by a Cantabrian, a worthy confidant of such a great lord. He too was a lord, an aristocrat of the low Pyrenees, a land of dancing where the humanity of his fellows had rendered a great many things utterly problematic. Neighbors were not neighbors. Brothers were not brothers. Fire and water only belonged to a small number of men more powerful than the rest, and although everything was common in the land, brothers and neighbors ate grass and died of thirst if they did not have the wherewithal to pay. At any rate, that lord was merely the valet of the other. Delegated to look after the machine, he had remained in the garden, accompanied by eight or ten Cyclopes, while Aristos tried to convert the two sisters to his opinions.

I cannot deny that Aristos was a man to fear in the art of tactics; he had given proof of it. As for mechanics, that was another matter; circumstance alone had made him a mechanician. One would, however, be forced to admit that he also possessed, to a certain degree, a knowledge of motive forces and equilibrium; but one would see at the same time that he was a reckless as he was vain, two great faults against which it is often good to guard.

Aglaonice, therefore, alerted to his visit, was awaiting him with no other witness than Bazilide, her sister. Aristos was introduced. It would have been stupid to open up straight away, so he adopted a light tone and only spoke at first about a discovery that promised him the advantage of meriting the hand of Aglaonice—whom he regarded as fundamentally impertinent, since she was nothing but a peasant.

"My ladies," he said, "I have learned that a rogue who aspired less to the honor of espousing you than to the profit he could obtain from his skill has robbed you of your jewels while amusing you with a telescope that he had stolen from the King of Egypt's museum,[16] which would have merited that Lord Cornelius have him whipped by his lictors. In truth, ladies, I find the Praetor and you possessed of a confidence and generosity of soul…you have not heard the history, then, of these refugees from the land of the Pharaohs?

"Anyway, the thievery of Bar-Cochébas and the trouble he must have taken are foreign to my object; let us only speak

---

[16] Author's note: "A learned Benedictine has rendered this probable. He is said to have read in an old manuscript that in the time of Ptolemy usage had been made of those optical substances by means of which hazard has since procured us the advantage of adapting lenses for approach magnification. I do not know why the quibbler L. Dutens casts doubt on the statement of that monk." The reference is to Louis Dutens (1730-1812), who published his *Recherches sur l'origine des découvertes attribuées aux modernes* [Research on the Origins of Discoveries Attributed to the Moderns] in 1766.

of his imposture—I mean the hope that he falsely gave you of revealing to you that which he was sure that you would never see. Yes, my ladies, his talisman is devoid of virtue; its mechanism is imperfect; he knew that very well; and believe that, as for his loudhailer, if he had had one, he would only have used it for himself.

"But even if you had read the stars distinctly, you would still have the regret of being separated from them by a distance that no man has thus far been able to cross. Consider the moon, and see there…what? Light and shadow; it is not of any interest from which any great satisfaction might result. The beautiful the marvelous thing, would be to transport oneself to the very heart of this planet, to see there with one's own eyes and touch with one's hands that which reason gives us the right to presume is there."

"That would be very fine, indeed," said Aglaonice, "but what means is there of getting there?"

"My lady, I flatter myself on succeeding in that; I will take you there, if you are curious to make the voyage, and if it pleases the twelve great gods, we shall marry up there."

The conversation was interrupted at that moment by the attention that each of them felt obliged to pay to a rather disagreeable sound that made itself heard, and was somewhat reminiscent of that of the friction to which the axle of a pulley that has not been greased for a long time is subject.

One could pause without error upon that conjecture; Cornelius, without anyone suspecting it, was present at the conversation, and even seated in a very comfortable armchair. A counterweight kept him suspended above floor level, in the middle of a thick section of stone wall once contrived or that purpose; a small opening made at the height of a man and masked by a light cedar-wood panel gave the listener the facility of hearing everything.

That balance, or whatever machine it might be, was not Cornelius' invention; it is easily believable that it had been used more than once when one considers that the house he occupied was the same one that had once been the residence of the tyrants. Cornelius was not one of them, but he had given some thought to Lord Aristos' proposition and, either by virtue of suspicion or pure curiosity, had made the effort to listen in.

Our three individuals were looking in all directions, anxiously, when a cat, which emerged from a neighboring room and appeared to their eyes, made them believe that the sound they had heard was merely that of the door, which the animal had caused to grate on its hinges by pushing it.

Aristos pretended to doubt that, however, and took advantage of the circumstance to explain the true objective of his visit.

"Do you feel completely secure, my ladies," he said, "in this part of the city where it is now not permitted for any Syracusan to live?"[17]

That reflection of a soldier, prompted by a cat, appeared to them to have a comical seriousness. They laughed at it wholeheartedly.

"Security is a fine thing," Aristos continued, undisconcerted. "Laugh as much as you please; for myself, I cannot accustom myself to the idea that this quarter of Syracuse is absolutely forbidden to us. It's a tyranny. For, after all, of what are they afraid? Supposing, in any case, that some good Syracusan wanted to shake off the yoke of Roman domination, would that be such a bad thing? Don't you think that an oligarchical government, composed of a few nobles, who would act in the interests of the people, would be infinitely more agreeable? You're Syracusan, my ladies: it must cost your hearts a great deal to see all Sicily thus become a Roman province."

"I don't see anyone complaining about it," replied Bazilide.

---

[17] Author's note: "As the isle of Ortygia was surrounded by two good ports, and also had a citadel, that part of the city became very important, and was reserved for the Praetor alone."

"Neither do I," said Aglaonice, "And furthermore, from what I've heard said of Cornelius is several conversations he has had with the wisest of men, I conclude that Syracuse is infinitely more fortunate in being governed in accordance with the principles of the Roman constitution that when it was necessary to obey the absolute will of the nobles. Cyaxare, the sage to whom I'm referring, doesn't think differently today."

"In that case," said Aristos, "I bear in my heart for your Cyaxare all the amity that I have vowed to the Demagogues. What a citizen!"

"But Monsieur," said Bazilide, "If it were the case that the Syracusans wanted to change situation now, it would be necessary for rivers of blood to flow; the walls of the city would be stained by it; let us try to forget it..."

"The conversation has certainly changed direction," said Aglaonice, looking at Aristos. That is not, I think, the motive that brought you here, my lord?"

"No other than that of uniting himself with you could animate anyone who has the good fortune to know you, and although you live here in the Praetor's house, people think too well of you to presume the good fortune of that aged foreigner."

"He serves me as a father," said Aglaonice. "I beg you to speak better of him."

"Good—but the advantage is all on his side. You would have had no lack of men as hospitable."

"Let us talk," said Aglaonice, "about what your talent for the mechanical arts has led you to undertake, or break off the conversation..."

Aristos thought that the young woman, whatever she said, was not sufficiently grateful not to allow herself to be caught by the charms of vanity.

"Well, my lady," he said, "on the subject of the machine about which you are questioning me, I will confide a secret to you that you will doubtless keep for me, when you know that it was constructed by design to favor the passion that I have for you. Beautiful as you are, you are born to reign; and I shall think about that from now on. If one could do at a stroke everything that one would like to do...

"But before anything else, it is necessary for this city to shrug off the yoke.[18] What you have to do in that circumstance cannot be treated as rebellion. Rome has stolen our liberty; nothing is more natural than that we should recover it."

"It was to liberate us, and not to dominate us," said Bazilide, "that the Romans battled our tyrants, and with them the Carthaginians who served them as supporters. The majority of us, animated by a long resentment, hoped to be defeated in order not to remain forever enslaved..."

Aristos had said too much for the ladies not to be tempted to denounce him to Cornelius. Aglaonice thought that it would be as well to know everything. Pallor, however, had spread over her face...

"One could listen to you for a long time," she said, if it were possible to have the slightest hope, but I foresee that too many citizens would be the futile victims of it."

"Don't be afraid," said Aristos. "It's not a matter of killing them all; a certain number would suffice. I can answer for a good third who are not as obdurate as your Cyaxare. Then again, we have a few intelligent men, especially the leaders. But the essential thing would be for me to be able to get in here under cover of darkness."

"And what would you do here?" asked Aglaonice.

"The salvation of Syracuse depends on the death of all the soldiers there are around this palace. Deliver them to my vengeance; immediately afterwards, I'll take you away. As for the Praetor, I consent to show him mercy if you still deign to take an interest in him..."

---

[18] Author's note: "Although this is only a historiette—which is to say, a mixture of fiction and truth, I am not so very far from the truth, from the history that serves as my basis. After the capture of Syracuse by Marcellus, there really were residual wars on the part of the partisans of tyranny, and it is also true that those wars had no consequences."

Aglaonice shivered.

"Then," he continued, "instead of only being the wife of an obscure citizen, you would command them all in the quality of the wife of one of the foremost in the State. Look...this machine that I've constructed can transport me to unknown regions. I've said more to you; I've spoken about the Moon, and I really don't despair of going as far as that..."

At this point, Aristos' eyes, and his entire physiognomy, no longer depicted anything but a man gone astray; his mind became unhinged at that moment.

"Now," he went on, "since the populace, whom we've tried in vain to seduce, is too stupid to listen to pour proposi-tions; since even our soldiers refuse to obey us, it's not moun-tains of gold that I'll go to search for up there; we have no lack of them. It's men that we need: a hundred machines like mine will bring down an entire army. The reservations of kin-ship won't hold them back like imbeciles in the presence of others. Thus, my lady, your individual happiness, mine and that of our partisans will be assured forever. As for the Ro-mans, Carthage will stand up to them again..."

The ladies scarcely heard the end of his speech. The madness of which he had just given proof in talking about his lunar army had given them time to recover their wits, and they ended up uttering a new burst of laughter, which did not fin-ish. Politeness demanded, however, that they justify that spe-cies of incivility. They gave him to understand that he ought not to interpret it as anything but the effect of a doubt, very pardonable in women whose knowledge was not as extensive as his. As it seemed necessary, at the same time, that they get rid of him, they flattered his hopes, pressing him to attempt the aerial voyage whose success was the only means of convinc-ing them that it was his destiny to make his party dominant and drive the Romans out of Sicily.

The double temerity of Aristos blinded him too much for him to doubt the sincerity of Aglaonice's final words. He took his leave of her and went straight into the garden to rejoin his dear Cantabrian, whom he took to one side in order to tell him what had happened. Then he went to the machine, to give the order to make it ready to take off.

VI. The tragic end of Aristos and the Cantabrian lord.

Aristos had not reached the bottom of the staircase when the Praetor appeared in the apartment with an expression as cheerful as usual, still gallant, and asked Aglaonice whether that equivalent of a private conversation had produced a good effect. The ladies did not know whether to laugh or adopt a serious attitude.

"You aren't saying anything!" said Cornelius. "Is that because your heart is already captured?"

"It's necessary to tell you," she replied, "and I can't hide it from you, that that lover, if he is one, is nothing but a monster that it's necessary to stifle immediately."

Cornelius secretly enjoying that sentiment of indignation, pretended to interpret it to Aglaonice's advantage.

"You're so charming," he said, "that it would be necessary to forgive a man who lost his head in your presence a good deal."

"It's not a matter of that," said Bazilide, excitedly. "Rather make sure of Aristos; he has formed a project to murder everyone in Ortygia, and your person is not safe from him."

"What! Is that all?" said Cornelius, smiling. "Oh, my ladies, you're accomplices. Why, Aglaonice is hiding it from me that she might have become Queen? However, she has every interest in my making her fortune; I even like her enough to assure her that a crown of flowers placed on her head by an honest citizen would honor her more than a diadem that she would receive from the hands of a new Agathocles."[19]

You can imagine the surprise of the two ladies at that observation by the Praetor; they looked at one another without saying a word.

---

[19] Author's note: "The tyrant who caused Syracuse to lose the liberty rendered to it by Timoleon."

Cornelius extracted them from their embarrassment by revealing the manner in which he had learned everything.

"Have no fear," he said to them. "There's more extravagance than reason in your Aristos' project. However, prudence requires that he presume that you have kept his confidence secret from me; otherwise, I shall be forced to take action, which would assuredly be futile. You'll see that within two hours, Aristos will have rid us of his presence.

Cornelius then went into the garden, as if he knew nothing about Aristos' perfidy, in order to see the preparations of the machine. It was a light chariot, to which to large wings had been fitted made of a fine linen fabric, supported by long struts of whalebone gathered together at the point where each wing was attached, and divergent that the opposite extremity. Those two wings took the place of wheels. They were deployed with the aid of hidden springs that were activated by means of a handle; then extended above the chariot, which they covered with their vast span, offering to the curious eye a motto that was not Aristos': *As the wind transports.*[20]

Time was pressing; they hastened to smear it, while waiting to be able to kill the author.

An awkwardness on Aristos' part had doubled the means. To the swingle-bar of the vehicle were hitched two large swans, which he had received as a present from a descendant of Cycnus, King of Liguria, and a relative of Phaeton.[21]

Aristos mounted his chariot. The springs continuing to move, the vast wings beat the air with so much force and

---

[20] The phrase *Autant en emporte le vent* [As the wind transports] subsequently became the French translation of the title of Margaret Mitchell's novel *Gone with the Wind* and the film based thereon. Nogaret doubtless derived it, as Mitchell did, from *Isaiah* 64:6: "our iniquities, like the wind, have taken us away." The "us" to which the Biblical verse refers are sinners.

[21] Cycnus of Liguria, who killed himself after Phaeton's fall, was probably his lover, so "relative" is euphemistic.

speed that the vehicle and its conductor rose up more than six hundred feet, always diminishing in volume, to the extent of soon seeming to be nothing but an owl. It was remarked at the machine's departure that the swans would have sufficed,[22] or that they were surplus to requirements, because the machine carried them away vertically, while they were making an effort to fly straight ahead. A worse augury was, however, that one of them was singing; that was the trumpet of death.

---

[22] Author's note: "Swans have been successfully employed for this purpose, it is said, by the Emperor Ki three thousand years before the Montgolfiers. See the *Memoirs on the present state of China* by Père le Comte, letter VI. A celebrated writer of our days believed it very sincerely, and I do too." The "celebrated writer" is Bernardin de Saint-Pierre, who commented at length in *Études de la nature* (1784) on Louis Le Comte's account in *Mouveau mémoire sur l'état present de la Chine* (1696), although he pointed out that other sources attributed the tale to the Emperor Tam, who reigned two thousand years after the (mythical) Kieu, or Ki.

A later version of the story, in *L'Antipode de Marmontel* adds a supplement to this note: "The Marquis de Vargas Machuca, it is said in a Naples gazette, possesses a manuscript printed in Bergamo in 1670 containing a long treatise on a "flying ship," which, with the aid of four copper balls, rose up to a certain height. The author explains the construction of those balls, and how the vessel can be steered with sails and oars. Another Italian writer, Bouilly, wrote the above in 1679, closely approaching Montgolfier's idea. He thought of enabling us to swim in the air, as fish do in water 'with the aid of a bladder that will be filled with a fluid lighter than the atmospheric air.'" The first reference is to a hypothetical design for a flying ship published by Francesco Lana de Terzi. The subsequent reference to an Italian document of 1679 is enigmatic, and Bouilly is not an Italian name, although by 1800 Nogaret would have been familiar with the French writer and Revolutionary Jean-Nicolas Bouilly.

Cornelius, then having no more to do than look up, had rejoined the ladies. A crowd of people had come from all directions to see the spectacle. The men, prompt to judge, said of Aristos that he had more genius than all the physicists of previous centuries, and that he would cause Icarus and the sun's bastard to be forgotten. One enthusiast even sustained that if the great Marcellus had been a witness to that prodigious ascension, he would be bound to agree that even Archimedes, a man so knowledgeable about statics that he called him a Briareus,[23] might not have imagined such a vehicle.

At the moment when the ecstasy reached its peak, however, a westerly wind plunged into the wings of the aristocratic machine and made it quit the vertical direction. The chariot, then drawn by the swans and pushed by the wind, followed a route parallel to the horizon, much more rapidly than the conductor would have wished.

It was about to brush, at the entrance to the port of Trogile, the tip of the Timoleon beacon, a famous obelisk two hundred feet high erected in memory of the liberty rendered to the city by the Corinthian captain, who defeated Denis and the Carthaginians. They thought that it was the end of Aristos, and that he was about to perish, hooked there. Let us leave him for a moment fluttering around the fatal luminary.

It is not possible, my dear reader, that you do not have some interest in his faithful Cantabrian and that you are not so much sorry as surprised not to see him here in the same cabriolet; I ought to tell you that, if he did not take his leave of the company too, it was because it had been agreed that he would remain behind for the benefit of service. His instructions included putting the world on the alert and also that, as a faithful observer of the voyage, he would be the first to publish an account of it. But it is necessary to show you the degree of

---

[23] Livy claims that Marcellus referred to Archimedes as a "geometrical Briareus" while complimenting him (posthumously) on his contributions to the defense of Syracuse, Briareus being a mythical giant with fifty heads and a hundred arms.

elevation to which the zeal of his minister bore him. He dominated all the spectators; he was on the platform of the citadel; he perched higher still...

Imagine twenty vigorous men, lined up in a square, their backs bent, with both hands on their knees, in the guise of flying buttresses. On those strong arches pose twenty standing men, their arms extended, holding very firm. Above those men are placed others, each of whose feet is carried on the shoulders of the robust champions forming the first stage—and so on, always diminishing and varying the attitudes. Suppose, finally, a pyramid whose summit is terminated by four men, arms in the air, sustaining a shield, on which our faithful confidant is standing, his eyes turned toward the beacon where his friend is in great danger. One presumes that his head is spinning at that spectacle, and that he is about to fall backwards on to the parvis.

He does, in fact, fall, but the cause has not been divined. The need or the desire to sneeze grips a good plebeian who is there, a near neighbor in the pyramid, his elbows leaning on the parapet. With the effort that he makes to disengage his head, his body being bent double, his backside bumps into that of one of the curbed Atlases making the angle and base of the pyramid. Instantly, all of them tip over, all of them fall. The Cantabrian and twenty of his caryatids tumble pell-mell to the feet of the walls of the citadel, like the Gauls once precipitated from the Capitol; but misfortune determines that a part of the military band placed there to play a fanfare at the departure of the vehicle perishes with them.

Music-stands, instruments, players and spectators were scattered everywhere. As for the rest of the children of Bel Babel Belphegor, who had only collapsed on one another and the Paros marble paving the platform, the majority were only crippled. But the poor plebeian, on whose body three quarters of the mass had landed, was so maltreated that only one breath remained to him. That was to finish like the terrible blind man who was crushed with the satraps, persecutors and tyrants of the Hebrews on whom he had wanted to take revenge. But the character of the dying man was not such as to be worthy of such noble comparisons. He had been cheerful all his life and he said, as he rendered his last sigh, that every cloud has a silver lining.

Let us now return our gaze to the winged machine and its conductor. A cry of dolor made itself heard on the part of a number of confederates placed here and there on the long chain of fortifications raised on the landward side and all along the coast. But the tragic end of Aristos would not have made enough noise if the Syracusans had been the only witnesses. The Gods wanted the death of that new Bellerophon to serve as an example to a large number of peoples.

A southerly wind, more impetuous than the first, carrying him away from the obelisk, caused him to traverse the Sicilian Sea and drive him in a straight line more than a hundred and twenty miles from Syracuse toward the northern entrance of the strait of Messina, a dangerous passage, where the gulf of Charybdis is located and the dogs of Scylla are heard barking incessantly. As he was completely lost to sight, it was necessary on either side to wait until the next day to discover what might have become of him.

Cavaliers dispatched by the Praetor, well mounted on Arab horses, set off for Messina at full tilt, and toward the evening of the following day, reported that the voyager, drawn down toward the sea, after having bobbed for a long time between the two reefs, had finally fallen on to the pointed rocks of Scylla, where laborers had even shown them the debris of the chariot, still suspended there. As for the individual, as no vestige of him had been found, the cavaliers added that the sea had surely engulfed him, along with all his great names.

That conjecture seemed as probable as it was satisfying to Cornelius and the ladies. However, those Syracusans who, not being fully informed, had only seen in the ascension of the machine a novelty in the success of which they were interested, were genuinely afflicted by the accident. As it was a discovery of which centuries to come would surely not fail to take advantage, however, and the invention would be attributed to them, their chagrin did not last long. On the part of the conspirators, it was mortal. All of them—with the exception of two, who threw the few drachms they had received in the faces of the others—departed for Messina, and engraved the following epitaph on a slab of marble they embedded in the rock:

It is noble, it is great, to fall from so high.

VII. The Flute-Player

"Another marriage failed," said Cornelius to Aglaonice, when the cavaliers had left his apartment. "It's a pity that I'm over sixty; no one could console me better than you for the annoyances of widowhood. A little vanity leads you to demand extraordinary things. If I read your heart correctly, your desires have the simultaneous objectives of youth, talent and fortune. If you were less pretty, you would not deserve to be pardoned for that excess of ambition. It would be necessary to diminish the extent of your pretentions, removing youth, for example, and the creative spirit so prejudicial to men who have too precipitate a confidence in their discoveries. Fortune is in my power; let it finally be sufficient for you, since you are now convinced that your mechanicians cannot succeed in contenting you."

"You would like me to limit myself to the advantages of fortune," Aglaonice replied. "Pardon me, my dear protector, but I am not sufficiently mistress of myself to stop there, and I believe you to be too generous to demand it of my gratitude. Let me tell you frankly that you have divined the secret of my heart. Yes, I do indeed aspire to everything that you have just explained in three words. But you despair of the accomplishment of my desires, while I have the greatest confidence in their fulfillment. The less one succeeds the more one strives to succeed. Self-esteem, and the desire to be talked about do indeed enter into it for two thirds, but you will allow me the small vainglory of attributing the rest to myself. Come on, agree that I merit grace on that article. You have said such flattering things to me so many times that it would cost me too much to think that you were deceiving me."

Aglaonice was not flattering herself without treason. Soon, two new competitors appeared on the scene, whose masterpieces would have caused hesitation over the choice if, when two things are equally admirable, the preference were not due to the one that brings a greater profit.

Of the two men in question, one, aged fifty, was an honest German, or rather a good Frank, a free man whose forefathers had lived on the banks of the Ister. One might have taken his talents and his politeness for Thamyris of Eritrea, a descendant of the celebrated Thamyris known as the rival of the muses. Our ancestors were not all as amiable.

As for his name, it resembled all the others, flaying the ears; it was Wak-wik-vauk-an-son-Frankestein. He excelled in the divine art of harmony, without every having learned music, and furthermore, was a very skillful mechanician. His bearing and his physiognomy did not leave Cornelius without anxiety from the moment he appeared before Aglaonice, tall of stature, clad in a narrow surcoat that, not descending below the knees, showed off the entire framework of that handsome body.

His homage consisted of a laminated metal statue as tall as a man, dressed in the Sicilian fashion, seated in a rolling armchair and holding a flute in each of its hands, which he announced that it would play at will. The figure could play twenty-two tunes, a list of which Frankestein gave to Aglaonice, saying to her: "You shall judge, my lady, whether there is a mortal that can refrain from falling at your feet. Command, and bronze itself will obey."

Aglaonice only convinced herself with difficulty that the automaton could fulfill such a fine promise, and Cornelius was even more incredulous, for he had never heard it said that a man had, so to speak, created his fellow. They both approached the statue, which bowed in their presence, and astonished them so much by that beginning, retaining the phenomenon of animal economy, that they took two steps back; they

43

thought it organized by a divine hand, as if there had been something to fear in assuring themselves of the contrary by touch, they recovered their composure, and drew away from it to a certain distance.

Impatiently, Aglaonice ordered the statue to play one of the advertised twenty-two tunes, which she designated. That air slowly expressed the chagrins of a heart ulcerated by amour. The statue, putting the two flutes to its mouth, far surpassed Aglaonice's expectations; she heard it extract the most varied sounds from the two instruments and execute the two parts marvelously. The prodigy caused her an emotion so keen that she almost fainted, her head leaning on Cornelius' bosom; he only brought her round by ordering the statue to play a livelier tune.

The author of that admirable invention had his share of modesty; he was flattered to have interested Aglaonice, but did not have the pride to believe that he would be her husband in consequence.

"I desire very keenly," he told her, "to have merited the possession of charms that would make the happiness of my life, but you are too amiable for me to be the last to have attempted prodigies in your favor. I saw, as I came in here, a man who is unknown to me, younger than me, covering with a veil the tribute he has brought you, and who, believing some regard to be due to the maturity of my age, demanded that I go ahead of him. If he is victorious over me, I shall be chagrined, but I shall not display any jealousy; I shall, on the contrary, see with pleasure that he has talents superior to mine; I shall believe that the gods have inspired him expressly to please you and I shall be more certain than ever that beauty can obtain the impossible."

It was not the ready-made jargon of an insipid gallantry that emerged from Frankestein's mouth; it was the expression of truth escaping a sensitive heart. Aglaonice resisted momentarily the invitation of that man, who was doubly interesting, by virtue of his talent and a modesty that increased its value. It is probable that she was composing herself, and secretly inter-

44

rogating herself as to whether she might not give him her hand; but as the Praetor whispered in her ear that she should distrust her senses, and she reflected that music is only a delightful thing for people who have dined well, she said to him, honestly:

"Sir, you can dispense with making entreaties on behalf of the person you have announced to us; you must believe that you will not be surpassed by anyone. Your colleague, who is surely not your rival, will only enter if you request it; we shall see him with pleasure render further justice to your talents, and assure you a triumph too modest for such a sublime art."

Frankestein insisting, the order was given to introduce the young man in question.

VIII. Nictator. His masterpiece.
The marriages of Aglaonice and Bazilide.

Nictator—that was his name—was a descendant of the shepherds of Chaldea, to whom the system of the heavens was known, almost as to the gods themselves. He had all the enlightenment of his ancestors, but in addition had devoted himself to mechanics, a science in which he had made progress that surpasses the conjectures of the human mind. He was also endowed with a perception that it was difficult for anything to escape, so that, after mature reflection, he had really been able to combine the agreeable and the useful.

Frankestein's flute-player had entered the apartment like an invalid who cannot make use of his legs; this time, as soon as the doors opened, a woman was seen to advance clad in the manner of vestals, walking without anyone's support. It was only when she had taken twenty paces that the handsome young man who was the father, taking her by the hand, presented her to the three individuals making up the company, raising his eyes to look at Aglaonice and lowering them immediately for fear of offending her.

Aglaonice perceived that, and blushed at the appearance of the new suitor. The nymph that he introduced to her deployed so much grace that she was obliged to suppose infinitely more of the person who had transmitted them. Without knowing what the statue was about to do, already vanquished by the seductive manner of its author, but taking a violent grip on herself in order to hide the sentiment he had made her experience, she said:

"Do you have enough confidence in yourself not to fear challenging an artist of whom Olympus might be jealous, as we are assured it once was of Prometheus? Still so young, you suppose that you have talent enough to put your work in parallel with the most extraordinary that they have ever engendered? Listen and judge..."

Then, in spite of the entreaties of Frankestein, who refused, Aglaonice had the statue play several tunes. Nictator was delighted by it, but the imposing tone of Aglaonice, and that marked predilection for a statue from which such melodious sounds emerged, so powerful upon a woman's heart, intimidated him to the point that he thought he was dismissed.

"That masterpiece has a right to please you, beautiful Aglaonice," he replied. "I thought that an artist more skillful than me would succeed in gaining your heart, and that it was an advantage reserved for experience, the companion of maturity. Music has charms for you... I have reflected a great deal, but that means of pleasing you, which is not foreign to me, has escaped my foresight! If I had been fortunate enough to think of it, perhaps the love that inspired me would not have left me at an extreme distance from my rival; but since, in sum, that victorious idea did not present itself to my mind, forgive me; I leave confused, even making a kind of crime of the hope with which I flattered myself."

"Stay," exclaimed Frankestein, "stay, amiable young man. My lady, if the idea of charming you with sounds has not offered itself to his mind, mine lacked the thought of imitating the laws of nature. I have not given my statue, as he has, progressive moment so natural that it imposed itself on me at first sight, so that an inanimate body appeared to me to be a living being."

"Let us see," said Aglaonice, "what this statue can do..."

She represented Plenty. She was seen standing up, bearing lightly in her fingertips the orifice of a long horn, artistically sculpted, containing fruits of a ravishing beauty; the other hand supported the curled extremity of the horn; and the motionless statue awaited stimulation. Under her drapery, however, a young child was hidden, who, as if giving in to a surge of impatience, raised the flap of the long robe under which he was buried, and, drawing a little bow, sent forth an arrow, terminated, not by gilded iron but by a rose-bud. That dart, directed at Aglaonice's heart, did not miss the target at which the mischievous bowman had taken aim.

A hidden trigger, adroitly brought into play, had caused the arrow to depart; another lowered the drapery under which the child had the appearance of mischievously taking refuge. That entire maneuver had taken place without any jerkiness or mechanical sound—in sum, in a manner so true that Aglaonice saw Amour himself in the little automaton.

She sensed all the amiability of such a declaration and could not help freeing herself from the cold reserve under which she might still have enveloped herself in order not to respond to it. Nature was the stronger. Aglaonice turned her tender eyes toward Nictator, stood up, extended her arms to him, fell back on to her seat, and let slip a question that laid bare the hasty wishes of her heart:

"Nictator...will you love me?"

Nictator remained silent; the statue spoke, saying: "Yes."

"What have I heard?" said Aglaonice. "Am I mistaken? It's your work that replied to me? No, it's you...it's you...but you're so timid that you fear to put yourself forward. Do you believe, then, that you haven't yet done enough?"

The statue replied: "No." At the same time, she took a step forward and offered the beautiful fruits contained in her horn to Aglaonice.

Aglaonice, deceived by the appearance, broke one, which she thought she could share with the ecstatic old Praetor, but the two lobes, coming apart, let slip into her hand large

47

diamonds and gems of every sort. A second fruit contained Oriental pearls of surprising dimensions.

The horn was inverted over Aglaonice's dress, and eventually covered it with more than a thousand gold coins; that river seemed inexhaustible. The beauty thought that she had been transported to a new world,

Then Nictator threw himself at her knees. "Forgive me," he said. "A thousand pardons, adorable Aglaonice, if, to the efforts that my art has attempted in order to please you, I have dared to join something more, but which you will agree is truly useful. Blind fortune has, it is said, forgotten you; I am only a shepherd, but if you judge me worthy of repairing a neglect so insulting, come with me to Chaldea."

"Go with him," said the Praetor. "I don't believe that you'll find such a handsome fellow, a man as rich and an artist as skillful in the entire world."

"Assuredly not," said Frankestein, in a enthusiastic manner, "and it is not difficult for me to admit it, as if I have told you. But my lady, since my statue was designed for you, deign to accept it, and that I shall at least carry away to my homeland that it has had the approval of a young man of whom, at my age, I would glory in becoming the pupil."

Aglaonice, incapable of taking aboard all that struck her eyes and ears at once, remained mute for some time. Finally, she said: "Dear Nictator, my desires are fulfilled beyond my hopes; I will go with you anywhere, I abandon myself to you; but since, by a stroke of fate above my merit, I find myself enjoying a happiness that a queen would envy, listen: I have a sister not as young as me; she is no longer pretty, but she is beautiful and worthy to make the happiness of an amiable man. If I had not given myself to you, Frankestein would have become my husband. I shall not offer him in exchange for his statue the magnificent gifts that I have just received from the hands of Plenty; give me the pleasure of enriching my sister with then, and that she should marry that gallant man. These jewels will be her dowry."

At these words, Frankestein, Nictator and the Praetor all began talking at the same time. The last abruptly gave orders for someone to fetch Aglaonice's sister, and for a magnificent feast to be prepared.

Frankestein was not unaware that the gravity of his fifty years was ill-fitting with the petulance of seventeen "Take back the jewels," he said, "and I'll accept."

"No," said Nictator, "no; and you don't have the right to refuse them, since it's not to you that they're offered. Do you want to wound the pure sentiment emanated by sensibility itself? Aglaonice does not want to be happy alone; she could not be. Be my friend, be my brother..."

"I shall be both," replied Frankestein, swiftly, with tears in his eyes, throwing his arms around him. "Young man, you have vanquished me today in everything."

Meanwhile, the tables were laid and Bazilide came in. I have no need to depict for you that new scene, in which the most tender sentiments succeeded surprise. The four individuals swore an eternal love in the presence of the Praetor.

Night was approaching; it was the perfect hour for celebration. Two thousand candles were lit around the palace, spreading a light that rivaled the light of day. In the middle of the island a flaming pyre was distinguished, composed of odorous wood, the symbolic blaze of which announced to the spouses that it was a law for them to maintain the household. The apartments were also embalmed by the perfumes of a hundred cassolettes, the voluptuous furniture of kings, which had never served such a beautiful occasion. The husbands supped with their wives that day, although it was not customary, but it will be remembered that the ladies were orphans, and could consequently do as they liked.

IX. The Last Supper.

The supper was all the more agreeable because there were only five guests and everyone could make themselves heard. The conversation, in consequence, went on long into the night. Each of them talked about the customs of his home-land.

Aglaonice's little ship came back to mind—or, rather, she remembered a comparison of sorts that the Praetor had made on the subject of its disappearance.

"Sir," she said to Frankestein, "I have a question to ask you. I had an ivory miniature, a charming little ship, which fell prey to polypes in a vase where I had left it. The Praetor told me at the time that the great ship of Lutetia would not have suffered such a fate. I know that Lutetia is a city in the land where you reside; of the remainder I am very ignorant. Give me, I beg you, the key to that enigma."

"Madame," said Cornelius, anticipating Frankestein's response, "it would have taken me a fortnight to explain that remark to you, which I repented as soon as it had escaped me. If I kept silent thereafter, it was less an impoliteness than an attention on my part. The idea came to me that boredom might ensue; and that was not too poor an augury at the time, for remember that since then, Cyaxare did not amuse you when he came to talk politics with us. But since, at present, your happiness is assured, one can without displeasing you, entertain you with something other than the sole object that could interest you then. I shall join with you in asking Frankestein to satisfy your curiosity; he will acquit himself better than me in that task."

Bazilide also joined forces with her sister in testifying the same urgency.

"My ladies," said Frankestein, "you have heard the Praetor; he spoke of nothing less than a fortnight to leave nothing to your desire, and he was not deceiving you. Fourteen days, pass, but not nights, I beg you, or I shall think you have the malign project of abusing your rights. We have all the time we need to understand one another; permit me to abridge.

"Lutetia is the capital of Gaul and its inhabitants are one of the sixty-four peoples who make up that formidable republic. The coat-of-arms of that city represents a ship, a symbol of the worship it renders to the goddess Isis, who has enriched it with wheat and the fruits that are harvested there in abundance. Isis herself was the pilot of the ship that carried that precious cargo.

"You can appreciate that gratitude made it a duty to consecrate that floating house as an eternal monument to such a great benefit. But as the vessel had made a long journey, it was not possible to conserve it for very long. Another was constructed, similar in form but of much greater dimension, whose flanks were also more solid. That second vessel, the emblem of the first, has nevertheless been replaced ten times, and the Lutetians always give it more strength and volume every time they construct a new one.

"That edifice, once afloat, does not cast off its moorings; it is perpetually at anchor between a pastureland surrounded by the waters of the Seine, known as the Isle of Swans, and the muddy island on which the building of Lutetia commenced more than six hundred years ago, from the moment when I am speaking to you. The siege of Troy and the reign of Sesostris are the epochs of its foundation; Rome did not exist and we Germans had not yet penetrated into Gaul.

"The ship of Lutetia was well-guarded on the two banks by a good number of citizen soldiers. I have also seen it served by the Druids that live there and the nymphs of the Seine who serve them as wives—without, however, losing their quality as virgins."

"How is that?" asked all the guests, simultaneously

"Such is the effect of the communication of peoples, that along with the best things, the most prejudicial are introduced. Isis, at the same time as she gave the inhabitants of the Seine the what she had taken from the banks of the Nile, also brought them the execrable abuse of the most civilized, and hence the most corrupt, people on earth. There exists in Memphis a very great distinction between the 'children of the Gods,' or 'children of the Vessel,' and the 'children of Men.' Young women, after having given birth in the vessel to a few babies 'of the Gods,' emerge therefrom and are espoused as virgins by the 'children of man.' The reason is quite simple;

there is such a vast inequality between the Almighty and humans that a young woman who has enjoyed the caresses of an Almighty is presumed to have gained by that celestial commerce and to be worth more for the earth than an entirely new young woman."

"Oh, what stupid credulity!" exclaimed Nictator. "And the inhabitants of Lutetia adopted that unworthy refinement of theocratic pride and lust?"

"What do you expect?" Frankestein continued. "It was not examined at first; people yield with heads bowed to superstition; devils appear to be celestial creatures; then evil pullulates like weeds, and it's the devil of a job to uproot it. For a long time, the Kings of Lutetia did all that they could, without success, to make the people lose confidence in the Druids, but the latter were dangerous, especially when they combined their ascendancy with the power of the nobles, or Iarles,[24] petty Regules that swarm in Gaul, and whose combined strength has more than once shaken the throne of the sovereign, to whom they give no other title that that of 'general of conquering soldiers.'

"'No one dared, for a long time, to resist the Druids, who took sole charge of the education of the young in order to inspire them early on and in an unalterable fashion with the most horrible opinions. Iarles have been seen to have the right of life and death over vassals whom they governed to their profit. Those two classes of citizens, one of which employed cunning and the other force to make itself feared, were balanced against one another, but they joined forces to tyrannize the people, whom they treated with sovereign scorn. I've seen that a man of the people could not succeed, among the Gauls, in fulfilling a public responsibility; it seemed that the nation was

---

[24] The Iarles are featured as contemporaries of the druids in Bernardin de Saint-Pierre's romance *L'Arcadie* (1781), which is set in a mythical ancient Gaul, from which the allegorical elements of this anti-clerical and ant-aristocratic tirade are taken.

only made for the priests and the aristocrats. Instead of being consoled by the former and protected by the latter, as justice required, the Druids frightened in order that the Iarles could oppress.'[25] The Kings who were most successful were, however, those who overtly took up the defense of the weak."

"You speak of all that," said Aglaonice, "as something past."

"A considerable fraction of those abuses no longer exists, in fact," Frankestein replied. "The Nation itself has destroyed them; but not without difficulty. It was first necessary to make the truth known everywhere, leaving no doubt as to the rapacity of the Iarles, who, taking advantage of the facile generosity of the King, had themselves given under the title of recompense, the major part of the tax revenue, which reduced the people to languishing in opprobrium, only procuring their subsistence be serving in the manner most dishonorable to humanity. It was necessary to prove that the Druids had caused weak minds to give them so many arpents of the best-yielding land that they alone possessed a third of the wealth of the republic of Gaul, without, however, wanting it to be touched, without contributing, other than under the title of loans, to the settlement of the State's debts; and that their intolerance had occasioned massacres that, if they were renewed, might depopulate the land. It was necessary to climb on to trestles to make the people hear that the king's counselors, charged with sending dispatches, abused his name, depriving honest citizens of their liberty in order to have their wives, and were no less predatory than the brigands stifled by Hercules. It was necessary to prove, in sum, that the plague was in the vessel.

"Weary of the miseries resulting from these tyrannical powers, the inhabitants of Lutetia then precipitated themselves with a kind of rage upon the mysterious ship; they devastated it with blows of the ax, after having let out the young women.

---

[25] Author's reference: "*Études de la Nature.*" *L'Arcadie* was reprinted in some editions of the later work, hence this slightly misleading reference.

The servants of the vessel and their friends the Iarles did not have a good time, but a short time afterwards calm succeeded the massacres and the burning. The same hands that destroyed the old poisoned ship have made a completely new one in which the children of men now replace the children of the gods. It is enormous in size and strong enough to endure for six thousand years and beyond.

"That is the key to the enigma. Furthermore, Isis has been banished; it is no longer her religious figurehead that is seen on the prow of the ship; it is that of the King of Lutetia, crowned with a civic branch, holding panthers on a leash in one hand and an olive branch in the other. At the top of the mainmast floats a large banner on which is written: *legum servi sumus, it liberi esse possimus.*[26] The gallery is ornamented with balustrades, from which emerges a lantern surmounted by a bonnet in the form of an epiroge."[27]

"Oh, you have charmed me," said Bazilide to her husband, embracing him in a bourgeois fashion, as was done in the times of Hector. "You talk about the change of fortune of the Lutetians with a kind of satisfaction that makes the greatest eulogy of your heart. I cannot tell you all the tender sentiments that you make me feel."

"Is the King of Lutetia beloved, then?" asked Nictator.

"Greatly," said Frankestein, "and not only by the Lutetians, but all the people of Gaul. Look, I have in my pocket two medallions that can give you proof of it. The first, imagined by gratitude, was struck a few years after the King, at the time of his coronation, had handed back certain onerous rights due to the chief of the conquerors on his accession to the throne, in the temple of Mars. The Gauls then came to experience great calamities; the people lacked bread; touched by

[26] We are slaves of the law in order that we might be free." (Cicero)

[27] An epiroge was a kind of cloak listed in many treatises on the French peerage as part of the ceremonial garb of the Greffier en Chef.

their misery, he reformed his expenditure; be had wheat imported from abroad at great expense, and distributed it first and foremost to the unfortunate cultivators. He is represented here in the emblem of the pelican, which bleeds itself to nourish its children."

"The idea isn't new," said Nictator."

"No," said Aglaonice, "but it has justice. Let us see the other."

"This one is very recent," said Frankestein. "It makes allusion to the reestablishment of the finances exhausted by depredations. The people are doing for their King here what he has done for them. You see the good city of Lutetia presenting her breasts to her father. Behind her is displayed the desire of all others to enjoy the same happiness as her."

"Oh," said Cornelius, "that trait of filial piety belongs to us, but the comparison is fortunate."

Aglaonice and Bazilide, indignant at the gluttony of the pontiffs serving the former vessel and the tyrannical spirit of the Iarles, wanted to know what had become of both parties after such an upheaval.

"Let it suffice for you to know, ladies," said Frankestein, "that all distinctions have been abolished: that the great Druids, the servants of the god Tor-Tir,[28] the Druid sacrificers who lived on pure wheat steeped in human blood, are reduced at present to a fine broth of lupins and beech-nuts, all washed down with the milk of goats of the race that once nourished the father of men; for that posterity of Amaltheia was imported specially from Crete, on the grounds that such a mild aliment would surely bring about a complete change in their mores."

As he finished speaking, Frankestein put his arm around Bazilide amorously. Nictator leaned toward Aglaonice with a voluptuous expression; her eyes did not react badly to that attack. Cornelius, who was only serving as a witness, did not want to put a longer obstacle in the way of their impatience;

---

[28] Another name derived from *L'Arcadie*.

he got up from the table and embraced all four of them, with tears in his eyes.

"One more word only," he said to them, "so that before I retire I shall know your projects."

Nictator had a father advanced in age, and could not renounce returning to him immediately

Frankestein made it a duty and a joy to introduce Bazilide to his family; he proposed then to take her to Aglaonice in the beautiful land of Sonar, in order never to separate again from her and Nictator.

"My friends," said Cornelius, "At least wait until the end of my Praetorship. If you leave me so soon, I shall think that I am losing all my children at the same time..."

He was promised what he requested; they swore it. They embraced again, and then they went their separate ways.

Mademoiselle de la Choupillière

by Jacques Boucher de Perthes

In a great and very beautiful city, which counted, as well as six thousand inhabitants, a sub-prefect, a president, a king's prosecutor and a lieutenant of gendarmes—in brief, everything that could contribute to utility and pleasure—there lived a curly-haired, clean-shaven, neatly-brushed fop of the species of those who, in the capital as elsewhere, turn around in a single movement for fear of disturbing the economy of their cravat.

A creature of new invention, wearing a corset and forming the intermedium between man and woman, Baron Léon de Saint-Marcel, twenty-six years rich, with a pretty face and an annual income of thirty thousand livres, playing society games and singing a ballad passably, had everything that constitutes a great man in the beautiful city of B***. Thus, he was the favorite of all the mothers who had demoiselles to marry off, and the target of every spinster or widow in want of a husband. There was not a single dinner party, ball, afternoon tea, lunch, picnic in the woods or excursion in a char-à-banc in which he was not obliged to take part.

The Baron was, in consequence, the busiest man in the arrondissement: putting on his morning suit, his midday suit, his evening suit, visits to receive, visits to make—he did not have a moment to himself. If, by chance, he had a few spare minutes, they were scarcely sufficient to read a fashion magazine, or make tender or polite replies—which were always costly, because he needed to consult the dictionary frequently, as much for thought as for style. Having left school early, he had only got as far as the fourth form, in which one does not learn orthography. He was, therefore, not a scholar; nor was he an intelligent man—which mattered little to him, because he believed himself to be both and, as three-quarters of the city also believed it, he enjoyed all the rewards of science and intellect without experiencing any of the embarrassments.

As we have indicated, Léon had illuminated profound passions among the young women of the locale; but as the demoiselles of our days generally have sage and mathematical views, the primary aliment of the conflagration was the Baron's annual income of thirty thousand livres; he would probably have turned ten times fewer heads had that figure been missing a zero. It is unnecessary to conclude that it was the love of money that made the hearts of those ladies beat—no, people think more nobly than that in the city of B***, and in any case, to love a rich man is not precisely to love the gold in his cash-box. One loves the proprietor because he is surrounded by all the prestige that makes a person appear lovable: fine clothes, beautiful jewels, lovely furniture; if he does not have all that, one knows that he can have it, or that one could have it for him, which comes to the same thing. That is why, in all civilized countries, the richest futures really are the most beautiful.

Monsieur de Saint-Marcel, whether for moral or political reasons, had not ceded to the seductions of his female compatriots. Although they were generally very nice, he had remained the master of his heart; only one woman had made any impression on him. That was Mademoiselle Louise D***, his cousin, a charming young person who had conceived a sentiment for him that seemed to authorize the projects of the two families. As good as she was beautiful, she possessed exactly what the Baron lacked: intelligence and education; but, her father's fortune having been successively reduced by unforeseen events, Monsieur de Saint-Marcel's passion had diminished in the same proportion, and in the epoch of which we are speaking, had fallen almost to zero. In vain, his mother, on her death-bed, had made him promise to contract that marriage; he was no longer looking for anything but an honest pretext to break off the engagement.

One day, he thought he had found it. After a ball at which Louise had danced with an officer of the garrison, he claimed that she had an intrigue with the soldier.

Thus defamed by the man who was the oracle of society, the unfortunate orphan soon found herself rejected by all the mothers and all the daughters for whom she had previously been an object of envy. Her despair was frightful; the ingrate was still dear to her. She fell ill and, instead of feeling sorry for her, her cousin said that she was play-acting. She played well, because she died.

Petty people who calculate nothing and marry like brutes, for the sentiment of simple nature, criticized the charming Léon severely; they considered him a hard and heartless man. People of status, however—which is to say, people with income—approved of the firmness that he had shown, and the innocent victim, dead of grief, was cited as an example of divine justice, which is always pronounced against young women who dance with soldiers devoid of fortune.

Rid of a redoubtable competitor, the demoiselles redoubled their provocative glances and flirtations. Unfortunately, in the arrondissement of B***, the largest landowners, apart from the Baron, had no more than a hundred thousand écus of capital; that is doubtless a tidy sum in the provinces, but it often happens that a pretty girl whose father and mother are thus provided has little sisters and little brothers, an insupportable rabble for a brother-in-law; or, if she has few or no co-inheritors, the parents are young and do not seem at all inclined to give pleasure to their son-in-law for a long time.

Léon had not, therefore, been able to fix the irresolution of his own wishes; he contented himself with those of all hearts, without granting any of them, which guaranteed him the continuation of politenesses, smiles, diners, compliments, handshakes, and even love letters—for a few sensitive individuals, whose only dowry was their virtue, ventured as far as that.

In that epoch, the arrival was seen in the superb city of B*** of one Monsieur de La Choupillière, a former émigré, former tradesman, former député, former prefect, former chamberlain and former gentleman of the chamber, for the moment simply a malcontent, but still a Comte and worth a million.

Everyone knew what the Comte had been, but no one understood the Comte at all. He was a man like no other, who gave the impression, absolutely, of a human machine. His gestures were regular and compassed, like those of a pendulum, or those of an actor trained in the royal school of declamation. Always on time, to the minute, nothing made him deviate from his route or his habits, and if by chance he made a false step, one might have thought that it was in the place where he intended to make it. He was often very taciturn, and not for anything in the world would anyone have caused him to unseal his lips, because when he began to talk, it was necessary for him to continue throughout a time that he seemed to have determined in advance, and, interruptions and incidents notwithstanding—including, sometimes, the departure of his listener—he carried on talking. His movements were firm and rectangular, as if moved by a spring, and his cycles seemed to be organized on the same principle. His voice, whether by dint of having spoken as a député, announced as a chamberlain, protested as a malcontent or sworn fidelity as a prefect, was exactly as sonorous as the mechanism of a turnspit.

The Comte was a widower; he had an only daughter who was absolutely the same model as her father—which does not happen often, but which ought to be the case invariably, for the facility of family recognition and the convenience of genealogists.

Mademoiselle Colombe seemed at first glance to be the antiphrasis of her name. Nothing in her physique was reminiscent of a dove. With regard to morality we cannot speak, but, leaving all resemblance aside, Mademoiselle de La Choupillière was pretty nonetheless, and very pretty, especially in the light, for her eyes were slightly ringed and her complexion slightly lustrous—certain signs by which one can recognize ladies of high society and the wearing effect of long plays, waltzes, gallops, and, in sum, all the nocturnal recreations slightly injurious to the general effect. However, the beautiful hair of the heiress, her pearly teeth, her forehead, neck, arms and hands whiter than alabaster, her nymph-like figure and her exceedingly tiny feet soon made one forget what the freshness of her coloration lacked. If nature was not present, at least there was art, taken to full perfection.

Mademoiselle de La Choupillière's intelligence, of which she was said to have a great deal, was of absolutely the same genre as her face; everything appeared to have emerged from the hand of the same maker. When she spoke, one believed one was reading a correctly-written book; when she sang, the ears were filled agreeably, but it was the song of a Barbary organ; one would have liked less precision and more soul. Her dancing was analogous; it was the elegant translation of her father's leaps and bounds. In brief, the entirety of her person seemed to be the finished work of which the Comte was merely a sketch.

The arrival of Monsieur de La Choupillière, who had rented a beautiful residence in the area, was, as one can imagine, a great subject of conversation. All the mothers trembled on learning that he was rich and had a daughter, and it was even worse when the demoiselle had been seen, and her charms were further emphasized by a beautiful carriage, elegant lackeys and a superb hunter.

By a strange circumstance, that retinue had the same nature as the master and the mistress; the horses, as well as the valets, had something stiff and jerky about them, which was initially striking. However, as everything was admirably well-chosen, well kept and perfectly regular, the eye adapted without difficulty to that eccentricity, which was attributed to the English origin of a part of the staff and the apparatus, and to the rather long sojourn that the family had made in the British Isles. In fact, English men and women, horses, dogs and mules—everything that originates from that country—all have a mechanical appearance, and an angular character that is not found elsewhere. Where does it come from? Is it the climate, the habits, the coal, the porter or the plum pudding? Chemists, anatomists and physiologists will decide.

When Monsieur de La Choupillière was installed in his château, had made his visits to the authorities and the principal families, and had sent cards to the others, he wanted to celebrate his arrival with a party. All the high society of the city was invited, and Baron Léon was not forgotten.

Before he had even met the young woman, her title of heiress had seduced him; as soon as he saw her, there was, as one would expect, a veritable surge of sympathy. Never, since Pyramus and Thisbe, Petrarch and Laure, the old and the new Héloïse, had a more violent passion set a heart ablaze, and when the superb silverware was deployed and he had heard its proprietress sing, and seen her dance, and was able to convince himself that the diamonds with which she was covered were not paste, what did he not experience? His bosom pounded as violently as if he had run a race on the Champ-de-Mars against the horse Phoenix or the mare Atalante. So he was all care and attention for the lovely young daughter, and manifested his admiration to the father, who, with a smile that one might have thought hewn with a chisel, replied: "She's the very image of her late mother."

Monsieur de Saint-Marcel, occupied with his new passion, had greatly neglected his old acquaintances during the evening—he had not even spoken to Mademoiselle O***, with whom he had danced regularly at every ball for ten years—with the result that the following day, there was a unanimous outcry against him.

The young men, excited by the others, and perhaps naturally aggressive in the city of B***, thought it appropriate to pick quarrels with him. They were all the more disposed to do so because Léon had just been deprived of his firmest support—his right arm, so to speak. That is a circumstance that it will not be futile to make known.

Our Baron, although very skillful with the épée, as with a pistol, did not like fighting, because he had noticed that one never gained anything whether one killed or was killed. In order to enjoy the pleasure of impertinence, however, and, at the same time, only to have to submit to its consequences as rarely as possible, he had for his second in all encounters a kind of cutthroat, a professional swashbuckler and the terror of honest folk for ten leagues around. One could not seek a quarrel with the Baron without having to answer to Captain Lapierre, a beast as malevolent as he was venomous, who had already murdered many a family's scion.

No one knew what regiment the Captain had served in; it was whispered in low tones that he was a former fencing-master, expelled from the capital for his evil deeds, and that all his campaigns had been fought in penal battalions. He had actively assisted, by means of malicious talk, in the ruination of the unfortunate D***, and prevented anyone from defending his memory by virtue of the fear he inspired. The young lieutenant, an innocent victim of calumny, having wished to give it the lie, had been challenged to a duel and killed by the said individual.

However, that redoubtable man was, for the moment, unable to fight.

The Captain had the habit of going every evening to the only café in the neighborhood, drinking and gambling at the expense of flatterers—for, whether by virtue of fear or something else, everyone has them. When he went in, he always put his hat on a table, where no one dared disturb it, under penalty of an immediate explanation, after which it was necessary to put the hat back where it had been found, or accept a rendez-vous for the following day—an encounter that no one sought, convinced that there was neither honor or profit to be gained therein.

One evening, when the terrible Lapierre and his redoubtable headgear were in their customary places, a stranger had come in, who, only seeing one vacant table, had removed the hat and sat down there.

The swashbuckler cries: "Respect Captain Lapierre's hat!"

At that interpellation the stranger looks up, not knowing whether it was to him that it was addressed. The other repeats it, adding a coarse oath. The impassive stranger approaches the stove, and puts the hat on it, to the amazement of the entire assembly, trembling for the imprudent, who probably did not know what he was risking.

As for the Captain, he stood up like Achilles, and the most terrible threat, accompanied by the obligatory challenge, emerged from his mouth.

The stranger's only response was to open the window, seize the arm of the unfortunate captain with an iron grip, and, without further ado, hurl him into the street.

It is difficult to fall on to a road from the first floor, however lacking in elevation it might be, without an inconvenient result, so the valiant Lapierre had his head cracked and his arm broken. He had been confined to bed for a month, vomiting fire and flame against the brute who had put him out of a condition to assume a fighting stance, while his pupil and protégé, Monsieur de Saint-Marcel, found himself the target of the animadversion of all the brothers and cousins of the ladies of the locale.

The Baron was sensitive to his situation; he had always been reckoned brave in the minds of fathers and mothers—which is to say, the people who did not know him—and it was important for him not to lose that salutary reputation. Knowing, therefore, that someone would definitely pick a quarrel with him, he thought it prudent to warn his enemies, and having examined the question of which of them might be the most maladroit and cowardly member of the coalition. He took advantage of the first opportunity to provoke him.

The rendezvous having been agreed, they went to the dueling-ground. As the Baron had anticipated, his adversary was afraid, and there was talk of lunch. The victor accepted, and took the opportunity to invite all his rivals, whom he treated to truffles and champagne.

There is no intimacy that can resist fine cuisine; the anger of young men is not tenacious, especially when it is only artificial and second-hand. It was, in any case, unimportant to them that Monsieur de Saint-Marcel adored demoiselles and was adored by them. He cleverly made them aware of that, and the peace treaty, whose preliminaries had been presented with the first course, was signed with the second.

With matters thus arranged, the elegant Léon was able to abandon himself entirely to his amour. The charming Colombe appeared to welcome all her admirers with equal kindness, but as she saw the Baron most frequently, it was to him that she listened with pleasure most frequently. The father did not seem at all inclined to oppose his daughter's inclinations; he had no scruples about leaving her alone with her visitors. Someone having made an observation to him in that regard, he replied that he had every confidence in Mademoiselle de La Choupillière, who was the image of her late mother.

One day, Monsieur de Saint-Marcel found his inamorata sitting on a grassy bank under a honeysuckle arbor. Everyone knows that arbors and grass are appropriate to sentiment in all countries, and they were no less so in the fine city of B*** and its environs. As soon as Léon had touched the bracken he felt suddenly inspired, and to be frank, he should have been; the semi-obscurity of the boscage, the simple and skimpy attire of the young woman, including the dress whose indiscreet folds allowed treasures to be divined, all seemed calculated to seduce him, if he had not been seduced already; I even believe that he would have fallen to his knees in his admiration if the tight trousers he was wearing had permitted him the possibility.

He commenced with a sigh, which was followed by a question that is slightly vulgar, but which had always been positive in the locality of B***: "Have you ever been in love, Mademoiselle?"

"I've heard a great deal of talk about it, Monsieur," Mademoiselle de La Choupillière replied.

"It's a burning passion, Mademoiselle."

"That's what everyone says, Monsieur."

The Baron had started badly, for he remained tongue-tied, as often happens during a matrimonial declaration—further proof of the malice of the demon that always murmurs accurately and effectively to us when it is a matter of an evil motive.

It was necessary to get out of it. What good was it to Monsieur de Saint-Marcel to have been the daring of all the local beauties for such a long time, only to remain mute, like an infatuated fifteen-year-old, on the day when it was most important for him to speak?

The second attempt was no more fortunate. He embarked on a definition of love. He was not very strong in the descriptive genre, and he took almost all of it from the valet in *Le Joueur*.[29]

Mademoiselle de La Choupillière could have said to him: "Love can no more be defined than air or light; it is sensed; it is inspired," but she did not, for she was very modest and reserved."

Finally, Monsieur de Saint-Marcel, after a profound sigh, exclaimed: "Adorable Colombe, it is futile to disguise my wishes any longer. I adore you; I offer you my heart, my life, my name, my fortune. Speak: it is my sentence that you are pronouncing."

"Monsieur," replied Mademoiselle de La Choupillière. "I'm extremely flattered by what you've done me the honor of saying to me, but, as you have had occasion to remark. I have a father; it's to him that you ought to have gone first to ask him for authorization to declare sentiments to me that, honorable as they might be, are entirely irregular at this point in time."

That was a perfect response, and as there is nothing to add when all has been said, the Baron found himself halted again, as if he had had less presence of mind.

"Oh, Mademoiselle," he continued, in a despairing tone "what would be the use of your father's agreement, if I did not

---

[29] Jean-François Regnard's comedy of 1787.

have the joy of obtaining yours? In the name of pity, for I do not dare to speak any longer in the name of love, pronounce your verdict; it is life or death."

For a second time he had the idea of throwing himself at her feet, but the wretched trousers still restrained him, and he swore that he would put on more ample ones when the opportunity presented itself.

"Monsieur," replied Mademoiselle de La Choupillière, "my father's wishes are always mine, and the will of a good child cannot be other than to obey."

That manner of expression was somewhat less than romantic, but, as we have said, the daughter and father alike only spoke in ready-made formulas, sentences and phrases, such as are found in all almanacs, gazettes, posters and announcements.

Léon hastened to respond as one responds in such cases, to wit: "Mademoiselle, it's not obedience, but love that…etc." His ardor carried him away to the point that he forgot the inconvenience of his attire, and the genuflection occurred.

Immediately, that which had to happen happened: the inflexible cloth was rent, not in the heart but in a less appropriate place—and that disconcerted him to such an extent that, although not timid by nature, he blushed, went pale, and could only retire, covering the vestment laid bare with his hat.

Having returned home, cursing the fragility of modern fabrics, he could think of nothing better to do than follow Mademoiselle de La Choupillière's instructions o the letter and address himself to her respectable father.

Meanwhile, the mothers, who were not unaware of the Baron's projects, were suffocating with chagrin. It was, in fact, hard to see a stranger winning such a victory over their daughters, merely because she was richer, more beautiful and more amiable, so it was necessary to hear what they were saying about the Comte and his progeniture.

After having exhausted all the resources of ordinary ill-speaking they came to calumny. According to the ladies, no one knew where the Comte had some from, although he had been many things. It was said at first that he was a nonentity, or even less, and was not even a man at all. It was claimed that at certain time, words suddenly failed him completely, and then movement, and that neither were returned to him until a certain agent, who accompanied him everywhere, had subjected him to some mechanical, chemical or surgical operation.

Such a rumor had nothing that could disturb a son-in-law greatly, but it was added that Mademoiselle de La Choupillière was in precisely the same state, and that during these accidents, no one was admitted to the house. It had also been noticed that on the days of balls, at a fixed time, the senior valet or steward, the only one who did not have the strained mannerisms of the rest of the household, came to extinguish the lights, and that at that signal, the Comte and his daughter wished their guess goodnight and withdrew. That had initially been taxed as arrant impoliteness; then people had got used to it, and now everyone was convinced that the master's health required it thus.

It was therefore believed to be an attack of catalepsy, which is nothing but a perfected epilepsy, and it was alleged that Mademoiselle Colombe was afflicted with the same disease. But Monsieur de Saint-Marcel saw nothing in these allegations but malevolence, and did not believe a word of it. In any case, the fortune was there, and with a few precautions, catalepsy could not have any effect on it.

The amorous Baron, having prepared his request carefully, went to see Monsieur de La Choupillière one day, and presented himself in the most respectable and filial manner that he could imagine. The Comte recited, one by one, all the words that do not say yes or no, and sent him back to Mademoiselle de La Choupillière, with his accustomed remark.

Sparing readers, mercifully, from preliminaries that would be as tedious for them as for the lovers, we shall say that after having been from daughter to father and from father to daughter, Monsieur de Saint-Marcel obtained the consent that he desired, with the aid of the steward, who seemed to have great credit with both of them. Convention dictated that

68

the marriage would take place in a month, and a mutual agreement was signed, under the guarantee of a large sum.

Now, it has long been embarked that, in counties where one wants to marry, everyone hears the news of a marriage before anyone has mentioned it; that is what happened in the great city of B***. The next day, it was the talk of every drawing room.

The anger of the mothers and daughters was terrible, and many might perhaps have died of it if, the day after the publication of the banns, the rumor had not spread that the Comte had just lost half his fortune in a major lawsuit.

The future spouse ran to his future father-in-law, who confirmed the verity of that unfortunate circumstance, and added. "But you still have Mademoiselle de La Choupillière; she's the very image of her late mother; you can't fail to be perfectly happy."

That reasoning, and the certainty that half of the Comte's fortune could still pass for a complete fortune, partly dissipated the disappointed Baron's concerns.

A few days later, it was said that the Comte had become involved in an affair on the Bourse, which had removed the other half of his capital. A further visit by Monsieur Marcel brought forth a further confirmation on the part of the Comte, who, after having addressed a superb speech to him, repeated: "But you still have Mademoiselle de La Choupillière."

That was, in fact, a great consolation. The future was still rosy. And then, the furniture, silverware and diamonds were worth a lot of money. The next day, however, it was said that the tableware had been sold and the diamonds seized.

A further race by the son-in-law followed, to whom the father-in-law replied with the same formula. Now, the contract had been signed, so there was a considerable forfeit; there was no more going back. In any case, it is necessary to say, Monsieur de Saint-Marcel was in love, and, even had he been free, he might have hesitated before renouncing his inamorata.

The wedding took place the following day. In spite of the Comte's misfortunes, a feast had been prepared; the entire city was there, some out of curiosity, some out of interest for the family, of which no one was any longer jealous now that it no longer possessed anything. The evening was quite cheerful, and, whatever the amorous Léon did to prevent it from being prolonged, it was nearly midnight when the steward, as usual, came to extinguish the lights and send the company away.

Monsieur de Saint-Marcel retired immediately to his wife's apartment; at that moment he forgot all the blows that fortune had struck him; he was the possessor of the most delightful of creatures, and an air of abandon and languor that he had not remarked before rendered her more seductive than ever. She was on a sofa; she sat down beside her; he removed the light gauze covering her shoulders, and those pure forms appeared to his enchanted eyes. Then his love burst forth in burning expressions.

She responded to it with a sight, and said "I..."

Then midnight chimed.

She stopped.

Léon thought that emotion alone was the cause, and even more smitten, he repeated his protestations.

To that his young wife made no reply. A curl of blonde hair tickled the amorous husband's cheek. He wanted to touch that charming hair; he asked to press it to his lips. She kept silent; that was a consent; He drew nearer, but at the first effort the curl came away from the forehead.

Astonished, he seized another; same effect. What! Was the interesting Colombe wearing a wig? He interrogated her; she remained mute. He took her hand; the hand did not respond to his own. He shook it.

Surprise! The arm came away.

The husband made a gesture of terror, and that movement, agitating the sofa, caused the head to slump. He tried to support it; it fell on to the floor.

Griped by horror, he thought that a baleful vision had troubled his reason.

He runs to the father's room. The latter is still up; he bombards him with questions; he comes to reproaches—the same silence. In his anger, he strikes him, and experiences a sharp pain. He repeats the blow; blood flows from his hand.

He returns to his wife, thinking again that he was deluded. He seizes the inanimate body, which yields to his efforts and separates into a thousand pieces. In a trice, he sees the parquet covered with cogwheels, screws, nails and springs, which collide with one another and roll around, with a silvery sound—and nothing remains in his arms but a dress and the stick of a doll.

He wants to escape that infernal house. In the antechamber he sees the lackeys arranged against the wall, upright, like mannequins after a performance at the opera. He calls them by name, and orders them to prepare a carriage, but not one budges. He launches himself into the courtyard; it is silent. He runs to the stable; he recognizes the coachman, the horses, the dogs, stiff and motionless, all seemingly deprived of life.

Beside himself, no longer knowing what he is doing, he wanders at random. Finally, he finds himself in front of his house; into which he goes, harassed and half-dressed. His servants are astonished and wonder what accident has set the Baron roaming on his wedding night.

Prey to a feverish delirium, he throws himself on his bed, but, ready to belief in magic, shades and revenants, he cannot chose his eyes.

When daylight appears, determined to clear up his doubts at any price, he arms himself, mounts a horse and, followed by his valet, goes to the château.

When he goes into the courtyard he hears a loud sound of hammering. In the vestibule he sees a great many workmen and crates, some sealed and others ready to be. Searching with his eyes for the master of the house he arrives in the nuptial chamber, where he finds the steward picking up the pieces of the Baronne.

On seeing him come in, the steward presents him with an invoice signed *Roberson, mechanician*, demanding 10,545 francs 25 centimes, for the cost of repairs to his two best automata.

Major Whittington
by Charles Barbara

Not far from the gardens of Paris, on the flowery banks
of the Seine, a vast and undulating plain extends, where various pleasure houses blossom here and there like great orange
dahlias in the midst of vervain. From one of the neighboring
hills, the view would be ravishing were it not for a quadrilat-
eral of gigantic walls that dominate the ensemble and obfus-
cate the scene. Those bare, solid, rusty walls imprison a terrain
of about three hectares. The stroller measures the enclosure
and runs an eye over them without noticing any other opening
than that of a little oak door, which seems to require, in order
to open it, the secret of some magical formula, since there is
no trace thereon of any lock, handle, knocker or bell. What
gives pause and completes the surprise is that, from a distance,
by posting oneself at a height and aiding oneself with a telescope, one sees rising up side by side from within, the gilded
dart of a lightning-conductor and the thin flue of a factory
chimney, from which smoke escapes incessantly in little intermittent jets.

The curious renounce seeing through those walls. Since
their erection, no one, to the knowledge of the people in the
vicinity, had penetrated into the enclosure and no one had
come out. So it was an event when three men arrived, on a
foggy afternoon, outside the little door. One of them, distinguished by a red ribbon, marched ahead, and the other two
followed with an air of deference. They were evidently representatives of the authority.

This is what had given rise to that domiciliary visit.

Eight or nine days before, a local bourgeois, climbing the
steps of the Palais, had been directed to the cabinet of the
procureur général and had asked to see that magistrate on a

matter of the greatest importance. His black coat, his white cravat and his respectable appearance had obtained him the immediate audience that he requested. To begin with, he reeled off his name, forenames, titles of ex-merchant and proprietor, and then continued in a grave voice in harmony with the singularity of his revelations:

"My wife and I, Monsieur le Magistrat, have no other ambition but to live tranquilly in our home; as Horace says: *Felix qui potuit rerum...*[30] I have sacrificed the satisfaction of having children to the inconvenience of bringing them up, the fear of hearing their cries and that of raising ingrates. We have not regretted it; it appeared wiser to us to divide our wealth into as many lots as months that remain to us hypothetically, to live. In that fashion we enjoy a perfect satisfaction without having to fear falling stock prices, crashes or bankruptcies. While she takes care of the house and supervises our domestics, I smoke, stroll, water our vegetables, occupy myself with the rabbits, trim the trees or pick fruits. Without flattering ourselves, I believe that it would be difficult to find two more virtuous individuals for a hundred leagues around. We have no debts, we never speak ill of our neighbors, we pay our taxes scrupulously, we do not infringe the liberty of anyone; it seems to us that the universe in bounded by the gate of our house."

Here the honorable bourgeois paused. He took a deep breath and continued:

"However, Monsieur le Magistrat, what ought you not to dread from my presence? You have doubtless already sensed it from my facial expression. Have I any need to tell you that our repose has been destroyed, our hopes disappointed, our plans disrupted, and that our happiness is no longer anything but a vanished dream?"

---

[30] Author's note: "In his trouble the excellent man commits blunders; it is not Horace who said that but Virgil, in book IV of the Georgics."

The procureur général, amazed, looked at his visitor with the expression that a physician adopts with a real or supposed hypochondriac. He asked him politely to get to the point.

"Beside our house," the bourgeois went on, "extends a vast terrain enclosed by high walls. The sight of it is somber and mysterious. Those walls, in the beginning, inspired in us the most entire confidence. The owner, jealous enough of his interior to hide it at so much expense, could only be, in our opinion, a tranquil man full of solicitude for the peace of his neighbors. Throughout the winter, in fact, events responded to our expectation. But, God in Heaven, this spring and summer, at this very hour..."

"Well?" demanded the magistrate with interest.

"Alas, Monsieur, imagine all the noises of earth and Heaven concentrated to the highest degree within that enclosure. How can I give you an idea of the racket that escapes from it? You would sometimes think it the barking of fifty assembled packs, then the sound of a locomotive pulling a train, then innumerable fanfares, then rifle fire, and then an orchestra of ten thousand musicians, or the din of a tempest with the accompaniment of thunder. In brief, Monsieur, from dusk until dawn, and from dawn until dusk, more often than not, one cannot hear oneself speak for a league around. My wife and I have lost our appetite and sleep, we are plunged into depression and terror, we are disgusted with life; it would not take much for us to die of chagrin and despair."

In the opinion of the magistrate, the grievances of the plaintiff were greatly exaggerated, if they were not entirely imaginary. Unable, at least, to believe that they were seriously founded, he put the supposed maniac off with a vague promise and hastened to get rid of him. In fact, no order was given and no measure taken. A few days later however, the unfortunate proprietor, beside himself, and with death in his visage, came to renew his depositions and his laments. The decision made by the procureur général could not hold up against the threat of being periodically obsessed; without abandoning his place, he delegated Baron de Sarcus, one of his most intelligent deputies, to verify the extent to which the poor man's strange assertions were exact.

The door opened by itself. Scarcely had the magistrate and the two secretaries that he had brought with him gone in, than the door closed as it had opened, by means of an invisible mechanism.

Everything that they embraced with a glance was strange: the house, the garden, and even the terrain that they had beneath their feet. A domestic came toward them. Their surprise was extreme: that domestic, clad in an ample hazelnut-brown overcoat, as straight and stiff as a pole, was not walking; he was sliding on rails; his eyes, of the finest enamel, lacked expression; it did not seem that blood flowed in his veins, and his lips designed a dry and inflexible line. He stopped. A noise of cogwheels was heard. As he raised his arm to shoulder height like a railway signal, he opened his mouth and articulated the single monosyllable: "There! There!"

At grips with an increasing astonishment, Monsieur de Sarcus headed toward the door that the domestic had indicated. He noticed in passing the curious pedestal on which the house rested: through thick glass as transparent as crystal his eyes plunged into a inextricable labyrinth of wheels, cylinders, pivots, escapements, anchors, teeth, hooks, pothooks and twenty other pieces of enormous dimension, all entangled and all in motion; it was enough to give one vertigo.

The visitors penetrated then into a vestibule, at the back of which the steps of a staircase began. A multitude of copper buttons dotted the walls. This warning, translated into a familiar idiom, invited prudence:

On pain of death, don't touch anything.

They went up...

The stairway ended in a rather poorly illuminated antechamber in which there were several doors. The door facing the staircase had two battens. A domestic in a powdered wig, dressed in the French fashion, in short trousers, silk stockings and buckled shoes, was standing sentinel there; his immobility was that of a tree trunk. Suddenly, he was animated. The two battens of the door, swinging on their hinges, unmasked the view of a vast room inundated by the most beautiful daylight. At the same time, with a stiff and angular gesture, the domestic invited the deputy and his secretaries to enter. They advanced rather timidly to the threshold and plunged anxious gazes into the interior.

"Come in, Messieurs," said a voice.

At first sight, the man who was speaking, a person dressed entirely in red, plunged into an armchair, produced the effect on them of an automaton, but he only had the appearances of one.

"Come in, Messieurs, come in!" he repeated, making a sign with his hand.

They bowed respectfully. The room in which they found themselves, high, wide and profound, admirably illuminated from above, did not contain anything except the red-clad man and his seat. On the other hand, there was no area larger than a handspan on the parquet or along the walls that did not appear to conceal some secret or mystery; the parquet above all, which creaked underfoot, was nothing but an assemblage of trap-doors and marquetry; a thousand intersecting stripes made it resemble a sheet of frozen water on which people had been skating all day. In addition to that, a singular sound, similar to that of the mechanism of a cathedral clock, filled the ears with a perpetual hum. In spite of the noise, one could hear, but as one hears next to the active wheel of a water-mill.

"Sit down, Messieurs," added the unknown man, pressing one of the gilded studs with which the arms of his chair were studded. Immediately, three comfortable armchairs slowly escaped from the wall.

Although Monsieur de Sarcus did not breathe a word, his eyes spoke for him; they were bursting with questions. His host seemed to have as much difficulty moving as a lizard numbed by cold. His external appearance respired strangeness. Already tall in stature, he was coiffed by a hat with gigantic horns, which made him seem even taller. That hat, buried under a flood of black plumes, crowned a face that was noble and intelligent, but dogmatic and impassive. White hair garnished the temples; the forehead was broad and undulating; between two eagle eyes, which shone in the shadow of thick gray eyebrows, an enormous nose was rooted, thin and curved, comparable to that of the Italian Polchinelle. A bitter disdain creased his lips; the strong square chin announced a powerful will; on the edge of his side-whiskers, no less white than his hair and trimmed at the level of the mouth, excessively small pink ears expanded.

The red coat in which the individual was dressed attracted the eyes at first; it was only later that one saw his black culottes, the buckles of which were lost in the legs of a pair of boots with golden tassels.

"I was expecting you, Monsieur le Baron," he said, phlegmatically.

By his accent, a foreigner was divinable. Monsieur de Sarcus was not mistaken about that.

"You know me, Milord?" he exclaimed.

"Are you not Monsieur de Sarcus," replied the man still calmly, "distinguished scientist and eminent magistrate? Are these messieurs not your secretaries? Is not the younger one your nephew. Philippe de Sarcus, a young advocate of whom much is hoped?"

"I have no need to inform your lordship, then," observed the intrigued deputy, "of the object of my mission?"

"And it will be a veritable pleasure for me, Monsieur, to aid you in the investigation confided to you."

One could not be more courteous.

"But you've had a long journey, Messieurs," added the Englishman. "Before we begin, allow me to offer you some refreshment."

Before the thought had even occurred to the visitors to refuse, he touched a pedal fitted into the parquet with his foot. A door opened; through that doorway a third domestic penetrated into the room, rolling, and stopped two paces away from his master.

"John," said the latter, "Serve Madeira for these Messieurs and me."

The domestic made a gesture of intelligence, pirouetted on his heels, and left as he had entered. He reappeared after a very brief interval; his right hand supported a tray on which four full glasses and biscuits were arranged, which he presented first to the deputy, then to the secretaries, and then to his master. They drank, but not before having bowed to one another politely.

After that, John, retracing his steps, and describing the same circuit, collected the empty glasses and disappeared. The door closed again.

A long silence fell.

"You see me, Milord," said the baron, suddenly, "confounded by astonishment. I can scarcely believe my senses; it seems that I am dreaming."

"Pooh!" said the lord disdainfully. "In these childish matters, Vaucanson was my master. Wait, Monsieur...."

At the same time as he had activated the pedal in the parquet, he had pressed the arm of his chair with his fingers; a carillon responded to it. Time went by; it was almost that of a alarm clock.

"It will only be a moment, Monsieur," said the Englishman. "You seem to be anxious to know how, without quitting my armchair, without receiving any paper or person, I am able to receive news, I had foreseen that anxiety. The carillon you have just heard will furnish me with the opportunity to respond to you."

With a scarcely perceptible pressure, he caused a small table to emerge from the floor to his right, at the center if which was a dial, and he continued: "At this moment, Monsieur, something new is happening in China."

The needle of the dial began to move and the carillon recommenced.

"The Emperor of the Celestial Empire," said the Englishman, his eyes fixed on the dial, "is decreeing gifts to industrialists who are coming to establish themselves in his country.

He is sending a commission of mandarins, in steam junks, to visit the establishments of Europe."

At that point, the needle stopped, which put an end to the carillon.

"That's fabulous!" exclaimed the baron, enthusiastically.

A carillon of a different timbre announced that the needle was about to speak again.

"Philadelphia," said the major. "The *Saturn*, a monster locomotive constructed in accordance with my system. Frightful accident. Pleasure train, carrying fifty thousand people. Ten thousand killed. One shudders at the thought of what might happen, etc..."

The vibrations of a third bell came in time to interrupt the consternation of the deputy and his secretaries.

"Aha!" said the Englishman, slightly emotional this time. "New Holland is in full revolution. The populations are rising from one end of the country to the other. Merchants are meeting in Melbourne to proclaim the independence of the Australian states. Separation from the motherland has been decreed. It's a question of constituting a realm. A convict has been chosen as king."

At the immobility of the needle, the Englishman, after a few minutes, declared that for the moment, there was no longer anything new or interesting under the sky.

However, a fourth carillon suddenly rang out.

"This time, Messieurs," said the Englishman, "the warning concerns you. The procureur général is anxious about the danger you might be running and is thinking of sending you help."

"Inform him, Milord, if it is possible," said the deputy, swiftly, "that we are safe and, better than that, in the company of the most amiable of men."

As soon as the lord had satisfied that request, he said: "Presently, Monsieur, you can see how easy it is for me to reach an understanding with suppliers. To hide nothing from you, the objects that I might need are not numerous; my chemistry and my industry substitute for almost everything. To cite only one example, the wine you have drunk and the biscuits you have eaten are of my composition."

"Is that possible?" said Monsieur de Sarcus. "My word! I give you my compliments, Milord, the wine and the biscuits were delicious."

"That's nothing, less than nothing," said the Englishman, modestly. "What merchant would not remonstrate with me on that chapter? I will confide to you summarily that the four walls of this property embrace an entire petty universe, of which I can call myself the creator. My science, my sagacity and my imagination have rendered me the rival, almost the equal, of nature; it would not take much for me to surpass her. Except for the art of creating living beings, which is, to say the least, unnecessary and vain, I do not know that I can be asked to execute anything impossible. You can judge for yourselves."

"I believe you, Milord," replied Monsieur de Sarcus, immediately, "I believe you. Only one detail confounds me: how is it that a man of your value is unknown?"

"Do you not know Major Whittington" said the red-clad man, in the simplest and most modest tone.

At that name, the features of the deputy betrayed a profound emotion; he seemed momentarily thunderstruck. Enthusiasm rapidly snatched him out of that stupor.

"Have I heard correctly?" he exclaimed, rising to his feet—and his example was followed by his two secretaries. "I have before my eyes the savant, illustrious and immortal Major Whittington, the incomparable astronomer, the fabulous mechanician, the inventor, the creator of the new panification, of the infallible macrobiotic, of the new telescope ,thanks to which the planets no longer have any mystery for us, and a thousand other marvels—the man, in sum, whom the century has proclaimed with a unanimous voice to be a Pico della Mirandola to the fourteenth power?"

With an inclination of the head, the major said yes to everything.

"Oh, Milord," said Monsieur de Sarcus, at the paroxysm of his enthusiasm, "this day fulfills my ambition, since I owe to it the honor of knowing the most marvelous genius that has illustrated or will ever illustrate humankind!"

Major Whittington was impassive before these eulogies; none of the muscles of his face stirred; his icy phlegm was inalterable. To his admirer, who was astonished to see such a great individual cloistered in an obscure retreat, hiding from glory, crowns honors, the throne and the worship that the universality of his contemporaries were yearning to award him, he replied: "A succinct account of my misfortunes will explain the legitimacy of my misanthropy; a few words will suffice..."

In those days, thanks to steam, gas, machines and innumerable human inventions, the level of dolor had considerably diminished on earth. What had once been only a simple prick with a lancet became, in view of that diminution, a large and cruel wound; the slightest contradiction produced on a human being effects as disastrous as what were once called woes and catastrophes. Under the empire of that state of things, Major Whittington had suffered horribly; his life offered nothing but an uninterrupted sequence of disasters. He had scarcely emerged from adolescence than his parents left him master of a considerable fortune and thus deprived him of being the child of his endeavors. Shortly afterwards, an aged bachelor uncle he had never seen had died of an indigestion of joys and bequeathed him, with a prodigious fortune, titles that constituted him one of the most important individuals in the realm.

With less energy he would have died of despair or committed suicide; his great virtue triumphed over cowardly discouragement. Scornful of prejudices, disdaining the duties of his estate, he confined himself in solitude and plunged into the study of the sciences, which had always been his passion: chemistry, physics, mechanics, astronomy, medicine, physiology, philosophy and metaphysics, he devoured everything and showed himself superior to everything. His late nights, his labors, his schemes, his industry and his imagination had enriched the arts and sciences with a series of discoveries and masterpieces each more astonishing than the last. Why? In order to see himself misunderstood, shamed, calumniated, pillaged and persecuted by the very people he enriched.

Judge by one example. He invented the famous telescope that bears his name; it is a known marvel. With that telescope, which only cost a million, one can stroll on the moon as in the gardens of the neighborhood. What a service! Well, it was claimed that he had bought that discovery at a price of gold from a poor and forgotten industrialist.

That was not all. Nearly two centuries before, a prize had been offered to the scientist who succeeded in reforming the tide tables. For him, it was child's play; his calculations were infallible. The elements conspired against him. Because brutal facts dared to belie him, because the sea had the impertinence to contradict his imperishable reforms by twenty minutes, the prize was refused to him. That revolting iniquity brought his misfortunes to a culmination. Resolved to end an existence forever withered and poisoned, he realized his fabulous fortune and bought a commission in the Indian Army.

"I had decided," the major said, at this point, "to allow myself to die, of the climate or war. Death refused me; there was no war, and the climate was full of respect for me. I thought that one could not be more miserable. I was wrong. My excessive riches were an irresistible magnet, which, at length had gathered around me all the adventuresses and dowryless misses in Great Britain; I was the focal point of the most beautiful and most dangerous eyes in the world.

"A blonde and rosy creature, truly angelic in appearance, succeeded in turning my head; I fell madly in love. Our marriage was celebrated with an extraordinary pomp. We had palaces, gardens on the banks of the Godavari, thousands of servants and elephants; we led a princely existence. I believed that I was understood, and the wounds n my heart were beginning to scar over when, at the hour when I least expected it, I surprised the person that I had made the equal of a queen…absorbed in the elucubration of stanzas to the stars. *I had married a bluestocking*! A thunderbolt would have caused me less surprise; I could have fallen from the tenth floor, head first, and the impact would have been less rude.

"Under the empire of the fury that possessed me, flames devoured the stanzas, and the caimans of the Godavari the perfidious creature. After that, I tried to die. The thrust deviated; I gave myself a wound that had no other consequence than that of changing the direction of my ideas. Impatient at having been until then, the most unfortunate of mortals, the fantasy took me to become the most fortunate, and to direct all my future efforts to that goal.

"My certainty, drawn from the springs of incessant speculations, was that the key to perfect happiness resides in the art of surpassing others. I quit India, I abjured my ingrate homeland and I came incognito to establish myself in this plain. Experience has proved me right; I have succeeded beyond my expectations; if I still suffer, it is from monotony, and I am sometimes reduced by it to causing myself some harm in order to be less happy."

Monsieur de Sarcus, deeply distressed, admitted that it would be necessary to go back at least a century to find misfortunes as poignant as those that had just struck his ears; he congratulated the major on the serenity that he had finally achieved.

"Although." he added, "I can only take account very imperfectly of the manner in which Milord, in a sequestration so absolute, can employ his time."

"Know, Monsieur," replied Lord Whittington, "that six weeks, at the most, would suffice for an examination of the distractions that I can procure without leaving home. It will please you, I hope, to see the principal ones. Let us proceed methodically. A man of your merit ought to like traveling, with all the more passion because his duties scarcely suffer that he can satisfy his penchant. Toward what country would Monsieur de Sarcus fly if, impossibly, he were suddenly impelled by wings?"

Meanwhile night had fallen gradually in the room; a profound darkness soon reigned there.

"Toward Pekin, Saint Petersburg, Philadelphia or even Japan?" continued the major. "Deign to tell me."

The love of travel had, indeed, always possessed Monsieur de Sarcus. He confessed, at hazard, the desire that had pursued him for a long time to see India. Immediately, a sort of creaking was heard, and the immense wood paneling at the back of the room disappeared gradually, to allow the sight, under the radiance of a bright sun, of perspectives of an incomparable splendor. The pagodas, the edifices, the gardens, the countryside and a thousand other details of the perspectives had the dimensions, the relief, the brightness and the animation of nature itself; it was magical, intoxicating and sublime.

Monsieur de Sarcus was able to compensate his passion in abeyance. Before his dazzled eyes filed, by turns, Calcutta, Benares, Delhi, Jaggernath and the most interesting viewpoints of Bengal and the kingdom of Mysore. His enthusiasm no longer had any limits; he was almost mad with joy. By means of an incomprehensible prodigy, the entire world had fallen, in a fashion, into his hand. He expressed the desire to go to China, to the Cape, to the heart of the two Americas, to Tierra del Fuego, and he was immediately transported there.

For the first time, the major quit his armchair. Because of his enormously long legs, he was even taller standing up that he had been judged to be when sitting down; his appearance really had something imposing.

"Now, Messieurs," he said, with his most automatic phlegm, "if it is agreeable to you, we shall go down into the garden...."

He had already obtained such an empire over his guests that, penetrated by an almost religious enthusiasm, they stood up without saying a word and followed him.

At the bottom of the staircase, the major said to them: "Would these Messieurs not be charmed to make a tour of my park? I have a locomotive at my discretion. While awaiting dinner we can chat as easily in a carriage, in the open air, as up there..."

Before Baron de Sarcus and his secretaries had recovered from the amazement that these offers caused them, a locomotive, docile to the orders of a mechanic, escaped from one of the lateral faces of the house; it was towing an elegant uncovered carriage, in which the major invited his guests to take places.

Immediately, the machine, with a mobile impetus, veered to the right without there being any need for a turntable, vomited smoke, blew out steam, whistled and set forth. Its speed was regulated to that of a pleasure train. The passengers were able to enjoy at their ease the views of the sites through which they passed. It was a varied and very curious spectacle: from the luxury, the brightness and the variety of the flowers, plants and trees that grew and flourished here and there, it was easy to experience an illusion and to believe oneself in the climate richest in plants and precious shrubs; exquisite odors embalmed the atmosphere; groves of orange trees, lemon trees and pomegranates, all laden with fruit, spread shade there in profusion.

On emerging from the woods, the eyes were struck by plantations of sugar cane, rice-fields, a nursery of coffee, cotton and tea bushes. Further on, they traversed a forest of banana trees, coconut palms and breadfruit trees, not to mention the fountains where all sorts of aquatic birds were playing under the intersecting fire of water jets, flowering bushes where warblers, finches and nightingales sang by turns, meadows in which a herd of gazelles reposed, and thickets where wild beasts were lying low.

Through all these riches the train described curves of an incredible boldness, turning to the right and the left, making a hundred tours and detours, without ever traversing the same landscapes, so well that after an hour, at a moderate speed, the major's guests did not believe that they had measured the full extent of the park.

Meanwhile, Lord Whittington, leaning on the cushions, his eyes full of fog, with a dreamy expression, spoke about this that and the other.

"Our ancestors," he said, "were afraid of everything; their eyes were closed to the simplest ideas. Thus, war and pestilence doubtless frightened them, and yet they were even more fearful of the radical annihilation of those scourges. They seemed to be convinced that such an annihilation would lead to a deplorable and deadly increase in population and would end up making the world too small. What an aberration! How did it escape them that, if room were lacking in breadth and width, we would naturally obtain it in height and build in the sky?"

"As witness, Milord," Monsieur de Sarcus hastened to add, "the plan submitted at this moment to the General Council of the Seine, which the council will not fail to adopt enthusiastically..."

"To superpose on Paris," the major continued, tranquilly, "by mean of open frameworks and glass floors, a city no less large and no less beautiful than that capital."

"You know that plan?"

"It's mine: one of my old ideas. The surrounding towns and villages will be razed and all that land delivered to agriculture, successively cleared, plowed, and sown and harvested with machines moving at twenty leagues an hour."

"Oh, with Your Lordship," said the baron, "steps to the sublime are required!"

"There is also the direction of aerostats," the major continued." Perhaps human intelligence has never shown itself more ingenious than in the examination of that problem, so I can't be sufficiently astonished that such a simple thing has escaped the sagacity of seekers for more than a century. Of what is it a question, in fact? Of tricking the wind, given that one cannot subjugate it. The air, in its variations and its caprices, must be subject to invariable laws. My observations have taught me those laws; I've drawn up a chart; it informs one, with infinite detail, for all latitudes and for all atmospheric layers, of the direction and degree of the strength of the wind from day to day, hour to hour and second to second; tempests, gusts of wind and whirlwinds are foreseen there. In

86

sum, with the aerostat of my friend Ottway and my chart of air currents, one can go by balloon, in any weather, from one point to another without running any risk."

The locomotive was still traveling.

"Now I think of it, Milord," said Monsieur de Sarcus swiftly, "are not the aerial sanitaria about which Doctor Pritchard is making so much noise, also yours?"

"That's very little, in fact," replied the major. "A child could have thought of that. You know that Pritchard cures all maladies with the aid of atmospheric baths. A very small obstacle hinders the general employment of his system: the difficulty of procuring instantly, in sufficient quantity, the quality of air required by the condition of the invalid. Pritchard was one of my friends; I communicated a plan to him; He is in the process of realizing it. Pretty cottages, drowned in flowers and shrubs, will be raised up by immense aerostats and maintained by cables that will permit them to be fixed in one region of the atmosphere or another. The doctor, equipped with a eudiometer, will make the ascension with his patients, install them, confide them to the care of an intern, and descend again to his home by means of a parachute."

Monsieur de Sarcus, wonderstruck, seemed to doubt that the major could furnish new elements to his admiration.

"Well, Monsieur," said the major, extending his hand, "cast your eyes around you. Everything that strikes your senses, these superb flowers, these rare trees, these golden fruits, these singing birds, these grazing quadrupeds, all these things are due to my artistry. There is not a grain of dust between these four walls that is not my creation. I wish I had the time to show you all the peripeties of a hunt; under these sheds a baying pack of hounds reposes, beaters who sound fanfares, grooms, and a magnificent horse, the gentlest in the world to ride. Or I could animate the fish that are asleep in the depths of those pools, and enable you to angle for eels, pike, trout or salmon. You could also feel all the emotions of a voyage through the stormiest seas, in the elegant gondola suspended over there between the branches of that cedar. But it's getting late..."

"In truth, Milord," said the confused baron, "I would scarcely dare to recount what I have seen; no one would be found to add faith to the things that are happening here; the story would be accused of being fabulous and extravagant, the issue of a delirious mind."

The carriage stopped.

"Let's get down, Messieurs," said the major. "I flatter myself that I've given you an appetite."

They went back into the house and went up to the first floor again.

A splendidly served table awaited them. Twenty enormous chandeliers wrought and sculpted in gold hung down from the ceiling, from the branches of which hung festoons and clusters of precious stones; under the floods of light that spread from the only one of those chandeliers that was illuminated, over the finest and whitest tablecloth, where four place-settings were arranged, wines, liqueurs, meats, terrines, etc. were distributed, along with sparkling flowers, silverware and crystal. Nothing was more magnificent or more rejoicing to see.

Each of the guests sat down at the place assigned to him. The table abounded in delicate and tasty dishes; everything was judged exquisite and succulent; every bite and every mouthful was accompanied by a murmur or expression of satisfaction. The magistrate and his secretaries began to be subject to the influence of the spirituous liquors; a kind of exaltation invaded them; they drank, ate, chatted and seemed henceforth to be beyond the state of being astonished, even by the resurrection of the dead.

Lord Whittington encouraged them.

"Eat, Messieurs," he said, "drink! You have nothing to fear in my home from poisons. All these aliments, all these wines, these cold meats, these marinades, conserves, spices and liqueurs emerge from my laboratory."

They reached the dessert. Heady wines flowed in abundance; they drank toasts to chemistry, to mechanics, to the major, and to nature. A slightly noisy gaiety gradually succeeded the serenity of the beginning. Even the cold Whittington took part in it; his tongue loosened, and he grave evidence of a surprising loquacity. His eloquence, overexcited by numerous draughts of liquor, attained vertiginous heights. The moment was propitious. His repugnance for metaphysical speculations was beyond measure; he had only devoted himself by virtue of ambition to resolving definitively the problem that metaphysicians delighted in resolving anew every fifty years. A volume in press, that would appear in due course, would impose silence forever on inventors of turbulence. He deigned, provisionally, to do no less than deliver his verdict on creation, on the origin, destiny and ends of the human species, and in terms so neat and limpid that the people least versed in those matters would have understood. In the opinion of the baron, it would be necessary to be devoted to a incurable intellectual blindness to refuse to believe, and to contradict.

Nevertheless, the latter, at the paroxysm of his enthusiasm, esteemed that Milord would by no less happy to see, from time to time, elite individuals, notably the faces of women.

"Oh," said the major, "I don't lack society. You'll see Milady, Miss Whittington, Miss Jeanne, Mistress Ingram...."

A clock chimed.

"Seven thirty-five and four seconds," added the major. "In the meantime, Messieurs, unless music irritates you, I shall have the honor of enabling you to hear the serenade of a great orchestra."

"What! His Lordship also has an orchestra at his orders?"

"Better than that, Monsieur: a creative orchestra, which improvises what it executes, and the ever-new combinations of which strangely eclipse the taste for the best symphonies of the past. The source of my enjoyments is inexhaustible. Fatigued by harmony, I have recourse to painting or plasticity; Apelles and Phidias would not disown the series of dazzling paintings and admirable sculptures that I obtain by means of the mechanisms of my invention. Time is lacking my desire to show you my resources; I shall limit myself to putting before your eyes, shortly, small-scale models of my most ingenious discoveries."

His Lordship had not finished speaking when the orchestra was already playing a prelude. It was still permissible to converse; a dozen instruments at the most were executing quietly an introduction of the most majestic slowness. The progressive selling of the sounds soon drowned out the major's voice; all instruments known and unknown vibrating successively and collectively aided the scherzo, which suddenly sounded and amused the ear with pirouettes and buffooneries. It would not have taken much for the volume of the racket to exceed the auditory sense, and yet, nothing of the sort happened.

A hymn inspired by the national anthem, "God Save the King," suddenly burst forth violently; the number of instruments, gradually tripled, quintupled and multiplied tenfold, was borne to more than a hundredfold as it approached closer to the terminus of development; in the last part of the finale, notably, the din achieved the furthest limits of the possible. Imagine for a moment the heat of a battle, when drums, clarions, rifles, canons, shells, mortars, the screams of the dying and the hurrahs of soldiers are resonating in chorus—and more! Perhaps, in order to complete the comparison, it would have do none harm to combine it with the rumble of thunder in the mountains. Oh, the shade of that monstrous composer, who dreamed of monstrous orchestras and monstrous concerts, and realized monstrous effects, which, of course, never made only the windows tremble...the shade, we say, of that great man, that precursor, would have been content!"[31]

---

[31] The intended reference is surely to Hector Berlioz (1803-1869), whose perennial interest in technology and the music of the future led him to produce the utopian fantasy *Euphonia* (1844).

However, Monsieur de Sarcus was drowsy; he fell asleep for about a quarter of an hour. Under the empire of digestion and the harmonic masses of the orchestra, slumber had gained him. Silence woke him up again; he opened his eyelids slightly, only to lower them immediately; the intensity of the light that inundated his eyes obfuscated them. Blinking furiously, he adapted to the blaze with which the hall was resplendent.

An unexpected, curious, dazzling spectacle struck his eyes; he imagined for a few moments that he was caught by the enchantment of a dream, or the hallucinations of a fever; the twenty chandeliers were ablaze; enormous mirrors, magnificently framed, covered three sides off the hall; between those mirrors, golden arms protruded from the walls, the fingers of which gripped candelabra with numerous candlesticks, similarly lit. A gigantic battle freshly painted, strewn with a multitude of bloody scenes, with distant horizons where army corps were maneuvering, covered the fourth expanse of wall, which measured a full sixty feet in width and forty in height. To the right, rich armchairs, arranged as in the theater, filled half the floor, empty a little while before. The center was occupied by an immense table, the cloth of which disappeared under small boxes incrusted with gold and tortoiseshell, veritable jewels destined for usages that their form did not indicate. To the left, at intervals, were a sideboard laden with golden vessels, an upright rosewood piano, an elegant occasional table on which a tea service was sparkling, and various gaming tables.

Three superbly dressed women and a young cavalier costumed as a naval officer were playing cards silently at one of the tables; a fourth woman, occupied in embroidery, completed the group. Further away, the major was sitting opposite a bald old man, with whom he was playing a game of chess. At two other tables, Monsieur de Sarcus distinctly saw one of his two secretaries tranquilly playing tric-trac and the other dominoes, each with a stranger. It is necessary to add that Monsieur de Sarcus could only see the backs of his nephew's adversary, that of his other secretary and that of the major.

Somewhat confused by his forgetfulness, the baron got up in haste and leaned over the group of women. On examining the group attentively, he thought once again that he was the victim of a dream, and raised his hand to his eyes. The oldest was an ardent blonde; she had a ruddy complexion; her porcelain blue eyes gazed without seeing; her smile, seemed to be stereotyped upon the violet lips; diamonds and rubies shone amid the gold of her hair; a magnificent pearl necklace embraced her long neck; floods of lace garnished her bodice and the three flaps of her dress. She was playing whist with two young women, one blonde and pink, the other brunette and pale, and a young officer.

Those five persons, including the other woman whose fingers were occupied in embroidery, had erect heads, inanimate faces, stuff bodies; the usage of speech seemed unknown to them; they only moved their forearms and hands, and those only jerkily. All of it was strange and produced the effect of a nightmare.

The peripeties of the game absorbed completely the major and the baron's two secretaries. Monsieur de Sarcus had plenty of time to examine their adversaries. Between them and the group sitting at the whist table, the identity was not in doubt; they were equally mute and equally impassive; their gazes and their features had the same rigidity; the forearms and hands were the only parts of their bodies that moved.

"Checkmate!" a hoarse voice suddenly exclaimed, amid a sound of cogwheels. It was that of the major's adversary.

The latter confessed that he was beaten; he raised his eyes, and only then perceived his guest.

"Pardon me, Monsieur," he said politely. "At grips with the emotions of the game, I forgot about you. Let me introduce you to my family."

He led the stupefied magistrate to the whist table. Scarcely had he touched the group than the three women and the young officer interrupted the game and bounded to their feet as if lifted up by springs. The woman who was embroidering nearby stopped her needle and stood up with the same vivacity.

"I introduce to you Milady," said Lord Whittington, indicating the woman with golden hair.

Monsieur Sarcus bowed. A singular noise was heard; Milady nodded her head, opened her mouth and stammered: "Milord handsome, Milord good, me like Milord."

With that, Milady nodded her head again, bowed, and glided toward the tea table.

"Miss Whittington," continued the major, his hand caressing the cheek of the blonde and rosy young woman.

In her turn, the latter nodded her head, parted her lips and articulated quite clearly: "Papa, Papa." Then she went to join her mother.

With less ceremony, the major introduced successively Henry Smith, a young naval officer engaged to Miss Whittington; Miss Anna, the young and pale brunette, the latter's governess; and Mistress Ingram, lady companion, the embroiderer. Like Milady and Miss Whittington, the three individuals bowed and then headed—with the exception of Smith, who sat down again—in the direction of the table where Milady was already pouring the contents of a fuming teapot adroitly into little china cups.

Then the major drew his guest toward the other gaming tables. He neglected to introduce the unknown persons, but limited himself to naming them.

"The bald gentleman," he said, "is the venerable Sir Norton, the most skillful chess player who has ever existed; he has just beaten me again; I must always resign myself to that. Your nephew is presently playing tric-trac with Sir George Chalmers, rear admiral, and Milady's father. As for your secretary, he's playing dominoes with Sir Barclay, esquire, former consul and one of my oldest friends. Let's not disturb them; they'll be finished soon."

Monsieur de Sarcus examined the players with a feverish curiosity.

"Lost! Lost!" repeated the baron's secretaries, almost simultaneously.

They stood up; their faces expressed chagrin, but not astonishment. Monsieur de Sarcus went to interrogate them. At the same moment, Miss Whittington, Miss Anna and Mistress Ingram offered the messieurs tea and sandwiches, with an exemplary good grace.

"Mistress Ingram," added the major, addressing his guests, "not only embroiders to perfection, she also plays the piano admirably. I hope she won't refuse to let us hear something.

The major took Mistress Ingram's hand and led her to the piano, where she sat down. There was no preamble, Mistress Ingram immediately improvised an original theme that she followed with five or six variations; the first was in triolets, the second in arpeggios, the third in tremolo, that last in cascades and runs. Her finger struck the keys stiffly, the ivory resonated as if under little hammers. One could not say that her playing was very expressive, but at least it had a perfect regularity and equality.

Then Miss Anna was asked to sing. She opened an enormous mouth, which disfigured her, and made vocalizations heard. Her sonorous contralto voice, striking and metallic, embraced four full octaves; that unique voice went from the lowest notes to the highest with a marvelous facility. She executed the liveliest trills, the most rapid runs and the most surprising perilous leaps, without fear and without fatigue. Nothing more perfect could be heard. The little audience was delighted; Milady, especially, approved with head, hands and tongue; at every phrase she repeated; "Brava! Brava! Brava!"

Miss Anna finally rolled back to her place. The orchestra was heard again. On perceiving Henry Smith seize Miss Whittington's waist and match her pace, Monsieur de Sarcus understood that the young couple were going to waltz. In fact, after a few slow measures and a pause, the orchestra burst forth in joyful tones and the two fiancés, holding one another at arm's length, spun in measure, rather like the wooden waltzers of Tyrolean toys. They did not remain in place but described a circuit around the tables and accelerated the movement at the whim of the incessantly more rapid rhythm of the orchestra. That rapidity increased constantly, the forms of the two fiancés becoming less and less distinct; finally, nothing was visible but a single form of indecisive color, the spinning of which resembled a veritable whirlwind. A sign from the major stopped them dead. They returned to their places without appearing to be either emotional or out of breath.

Monsieur de Sarcus did not yet have the assurance of being fully awake; his doubt in that regard caused him a kind of torture. Inclined to believe that he was the victim of a hallucination, however, he was astonished by a perception so clear and persistent of the same milieu, the same people and the same things. Could he admit that a dream might last such a long time, and be connected with so much logic, without any kind of dissolution of continuity?

He was feeling a sort of dolorous oppression, which he attributed to those reflections, when the major said to him: "Presently, Monsieur de Sarcus, while Milady resumes and finishes her game of whist, and while awaiting the ballet-pantomime that I count on having performed for you, we can, if you wish, make a tour of this table and pass in review the ensemble of my finest discoveries."

They went along the long table encumbered by veneered and varnished boxes. Those boxes differed from one another in form and dimension; some were no more voluminous than a snuff-box, whereas others had the caliber on a traveling-bag. Monsieur de Sarcus' memory, although excellent, was insufficient for the number of small-scale models that the major set before his eyes. Each box contained a microscopic machine. Included in the collection were a machine to tailor clothing, an embroidery machine, machines for manufacturing beer, tea and coffee, a machine for trimming beards, others for producing vegetables and fruits, wrapping chocolate, laying eggs, curling hair, washing linen, forging iron, etc., etc. The major did not neglect to put in relief the inappreciable benefits of all these discoveries. With the complete assemblage of agricultural machinery, a single peasant was sufficient to farm ten hectares and more; with another, only one worker would be needed for the exploitation of the largest factory. At least two thirds of men would no longer have anything else to do but fold their arms. Tasks that had once required the hand of a skillful worker could now be obtained with the aid of a mechanism.

The majority of those marvels only obtained a rapid glance from Baron de Sarcus; he was scarcely interested in any machines except those that tended to suppress intelligence; the machine for drawing and painting, for example, the machine for sculpting, the machines for composing music, versifying, carrying out the most complex mathematical operations and, above all, the sketch of a machine for calculating the probabilities of anything, struck him with admiration.

"Truly, Milord," he cried, "one can say that human genius cannot go any further, and that after you, it will be necessary to close the era of inventors and inventions."

He did not turn his head, however, at the very end of the field; certain noises troubled him; the two battens of the door to the drawing room never ceased opening to give passage, sometimes to a military man decorated with medals, sometimes to a gentleman in a black suit, sometimes to a woman clad in velvet, covered in flowers and jewels. Those individuals, in the most various guises, could not hide their family resemblance. Announced successively by the barking of the domestic standing at the entrance, they filed, smiling, as far as Milady, inclined before her and went in an orderly manner to take possession of seats facing the painted wall.

The baron forgot momentarily to take account of those details. He suddenly perceived that the seven or eight long rows of armchairs were filled by a numerous and brilliant company. Whispers comparable to the sound of twenty thousand watches in the same room filled his ears.

His amazement was boundless. On seeing all those stiff and motionless people sitting like rows of onions, folded at right angles, he thought for a moment that he had gone astray in the middle of an assembly of Egyptian gods.

Gradually, the music covered the sound of conversations. The major had already warned his friends, obligingly, that the ballet was about to start, and asked them to take their places.

A ballet! thought Monsieur de Sarcus, confused. *Where? How?*

He attached himself once again to the idea that he was dreaming, that all the things that filed before him participated in slumber or the phantasmagoria of fever.

Once again, he did not have the leisure to verify that hypothesis. Under the influence of the nebulous motifs of the orchestra, he plunged rapidly, involuntarily, into the realm of enchantment.

The immense painting that covered the side of the room toward which the spectators were turned shuddered unexpectedly, like the surface of a pond under the evening breeze. What had at first had the solidity of a wall was no longer anything but painted canvas. About two-thirds of that canvas, gradually raised, unmasked a wide and profound theater, and, to the sounds of a music doubtless appropriate to the pantomime of characters, the performance commenced.

A guide would not have been superfluous; the most intrepid decipherer of hieroglyphs would have recoiled before the task of penetrating the action; no more obscure scenario had ever served as a pretext for dancing. It was evidently a matter of a prince and princess whose union, inscribed in the book of destinies, suffered ten or twelve tableaux of delay. The powers of the fantastic world, interested, some in the mortification and others in the glory of an invincible amour, struggled mightily with ruses, prodigies and acts of courage.

Furthermore, nothing could be imagined more beautiful than the stage setting; it was enough to make the sun itself pale. The sets changed every scene, and the changes of view were operated with lightning rapidity; there was scarcely time to see them; it seemed that one was at the window of a carriage traveling through beautiful landscapes.

A castle besieged by giants and defended by dwarfs was succeeded by a legion of fays fighting hand to hand with genii; an oscillation of hideous witches around a cauldron gave way to quadrilles of butterflies in the middle of a garden where the flowers were animate and joined in with the dances; there were also caverns full of reptiles and monsters, perilous forests populated by phantoms, bats and a thousand chimeras.

All those characters crossed paths, dancing in a fashion to make one faint with ease. Turning their heads to the right and the left, rolling their eyes, they moved their arms like fantoccini, while, sometimes sliding on one leg, sometimes on the other, they seemed held to the floor like iron to a magnet. A pond charged with semi-frozen skaters would not have caused a more singular sensation. Magnificent costumes distinguished the subjects; the principal dancer, for instance, was covered with precious stones. It was necessary to place her in the number of the greatest artistes. She executed various steps and pirouetted on tiptoe with a lighting rapidity that excited the transports of the public periodically.

The curtain finally fell on the inevitable triumph of the two lovers in an atmosphere resplendent with fireworks. Monsieur de Sarcus had understood absolutely nothing; nevertheless, incessantly solicited by a music that was dramatic and joyful by turns, by the changes of scene, by the beauty and richness of the costumes, by the *coups de théâtre*, and by the strangeness of the mimes and the dancers, he had forgotten himself to the extent of laughing, crying bravo and clapping his hands.

Entirely entered into the magic of the performance, his singular neighbors, with their mechanical cries and applause, had scarcely preoccupied him. He remembered them when the curtain fell; he saw them, during the peroration of the orchestra, get up one after another, turn left, slide as far as Milady, salute her and disappear through the door, as they had come. When the orchestra struck the last chords of the *tutti*, only the actors of the soirée's first scene remained in the room. Rear-Admiral Chalmers got up in his turn, shook his son-in-law's hand and left. Henry Smith, John Barclay, esquire and the venerable Sir Norton did not take long to follow his example. Standing and surrounded by his daughter, Miss Anna and Mistress Ingram, Milady received the bonsoir of her husband. Baron de Sarcus ran to her, seized a hand that she abandoned willingly, and said to her:

"Oh, Milady, ideal woman, marvel of grace, model of fidelity and discretion, permit me to kiss your hand."

In response. Milady jabbered a few foreign syllables, in which the baron had no difficulty in detecting a line from Sophocles:

"Go then, if you must, but remember..."

The chandeliers were extinguished one by one. Everything returned to the initial noise of cogwheels, which had struck the major's guests to begin with. Several times, Monsieur de Sarcus, having run out of praise and admiration, had manifested the intention to withdraw. Strange sounds suddenly struck his ears; the voice of a parrot, which seemed to be coming from the ground floor, began to whistle: "Long live Henri IV! Long live the valiant king..."

A little snigger escaped the major's lips

"What does that signify?" cried Monsieur de Sarcus, stupefied.

"Let's go downstairs Messieurs," replied the major, tranquilly. "You appear to be fearful for my riches; my walls seem to you to be easy to surmount, my doors easy to force. Let's go downstairs. A fortunate chance is taking charge of answering for me."

They went down. At the foot of the staircase, the major, instead of leading them into the garden right away, asked them to follow him to the left and to penetrate with him into a room whose door stood ajar. The darkness therein was profound. Scarcely had they entered than sighs alerted their attention.

Twenty gas jets suddenly illuminated a scene that astonished them at first, but soon excited their gaiety.

To the left of the entrance, in the corner of a room full of precious furniture, in front of an immense strong-box with both battens open, a poorly dressed man was standing, who was wailing. They could only see his back and could not imagine why the wretch, without being alarmed by the sound or the light, was not thinking even of withdrawing his hands, plunged into the safe.

The major invited them to approach. They understood then why the unknown man was standing still. His wrists were blue-tinted under the pressure of iron bracelets, and his hands, stretched by the torture, were suspended piteously over several piles of gold and silver arranged in battle order on the shelves.

"Aha, my lad!" said Monsieur de Marcus, gaily. "It was a bad idea you had to attack His Excellency's guineas."

Those words were greeted by a general hilarity. The thief kept quiet. He was young, with long brown hair falling in disorder over his shoulders. His face thinned by privations, did not lack nobility or charm; his forehead shone with intelligence; the wings of his aquiline nose announced an extreme sensitivity; his mouth and chin disappeared under the waves of a silky beard; a distressing sorrow flowed from his large blue eyes.

Soon freed from the handcuffs that were martyrizing him, he bowed his head ashamedly before those who were examining him.

"How is it," the baron suddenly said to him, severely, "that a young man with your distinguished features has not recoiled before an attempted theft?"

"Alas," replied the poor devil, with an air of irresistible candor, "I wasn't thinking of stealing; I was seeking shelter."

"That's surprising," exclaimed Monsieur de Sarcus. "You have no profession, then?"

"Pardon me," stammered the wretch, in a low voice, blushing. "I'm a poet..."

At that confession the major and his guests looked at one another in amazement.

"A poet!" said Monsieur de Sarcus, finally. "A poet! The unfortunate fellow! They still exist, then! Oh, Milord, for the curiosity of the fact, let's call it quits and let him go."

"Mercy, Monsieur, pity!" said the tearful poet, immediately. "I beg you with joined hands not to throw me out! Where would I go? I have no shelter and no bread; put me in prison!"

The first movement of Lord Whittington, at that plea, was to take a pile of gold from the shelves of the strong-box and put it in the young man's hands. Stimulated by that example, Monsieur de Sarcus, stung by honor, plunged his hand into his fob pocket and pulled out a few silver coins, which he added to the major's gift. The poet changed color; by turns he became pale, green, and red. He opened large haggard eyes; his hands remained open; he evidently thought that he was dreaming, or the victim of a cruel trick.

"Take it, take it!" said the major, generously, "and correct yourself; embrace a career."

Monsieur de Sarcus shook his head dubiously.

The young poet seemed anxious to prove him right; convinced that he was not asleep, that he had the gold, and that he was free, he was gripped by an intoxication neighboring delirium.

"Thank you, Messieurs, thank you!" he cried suddenly, with enthusiasm. "You're noble hearts! Posterity shall know it. Thanks to you. I shall finally be able to devote myself to the composition of my odes to the moon."

"What did I tell you?" said Monsieur de Sarcus, looking at the major significantly. "Incorrigible! Incorrigible!"

The poet did not hear. Full of joy, he had already disappeared into the shadows of the night.

"That incident, Messieurs," said the major, "makes me think that the roads are not safe. Permit me to offer each of you an overcoat of my invention."

He unhooked bearskin cloaks from the wall, on the fur of which the barrels of pistols and the blades of daggers were symmetrically arranged, and invited his guests to put them on.

"Take note of the three olives lined up at the place of the heart," the major added; the first arms the engine, the second activates it, the third puts it in repose."

Monsieur de Sarcus, and the two young secretaries, following his example, moved the first olive; the blades and gun-barrels stood up in a threatening manner. One might have thought it the back of a porcupine on the defensive.

"I case of a bad encounter," the major continued, "It will be sufficient for you to press the second olive; twenty bullets and twenty dagger-thrusts will immediately rid you of your enemies. I call this garment the infernal cloak. Please keep them in memory of me."

The baron muttered confused thanks. He put himself entirely at His Excellency's discretion, and expressed how proud and glad he would be to be agreeable to him in one way or another.

"It is presumable," said the major, as he showed his guests out, "that my neighbor will have reason to complain again more than once, and will not fail to do so. Be so kind, if possible, as to inspire a little patience in him; my neighborhood won't inconvenience him much longer, and I hold honorable functions in reserve to indemnify him for his insomnias...."

Monsieur de Sarcus insisted that His Excellency should not take any notice of the petit bourgeois."

"Adieu. Messieurs," said Lord Whittington with that, "adieu! May science and progress bring you joy. Before long, you'll have news of me..."

The unhappy bourgeois did not, in fact take long to return to the Palais de Justice to make his complaints heard; he was gradually getting the habit of it. He and his wife were visibly perishing. He was sent away, initially with benevolence, then rather coldly, and soon rudely; the procureur général finally decided to forbid him his office door. The unfortunate fellow had recourse to petitions; they were thrown in the waste paper bin. The last one, however, was menacing:

We have come, it was said therein, *to desire a prompt death in order to be delivered as soon as possible of an existence henceforth poisoned and intolerable, Beware, Monsieur le Magistrat! Unless you put an end rapidly to the conspiracy of which we are victims, you will have to reproach yourself for the premature end of two excellent beings, models of all the virtues, who still cannot believe themselves unworthy of a happiness bought with twenty years of commerce, order, economy, privations and good housekeeping...*

These sinister previsions only found insensible hearts.

The good bourgeois no longer took counsel from anything but his despair. *Ab irato*,[32] he immediately fixed to his garden gate the following notice:

Comfortable house for immediate sale, by reason of decease.

A buyer presented himself. The contract of sale was promptly drawn up; it only lacked the signatures. One terrible night changed the dispositions of the honest proprietor unexpectedly.

It might have been an hour after midnight. By the scintillating light of the stars, nature was in repose. Dull rumbles troubled the silence of the plain at intervals; one might have thought that a storm was approaching, or that an earthquake was threatened. Gradually, the rumbles increased in intensity and became formidable; nothing similar had been heard before; there was no rain or wind; the din, without being reminiscent of thunder, was more horrible; it was a singular mixture of a thousand uncomfortable sounds, a gathering, at a single point, of all the noisy métiers of the entire world. At that game, Vulcan and his cyclopes, working in concert under the sonorous vaults of Etna, would have admitted themselves vanquished.

For about two hours, it seemed that millions of hammers, millions of files and millions of saws, confounded with as many factory bellows and whistles, were beating, filing, tap-

---

[32] "By one who is angry."

ping and sawing iron bars, sheet metal, wood and stone at the same time. That giant, monstrous, terrible symphony was followed by an explosion that caused the houses to vacillate for two leagues around and bore fear into the hearts of the most intrepid; many people thought that their last hour was nigh.

Nevertheless, that was all. A mortal silence followed...

In the morning, the poor bourgeois, half dead with fear, took the risk of looking out of the window. What he perceived made him believe that he was not really awake. He rubbed his eyes. No mistake was possible. A few seconds of astonishment nailed him to the spot and paralyzed him. Shortly afterwards he ran to his wife, and, mute with the force of emotion, drew her by the skirt to the window. His wife was no less profoundly astounded.

Instead of the high and somber walls that had masked their view the day before, a beautiful golden gate presently embraced a vast square, in the center of which stood a monument of sorts.

The man and the woman, soon at the foot of that grille, did not take long to join their conjectures with those of the crowd that was gathering incessantly before that miraculous transformation.

At the head of the alerted authorities, Monsieur de Sarcus arrived later, in whose memory the prophetic last words of the major resonated once again: "Before long, you'll have news of me...." He cleaved through the groups, penetrated into the garden and marched straight to the monument.

It was a grandiose and bizarre mausoleum. Ten pages would not suffice to give the details of its composition. Its form was impossible to describe. On its granite base reposed a gigantic group skillfully conceived, in which one distinguished, among a thousand other things, a locomotive, an aerostat, a ship, electric cables, helices and telescopes. The ensemble was dominated by a little pyramid and a lightning-conductor. On two of the four faces of the pedestal, a marble plaque awaited inscriptions.

On one side, the entrance to a cellar opened in the base. Monsieur Sarcus had torches brought, and descended bravely. Twenty steps conducted him to a vast hall sustained by pillars and buttresses. Along the walls, heaps of manuscripts and several cupboards were arranged in an orderly manner, while in the center there was a marble tomb. The baron approached it; thick unsilvered glass covered it. Through the crystal, Monsieur de Sarcus perceived the major lying on his back; he was clad in his red coat and coiffed in his hat with cock's plumes; apart from his head, which was entirely visible, the rest of his body was plunged in soft cushions. It seemed that a thin layer of wax was spread over his features. One of his hands was holding a scroll of paper.

Monsieur de Sarcus ordered his men to lift the lid of the tomb. The scroll of paper was addressed to him; it contained the expression of Lord Whittington's desires.

One could not say that it was a testament.

I am not dead. Life is simply suspended in me by an anesthesia of my invention.

Thus the major began. He continued:

The recipe will be found among my papers. I desire to see with my own eyes the world in sixty years. To dissimulate nothing, in the very bosom of my unalterable happiness, a certain malaise slyly germinated and prospered, something comparable to ennui or spleen. Suicide would have delivered me from it, if I had not had the resource of going to sleep.

During the next sixty years someone might have found a remedy for the tapeworm before the development of which all my discoveries have thus far failed. That is the question. My neighbor, during his life, should be charged with guarding my body in return for twenty pounds sterling for month; it is a sinecure, the privilege of which I bequeath to him with the intention of enabling him to forget my turbulent neighborhood. His task will consist of dusting me from time to time and renewing the layer of wax over my face once a year. He will choose his successor himself among the honest men of his acquaintance. After sixty years, the person who finds himself constituted my guardian in that fashion will observe scrupulously the instructions consigned in my papers, in order to recall me to life.

Following a number of other dispositions, the major added:

All the manuscripts in the cellar should be confided to the care of the members of the Académie des Sciences, who should be kind enough to appoint a commission to put them in order, annotate them, publish them and aid with all their influence the popularization of my discoveries. In addition, those messieurs are requested to deign to found an annual prize of eight hundred pounds sterling to the benefit of the person who discovers a means of being perfectly happy when dolor comes to be radically abolished. In the presence of the incurable wellbeing with which science, the industrial arts, mechanics and drainage threaten to endow humankind, that foundation appears to me to be essentially philanthropic...

I bequeath to the Académie des Sciences, as a mark of my profound admiration and high esteem, a perpetual income of eight thousand pounds sterling, to be divided annually between the forty armchairs of the section. Half of the sixty millions contained in banknotes in my cupboards will suffice amply, I hope, for these various legacies.

The honorable mission of supervising the rigorous accomplishment of those express desires was conferred to the good will and intelligence of Baron de Sarcus.

That news produced a prolonged sensation in the scholarly world. Various periodicals, including the *Journal of Practical Mechanics*, appeared framed in black for several months. A commission was immediately appointed to coordinate, examine and explore the major's papers. At the innumerable marvels of which they contained the seed, the members of the sciences section of the Académie were seized by an extraordinary enthusiasm. They got up as one man and went in procession, in formal costume, to the dwelling of Lord Whittington.

By their cares, on one side of the pedestal was engraved in golden letters:

TO THE SCIENTIFIC MESSIAH

And on the other:

THERE IS NO OTHER GOD THAN MAN
AND WHITTINGTON IS HIS PROPHET

So be it!

The Automaton

A Story Taken from a Palimpsest by Ralph Schropp

The heart is everything.

Preface

During a long sojourn at the Château de Beauregard in the south of France. situated in the middle of an ideally pictur-esque mountainous region, we employed long hours in ferret-ing through the shelves of the vast and rich library of that old manor. The books and manuscripts contained there in such large numbers originate, for the most part, from an old con-vent constructed in the vicinity, but nothing remains today of that specious monastery but walls and ruins. The vaults under which the numerous and venerable monks with silvery hair ambled slowly while reciting the hours have suffered the de-structive action of time; silent and deserted, one no longer sees anything but climbing plants that hide the fissures. Not the slightest trace any longer remains of the narrow cells that once gave birth to so many manuscripts, sometimes so precious!

One day, while extending our curious research as far as the château's archives, we found a parchment covered in mil-dew and spotted with the dust of centuries. After an attentive examination, we recognized a palimpsest. While striving to divine a few precious fragments of Latin or Greek literature that the sheets might have contained, the original characters of which had been washed away in order to make use of the parchment for a second time, we read, involuntarily at first, the new text that had been superimposed there. The Latin was very defective, but the story it contained captured our attention completely from the very first lines.

We give here a translation as faithful as possible, given the deterioration that time has inflicted on the original. Words that have been effaced or have become illegible have had to be reestablished. The monk Theodulus whose name figures at the end of the manuscript seems to have been a man of the world before his entry into holy orders. He probably composed this story in accordance with the memories conserved in the cloister, based on the relation that was doubtless made by the two monks mentioned toward the end of the story.

Nice-Maritime, 28 November 1878.

R.S.

Albert the Great, the pious Dominican and celebrated magician, had just finished his famous automaton. With joy he considered his work, the fruit of long sleepless nights and profound thoughts. He had been obliged to sacrifice the best years of his life to numerous trials; now, having almost arrived at the end of his career, the sight of his work consoled him for the past troubles and infinite difficulties that he had had to overcome. A most complete success had surpassed his expectations and crowned his desires. He had succeeded in executing in perfection the ideal that he had borne within him since the time of his youth, when he had concluded his studies in Padua.

Homunculus—that was the name with which the new Prometheus had baptized his creation—left nothing to be desired. He resembled a veritable man of flesh and bone closely enough to be mistaken for one. So, in order to trace his portrait, it is a celebrated mortal rather than an automaton that is to be described.

Albert the Great possessed in his soul, in his capacity as a scholar, no trace of the divine breath of the artist, so his creation, purely mechanical, absolutely lacked the imprint of beauty. He had been content to copy a human face and to reproduce nature exactly, without giving the slightest thought to poeticizing it. The features that he had succeeded in imitating were passably regular and agreeable enough; the physiognomy was more pleasing, in several regards, because he had chosen for models certain plastic figures, but empty of expression, such as one encounters in society, the sight of whom soon engenders lassitude. One could allow one's eyes to linger on the visage of the automaton without experiencing either surprise or repulsion, and one always saw that physiognomy again with an equal pleasure.

He had a good complexion, neither pale nor highly colored, and, as a whole, Homunculus was not remarkable, whether by an excessive stature or an exaggerated stoutness. He was the image of one of those men who can be counted in thousands, people who pass unperceived, giving no purchase to criticism, but not exciting any admiration either.

His creator and master had dressed him in the latest fashion of the era; as regards elegance, his exterior was irreproachable. With the aid of an ingenious and well-designed mechanism, the secret of his inventor, Homunculus executed with facility and grace all the movements indispensable to material life. Everything about him was regulated and studied to such a point that he would never be able, in the sphere of action, to offend or irritate even the most susceptible people by abrupt or thoughtless behavior.

Thanks to mechanisms that only their author could set in movement or return to repose, Homunculus' thoughts took on the imprint of the character, intelligence and sentiments of the person speaking to him. In that fashion, he always found himself in perfect harmony with his interlocutor, and he made the most favorable impression from the outset.

Although superficial, the automaton's education had been well directed and was sufficient to his needs. He possessed notions of all things, and, as his mechanical resources could not let him down, he emerged victorious from the most arduous debates.

His voice, established in a monotonous, indifferent and authoritative register, free of intonations and modulations, was perfectly suited to his nature. For those who make use of it, that manner of expression has something divine about it, for they believe that they are floating above various human situations, as in the time of the creative Spirit floating above the waters.

That genre of conversation, which is merely a studied form in many people, was natural to Homunculus. Nothing was capable of gladdening him or saddening him. Like a god, he could traverse the keenest joys and the sharpest pain without feeling the slightest emotion; a stereotyped smile sometimes wandered faintly over his lips.

Those particular features of his character, enviable in some respects, are easily explicable. The great magician had succeeded perfectly in imitating a human similar to all others in gesture and thought, but he had been incapable of giving him a heart, of causing to spring forth within him the divine spark that warms all beings, as the sun exercises its benevolent attraction on the earth.

The monotony of Homunculus' voice, and the general lack of expression in his person, derived from his irremediable imperfections, caused by the impotence of his master to take any further a work above the range of mere mortals. That imperfection deprived the automaton of the sentiments and passions that ennoble humanity, and which flow from the principle of sensibility that we bear with us from birth, but which produces totally different effects in different individuals.

A man who, living by the soul as well as the body, was put in direct communication with the automaton, would not have taken long, in the presence of those impassive features and that unmoving gaze, to feel a chill penetrating his heart. Albert the Great himself often experienced a pain in his ribs, and the sight of that living and yet artificial being, who was his work, sometimes plunged him into a kind of indefinable trouble and terror.

By the efforts of his powerful intelligence, Albert had arrogated rights that only belonged to the Creator. Now, alas, he was about to suffer the consequences and submit to the immutable rules of destiny, which even a god cannot escape.

The individual who creates always forms his work in accordance with plans based on fixed principles. If he submits his work to certain laws, he imposes them on himself by the power of reciprocity. As a creator, he can doubtless liberate himself when he pleases from those voluntary chains, but only by destroying his work. Thus, by the effect of those primordial laws, the master inevitably makes himself the slave of his creature.

Many a time, Albert had been seized by regret for having conceived his insensate dreams and had forged needlessly, in realizing them, annoyances of all kinds. In his moments of discouragement and overexcitement, only self-esteem, combined with the memory of many lost hours, prevented him from destroying his work.

The automaton was beginning to become a burden to him. He did not know how to utilize him. He could doubtless render him motionless, simply by pressing a switch known to him alone, but he would run the risk, in leaving him for more than a day in that fictive sleep, of causing serious damage to his work. The machine was so constructed that it was necessary, under pain of derangement, for it to be continuously active, for movement developed movement within it, giving heat to its limbs and thus becoming the source of Homunculus' apparent life. He had no need of repose, his artificial existence only being the result of fortunate mechanical combinations.

Those reasons obliged Albert only to immobilize him very rarely; in any case, that was not necessary, because the automaton, docile and diligent, carried out his master's orders to the letter. As he never left he Dominican's cell, there was no reason to fear any misfortune occasioned by his intervention, or that might be prejudicial to himself.

But idleness is always dangerous, even for an automaton. That was what Albert the Great also thought. Not being able, even so, to open a career for Homunculus immediately, he made him his secretary and domestic. He retired to the bottom of a drawer the gentleman's costume in which he had initially dressed the automaton and replaced it with a monk's habit entirely similar to the one he wore in the cloister. From then on, Homunculus devoted himself to all kinds of work. He had no equal as a domestic, for what is more agreeable than to be served by machines? The master's correspondence was also handled by him with a rigorous punctuality, and Albert, thus aided in his everyday occupations, was much better able to devote his time to new research and new inventions.

Several months went by in the most perfect harmony between the master and his secretary, and their union would have lasted for long years but for certain circumstances that came to interrupt them.

Homunculus began to be subject to the common laws that claim their rights over all created beings; he experienced a need to exist for himself, for, from the day that he had been finished, he had been capable of providing for himself. Dependency weighed upon him, since he sensed the faculty of living and acting without outside help.

The letters that he was responsible for writing, and his reading in his master's library had awakened intelligence and given him an irresistible desire to see the world. An anxious ardor drive him to leave the cell in the convent, but, never daring to communicate his desires to Albert, he conceived his escape plan in silence.

There is no deep-rooted habit that cannot be surprised by negligence. One day, Albert forgot to lock the door of his cell, or perhaps left it open intentionally, intending to take a walk in the garden of the cloister.

Homunculus quickly perceived that negligence and took advantage of it immediately. From the drawer where it had been deposited, he took out his gentleman's costume and, having made a bundle of it, hid it carefully under his robe. As he had learned that money is necessary to live in the world, which he only knew by name, he took possession of the convent's cash-box, which received alms for the poor, and filed his pockets with the contents. Then, after having left the door of the cell ajar, he solely went down the common staircase. A few moments later, he was outside the cloister and in the world that he had such a keen desire to see and know.

Thanks to his habit he had been able to emerge freely from the monastery. The porter had no paid any attention to him, doubtless thinking that he was a brother going out to collect alms.

Scarcely was he outside the walls of the cloister than Homunculus wondered what he ought to do. To begin with he walked rapidly for some time, with the sole aim of getting away from the convent as quickly as possible. All the unfamiliar objects that struck his gaze only caused him a mediocre astonishment. Because of his lack of a heart, he remained a stranger to all impression. The springs that served him as a soul had been so well designed and executed that the automaton admitted the most astonishing things as simple and natural. Thus, he found himself all the more at ease in the world that he was seeing for the first time because his purely mechanical constitution inspired in him nothing but a superb indifference.

Wandering at random, he had arrived on the bank of a river. Instinctively, a good idea occurred to him. He went to hide behind a bush, took off his monk's habit and threw it, not into the nettles but into the water. Then he put on the gentleman's costume and found himself suddenly metamorphosed and embellished. Over the next few hours he continued his route through the countryside, all the way to a highway, which he followed. After a day's marching, it brought him to the gate of a large and prosperous city.

In the interim, Albert the Great, his unfortunate inventor, abandoned himself to a profound despair. After his stroll in the cloister garden, he had returned to his cell. Finding it open and not seeing Homunculus, he had called out to him and looked for him in the vicinity but, being unable to discover him, he ordered a minute search in the enclosure of the convent. Everyone was put to work to rediscover the automaton. Albert did not believe definitively in his escape until the brother in charge of the door told him that he had opened it to a monk a short while before. Messengers immediately departed in all directions, but they came back without being able to report any precise news.

Two days after Homunculus' flight, a fisherman brought a habit to the convent. Albert immediately recognized it as his automaton's.

"Alas!" he exclaimed, desolate. "Must I lose the fruit of my late nights, the preoccupation of my entire life, in this fashion? Can I expect a similar destruction of my achievement? I have kept my invention secret; my name will not pass to posterity!"

He continued to lament his negligence and his misfortune for a long time, without being able to resign himself to it.

Meanwhile, the automaton was enjoying the supreme happiness of conducting himself in accordance with his own will.

The great city to which hazard had led him soon offered him countless pleasures. He had taken a room in the principal hotel. A secret instinct having driven him to visit the city's fencing and riding schools, he did not take long to cultivate the best of relationships with the young men who routinely frequent those places. Thanks to his particular organization, he possessed a remarkable aptitude for all bodily exercises that only demanded flexibility of movement. The most spirited horse became immediately docile in his hands, and the most skillful fencing-masters feared his blade.

In a matter of weeks he had made numerous friends. In order better to position himself in their society he passed himself off as the son of a good family whose youthful follies had caused him to quarrel with his parents. He only became more interesting for it. Soon, women of the world, whose friends had described some of his brilliant qualities, desired to get to know him. That was not difficult. Two months after his escape from the convent, Homunculus was shining in the foremost salons in the city. Everyone admired his rare distinction, his exquisite tact and, above all, his imperturbable assurance.

Only a few envious individuals permitted themselves to criticize him. They claimed to have sometimes detected in him the manners of a *parvenu*, contracted in another society than the one into which he had now introduced himself. They suggested that he only paid scant or no attention at all to those who did not have a high position or who were merely his equals. They alleged that he deliberately disparaged all those who were praised in his presence, and that in his conversation he incessantly had the sufficient tone that permitted no reply. They regarded him as one of those people who take pleasure in expressing their own opinions but do not permit others to express theirs. Finally, they reproached him—which was much more serious—for behaving basely and crawling with people of influence superior to his rank, especially with those from whom he hoped for some advantage, if only to receive invitations to dinner or obtain via their intermediation one of those facile decorations not earned on the battlefield, but accorded solely as a testimony of favor.

These calumnies had certainly only been invented by the jealousy of a few rivals. What could not be denied was that Homunculus was generally liked. His absence of heart facilitated the means of worldly success. He was especially able to attract the sympathy of women, and thanks to their protection, which he owed to the sentiments that he was clever enough to inspire in them, he shone in all their salons. To conquer their favors, he had begun by making each of them believe individually that he only burned with passion for her, whereas even the most beautiful was incapable of awakening an elevated love in him. His speech only expressed false sentiments; he could repeat the same nonsense to all women, without running the risk of being caught in the nets of his own lies. His natural indifference always made him the master of the situation. By means of that conduct, which derived from his constitution, it did not take long for him to be invited everywhere.

A great lady, very fashionable then for her supreme elegance and also vary sensible although she was no longer very young, having no fear, in spite of her recent widowhood, of showing that Homunculus had conquered her heart, and she put the cap on his success. Soon, the other women were competing with her to excite the attention of the automaton. From that moment on he was so sought after that he became the object of all conversations, and it was regarded as an extreme favor merely to receive a note in his handwriting.

The perseverance of the beautiful widow carried him away. Homunculus, faithful to his nature—which is to say, his mechanism—had remained insensible for a long time; the exhaustion of his money finally advised him to allow himself to be touched by so much love. He consented to marry the great lady, declaring in a negligent tone to his friends that it was not because he loved her, but because he was madly loved himself, that the marriage had been decided.

By virtue of Homunculus' indifference, the union that he had contracted was untroubled by any cloud. His wife adored him and lavished care and attention upon him. She never perceived, fortunately for her, that no heart was beating within her husband's breast. The only thing that she found strange in him was that sleep never came to close his eyes. After a few months, however, she had succeeded in getting used to the phenomenon, and as Homunculus did not begin to waste away, she ended up congratulating herself for having found a second husband who combined with so many other qualities that of never sleeping.

Three years had gone by since Homunculus' escape, and he had become he father of two delightful children, who took after him and their mother. They resembled her externally, but, having no heart, the same insensibility and egotism was found in them as in their father.

Albert the Great had had time to console himself, apparently at least, for the irreparable loss that he believed that he had suffered. He was now attempting other inventions, without thinking overmuch about creating a second automaton.

Around that time, the story of an unusual event came to trouble the ordinary quietude of the cloister. It was said that the inhabitants of the nearest big city had suddenly risen up against a gentleman of noble birth, and that public tranquility had briefly been in danger, but that calm had been restored.

The fact, however, were sufficiently important for them to have spread of their own accord all the way to the silent walls of the cloister.

One feast day, in one of the busiest streets of the city, an aristocrat's carriage had run over a child. Members of the crowd had immediately hurled themselves in front of the horses, and in spite of all the coachman's efforts, exciting them with words and the whip, had succeeded in holding on to them. Furious people had scaled the carriage, uttering cries of vengeance. The great lady who was inside the carriage was terrified; as for the gentleman sitting beside her, his face had not been pierced by any emotion. He had contented himself with throwing a few handfuls of gold into the crowd, in a negligent and impassive fashion. At the sight of that magic rain, the common people had suddenly calmed down. The horses had been released, and the coachman had taken advantage of that to drive away rapidly.

The manifestation seemed to be concluded, and would have been, in fact, but for an unexpected incident. At the moment when the carriage set off again, the lady, who had recovered her composure, had said a few words to her husband; the latter had replied, in a loud voice and in the most indifferent tone with a remark that had, unfortunately, been overheard by a number of people: "There are enough children in the world without that brat."

That cruel comment had run from mouth to mouth. Toward evening, the crowd had pressed, like the turbulent waves of the ocean, beneath the windows of the house inhabited by the man who had pronounced such harsh words in public. People were crying vengeance, and several agitators were already trying to break down the main door. In order to reestablish order and tranquility, it was necessary to have recourse to armed force, and there had been casualties, some of them fatal. Gradually, however, the multitude had dispersed and the night had rendered calm to minds—except that the gentleman as advised not to show himself in the streets of the city for some time.

When that tale reached the ears of Albert the Great, a sudden flash of enlightenment passed through his mind; his face cleared; the expression of his features, melancholy or a long time, became cheerful, and he cried, full of enthusiasm: "My work is not lost! By that absence of heart, I recognize my automaton! Homunculus lives; I shall go to recover him."

He left for the great city that same day, accompanied by two brothers. In less than twenty-four hours they had arrived at their destination.

Rightly presuming that their habits might alarm the automaton, they disguised themselves as men-at-arms and went, the very next day, to Homunculus' house. Albert, transformed into a knight, asked to speak to the master of the house. Far from inspiring suspicion, their disguised served to facilitate their passage, because, since the recent events. Homunculus had been put under protection of the army.

When Albert was in the presence of the pretended gentleman, he recognized his automaton joyfully. As soon as the valet who had introduced him had withdrawn, he ran to his creation and, rapidly pressing the hidden switch that was known to him alone, immobilized Homunculus immediately.

In a matter of minutes the automaton was dismantled, and, the two brothers who were waiting at the door having come in, each of them hid several pieces of the machine under his cloak. Albert took the head and shoulders, and thus, as Roman senators had once caused their first king to disappear, the monks carried poor Homunculus away without being seen.

A few days after that event, the automaton was installed in the cell again, submissive as in the past to the orders of his master and inventor. As before, he fulfilled the double function in his regard of secretary and domestic. Albert was radiant with joy, and now kept watch on his work with jealous care. There was no more chance of escape for the unfortunate Homunculus henceforth. Fortunately for him, his lack of a heart spared him from all regrets and all sadness.

A month after that forced return, the celebrated Thomas Aquinas, nicknamed the Great Ox of Wisdom, came to render a visit to the Dominican convent; he had undertaken the voyage with the objective of seeing Albert and appreciating his marvelous inventions for himself. Scarcely had he arrived than he asked for the celebrated magician. A brother indicated to him the cell he inhabited and then withdrew.

Thomas Aquinas having knocked on the door, Homunculus, following his master's orders, immediately came to open it. At the sight of him, the man inspired by the Lord was gripped by fright; he had immediately sensed the absence of the heart, and divined the artificial man in the Dominican's domestic. He must even have mistaken Homunculus for the spirit of evil, for, having raised a knotty oak staff that served him as a support, he struck the automaton on the head with a blow so violent that this time, the machine was permanently destroyed.

The arguments that followed the automaticide were violent. Albert did not spare the future saint, but all his anger was futile. The master's work was irredeemably annihilated.

Why had Thomas Aquinas not come to the convent before Homunculus' escape? What annoyances poor humanity would have been spared!

In time, the Dominican succeeded in resigning himself and almost consoling himself for the loss he had suffered. It was not the same for the wife of the automaton. The great lady could not explain her husband's sudden disappearance. Incapable of reconciling herself to that inconceivable separation, she set everything in motion to find him.

Her research was devoid of result. Albert maintained an obstinate silence and the brothers who had lent him their aid in the abduction of the automaton were also constrained to silence, because the Dominican had compelled them under the most severe menaces. It was only after his death that they talked, and it is to them that the relation of this story is owed.

Many years have gone by since that epoch. The events recounted above have been partly forgotten, but the automaton's descendants are still alive, alas. The two sons he had by his marriage have perpetuated his race. Sometimes it seems to be extinct, but suddenly, be the power of the phenomenon of atavism, individuals entirely identical to the first Homunculus reappear on the world stage.

You ask with astonishment: "Where are they encountered?" Without looking very far, you can find marvelously accomplished specimens; they can be seen in all ranks of society; each sex counts its representatives, and it will be particularly easy for you to find examples among courtiers and men of the world.

The Man of the Sea

by Arnold Mortier

It was in Dresden two or three years ago.

A friend of the signatory of these lines, passing through the capital of the kingdom of Saxe, was in a shop of comestibles where he was purchasing a few provisions for the journey, The service as slow, the packaging careful. Slightly fatigued, he sat down next to the counter and, while the merchant was arranging ham and sausages in a small basket, his eyes fell on some old sheets of manuscript, doubtless destined to wrap the greasy acquisitions of clients.

One of them was torn in half, the truncated phrases of which he tried to reconstitute:

What he had perceived in the waves was...
...a Parisien, a Vien...
...an inhabitant of...Dresden flee...
..It was a bath...
..a naked...
...tracing a pink...
,,,in the somber sea...
..What...
...satanic, what redoubtable spe...

Other sheets lay scattered among various pieces of meat. He scanned them, and the reading interested him enormously.

"Where did you get these manuscripts?" my friend asked the shopkeeper.

"In truth," the fellow replied, rather astonished, "They've been in the house for a long time; a musician who came to lodge here with my grandfather in 1813 left precipitately one day, only leaving to settle his rent a trunk full of papers. The musician having never come back, we conserved those scribbles, father and son, until the moment when I decided to utilize them in this fashion. There were a large number of them, but those you see there are all that remain."

My friend easily obtained from the typical Teuton the gift of those few yellowing sheets "Which aren't even worth as much as printed paper for making good bags," and, having returned to his lodgings he started rereading the German text, of which the rats had nibbled their share, and which time had rendered almost indecipherable.

The more he studied the semi-effaced lines, the more he was struck by the strange and quasi-symbolic form that he discovered in them. He repeated to himself obstinately: "One might think it an unpublished tale by Hoffmann."

Evidently, nothing permitted the supposition that the disorderly and ever-needy author of *The Cremona Violin* had neglected to have a single one of his literary and philosophical fantasies published. But my friend gave himself excellent reasons nevertheless and ended up, for want of material evidence, bringing together a series of probabilities that appeared to him to be conclusive.

After having observed that the manuscript must be a copy, since it did not resemble known autographs of Hoffmann, he recalled very appropriately that the celebrated author of the fantastic tales had been brought, by the hazards of a more than agitated life, to occupy in Dresden he much sought-after post of the leader of the orchestra of the National Opera. That happened in 1813.

Now, it was the same year, 1813, that Napoléon entered Dresden.

The arrival of the victor of Lützen and Bautzen must have had, as a consequence, the precipitate flight of the German writer, who, apart from his great literary and musical value, possessed a talent for drawing that had permitted him to publish bloody caricatures of Napoléon. The great captain, who was very sensible to attainments of ridicule, would certainly not have spared their author.

It then became explicable how Hoffmann had come to hide, probably under a false name, in the home of a local pork-butcher, and how he had departed suddenly without even having the time to take the unknown works, of which the tale in question must be the sole recoverable relic.

For want of the illustrious Xavier Marmier, who has faithfully rendered into French the literary baggage of the great German storyteller, my friend was forced to furnish me with a very conventional translation of the text reconstituted by him. It is that translation that I am reproducing here without further commentary.

Nature, which has multiplied on the coasts of Norway the gigantic cliffs crowned with pines, has not shown herself anywhere more fantastic and more picturesque than in the splendid bay of Vaagen, in the depths of which the white and red houses of Bergen appear.

It was on the occidental point of the bay, that a jagged rock eroded by the sea was found, posed as if on a pedestal of seaweed and wrack, but covered nevertheless by mosses and evergreen trees, where Christian Vogt loved to come to dream.

Few human beings are as rudely tempered as Christian was for the struggles of life. An elevated noble and virile soul in a body of steel, an extraordinary intelligence developed by sane and forceful studies, he was entirely out of place in Bergen, in the midst of a buy population of fishermen and mariners, and fat merchants whose life was spent behind a counter or astride a barrel. He avoided worldly seductions, never frequented taverns, and seemed to be reserving himself for some great unknown task. He was the kind of man of which celebrated heroes and benefactors of humanity are made, and who become the instruments of destiny when destiny condescends to make them its plaything.

Christian was taciturn, not because he was misanthropic, but because he saw nothing around him but futile minds; apart from the old priest who, before dying, had had time to make of him a man of courage and knowledge, he never found anyone to whom he could talk, or who could respond to him.

God had isolated him on earth, first by rendering him an orphan in his early years and then by attributing to him a total of superiorities that so many other men lacked.

Every day, when the sun was already in decline over the horizon, Christian came to contemplate the immense infinity of the ocean from the height of the cliff of the promontory, which the mysterious work of the centuries had erected like a fantastic sentinel at the entrance to the bay of Vaagen.

In his mute and mystical observation, in his sublime and profound meditation, Christian was never alone. He believed that he was living in the midst of an unknown world, surrounded by supernatural spirits who understood his thoughts, his dreams, and his vague and as yet undetermined ambition.

One day, lending his ear to the muted chant of the ocean and seeking to imagine what the distant horizon was not showing him, he had just cried out with a noble impatience: "What can I do that is great?"

His attention was drawn to the foot of the cliff by a slight slash that, in spite of its lack of intensity, made itself heard in the midst of the more imposing sounds of waves breaking against the rock.

Christian leaned over, looking down below, uttered an inexpressible cry, got up with one bund and fled without looking back.

What he had perceived in the waves would not have made an inhabitant of Paris, Vienna or Dresden flee.

It was a bather, a naked woman, tracing a pink furrow through the somber sea.

What a satanic dazzlement, what redoubtable spell for that chaste and robust man!

The sight of the body with the voluptuous contours maddened him, and the smile of the pretty swimmer remained engraved in his eyes and in his heart; for, in spite of the rapidity of his retreat, he had had time to see that the woman was smiling at him. She had smiled at him, in fact, blissfully, immodestly, without embarrassment and without any apparent concern for her improbable nudity.

The next day, Christian did not come back.

He shut himself away, entrenched in a vain and sterile meditation, thinking even so and against his will about the apparition of the previous day.

That apparition was reproduced in a dream, and the awakening seemed full of shame.

Christian understood that retreat could only add to the obsession, while the great horizons that were familiar to him might perhaps deflect the course of his ideas.

In any case, the bather could only have come to that almost inaccessible place by chance. She certainly would not reappear there; he would never see her again.

And he returned to the cliff, full of assurance. The sea was calm. The waves were dying slowly at the foot of the rock.

Christian remained plunged in an anxious reverie. She was no longer there. That was what he had hoped, but he was surprised to regret the accomplishment of his hope. After a little while, however, he heard a slight splash and he saw again the beautiful body, to which the fluidity of the sea in which it was playing scarcely lent a silvery gauze.

Christian was no longer afraid now.

Far from fleeing, he contemplated the perfidious spectacle and abandoned himself to unknown sensations.

On his knees at the edge of the cliff, in the posture that he had only ever adopted in order to elevate his soul toward God, he looked down—a man who had always wanted to look too high! He gazed, with a superstitious joy that he no longer tried to dissimulate, at that marvelously beautiful woman, whose smile gradually intoxicated him.

It was strangely lascivious, that smile, calm, incessant and as if fixed to the vermilion lips of the admirable creature.

Vanquished and fascinated, Christian wanted to get closer to the unknown woman; like a fanatical Hindu who slips into the temple by night in order to see the divinity, he would take advantage of the declining daylight to descend without being seen, he thought, and surprise her at his ease.

The enterprise was rude and perilous, the cliff being sheer and rather high, but Christian was strong and adroit. Furthermore, his natural vigor was multiplied tenfold by a truly unusual overexcitement, which metamorphosed him in his own eyes.

Twenty times, on the improvised route in the midst of rocks ready to fall away, he was nearly dragged down. He resisted everything and continued his terrible descent even so.

The sinuosities that he was constrained to follow grew increasingly steep and caused him in the end to lose sight of the sea, and the bather, and the smile that attracted him.

When he finally found himself on the strand, at the angle of a colossal rock, the unknown woman had disappeared.

Where was she? There was no trace, no vestige on the shore.

Where had she come from, then, via the high sea?

Poor Christian went home timidly, searching in vain for the key to the enigma.

For two more days, the two following days, he saw the pretty bather again in the same circumstances, and recommenced the same descent, with the same lack of success.

On the third day, he sat on the strand and waited. For certainly, if he were not the victim of some diabolical mirage, the mysterious creature would come back, and nothing could frighten her or put her to flight, since instead of the descent along the rock face, as on the other days, he would be there, at the moment of her arrival, very close to her, close enough to speak to her, and even to reach her.

Night fell, arm and starry. Christian did not sleep. He counted the hours, lending his ear to the distant carillons of Bergen, impatient and feverish, saluting with a cry of joy the first light of the rising sun. Would he see her again? From which direction would she come? Would she arrive in the bay from the open sea, or would she surge forth abruptly from behind a rock?

The wait was long. The hours of the day flew by without him being able to discover anything on the surface of the waves but the rapid flight of gulls, full of undulations and the inflated sails of fishing boats. He felt despair invading his soul; then everything was forgotten before the sudden vision of the beautiful swimmer. She was there, a few meters from the shore, and he did not even try to explain her sudden and supernatural appearance. He devoured her with his eyes, intoxicated himself on the sight of her. And she was still smiling.

She approached the shore, darting a strange gaze at him, fixed, troubling and unsustainable; then, suddenly, she described a semicircle and drew away, as if to reach the open sea.

Christian was a exceptional swimmer. He threw himself into the water with the impetuosity of young charger launched on an endless trail.

In a few moments he had caught up with the unknown beauty, who was swimming with a sustained and regular rapidity, not seeming disposed to do anything whatsoever to abridge or complicate the difficulties of his nautical course. When he arrived beside her she neither relented nor accelerated her speed.

She did not make any gesture of surprise, nor let any exclamation of joy or terror escape; she smiled—that was all.

He remained silent, content to admire hr and not daring to speak to her. But hat mute contemplation could not last. The passion of the young man, stimulated by the sight of that marvelous immodest body, was soon exhaled in ardent confessions.

"I love you! I adore you!" he said, with each stroke that carried them into the Immense ocean. She did not reply; she smiled.

"Respond to me, adored darling," he sighed.

She continued smiling.

"I love you!" he repeated, with a rage of obstinacy.

But there was always nothing but the eternal smile.

The day declined. Already, they had both been swimming for a long time, unrelentingly, without a rest, and without even changing the monotonous regularity of their movements.

How far would she take him?

She did not seem to experience any lassitude.

The young man, on the contrary, felt fatigued; he was maintaining himself by means of painful jerks, and he darted a long glance behind him.

A grandiose and imposing spectacle!

It was the hour when the setting sun modifies at every second the multiple coloration of the sea. The sheet of water traveled seemed immense. He could scaly see the first reefs blanched by the waves. As for his favorite rock, he perceived it, confused, indecisive and imperceptible, as if surrounded by a sinister vapor. The promontory was no more than a pin-head, and Christian told himself that it had been sufficient for him to follow that silent and admirable creature for everything that he had believed to be large to appear to him very small.

However, his strength was exhausted. Every new wave seemed only to be coming toward him in order to engulf him in the vast ocean, the depth of which he sensed augmenting as he lost sight of the land.

He appealed to the woman to help him. She did not even appear to hear him, continuing to smile. That was too much. He succeeded in reaching her, by means of a supreme effort, and tried to seize her, mingling the voluptuousness of the first touch with the reckless grasp of a drowning man. But his hands only encountered icy arms, and shoulders over which they slid.

At the same time it seemed to him that beneath him, an abyss was hollowed out; the sea opened up and everything began to whirl. He thought that he had been transformed into a top, so rapidly was he spinning. The clouds in the sky were spinning too, and the big waves were spinning, sucking him in, drawing him into a gigantic funnel. Crabs of colossal dimensions were climbing along his legs, tickling the soles of his feet, while gigantic octopodes enlaced him with their tentacles.

All the monsters of the sea attacked his body, in order to drag him to the bottom. He wanted to scream, but the water closed his mouth. He saw, above him, in the vapors of the twilight, horrible heads that were laughing at his agony; in the foam of waves, huge phantoms extended arms to him; then the water closed his eyes. Then he heard again, in a muted roar, yapping voices that cried: "You're ours! You belong to us forever!" At that moment, the water closed his ears. At the same time as the great and eternal silence commenced for him, he clung to the beloved creature in a final convulsion.

Dominating the sound of the waves, a strange cracking sound was immediately produced, something like the mechanism of a clock breaking.

The man and the woman sank; the water seethed for a few moments.

The following day, in the depths of the bay, the tide washed up two bodies, tightly enlaced; one as the lacerated cadaver of Christian Vogt; the other was a mechanical woman, an automaton whose mainspring had broken.

The man's face expressed he tortures of a terrible agony.

The woman was smiling.

The man was buried and the woman was repaired,

She will always smile, for the smile of dolls is eternal—like evil.

Industria

by Didier de Chousy

I. The City

In the era that we have now reached, the founders of the Central Fire Company have perfected their work. For some years, the city whose first stones they laid at the same time as they made the first pick-axe blows of the excavation—the city that was confidently mapped out around the rim of the geothermal well, Industria—has flourished in a prosperity exceeding all hopes.

Not only has the Central Fire kept its word and delivered to its shareholders their daily million horse-power, but the force and the heat have unexpectedly exceeded that quota—a circumstance doubtless brought about by some internal lesion opening up a more direct access to the heat, augmenting the heating surface, which initially made the engineers anxious but without anything justifying their fears. The functioning of the well, having become more intense, became regular and merely provided a surfeit of riches that permitted the distribution of the shareholders of a greater dividend of well-being.

For the traveler arriving from the east across the cold fields and desolate vegetation of that part of Ulster, it was a marvelous spectacle when the panorama of Industria City unfurled before his gaze: an immense plain adorned with all sorts of flowers, limited by a circle of hills planted with woods and vineyards, which enveloped the territory with a mantle of green foliage and vines.

At the center is an Oriental city deposited in Ireland, along with its sky, its climate, its palaces in lacy stone: a city of scattered villas, white and shady, mounted like daisies in a lawn, open to all the breezes of the air and all the perfumes of the fields. On the far side of the plain, beyond the city, the girdle of hills opens to give access to the sea, where a life-sized image of this prosperity is reflected, on a sea with gently blue waves, which come, shaking their foamy manes to present their mirror to the Venus of the shore.

The approaches to Industria's port are defended by electric eels, motionless living torpedoes hidden in the sand, which reveal two gleams, two semi-extinct eyes like dull lanterns; guardians chained to the shore by the wires transmitting their signals. The power of these fish—already great enough to kill horses, as Humboldt has observed—has been further developed by means of Ruhmkorff coils wrapped around them. They cannot sink ships, but their discharges into iron hulls reach the crews, paralyzing them or killing them.

Ships swarm in the harbor; carriage-boats, improved chariots of Amphitrite, whose disks skim the water, and, like halcyons, only dip the tips of their wings into the sea; which cross the Atlantic in twenty-four minutes, without paying any more heed to storms than a cart pays to potholes—for, properly speaking, there are no more ships and what people call navigation no longer differs from journeys overland. From Ireland to India, from one antipode to the other, journeys are made without changing carriages, without the voyager noticing whether he is moving over land or sea. The wagons descend to the shore by means of a ramp, their wheels boxed in drums which float like barges and turn like wheels; a locomotive, carried by these paddle-wheels, is detached from the shore and harnessed to a train that takes to the open sea and draws away, whistling. If the weather is good, the voyagers go up on to the imperial and savor the marvelous skating with their gaze; if it is bad, they close the windows and the express train, sweeping aside the little waves and hollowing tunnels through the big ones, pursues its course more rapidly than the wind and more furiously that the tempest.[33]

---

[33] The author inserts a footnote here: "A few items of practical information will be useful to readers who might be called up-

For the transport of goods, at low speed, a few bad habits of the old systems have been preserved; even so, the boats no longer go over the water but under it, fifteen or thirty meters deep in the tranquil zone that begins beneath the pellicle of the waves. One can get an idea of ships of this type by imagining large swans with two necks, only allowing these necks to emerge, like the piers of a bridge, sustaining a gangway above the water where passengers stand. Giant ferries, these steamboats! Enormous Saint Christophers marching on the sea-bed, bearing their passengers in their extended arms! Marine monsters as large as islands, frightening to see emerging within

---

on to take one of these express trains. On terrestrial railways, the longest journeys extend for a few hundred leagues; stops are frequent, bends numerous and inclines considerable. This combination of causes restricts speeds to puerile proportions of 80 to 100 kilometers per hour. It is only on the sea that serious speeds can be obtained. Straight lines are almost infinite there: no bends, no slopes, the spherical surface of the globe being level everywhere; no obligatory stops between one continent and another. From the port of Industria to New York is 4,000 kilometers in a straight, flat line. What a magnificent racecourse! What a prey for those hungry for space!"

"Now, it is a scientific notoriety that speed suppresses weight; that a wheel—a disk as well as a planet, animated by a rapid velocity, is freed from gravity to the extent of losing a large part, if not the whole, of its weight. It is for that reason that a locomotive in motion weighs on the rails less than a locomotive at rest; in going faster, it weighs even less, and at the extreme limit of speed no longer weighs anything at all. As speed increases, weight diminishes; as weight diminishes, speed increases, without one being able to determine any other limit than the insufficiency of space. Long distances are indispensable, and the 4,000 kilometers that separate Ireland and America are scarcely sufficient for maritime trains to be able to launch themselves to the limit and stop time. They would arrive sooner if they had further to go."

133

view of a port. When they dive to depart, one might thing that a portion of the coast is sinking.

The Protean manifestations of the great source of fire and force can be seen spreading out into the distance and beyond the sea as easily as they do in the plain of Industria City, where hot air and steam, channeled as in a drainage system, warm the soil, excite its vitality, activate organic decompositions and impregnate the atmosphere with a fecundating mist. Thus organized, the countryside is a veritable hothouse! A hothouse in the open air, without any other shelter than the ring of hills, provided that that the thermosiphons are powerful enough to vanquish the Irish weather and to create a tropical climate.

Following the admiration caused by the aspect of the landscape and its flora, a new astonishment takes hold of the visitor, at the sight of the creatures that cultivate these fields, of those country-folk of an unknown species, triple crosses of humans, animals and machines—a fauna unclassified and unclassifiable, as strange as the most peculiar animals of antediluvian nature.

Here, in a field that is being prepared for sowing, is a biped whose enormous breast roars and shakes like a pressure-cooker. Like the angel of the Apocalypse, the legs supporting the trunk are two columns that march stiffly and heavily. It is dragging a ploughshare attached to its waist, which is so heavy that the beast's entire body sweats an oily and rancid mist. No human being guides this laborer, which, from time to time, unhitches itself and goes to a spring, from which it drinks long draughts. Thus refreshed, it resumes its work.

Another worker follows, in the same furrow. Long and flat, it resembles a crocodile whose jaw has been made into a rake; its teeth rake and harrow the soil, completing the work of the plough, and when it has passed, the earth is ready for seeding. Then the sewer advances, launching cascades of grain from its open mouth, like the nymph of a fountain, which spread out all around: Ceres, thin and bronzed, a farmer's daughter rather than his wife; a Ceres of iron, forged by Vul-

134

can. A second crocodile follows in the footsteps of the sewer and buries the seeds with its rake.

In the neighboring fields, where the harvest is under way, there is no less activity. Snakes with steel teeth hiss as they undulate through the fallows and bite the bases of the ears of corn, which lean over and fall into the ties extended to them by others in charge of the gathering. Reapers are shaving one field, and there are haymakers that one might take for lunatics, so agitated are their long thin arms, hurling the hay to ridiculous heights, which falls back and settles over them.

These creatures, or people, fill the countryside with their activities, as diverse as their forms, enveloped like phantoms in the clouds of steam they exude. One might imagine that one was seeing a swarm of insects: scarabs with bronze wing-cases and prothoraxes gleaming like suits of armor—but insects promoted to the size of pachyderms.

You will already have recognized the pseudo-human race conceived by Lord Hotairwell and brought into the world by his skilful engineers: the *Enginemen*, or, rather, the *Atmophytes*, for the latter appellation has prevailed; the rural Atmophytes, bloated peasants, as inferior to their colleagues in the city as a farmhand who grooms horses is to a valet who grooms human beings. Only the latter merit the name of Atmophytes—steam-men[34]—for one cannot call facsimiles of humans so closely resembling their creators "animals" or "machines". They are men of iron and copper, similar to diving-suits or knights in armor; bodies in which steam has been substituted for blood, in which electricity animates mechanisms so refined, so subtle and so steeped in human genius that they immaterialize themselves by the virtuosity of their

---

[34] The Greek *atmos* means "vapor", and as the French word for steam is *vapeur*, the first part of the synthesized term can easily be held to signify "steam", but the Greek *phyton*, which gives rise to the English and French suffix –phyte, means "plant", and not, by any stretch of the etymological imagination, "man".

matter, and their gestures are less reminiscent of products of force than manifestations of life.

They are creatures perfect enough to disquiet their creators with the possibility that these strange beings might one day cross, by means of their acquired speed, the narrow frontier within which intelligence confines instinct, trying in their turn to scale the heavens, to stifle their bewildered masters against breasts of bronze, and to render into their native dust the human clay that they once took for gods!

II. A Comfortable City

It is to the outskirts of the city, to the bosom of the active anthill of the suburbs, that one must go to see this population of automata eagerly about the work that is entrusted to them: the express porters and the steam messengers; the compressed-air warehousemen, heavy-treading iron Hercules carrying mountains of goods on their shoulders; the high-speed taxi-cabs, retained with difficulty by their mechanical drivers who sting the metal plebs with lashes of their electric whips to urge them on, making them howl as they receive the discharges and leap forward; the phonographs that transmit orders and news, reading in loud voices the newspapers with which their bellies are filed; the microphones with keen ears, indiscreet jeering street-urchins who pass on everything they hear, crying out the secrets they have discovered, roaring like bulls in deaf ears and adding the excess of their joyful capers to the busy tumult of the populous streets.

These innumerable servants are animated by a love of their masters unknown to the domestics of old, and would kill themselves in their service if death were able to claim such solid bodies. They come and go in every direction, their paths interweaving at top speed, skillfully avoiding collisions that would be terrible between such vigorous individuals; they anticipate one another, and converse between themselves by means of a guttural croaking, of which the talking machine at the Paris Exposition[35] might give you some idea. These ardent workers only pause on the orders of their manometers, in order to drink at the public fountains that fill them up with compressed air, electricity or steam—which is to say, with strength and life!

As one crosses the exterior boulevards, the proletarian tumult suddenly falls silent, this population being swallowed up by the subterranean streets designed for them—for the city is built, in its entirety, over a cellar; it covers a crypt as vast as itself, dedicated to the residence and labors of Atmophytes. It is there that the factories, storehouses, laboratories and steel-yards are located, from which ships emerged fully-armed and houses fully-built.

Beneath this vault is a labyrinthine network of sewers and channels, telegraphic and telephonic wires. Trams suspended from the vault are in motion there, atmospheric tubes unroll there: enormous serpents which swallow and vomit unrelentingly; long culverins which load up travelers at the breech which they fire to their destinations. Rails, tubes, wires, countless engines, to which this civilization is appended, unroll at the foot of their city like the roots at the foot of a tree that enable the flowers to grow in the crown: a city organized like those well-designed modern dwellings which hide the kitchens, the pantry, the servants' quarters and the servants themselves underground, only revealing the glorious face of the master and the façade of the château; a residence of happiness, perfect happiness without deficit and without plethora, without the satiety of an excessively blue sky nor the regret of fog and rain, since the engineers create their own rain and fog when needed.

The houses of Industria, with no shutters other than their blinds of climbing plants, and no defenses other than their masters' probity (that of Atmophytes is beyond question) are

---

[35] There had been two *expositions universelles* in Paris when the novel was first published, in 1855 and 1878; it is the second to which the author is referring.

far enough apart to leave frontiers of foliage between them, but close enough to one another to defy solitude: family life and public life at the same time; salubrious life in a climate maintained at fifteen degrees centigrade—the lukewarm temperature of orange-groves and marriage, propitious for the nurturing of durable sentiments, which evaporate like liquids when one brings them to boiling point.

Most of the habitations are fabricated from blocks of translucent glass, rendered unbreakable by the Bastie process[36] and furnished at a low price by the glassworks of Industria, where the sands of the sea-bed, the central fire and the handiwork of Atmophytes cost nothing.

One of the most curious specimens of this architecture is an edifice in polished crystal, as dull and fleecy as frozen snow, whose first story rests on a heap of little icebergs and which is coiffed, by way of a roof, by an ice-floe surmounted by a polar bear. This construction, which exhales the mists and frosts of the pole, is the head office of the General Company for Perpetual Breakage, whose offices had to be transferred from the North Pole because of their growth.

The importance of this enterprise merits its introduction to the reader. Struck by the inconvenience of the variety of seasons, which subjects humans to the elements and whirls them around like leaves in a tornado, without respect and without prophylactic transitions, the engineers of Industria, inspired by Lord Hotairwell, have undertaken to obviate it.[37] It is well-known that on one part of the European continent, the atmospheric variations depend on the fracturing of ice-sheets that break off from time to time from the belt of circumpolar ice. When winter is harsh at the pole, the thicker ice is less easily dislocated; the break-up is slower and, as the rains re-

---

[36] Tempered glass was invented by François Royer de La Bastie in 1874.

[37] Author's note: "*The Domestication of Climates* by Lord Hotairwell, 10 volumes, London: Watbled & Sons, Publishers."

main crystallized in their sources, spring is cold and summer rainy.

The General Company for Perpetual Breakage was proposed, as its name indicates, to produce the breakage of the polar ice itself, and to break the ice wherever need dictates, managing the progress of the thaw in the best interests of the countries whose climate it had taken over. Its means of action consisted of cracking the polar ice with the aid of enormous torpedoes submerged in the sea subjacent to holes drilled in the ice; the internal tempests resulting from the explosions disaggregated the ice into floating blocks, which a marine current conducted to Newfoundland, where their melting determined the desired meteorological effects.

The benefits of the enterprise consisted: firstly, in royalties paid to the countries subscribing to the breakage; secondly, in sales of ice, dispatched loose, as complete icebergs; thirdly, in toll-charges to be levied on the polar passage, as soon as the Company has finished breaking the ice and freeing up that passage; and fourthly, in polar bears surprised by the explosion of ice-floes, drifting with the to Europe and sold for acclimatization or for their fur.

Like everything else in this world, the General Company for Perpetual Breakage had suffered a few setbacks. Its most recent exercise had gone awry; the administrators having pushed the breakage too far, and sent the ice-floes in the wrong direction, an avalanche of icebergs had descended upon England. Greenland had blockaded Great Britain. That year, the polar sea was free, but the Channel was blocked; whole populations perished from colds and chills. Only the inhabitants of Industria, huddled by the side of their central fire, had observed no lowering of the thermometer or variation in the condition of the air.

The Company had paid substantial indemnities—but such accidents are merely the sacrifices necessary to avert the caprices of fortune, and besides, important as the principal element of its wealth was, the Company has other sources of prosperity; it has many other stocks of the same sort in its

139

portfolio, and other projects of the same value—which puts the future on a safe footing, and demonstrates that the architecture of the abode of the General Company for Perpetual Breakage is perfectly appropriate to the enterprises that are perpetuated there—that chaos surmounted by a bear really is its emblem and its sign, so eloquent that passers-by, especially shareholders, cannot look at that head office, nor sit down there, without experiencing a shiver.

It is, however, impossible to give a complete description of the marvelous enterprises born around the geothermal well; one would heap up volumes in listing the names of these exploits of industry and science which, to the gaze of a stranger, seem to be prodigies, but which, to the inhabitants of Industria, are merely vulgar manifestations of its power over all the realm of nature: over the flora redesigned, recolored and remade by incomparable chemists; over the fauna manipulated by hybridizations so bold and grafts so strange that some of the resultant beasts no longer resemble the animals of the Creation. Adam would not have recognized them, and Noah would have chased them out of the Ark as paradoxical animal creations, travestied with the manifest aim of annoying nature: furry birds and feathered serpents; white blackbirds rendered yellow by infusions of bile; canaries turned blue by nourishment based on pepper. Even men, or at least their wives, took part in these masquerades, grafting coiffures of living hummingbirds on to their heads, hanging Cleopatra necklaces of sea anemones in aspic around their necks, or even—in imitation of squids, which owe their whiteness to their blue blood—turning their blood blue to whiten their skin, risking their lives by substituting dialyzed Pravais copper for the dialyzed Bravais iron that is the basis of good blood—a dangerous counterfeit.[38]

---

[38] Bravais is presumably the crystallographer Auguste Bravais (1811-1863), whose relevance to the iron-containing hemoglobin in blood is rather slight; it is unclear who "Pravais" is supposed to be, although the author presumably has the color

Let us hasten to add that these excesses are exceptional, and that the science of breeder-chemists is ordinarily applied to more elevated problems, as evidenced by the magisterial creation of the beautiful species of Horse-Dogs, saddle-dogs and equine pointers, incomparable for riding out and hunting.

The habitations of Industria, almost all in glass, are mostly more prepossessing in form and color than that of the General Company for Perpetual Breakage. Violet glass, recognized as extremely tonic, as favorable to human health as to that of plants, is employed for hospitals, which are, in any case, few in number in a city where public health is excellent. Madhouses, which are much more numerous, are constructed on the model of the one run by the celebrated physician who treated mental illness by the homeopathy of colors, *homeochromopathy.*[39]

These houses are in glass of different shades, according to the madness in question. Furious madmen generally obtain benefit from a sojourn in authentically unbreakable bright red double-glazing. Hypochondriacs recover their cheerfulness in padded cells of polished black glass. Overexcited poets calm down when imprisoned in sky-blue glass. Sluggish or anemic intelligences, dotards or idiots, come on miraculously when placed in sunlight, with their eyes wide open, beneath melon-shaped bells—a method imitated by nature, which has made the eye in the form of a globe or a lens, in order that the solar rays are concentrated there, activating the maturation of the brain. Few patients resist these treatments; a few, however, although fully cured, leave the establishment afflicted with

---

of copper sulphate in mind in imagining a copper-based substitute for haemoglobin.

[39] Homeopathy and chromopathy were both fashionable therapies in 19th-century France, but this fictitious combination is fanciful.

Daltonism,[40] having lost the notion of colors, and even that if ideas.

The most elegant private dwellings are Oriental in style, in muslin-glass that is transparent or opaque, according to the owner's mood. When the solar spectrum impregnates these translucent walls, as iridescent as soap-bubbles, one might think them fragments of a rainbow. This is charming by day, but the nights are enchanted in that city, illuminated by all its houses, which light up like lamps within their globes.

In addition to electrical apparatus, a superior system is available for lighting, which consists of storing sunlight by means of a substance called *heliovore*. Every ray of sunlight that falls on a surface coated with heliovoracious glue is captured like a bird in a trap, and the entire city, its inhabitants, their nightclothes and their winter clothing are coated with sunlight by this means, rendered bright and warm. That kind of lighting would supplant all others if it were not necessary to take account of the collection time, in view of which the old Gramme apparatus and Jablokoff moderator lamps are conserved for emergencies.[41]

The lighting of the countryside is obtained, without expense, with the collaboration of local glow-worms, the careful selection and skilful cross-breeding of which have increased their size and develop the photogenic aptitude, and to which other luminous insects imported from tropical climates have been added. South-American Elaters, whose vivid gleam per-

---

[40] Strictly speaking, Daltonism—named after the atomic theorist John Dalton, who suffered from it—is red/green color-blindness, although the author appears to be using the term as if it applied to general colour-blindness.

[41] Zénobe Gramme (1826-1901) patented a direct current generator in 1870, which was used in some early electric lighting systems. Jablokoff is a once-common rendering of the name of the Russian Pavel Yablochkov (1847-1894), who developed a kind of electrical arc-lamp, known as the Yablochkov candle, in 1876.

mits travelers to read by their light, mark out the roads by night, flamboyant road-workers illuminates on the verges, and millions of Italian Lampyra are distributed in the fields like minuscule lighthouses, emitting their intermittent flashes at regular intervals, along with Pyrophores, secreting droplets of oil that sparkle as they oxidize, and Lucioles, perched like lamps at the tops of blades of grass, their abdomens extended and rounded like opaline globes, constellating the verdure and illuminating the foliage.[42]

You can imagine what decisive elements of success are achieved by nocturnal fêtes with such a provision of lights of all the colors of the prism, and others recently invented, and what a décor in provided by those fields inundated with fires, that city sweating sunlight and those streets parqueted with radiance, populated with sparkling crowds wearing resplendent clothes, in which every passer-by is a gleam, a glare, a scintillation, a flame of joy, an animalcule of phosphorescence!

These beautiful soirées are prolonged until dawn, until the exhaustion of strength, until ophthalmia takes possession of eyes overloaded by such glare. Then, saturated with pleasure and fleeing the heat, everyone goes home and opens fountains at the summits of their roofs, which shroud the houses with their cascades. If anyone desires sleep and silence, blinds like vast wings are deployed over the dwellings and the houses, as brilliant as beacons a moment before, disappear into semi-darkness—and a spectator in the sky would take those dim lights lurking beneath the foliage for a colony of sleeping glow-worms. If anyone is sad, and has need of noise and day-

---

[42] The names of these various bioluminescent insects seem to be confused by accidental redundancy; the members of the family of *Elateridae* (click beetles) possessed of this property belong to the genus *Pyrophorus*, while "lucioles" is an alternative term for members of the beetle genus Lampyridae, whose most familiar member is *Lampyris noctiluca*, the common "glow-worm" or "firefly".

light, the night that gives birth to dreams is dissipated as easily as it is created; the blinds are removed, the windows are opened, and one is refreshed by the borrowed happiness of neighbors; everyone can see everyone else while remaining at home, separated and united in wire-netting enclosures in the same aviary, taking part, to the extent of their desire, in the same concert of bird-song and colored plumage.

III, Yet More Happiness

The inhabitants of Industria are so happy at home that they hardly ever go out, although they are able to stay where they are and go out at the same time. Absence, that sickness of tender souls, has been eliminated. Everyone is ubiquitous, simultaneously at home and elsewhere—a result obtained by perfecting a means formerly proposed for sending telegrams without wires, without any other conductor than the ambient medium: a means abandoned because the first telegrams delivered by their own instinct went astray, the fickle electricity accepting too many conductors and delivering itself to any and all electrodes, but then restudied and made workable by the engineers of Industria, who have succeeded in domesticating the fluid, creating affinities—not to say affections—for it, which render it faithful to a single conductor and a single pole. Electricity is thus animalized and domesticated, only having to be put in contact with its master once, to smell and touch him, for that veritably canine magnetic current to come to heel or recover his trail.

The telechromophotophonotetroscope, invented at the same time, by the same physicists, eliminates absence in an even more radical fashion. The telechromophotophonotetroscope is, as everyone knows, an almost synoptic succession of instantaneous photographic prints, which reproduces electrically the face, speech and gestures of an absent person with a verity equivalent to presence, and which constitutes not so much an image as an apparition, a duplication of the absent individual.

144

This very simple apparatus consists of a chromophotograph that provides color prints, a megagraph that magnifies them, a stenophonograph that receives and transcribes the subject's speech, aided by a microphone that amplifies it, enclosed in a telephone conjoined with a tetroscope, to propagate the image and the sound. The different parts of the instrument add their efforts together and emit the product into a recipient commonly called a phenakistiscope—an acoustic and visual instrument by means of which one can see and hear. It works in such a way that, by modifying the operation of the system as required, one can make the absent individual appear, or appear in ones turn to him, at will.

The creation of the various parts of this apparatus go back some years, but the honor of contriving the synthesis and the physical combination is due to the scientists of Industria. You can imagine all the benefits of such an instrument and all the vitality that it lends to relationships. No more isolation or solitude; whether one likes it or not, one receives spectral visits from absent friends, provincial relatives or idle neighbors at all hours, arriving unceremoniously to spend an hour or a few days in your home. What a unification of all the inhabitants of the country, linked into a single family by threads so tight that one could not sever a limb without making the entire body cry out, nor pull out a single hair without tearing off the entire scalp!

The invention just described was also applicable to performances, to which no one went, since everyone could procure their charms at home—so theaters were, in spite of their magnificence, merely music-boxes, drama-factories whose produce was carried into domiciles by the telechromophotophonotetroscope, and whose overflow, escaping through the diaphonic cupola with which every room is provided, expanded into the atmosphere and impregnated it with harmony.

Music was also brought within everyone's range by a method that is not without analogy with that of Messieurs Cailletet and Pictet for the solidification of gases, and which consists of compressing the sonorous vibrations without extinguishing them, as one compresses a spring without breaking it, and of concentrating them to the point that an operetta can be held in a liter, and a drinking-song in a wine-glass. One of the greatest pleasures of the table was to uncork a brindisi, a polka or a waltz during the dessert, whose notes, as sparkling as Champagne wine, would burst forth from the neck. Sometimes, young Atmophytes would amuse themselves by giving microphones and phonographs the mingled dregs of these harmonic bottles to drink, which would then go out in a drunken state to dribble the discordant concert in the streets.

Although absence, as we have seen, had been averted, material distance had been no less happily vanquished by the most advanced means of transport. In addition to tramways and express tubes, it is appropriate to mention the aeroscaphs—the aerial boats that await use moored to windows like birds, attached by their beaks, constructed in aluminum, that weightless metal, and powered by compressed air—fifteen pounds of which, reduced to a volume of 100 liters by a pressure of 200 atmospheres, is sufficient to fuel a six-hour journey. Navigation is delightful when, opening one's window and leaping into one's boat as evening approaches, one sets off into the sky, when the enslaved breeze cries the gondola and inflates the sail with perfumed effluvia! Humans become sylphs and sail in a dream, landing on a cloud or skimming the terrestrial soil, protected from ruts and potholes.

But the roads of this region have neither potholes nor ruts, and the wide circular boulevards of the city can, like rivers, be called "moving roads". They do move, their causeways roll on moving cylinders installed in the crypt, dividing into equal sections the quarters inscribed between their borders. Without taking a step, one can make a tour of the city on foot, on these roads that travel, rotate and return, tranquil and majestic. Thus this city and this civilization rotate around their axis and their soul: the Central Fire, whose palace, the center of all these circles and the focal point of all these sectors, appears from all directions in the place of honor that is its due.

The edifice dedicated to the Central Terrestrial Fire, to the god Power, whose name is inscribed in Greek on its fronton, is both a temple and a town hall. The order of its architecture is naturalist, something like the Parthenon reconstructed on the plan of an *assommoir* by Monsieur Zola, architect.[43]

One of the most fortunate inspirations of its constructor has been to give this temple the form of a gigantic locomotive, nine hundred feet long and three hundred wide, surmounted by a copper cupola forming its steam-funnel. The body of the boiler, or the nave, is in sheet steel rendered un-oxidizable by steam-annealing, which preserves all of the metal's shine. Thus, when the sun lights this cylinder with the copper-girded flanks, it is difficult to bear the sight. That metallic surface becomes a reflector that returns the sun's rays blow for blow, and one cannot fix one's gaze upon it without falling into hypnotic ecstasy—a circumstance permitting the impregnation of crowds with the sentiments of mysterious attraction and dread that make the fortune of Sibylline temples.

You must not think, however, that any mysteries are accomplished in this temple and in the religion of a new humankind, promoted by its genius from the rank of creature to that of Creator: a race of Promethean conquerors, having finally discovered the secret of life, having broken its chains, overturned its rock and recovered its entrails from the vulture in order to take its seat at the banquet of the gods.

The interior of the temple is pragmatically adapted with a view to various uses. In the apse, at the rear of the actuary, is the God: the well of the Central Fire, linked by gross nozzles to the dome in which the great flux of the mounting waves of hot air is accumulated. That dome, whose superior hemisphere floats above the edifice like a huge copper aerostat, penetrates

---

[43] The word *assommoir*, which provides the title of one of Émile Zola's most famous "Naturalist" novels, published in 1877, is not usually translated when that novel is rendered into English, so I have preserved it here; it refers to a drinking den where cheap liquor is sold.

into the apse to the full extent of the other half of its sphere, which it deploys like a cup.

A colossal statue serves that cup as a pedestal: the statue of the goddess Antrakia,[44] coal: the daughter of the Central Fire, born of its endeavors in the first ages of the world, when its heat, still close to the surface, caused the growth and distillation of vegetation. Now, the goddess Antrakia, vanquished, chained in the pose of Michelangelo's captives, lifts the arms of a black slave above her head to support the sphere that envelops the bristling braids of her hair like flames.

Around the Central Fire are grouped the emblems of its power, the objects of its usage and the tools of its labors: all the forms that the iron, copper and bronze softened by its flame and molded by man can acquire, as manifestations of its force: stout shiny tubes in which steam respires, oppressed and hoarse; guiding-rods and driving-rods which move back and forth like a carpenter's arms; valves and alarm-whistles, and the manometers that their tension causes to quiver; pipes that creep, interlacing and coiling, brazen serpents with monstrous taps for heads; piston-pumps that plunge into cylinders as deep as wells and return spilling out rivers; condensers, reminiscent of huge organs, into which steam surges noisily, then murmurs a sad song that grows ever-fainter. An Apotheosis of boiler-making!

To the right of the Central Fire, in the place of honor that a decorous god offers his colleague, stands the statue of a mysterious deity—a *Deae ignotae*, still almost unknown, so reticently does it reveal itself—hiding away from mortals, not in the shadows but in the blinding glare of its radiance. I have named this god Electros, electricity, a close relative of the Central Fire, its equal, perhaps its superior—a benevolent and terrible god, who alternately fulfils his worshipper' wishes humbly or strikes them down carelessly; the soul of matter, matter impalpable as soul, similarly endowed with love and

---

[44] This name is improvised from the Greek term for a type of coal, which also gives rise to the term "anthracite".

hate, attraction and repulsion, at the whim of his two poles, his two sexes, which hate the similar and seize the contrary.

Formed of metals that this divinity has chosen as his servitors, the statue of Electos rests, isolated from the ground, on a rock of crystal; seated before a spinning-wheel, he moves a glass disk, and his spindles unwind electrical wires; one might imagine him to be the Fate Lachesis spinning the lives of humans—but this terrible spinning-wheel engenders thunder, and those wires impregnated with human thought wind around the terrestrial globe like a neural network within a body.

At the feet of the god are scattered the souvenirs of his infancy, the emblems of his works: the zinc and copper that coupled to give him birth and nourish him by devouring one another; the piles and the Leyden jars, the statuettes and galvanoplastic medallions that Electros has taught human beings to sculpt.

So much for the lay-out of the apse.

The nave is fitted out as a legislative hall; it is here that the Assembly is held on solemn days. In the ordinary course of parliamentary life, the sessions are held in a cupboard that holds two hundred telephone receivers, linked to those of the two hundred delegates, who can attend the sessions and take part in the debates by that means, without leaving home. Positioned on a table at the center of these items of apparatus, a presidential Phonograph records the discussion and issues rulings.

These kinds of meetings are usually peaceful; sometimes, however, storms burst out in the cupboard, which might then be mistaken, so loud is the racket, for a drum filled with enraged drummers. On such days, people gathered outside the cupboard, as fond as anyone else of seeing the political wheels in motion, amuse themselves by collecting the crumbs of noise that escape through the cracks.

In any case, thanks to the telephone network, all the citizens can attend the sessions from a distance, like the delegates; in emergencies, they can also invade the hall telephonically, mount the podium, expel the phonograph and overthrow the government, without any physical displacement or loss of time, without fatigue and without absenting themselves from their customary occupations.

The remainder of Industria's form of government is pantopantarchic, which means the rule of all over all. Every citizen, at birth, finds a crown in his cradle, and, on reaching the age at which he can wield a scepter, exercises absolute power, without any limit other than the absolute power of his neighbor. The necessary authority and the even-more-precious liberty are thus exactly balanced.

This mode of government has been denigrated by people who do not understand it, although a similar kind of crosier could not have sufficed the kings of old, pastors of poor, suffering flocks inclined to revolt, it does, by contrast, suit a population of contented millionaires, happy enough and rich enough to satisfy the most avid, in a social estate arrived at true equality: an equality obtained without lowering summits or scything down tall stems; a lofty equality, by virtue of the accession of all stems to the light, consisting entirely of crowned heads, by virtue of the elevation of an entire people to a throne solid enough and large enough to seat them all.

What simplicity there is in the workings of that society and its government: no universal suffrage, no elections and no electors, all elected! Nevertheless, as sages have observed, every good rule needs confirmation by exceptions that violate it, and there is no embarrassment in saying that Industria possesses a Parliament, an administrative council elected in by the best possible method, since it is nature, more impartial than man, that elects—or, rather, selects—it.

The intelligence of an individual is, as everyone knows, proportional to his encephalic mass, just as his appetite corresponds to the dimensions of his stomach, so every candidate for the legislature, having passed a preliminary examination by Dr. Mosso's plethysmograph[45]—which measures the inten-

---

[45] The Italian physiologist Angelo Mosso (1846-1910) did not actually invent the first plethysmograph (that was probably

sity of the blood-flow to the head—is then submitted to the measurement of the cubic capacity of his cranial cavity: the depressions and protrusions, the slightest phrenological circumstances, are measured by a jury of strong minds, who are hardly ever mistaken about the quantity of cerebral labor and intellectual sap that the subject can furnish.

Every brain weighing less than two pounds is excluded from the management of affairs. It is not that exceptional intelligences are taken—monstrous brains like that of Pascal, which weighed 1,784 grams, or Cuvier's, which attained 1,829 grams.[46] On the contrary, they are wary of these anomalies, which are, in any case, rare among men who, under the influence of the climate they have created, have become luxurious Orientals whose health is superb but whose minds and facial angles are rather obtuse. Their souls have not swollen in proportion to their abdomens. The legislators, therefore, exclude geniuses of excessive magnitude from affairs of state, by necessity and also by reason; recognizing the inconvenience of uniting disparate intelligences is a single assembly, the most luminous of which would seek to extinguish the rest, as would occur in a room simultaneously lit by electricity, gas, oil and smoky candles—either the electric light oppresses the lesser lights, which represents despotism, or a general fog is produced which symbolizes anarchy.

Francis Franke), but he was the first person to report (in 1878) on extensive experiments carried out with one. He subsequently invented a sphygmomanometer for measuring arterial blood pressure.

[46] The author inserts a footnote here: "It is well-known that, from the viewpoint of encephalic development, humans, canaries and robins are best-favored by fortune, the mass of the brain proportional to that of the body being, for a human, one thirty-fifth, and for a canary, one thirty-second. The latter creature, long assumed to be stupid, is thus, in realty, better endowed than a man.

151

There is nothing similar in this parliament, where all brains are identical in weight and think as one, except for the brains of Lord Hotairwell, estimated at 3,800 grams (nearly four pounds heavier than Cuvier's) and Dr. Penkenton, which, by contrary excess, only attains the minimum for admission. That emptiness in such a large head, combined with a collection of phrenological protuberances better suited to the skull of a wolf than that of a geologist, had left the jury somewhat nonplussed, as well as exciting the mockery of its chairman, William Hatchitt, and Penkenton had only been admitted by virtue of a favorable weighting.

Apart from these two exceptions, there is not ten grams of difference between the cerebral engines of the two hundred delegates, which are all stamped by the same pressure, presenting identical heating surfaces, the same length of travel, and delivering an equal number of piston-strokes within the cylinder. Thus, arguments are rare between these colleagues, who are all seated on the right, all conservatives, not only because they are mostly over sixty, but more especially because they have attained the extreme limits of well-being and progress.

There is no more agreeable and serene spectacle than that assembly: that family of two hundred brothers exchanging conciliatory ideas and emitting exactly similar opinions without passion; those beautifully-formed ivory skulls, so similar that they seem to be united, oscillating in signs of assent and benevolence for the orator who expresses, from the podium, the opinion that is their own.

Such is the usual state of these parliamentary debates, but there are exceptions, as we have said, and the present session, which commenced yesterday and whose end is not yet in sight, will go down as the longest and most exciting page in Industria's history.

IV. A Stormy Session

Since three p.m., Lord Hotairwell has been presiding, not over an assembly, but a tempest, without his tranquility and impartiality failing for an instant. He is like a pilot at the helm, lashed to the presidential armchair, which the waves submerge, the currents drag away and the crazed crew cover with dribble and foam; he is thrown into the sea ten times over but rises to the surface and fight the storm with broad sweeps of the tiller, still steering even though the ship is sinking, holding its course even underwater, anxious to damp down the wreck on the deep strand where sailors and ships sleep, to wait in the shelter of the winds, beneath the vault of the waters, until he can set sail again.

James Archbold, William Hatchitt and Edward Burton, clinging to the ministerial bench, where the tempest is also unleashed, support the valiant commodore as best they can. Dr. Samuel Penkenton is absent on leave, as often happens since he has unexpectedly launched himself into commerce, against all probability and in spite of his aptitudes, and has become a ship-owner. At least, he has taken delivery, a few days before, of two fully-laden ships, which he piloted personally into a safe harbor, with a thousand precautions, as if their cargo were particularly fragile or mystery were indispensable to the success of his speculation.

A storm as violent as it is unexpected is, therefore, raging in the assembly. Parties whose existence was previously unsuspected have suddenly surged forth. For several hours, the parliamentary body has had a right and a left, center-rights, center-lefts and center-centers, groups and sub-groups, which deliberate, shout, fuse or break up, choking in an excess of wrath or strangling in furious alliance. It is a hydra with two hundred heads; a maddened octopus tangled up in its own tentacles, fighting itself fiercely; a mêlée of opinions that collide with one another, raise bruises and howl in pain; a confusion of arms that vote, torsos and legs that rear up and kick beneath the president's whip, which no longer draws any distinction between its right and its left, its friends and its adversaries, distributing the stings of its discipline aimlessly.

A calm materializes, by virtue of hazard or lassitude, and Lord Hotairwell hastens to take advantage of it. "Gentlemen," he says, "for the tenth time I give the floor to the honorable Sir William Barnett, who has not yet succeeded in taking it. The floor is yours, sir."

"Gentlemen," said Sir William Barnett, "I come to appeal for the solicitude of the honorable gentlemen who sit with so much luster in the councils of State, on matters of the utmost gravity, perils all the more redoubtable because these gentlemen are showing themselves indifferent, to the extent that you can see them sleeping, lying full length on their benches, in the naïve quietude habitual to all governments."

(*"Hear hear!"*)

"Symptoms of revolt have appeared among the Atmophytes. These machines have proffered seditious squeaks; these slaves have insulted citizens; and several among them, emerging from the subterranean region to which our constitution restricts them, have taken the air in the street. These fits are the result of the excessive development that you have allowed the Atmophytes' organs to acquire—unconsidered improvements by which you have given them not merely instincts, but souls and the power of thought.

"Yes by a deplorable effort of the genius of your engineers, you have raised to the level of human intelligence these coarse organisms"—(*murmurs*)—"whose inept brains, maladapted to so much light, have been dazzled and crazed in seeing themselves become as intelligent, or even more intelligent, than you!"

(*Urgent denials on a large number of benches.*)

"They are dreaming now of replacing you and destroying you, or perhaps letting you live, to make *you* into *their* Atmophytes."

(*Protestations and ironic laughter.*)

154

"Gentlemen, if there is a Hercules among you capable of taming a hydra with the size and strength of two million horsepower, let him rise to his feet and take up his club!"

(*Prolonged sensation.*)

"Personally, I demand exemplary punishments for these criminals; I demand the immediate destruction of any Atmophyte whose cerebral equipment surpasses in perfection the quantity useful to a good domestic."

On descending from the podium, the speaker receives the congratulations of a great many of his friends.

"The floor is given to the honorable Mr. Greatboy, who has asked for it," says the president.

"Gentlemen," says Greatboy, "as I lent a saddened ear to the discourse to which you have just been subjected, that envenomed accusation leveled against the progress and well-being of Atmophytes, I asked myself whether, by a curious coincidence, my eminent opponent might not have lost precisely the quantity of intelligence that he reproaches these poor individuals for having found."

"Your language is not parliamentary," a member to the right puts in.

(*Cries of "Order! Order!"*)

"I invite Mr. Greatboy to explain his words," says the president.

"Out of respect for Mr. President's authority," says Greatboy, "I shall explain my meaning, even though it is sufficiently clear; and I shall say that the intelligence of my eminent friend seems to me to have fallen beneath that of a brute."

(*Loud protests. "Censure! Censure"!*)

"The speaker having explained his words," says the president, "these protests are pointless."

"But in explaining them," says Mr. Powell, "he has aggravated them!"

"You do not have the floor, Mr. Powell," says the president, "and the president believes that he knows the rules as well as you do. Now, the rule demands that the speaker explain any regrettable words that have escaped him. Mr.

Greatboy has explained his, and I call the interrupters to order. The matter is closed."

"I demand to speak against the closure," says Powell.

"What closure?"

"The closure of the matter."

"No," says the president, "you can't reopen a matter that I've closed."

"Gentlemen," says Powell, "The interpretation that Mr. President..."

"You're reopening the matter..."

"By breaking the closure," put in Lord Calhamborough.

(*Laughter*.)

"I withdraw the floor from you," says the president.

(*Protests from the center-right and the center-center. The president is abused. Discordant cries are heard, and the disorder threatens to mount.*)

"If I can identify those responsible for these cries, I shall not hesitate to reprimand them."

(*"All of us! All of us!"*)

"I call the chamber to order."

"There's no justice anymore!" says Powell.

"Who said that?" says the president.

"You're presiding with a disgusting partiality," Powell retorts.

"Who said that?" repeats the president.

(*"All of us! All of us!"*)

"I invite the persons who say that I'm presiding with disgusting impartiality to come to the podium to explain themselves."

The Assembly rises to its feet in order to mount the podium; Mr. Powell, arriving first, takes the floor.

"Gentlemen," says Powell, "It is only my profound respect for the President's authority that has drawn me to the podium, since I have nothing to say."

"Then why have you mounted the podium?" asked the president.

"Because you invited me to, along with everyone else—but since you oblige me to, I'll speak, in spite of the fact that I have nothing to say, and I hope that, silence being the last of our liberties, you will leave it to us. I shall, therefore, speak..."

"No, don't speak!" several members put in.

"You have a right to shut up—use it," says William Barnett.

"Don't speak," other voices advise. "Get down from the podium!"

Powell quits the podium and receives the congratulations of his friends.

"The speaker having refused to explain himself," says the president, "the matter is closed, and I give the floor to Mr. Greatboy for the continuation of his speech."

"As I was saying, Gentlemen..." Greatboy begins.

"You weren't saying anything," says Mr. Stopman, "and since you're preventing our orators from speaking, you shan't say anything."

"Besides, there are more of us," says William Barnett.

"One is still sufficiently numerous to speak, and I shall speak," says Greatboy.

(*"No! No! Yes! Yes!"*)

At this juncture, the right descends to the floor and heads for the bar.

"Yes," Greatboy continues, "I shall speak, if only to condemn the scandalous exit of a part of this Chamber, a seditious manifestation that I denounce to the severity of the rules and the judgment of the nation."

All the members who left come back in and take their seats again.

"Yes, I qualify as seditious..."

"There was no sedition," says William Barnett, "just some people going to the bar."

(*Incredulous murmurs and smiles.*)

"It is physiologically implausible," says Greatboy, "that all of you had the same need at the same moment. The nation shall be the judge! The truth is that you were obeying an order."

(*"No! No!"*)

"We went out because the president of our group offered to buy a round," says William Barnett.

"I don't care," says Greatboy. "I protest, and I say that a parliament in which..."

"Whoever speaks, lies," put in Lord Calhamborough.[47]

(*Laughter.*)

"That pun isn't parliamentary," says the president.

"I don't claim that the orator who is speaking is lying." (Laughter.) "On the contrary, he says excellent things; and I cannot, when people speak to me on the subject, keep quiet."[48]

(*Laughter.*)

"I was saying," Greatboy resumed, "that a parliament in which such mores become established, in which every opinion prompts a need to walk out in order not to listen to the opposing opinion, will sooner or later be dissolved. I've said it, and I repeat it, because I'm right; such actions are unintelligible, seditious and indecent, so far as the country is concerned."

(*Cries of "Order!"*)

The right gets up and heads for the bar again, but the president, strongly supported by the secretaries, lands such blows with his hand-bell on the heads of the column emerging on to the floor that they stop, indecisively.

Mr. Greatboy hastens to take advantage of the pause. "I resume, Gentlemen, and I shall be brief...the honorable Sir William Barnett demands severe punishment for the childish behavior of a few Atmophytes, but I say to you: do nothing! Don't force springs that are already too taut; don't squeeze steam that is roaring and water that is boiling into narrower

---

[47] This old joke does not translate; the French *parlement* [parliament] can be separated into *parle* [speaks] and *ment* [lies].

[48] Again, the pun (*quand on m'en parle, m'en taire*), this time on *parlementaire* [parliamentarian] does not translate.

dikes, for their pressure, rendered uncontainable, will bring down their prison walls on their jailers."

(*Prolonged sensation.*)

"Does that mean, however," Greatboy continues, "that there is nothing to be done—that there is no crisis, or that there is no remedy for the crisis? If there is a crisis and there is a remedy, it is necessary to apply it quickly, but above all: don't punish severely, forgive! Don't tear apart, cure! Improve, instruct, elevate these Atmophytes, your creatures, your children, to the dignity of men! Lose slaves and win friends! I ask the Government to give its opinion."

This speech is followed by a long agitation. The session is suspended *de facto*. James Archbold, Edward Burton and William Hatchitt, the only ministers present at the session, hold a hasty conference on the floor, and decide to delegate William Hatchitt, in whose supple and insinuating ways render him more likely to find the juncture between two pinions and penetrate their interstices without bursting them asunder. After an interruption of a quarter of an hour, the session resumes.

"Mr. William Hatchitt has the floor," says the president.

"Gentlemen," says Hatchitt, "to the honorable gentleman who asks our opinion on the opinions successively expressed at this podium, it will suffice for me to reply that the Government has gathered those opinions carefully, that it shares them, and that it will regulate its conduct accordingly."

(*"Hear hear!"*)

"The Government thinks, with the honorable Mr. Barnett, that the maintenance of order is the primordial interest to which all others must be sacrificed—to a certain extent, of course. The Government is convinced, like the honorable Mr. Barnett, that it is appropriate to oppose violence forcefully, and to reduce by pitiless repression any rebellion devoid of excuse."

(*"Hear hear!"*)

"But it agrees with Mr. Greatboy in the firm resolution only to employ force united with gentleness."

(*"Hear hear!"*)

159

"Such are our rules of conduct, immutable but ready to bend to the will of the advice of our friends seated on this side of the Chamber, and in the direction of the indications of our adversaries seated on the other side. For, Gentlemen, if we are the Government, you are the Opposition; if we are the strength, you are the light; if we are the power, you are another. We steer the cart, we are the coachmen, but it is you who choose the route. Sitting on the seat, we hold the reins and crack the whip, but from the depths of the carriage you are the guides."

(*Denials and murmurs.*)

"Gentlemen, when it pleases you to climb upon the seat, we shall hasten to get down therefrom, to replace you in the carriage, or, preferably, to go on foot. But while awaiting the day you have appointed for discharging us of the burden of power"—(*Further denials*)—"trust that we shall apply ourselves with even greater zeal, not only to the satisfaction of your demands but to anticipate the development of your desires, and to give you all the satisfactions that a government is happy to offer to its friends, because it loves them, and to its adversaries, because it fears them."

Loud protests are heard in the ranks of the opposition, and Mr. Greatboy, its leader, heads for the podium, very pale and emotional.

"Mr. Greatboy has the floor," says the president.

"Gentlemen," says Greatboy, "the protests against the Minister's words that are still resounding, have already paid that man his wages." (*"Order! Order!"*) "I shall therefore not delay in taking seriously his requests for advice and his offers of alliance. I shall content myself with asking him two questions, to which I shall provide my own replies. You have, Mr. Minister, just promised us satisfactions. Is your promise sincere? No, you say? Then it is despicable."

"I didn't say anything," says Hatchitt.

"Don't interrupt," says the president.

"I shall continue your interrogation," says Greatboy, "and I say again: is your promise sincere? Yes, you reply, this time. Oh! Then it's redoubtable and subversive, prejudicial to the constitution and the very foundations of parliamentary rule." (*"Hear hear!"*) "You don't know, you say?"

"I say nothing," says Hatchitt.

"Your interruption is nonsensical, since I've warned you that I shall provide the questions and answers myself. So you say—a childish excuse—that you don't know! So, under your reign, in my country, the primary instruction has come to the point of superior ignorance, and it is incumbent on me to inform you that the primordial law of parliamentary rule excludes any transaction and any truce between the ruling power and the opposition. And you, Minister, a crank violator of this dogma, have just offered us alliances and to permit us satisfactions! Ah, in truth, it is as smooth as it is perfidious, this Calino-Machiavellian[49] politics, consisting of curing famine by plethora, of giving everything to prevent anything being taken, of keeping our mouths full in order to shut us up, tying our hands by embracing us in your arms."

(*"Hear hear!"*)

"No, Mr. Minister. 'Never strike a woman, even with a flower,' says the poet Saadi;[50] never enchain a people even with benefits!" (*Cheers and applause.*) "To each his task, and no misalliance. You are the Government! We are the Opposition! Our job is to attack you, to undermine your bases, to saw through your roots, to break your branches and gather your fruits."

"Your job, Minister, is to defend yourself. If we knock you down, get up again; if we chase you away, come back; if we break your ministerial bench, sit down on it more forceful-

---

[49] The first part of this portmanteau term is presumably derived from the French verb *caliner*, meaning to coax or wheedle.

[50] Saadi was the familiar signature of the Persian poet Abu Muslih bin Abdallah Shirazi (1184-1283), whose principal works were *Bustan* [The Orchard] (1257) and *Gulistan* [The Rose Garden] (1258). The quotation is probably apocryphal.

ly; and know that it is only by the observance of these principles that you render your profession of Government almost
blameless.

"I think I have painted a portrait of Government as everyone knows it"—(*"Yes! Yes!"*)—"and which he alone con-
trives not to understand—which proves that he's none too
strong. Now, what we want is a strong Government, a Government that can be attacked without crumbling, can been
doused without drowning, knocked down without breaking—
that can, finally, be undermined generally with the patriotic
certainty that it will not collapse as a result!" (*Cheers, and a
salvo of applause.*) "But if you capitulate at the first critical
word and demand mercy at the slightest blow, how can we
undermine you? If we can't undermine you, who, then, should
we undermine? And if we don't undermine anyone, how do
you expect us to be crushed?" (*"Hear hear! That's right."*)
"Our job, thank God, is neither to be governors, nor governed,
nor governable!

"Such is the conclusion of the non-welcome that we oppose to the Minister's offers; and in truth, this paints a..."

"Oh," says Lord Calhamborough, "you shouldn't say
that..."

"I don't understand the meaning of that interruption,"
says Greatboy.

"You said: *This fool...*"[51]

"What!"

"You don't use the word *fool* in talking about a Minister."

"Indeed," says the president. "I must ask the speaker to
make use of another expression."

Greatboy tried again. "I said that this paints a..."

"Precisely," observed Lord Calhamborough.

"I didn't say *this fool*; I said *this paints a*...but if the
words offend you, I withdraw them."

---

[51] Yet another bad pun. Greatboy said "*Cela peint la....*";
Calhamborough construes it as "*Ce lapin-là....*"

"Yes," says Calhamborough, "withdraw the fool."

"With respect to the verb *to paint*," says Greatboy, "I shall select another tense..."

"That's right," says Calhamborough. "Pick better weather."[52]

"I shall therefore say that what the Minister has painted..."[53]

"Point of order!" cries Calhamborough.

"What point of order?" asks Greatboy.

"You said Scapin the Minister—you called the Minister Scapin."

"I didn't say *Scapin the Minister*; I said that *what the Minister has painted*...but I'll change the construction yet again, and say that, in a word, the Minister would paint."[54]

"What! The Minister, that dauber! You call the Minister a dauber! Withdraw that word."

"Since that's the way it is," says Greatboy, "I'll withdraw my entire speech and come down from the podium."

"Yes," says Calhamborough, "withdraw yourself, as well as your speech."

"Anyway, I've accomplished my task—I've notified the Government of our wishes."

"Your desires," says Mr. Stopman.

"No, our wishes," Greatboy insists, "for the majority has the right to wish, and we're the majority."

"But you're only four in two hundred," Stopman objects.

"That many be," says Greatboy, "but we're the majority in the country."

---

[52] *Temps* means both "tense" (in the grammatical sense) and "weather" in French.

[53] *Ce qu'a peint le Ministre*—inviting Calhambrough, inevitably, to misconstrue the phrase as *Scapin le Ministre*, recalling the protagonist of Moliére's farce *Fourberies de Scapin* (1671), a knavish servant.

[54] *Sera peint*, misconstruable as *ce rapin*, if the silliness is extrapolated to its ultimate limit.

(*Protests*.)

"If the members who are interrupting me were more knowledgeable in history," Greatboy continues, "they would know that in all times and all countries, in the bosoms of the most respectable of the oldest Parliaments, it has always been the custom for the minority in the Chamber to say that it is the majority in the country; besides, it's true."

(*No! No! Yes! Yes!*)

"Yes, it's true, because the minority is the opposition, and opposition is natural, while Government is merely a fiction brought forth by the people, as imperfect as its creators: an artificial creation, more often than not deformed—a sort of monster!"

(*Loud protests from the Ministerial bench*.)

"For the fourth time, I shall sum up, and resume my speech at the point where I left off, in order to talk about something else. I sum up our position, in demanding, for our slaves, the right to daylight. I demand that their working hours be reduced and that they be allowed, when their work is done, to go out to take the air and mingle a little oxygen with the carbon dioxide that corrodes their lungs in their workplaces. And with the aim of hastening the hour of justice when they will be admitted to sit within these walls"—(*loud protests from a large number of benches*)—"I demand for the Atmophytes the means of self-education. I demand the creation, for the most advanced among these machines, of a College of Applied Mechanics, to which our eminent engineers will surely be proud to lend their collaboration, in order that these poor people may learn to know themselves, and also to reproduce themselves and to love one another."

(*Cheers*.)

"On the subject of rumors of alleged revolt, I would be glad if someone would procure me a few moments' conversation with the insurrectionists, taking the responsibility upon myself of immediately resolving any difficulties that they will have the honor of submitting to me."

(*Approving laughter and applause*.)

164

At this moment, Mr. Stopman, coming in from outside, climbs up to the armchair and exchanges a few words with the President.

"Gentlemen," says Lord Hotairwell, "I have learned from a source, which is the very mouth of our honorable colleague, Mr. Stopman, that the revolt of the Atmophytes is assuming the gravest proportions." (*Laughter on several benches.*) "They have quit the workshops in large numbers and are running tumultuously through the city."

"That's a false report, intended to influence the vote," says Greatboy.

(*"Yes! Yes! That's what it is!"*)

"I call you to order, sir," says the president.

"You'd do better to call the Atmophytes to order."

(*Laughter.*)

The president continues: "In view of this grave news..."

"Alarming!" says another voice.

(*Laughter.*)

"Frightful!" says another.

(*Laughter.*)

"Grotesque!" says Greatboy.

(*Laughter.*)

"In view of this news," the president insists, "I propose that a special committee, representative of various sections of the Assembly, should go immediately to the top of the dome, from where it will be easy to establish the essence of the situation at a glance."

(*"All of us! Let's all go!"*)

The session is interrupted, and the Assembly heads for the staircase of the dome.

V. A Mechanical Mob

In a matter of moments, the Assembly arrived on the balcony, where a terrifying spectacle was offered to their eyes.

Like geotrupe insects extracting themselves from the dirt, discarding their pupal husks and spreading their wings, that catachthonic population was exhuming itself from its limbo, escaping from its jail through every possible issue from the crypt: through ventilators and drain-openings, crevices and fissures, swarming, innumerable and terrible. The Atmophytes were in open revolt—and in their wake, machines of an inferior order, less intelligent and more sedentary, which ought to have been retained by their weight or difficulties in mobility, were quitting their workshops and invading the city.

As they approach, following custom, shopkeepers close their shutters to protect themselves from the mob, but leave their doors ajar in order to enjoy the sight of its passing.

Barricades are already obstructing several avenues, and the mechanical coachmen of steam-cabs and omnibuses, exhibiting a human intelligence, are overturning their vehicles across the streets. Behind these advance positions, still hesitating to cross them, an unspeakable confusion of vagabond automata is swarming: riotous machines and Atmophytes attained by furious atmomania, staggering around, drunk on the electricity they have consumed to excess—for the majority of these wretches are less ardent for insurrection than intoxication, and the fountains of hot air and steam, along with the electrical reservoirs, are the primary objects of their covetousness.

Menacing gangs besiege the fountains, howling. The earliest arrivals and the most drunk, squatting on the outlets, deaf to their manometers, open their enormous valves and aspire torrents. Others, more sensual, athirst for more acrid liqueurs, have invaded the telegraphs and are drinking from the acid-baths, plunging into them and emerging streaming with sparks. They are trying to operate the apparatus, peppering one another with enormous discharges—intense voluptuous sensations which shake and sting them, provoking outbursts of sardonic laughter that conclude in screams.

While these odious scenes are being played out on the upper stages, other insurgents, which have descended into the cellars, re-emerge carrying baskets full of Leyden jars. They break them open and drink gluttonously. Their platinum brains turn red, madness advertising itself therein. They are flaming lunatics that set alight everything they touch, carelessly propagating fires that make them laugh, into which they hurl themselves to cause explosions.

It is necessary to see such things to believe them, and yet the spectacle has actors more hideous still: the women, the Furies and Bacchantes of the mob, its most ferocious bit-part players, the most ardent to wallow in the cup of the public orgy. They rise at the dawn of every bloody day in history, marching in the front rank of violent revolution, and are not lacking in this one.

Here are sewing-machines, good working-girls a short while before, dedicated to their tasks, which, now furious by virtue of irrational contagion, are gnashing teeth as fine as vipers' tongues. Their needle-bearing jaws move in empty space, with a silent and crazy velocity, like people so overwhelmed by anger that word quiver on their obstructed lips without emitting any sound. And here are other female machines, coarser still, vomiting monstrous utterances: obscene emissions of all the filth that the belly of a mechanical charwoman in a state of drunkenness can contain.

From all of this rise the unspeakable gusts of an indecent, noisy, fetid racket: the reek of the crowd, the clink of metal sweating rage, grease and oil. The conflagration spreads, everything bursts into flame on contact the incendiaries. To see these demons in this sea of flame, one might think that Hell has overflowed, that the geothermal well had broken through its floodgates, unleashing its steam-horses,[55] which have taken the bit in their teeth, foaming at the mouth, whinnying, rearing up and kicking their coachmen in the face.

Night, which descends over these horrible scenes, does not seem likely to put an end to them; on the contrary, the fire spreads, the destruction extends as far as the port, where the

---

[55] The French measure normally translatable as "horse-power" is *chevaux-vapeur* [steam-horses]; I have used the literal translation here to comply with the wordplay.

167

two ships so carefully towed in by Dr. Penkenton suddenly sink and disappear, as if a mysterious hand has just pierced their hulls.

There are symptoms more frightful still: through the semi-darkness, rallying in the suburbs, the mob's reserves are glimpsed, and the prudent machines only desirous of rebellion if success is guaranteed. Further away, beyond the city limits, the Atmophytes of the countryside, in tumultuous disorder, are filling the roads and hastening toward the city: rural populations, gentle and hard-working, broadly-built, with smug faces; lions concealed beneath the pelts of oxen, which study the horizon with an oblique gaze as they work, and which, when the clouds gather and the storm bursts and endures, cast their disguises aside and expose their manes; good people who do not sew revolt, but which, when it is ripe, lend a hand to the harvest.

Already, with a marvelous instinct, mechanical reapers have beaten their blades into swords and pikes. The harvesters are sharpening their scythes. The haymakers, who have quit work at the first indications from emissaries, come running, hampered by their wigs of hay, and the plows follow them, taking the middle of the road and tracing their furrow in that turf with their plowshares.

The darkening night renders this spectacle even more fantastic. All these monsters have lit up their eyes, but their bodies, steeped in darkness, only reveal themselves by the gleam of their gazes, which project and intersect like flamboyant épées in the hands of invisible fencers.

Could so much aptitude to imagine evil action, and so much skill in committing it, be spontaneous, even among the most advanced Atmophytes? Was it necessary to believe, with William Barnett, that the engineers had imprudently exaggerated the provision of instinct in these machines and inadvertently inoculated their brains with a little of the human virus? Was it, in fact, among the Atmophytes that the insurrection had found its organizer and its leader? For it had a leader, there was no doubt about it. The king of the mob could be glimpsed, here and there, in the great clearings that the flames cut out of the darkness; he could be followed by the track of the popular acclaim that greeted him as he moved from quarter to quarter, inspecting his barricades, stimulating his insurgents, sewing along his route a trail of more devouring fire, more frenzied intoxication.

Lord Hotairwell, leaning on the rail of the balcony, silently watched his work destroying itself, crushed by his impotence to hold his creations in check. What could oppose such assailants? Neither force nor persuasion. One cannot reason with a runaway locomotive; one cannot employ force against a cannonball.

As I looked at him, similarly downcast, without saying anything, but seeking to penetrate his thoughts, he said: "Mr. Burton, the work that is being carried out surpasses the range of the most intelligent of our Atmophytes; they are the perfect instruments, but a human hand and a human mind are directing them. That hand..."

Lord Hotairwell was unable to finish. A more intense clamor, of cries of joy, signaled a more ferocious and decisive attack enveloping the temple like a whirlwind, from the bosom of which an enormous monster advanced—pulled, pushed and carried in triumph.

It was the god of this apotheosis: a sort of elephant armed with a club sheathed in its trunk, something like a living anvil brandishing its own hammer. It was a pile-driver weighing 200,000 kilograms, which the insurgents, with prodigious strength and skill, had extracted from the crypt and were setting up before the gate as a battering-ram.

At the same time, having rendered themselves masters of the entire network of wires and tubes centralized at the town hall, they had tangled the tubes in the wires to the point of rendering transmissions unintelligible and dangerous; they were sending electrical discharges through the conductors, enormous lightning-bolts, impregnating the walls of the edifice so that no one could any longer touch them without receiving a shock. The atmosphere of the hall was saturated with it; a handshake led to an exchange of sparks between the electrified bodies, shaken like frogs by the Voltaic arc—less reminiscent of men than electrical vibrators, automata, Atmophytes with no authority over their limbs, incapable of maintaining the dignified attitude required at such a moment.

All the transmitters, thus transformed into malevolent agents and instruments of revolt, were vomiting, according to their aptitude, hails of projectiles or torrents of insults, which the microphones took care to amplify and the phonographs recorded and repeated with mechanical obstinacy, mingling their shrill voices with the thunderous blows of the pile-driver. Telephones became cacophonic and phonographs cacographic: a confusion of tongues embroiled in skeins of steel wire. Atmospheric tubes were transformed into artillery pieces which the barbarians loaded with peaceful citizens, launching themselves with such violence that, departing as cannonballs, they arrived as grapeshot—a grapeshot of human shreds.

It was thus that we had the incomparable pain of seeing the return of the disfigured remains of the engineer William Hatchitt, who, with his obliging nature and habitual devotion, proud of his great familiarity with underground travel, had undertaken a reconnaissance mission in a tube, in order to obtain a better appreciation of the revolt and to attempt, by taking it by the tail, to hold it in respect.

Industria's final hour had sounded. The doors of the temple yielded to the redoubled blows of the hammer. Through the gap came ferocious stares, whistling blasts of air, claws that attached themselves to fissures in order to enlarge them, scythes and sickles attempting, with professional skill, to mow down men like ears of corn.

The Assembly had resumed sitting. Its members, having become calm in the face of the supreme anger, was no longer thinking of anything but dying well, when James Archbold, having consulted his watch and asked for the president's authorization, headed for the apse at a rapid pace. As soon as he arrived he closed the tap that distributed the motive force emerging from the well to the Atmophytes of the city and the countryside.

A thunder of applause saluted the execution of such a simple idea, which cut off the fuel, and the very life, of the insurgents, ensuring a spectacular victory, and a decisive repression. A second salvo of cheers welcomed Archbold when he returned to his place, having saved Industria with that small expenditure of common sense…or, at least, would have saved it if he had acted sooner. Unfortunately, at that extreme hour, would not the work of the insurrection be completed by virtue of acquired momentum, before the motive force drained from the channels had ceased to fuel the Atmophytes?

Every effort of the pile-driver made a more prominent dent in the doors. The encouraged assailants were increasing their pressure, scaling the walls and crowning the edifice, which was crushed beneath the crowd like a tree collapsing under the weight of its own fruit.

Inside, no one any longer had any fear of death; they desired it, and would have called out to it if there had been any chance that it might hear in the midst of such a tumult. Lord Hotairwell stood up at the armchair, and put his hat on in order to receive the mob, while Archbold attentively followed the flea-jumps of the second hand on his watch.

Suddenly, under the effort of a more formidable shove, the doors gave way and fell, opening to the gaze of the besieged the indescribable spectacle of the battlefield and its combatants: an undisciplined and frenzied mass of furious machines and ferocious scrap metal, into the hands of which the disarmed masters were finally about to fall…

Against all expectation, however, it was not a cry of triumph that went up from the bosom of that crowd, but a death-rattle. The clamors, oaths and threats were frozen in their throats, or died like plaints on platinum lips—and the pile-driver, its fist lifted, remained stuck in that attitude.

Paralysis struck the Atmophytes as the power flowing to the fountains ran out and drained away. Stupefied by the transition from plethora to dearth, from the paroxysm of strength to overwhelming inertia, they tottered, fighting for life—but their eyes were extinguished in their orbits and their limbs fell limply beside their bodies, which collapsed like empty suits of armor. Progressively, by rapid contagion, as the wells dried up, holes were cut through the crowd from the threshold of the temple to the extreme suburbs, as if a haphazard harvest had commenced.

Industria was saved.

The four hundred hands of the two hundred members of the Legislative Body joined together in a cordial handshake, and extended toward those of Mr. Archbold, who was busy replacing his watch in his waistcoat pocket.

"Gentlemen," said the chief engineer to his colleagues, who surrounded him, "our slaves leave something to be desired, but our other machines are excellent. I calculated that the insurrection would cease twelve seconds after the closure of the conduit distributing compressed air to the fountains, where the first ranks of the insurgents were refueling themselves, but my chronometer has shown me that eleven and a half seconds were sufficient. The compressed air has therefore taken action, watch in hand, in conformity with my calculations—and if it had been three-quarters of a second out, the hinges of the door would have burst asunder and the insurgents would have invaded this refuge. Yes, the character of the Atmophytes needs to be retouched, but our other apparatus is excellent!"

Concluding thus, Archbold, in a fit of extreme satisfaction, forgot himself so far as to rub his hands together, without taking account of the expenditure of energy and frictional losses that the gesture would occasion.

Mrs. Little

by Edmond Thiaudière

Prologue

There are people (I am a sorry example) who generally obtain more ennui than pleasure from social relationships. There are some whose idleness is disturbed thereby, because one has to get dressed at fixed hours; there are others whose vanity is compromised, because one cannot always flatter oneself with presenting the image for which one is ambitious; some suffer from their frankness, because one is exposed to saying, or at least hearing said, many white lies; others, finally, without being retained at home by idleness, vanity, or even a grim integrity, renounce society after a few attempts, for want of ever finding their intellectual and moral milieu there.

When I say "their milieu," I do not suppose in the slightest that no sort of divergence of opinion is produced between the habitués of the same society, which would be monotonous and, moreover, impossible, but I am supposing that there is no magnetic antipathy between them.

And that is quite rare.

For myself, I only know of one salon where I have found my milieu, and which I continue to frequent, and that is Madame ***'s. A little more and I would have named that sovereignly amiable woman, whom one of the most fortunate hazards of my life enabled me to encounter in Rome, in May 18**, and who was kind enough, on my return to Paris, to admit me into the restricted number of her familiars.

We meet in her drawing room every Wednesday, ten persons at the most, among whom are four wives with their husbands, women who are neither prudes nor coquettes, but simple and good, like the mistress of the house.

People chat there at their ease, and if there are sometimes differences of opinion, there is always the same humor. Everyone enjoys themselves there effortlessly, because honesty, benevolence and a certain jovial philosophy are equally shared by everyone.

I doubt that another salon like it exists in Paris. One of us, with good reason, has called it "the worldly paradise." And it is a paradise that we shall not lose, for if we form multiples of Adam and Eve there, at least no one can say that there is a serpent among us, nor any apples, except for the golden serpent with emerald eyes worn on the finger of the mistress of the house, and the pommel of the cane on which the metaphysician Morini has the custom of supporting his chin while he divides the spidery thread of our transcendent conceptions.

One evening we had a full complement. The conversation revolved around the force of habit in amour. The beautiful and virtuous Mina—I believe that I can give the true forename of our hostess—talked to us in an emotional voice about the husband she had lost many years before, and the portrait of the latter, so lifelike was it, seemed to detach itself from the wall and discuss fidelity with us.

In thinking about the great misfortune that had overtaken their friend and which might overtake them in their turn from one day to the next, the women were almost weeping, and not one of the men, I am convinced—even the bachelors—felt born within him the foul and vile desire, so frequent in banal natures, to soil with their caprice or passion a sentiment as sacred as that of a widow's mourning.

Suddenly, the door of the drawing room opened and Mina's chambermaid, the worthy old Gervaise, whom we called between ourselves "the chamberlain," announced Monsieur Le Bref.

The name was unknown to all of us, except Mina. So, in the moment when she got up to go and greet Monsieur Le Bref, with her familiar grace, we looked at one another, and it was easy for me to see, painted on all the faces, the same apprehension regarding the newcomer.

Was he not destined to trouble in some manner the precious harmony that reigned among us? Such is the question that we were asking one another with our eyes.

In order to resolve the prevision as much as it was possible for me, I examined Monsieur Le Bref very attentively

He was a tall and handsome fellow, about thirty-five years old, elegantly dressed, with a simple and grave deportment, of a rare distinction, extremely sympathetic from the outset. The first words he pronounced revealed to me, in addition, the timbre of a charming voice and a good deal of intelligence.

There is a locution that is generally applied to people much less well endowed than Monsieur Le Bref appeared to be: it is said that they have "everything going for them."

He gave the impression of being such an accomplished fellow that I thought, privately: *There's a man who has everything going for him, and quite a lot more!*

A perfection so overwhelming could not help but make me anxious, because of the women. And I feared immediately that it might be an element of dissolution for the circle, if only by giving umbrage to the men, were Monsieur Le Bref to become one of us.

"My dear friends," exclaimed Mina, "I introduce to you Monsieur Le Bref, a nomad who is incorrigible to the point that, in coming to see me this evening in Paris, where he only arrived yesterday from Rome, he tells me that he is departing tomorrow for England. I regret his precipitate departure all the more because, belonging to our school, he would become one of the pillars of the Academy of Joyful Melancholics."

"If you would care to admit me as a corresponding member," said Monsieur Le Bref, I will formulate the wish that everyone resume the conversation that was in progress before my arrival."

"The question that is the order of the day, or rather, of the evening," replied Mina, "cannot interest you."

"Am I not a joyful melancholic?"

"Yes, but..."

"But what, Madame?"

"Would you like to know?"

"Certainly."

"Well, we were talking about the force of habit in amour…now, you travel far too much to have ideas on that subject."

"I have them, however, and the best."

"Oh!! The best?"

"And the freshest," he said.

She started to laugh and said: "I'm sure that you're of the opinion that habit is the greatest scourge of amour."

"Entirely the contrary, Madame, I am of the opinion that the only true amour is born of habitude."

"For a nomad, you astonish me."

"Alas, you know full well," replied Monsieur Le Bref, "that the ideas that are dearest to us are precisely those that we have not been able to attempt in practice—but I have encountered in my travels an English eccentric who has taken the practice of the idea of force of habit in amour as far as, and even further than, it can reasonably be taken."

"Come on, tell us about that," cried Mina. "It will be your speech, or rather your narration, of reception into the Academy of Joyful Melancholics."

"I must warn you, though, that the story is a trifle long," Monsieur Le Bref replied.

"So much the better for us," replied another lady.

Monsieur Le Bref yielded to that graciousness, and, as we all demanded the story of the Englishman, he began to tell it.

PART ONE: IN SPAIN

I

In August 18**, following a cruel family misfortune that had caused me sufficient chagrin to affect my health profoundly, my physician, thinking that I had need of both a tonic and distraction, prescribed the sea-baths at Biarritz for me.

In truth, the listlessness in which I found myself then was so great, and I was so isolated by my sadness from the ordinary course of human things, that I was reluctant to displace myself. My physician insisted. I tried at least to obtain from him that I might simply go to Luc, in Normandy, where I had my habits so to speak, for I had spent several summer seasons there, but he closed my mouth, saying to me that I would derive all the more benefit from my voyage if my destination was more distant and quite new to me.

I therefore decided in favor of Biarritz.

As I had a friend to see in Bordeaux I stopped there for a full day, which also permitted me to rest, for the journey from Paris to Bordeaux cannot help but be somewhat fatiguing.

When I arrived, two days later, on the platform of the Gare Saint-Jean, the train for Bayonne was already full. After having searched from carriage to carriage for an empty seat, I spotted a compartment in which, apart from two good English figures—a man and a women—who were blocking the door, there seemed to be places free.

I approached in order to climb in, but the man exclaimed: "No, you can't!"

I attempted to infringe that order, whose legitimacy seemed all the less explicable to me because there were, in fact, six vacant seats in the compartment.

Immediately in the same way that a guard dog launches itself out of its niche to bark loudly at any individual bold enough to approach, the lady irrupted out of carriage window and an ill-defined screech emerged from between her elongated teeth. I heard something like: "Loa! Loa!"

In my stupefaction, I stood there at first with my hand on the door handle.

What the devil did that Englishwoman mean with her *Loa, loa*?

I thought of Alfred de Vigny's *Éloa*,[56] but without settling on the idea that the Englishwoman might want to compare to that celestial creature a monsieur who persisted in trying to climb into railway carriage.

Then I reflected that she might be insulting me and shouting: "L'oie, l'oie!"—which is to say; "You're a goose!" although I found such an insult excessive.

Finally, I was extracted from my perplexity by the conductor of the train, who, having heard the Englishwoman's peacock screech, approached me and said, politely raising his cap in one hand while he used the other to show me an indicative placard: "You see, Monsieur, this compartment is reserved until Bayonne.

"*Loué!*" I exclaimed. "Ah—I understand."

So, the Englishman, in saying to me "No, you can't" and his worthy companion, in crying "Loa! Loa!" or "L'oie, l'oie!" had simply wanted to signify to me that they had an exclusive right to the compartment.

In fact, did they really? I don't know. Perhaps they had simply brought, in return for a good tip, the complicity of the train conductor—which can be done, so it's said.

At any rate, I did not persist, and I allowed myself to be led meekly by the conductor, guilty or not of private enterprise, to another compartment, where, by some miracle, one seat remained unoccupied, and for his trouble I even slipped a fifty-centime piece into his hand.

In those days the railway did not go as far as Biarritz, but there was a very rapid diligence service from Bayonne station to Biarritz. When, having arrived at Bayonne station, I had reclaimed my baggage, I raced to the diligence and installed myself in a corner of the coupé.

---

[56] In Alfred de Vigny's poem, a classic of French Romanticism, Éloa is female angel who falls in love with handsome male angel, not realizing that he is about to start a war in heaven and be damned, drawing her to damnation with him in spite of her innocence.

I thought that the coupé was for first comers, but to tell the truth, I was not certain of that, only knowing one thing, which was that I had bought a first class ticket in Bordeaux, diligence included, to Biarritz.

I was therefore, stuck in my corner of the coupé, at hazard, watching the passengers arrive, and sometimes shuddering when the factors threw their heavy luggage up on to the impartial.

Suddenly, here come my English couple again, heading straight for the coupé, and the husband says: "You can't stay," and the wife adds "Loa, loa," or, again, "L'oie, l'oie."

"Good, good," I said, laughing, I should have expected that."

And I got down through the other door and climbed philosophically into the interior.

The Hôtel des Ambassadeurs had been recommended to me as one of the best in Biarritz.

On arriving in Biarritz at the diligence office, I spotted a commissionaire attached to that hotel, the name of which he wore inscribed on his cap.

"Under the tarpaulin of the diligence," I said to him, "there's a trunk and a hat-box with the name of Monsieur Le Bref, will you take them?"

Before he had time to reply, the Englishman, having approached us, asked him: "Boy, you were the boy of the Hôtel des Ambassadeurs?"

"Yes, Monsieur," said the commissionaire, without paying the slightest attention to me.

"Oh, I thought so. Since you were the boy of the Hôtel des Ambassadeurs, come a little, take the trunks of me. to carry them to the Hôtel des Ambassadeurs."

"Yes, Monsieur…I have others to take as well"

"You take those of me first."

On hearing that injunction, I felt a surge of impatience that I could not master. In sum, it was becoming a challenge. That beastly islander, then, had sworn to cut the grass from my feet in every circumstance. Not content with nearly making me miss the train in Bordeaux by forbidding me to climb into his compartment, under the pretext that he had reserved it, and having thrown me out of the coupé in Bayonne under the same pretext, now he was demanding that the commissionaire of the Hôtel des Ambassadeurs serve him before me, although I had commandeered him first.

"In truth Monsieur, in truth," I said to the Englishman, in a very acerbic tone, "you don't inconvenience yourself as much as politeness requires in our land of France. I commandeered this man before you and he has no reason to serve you before me."

"It was you who lack politeness and me I won't suffer it," replied the Englishman. "I had a sufficient motive for demanding the work of this porter. Me I have retained the place of me and my wife for more than a fortnight at the Hôtel des Ambassadeurs."

"L'oie," I said, ironically.

"Oh yes, said the Englishwoman. "This porter is loa."

I had a desire to reply: "L'oie is your husband! L'oie is you!" But I contented myself with saying, with an ironic smile, of which they certainly did not comprehend the full range: "May the god Lord bless both of you!"

And after having given my instructions to the commissionaire I went to the Hôtel des Ambassadeurs in order to book a room, in the event that—which I did not know—the English couple had left any available.

I asked when I arrived whether it was possible to give me a room with a view over the sea, to which the reply was negative, because there was only one vacant with that situation, which had been promised to an English couple who were expected at any moment.

I ought to have expected that. It was added that there was another next door to that one, which did not have a sea view but which was no less comfortable.

"Next door to the English couple!" I exclaimed. "Oh, no, not next door to them, I beg you, I implore you."

It was to the landlady of the hotel that I replied in those terms. She could not help laughing.

"Monsieur doesn't much like the English, I see."

"On their island, yes indeed, on their island. Oh, my God, you're not of my opinion, Madame and you prefer them in your hotel—that's understandable."

"The ones who are going to occupy that room," she said, gaily, pointing at the door, "a lady and gentleman, reserved it a fortnight ago."

"Yes, yes, I know."

"Monsieur knows them?"

"Far too well. And I announce to you that they'll be here momentarily. Try, then, to find me a room a hundred leagues from theirs...a hundred leagues is very little...a thousand leagues."

She evidently found the animadversion that I professed for the subjects of Queen Victoria very amusing.

"In that case," she said, "it would be better to give Monsieur a room in the other wing of the house."

"Yes, Madame," I cried, "that's right...the other wing, if you please."

II

The room that I had been given simply had a view over a small courtyard where there was a small basin in which a few ducks were paddling. It was not the sea, but nor was it the English couple, and yet the ducks reminded me of the Anglo-French exclamation that had aggravated my nerves so much: "L'oie, l'oie!"

After having taken a few turns around the beach, I came back for dinner. I arrived slightly late; everyone was at table.

There were only two places free, and by virtue of a slightly grotesque fatality, one of those places was next to the English couple and the other facing them.

Between two evils, it is said, it is necessary to choose the lesser. But there was still the question of knowing which was the lesser. That was what I asked myself as I hung my hat on one of the pegs in the dining room.

If I sat facing them the viewpoint would not only be not amusing for me, but exasperating. If, on the contrary, I sat alongside, might I not pick a quarrel?

I made a reflection that cut short my uncertainty.

They're capable, I thought, of having reserved the place next to them, and if I go sit down there, the Englishwoman will doubtless screech once again: "L'oie! L'oie!"

That idea amused me so much that my rancor against the English couple was disarmed and, having arrived at the place that was opposite them, I began contemplating them one after another with a very equable and even cheerful, humor.

The Englishman might have been thirty-five or forty years old, and the Englishwoman not much younger. For faces, they possessed two marvelously matched ruddy balls, which did not lack analogy with a Dutch cheese in their integrity. There existed between them a family resemblance such that one would more readily have taken them for brother and sister than husband and wife. And yet, they were definitely spouses, for the Englishman, in speaking of the Englishwoman during our little altercation in front of the diligence, had said: "my wife."

It is necessary to admit that nothing about them suggested that they were nasty people. On the contrary, their placid gaze was imprinted with bonhomie.

As true English people, of course, they did not have any expansion, although they seemed happy to be beside one another.

At intervals, the husband said a few words to his wife, to which she replied with a single word: "Yes," or "No," depending upon the circumstance—nothing more.

The following morning, as I was looking at the names of the bathers staying at the hotel, I noticed, not far from mine, those of Mr. and Mrs. Little of Chester, with the indication that they had arrived the day before. It was of no importance to me to know what the name of admirably matched couple was, but, in any case, I knew.

From that day on, and for twenty more, I stayed in Biarritz. My life was spent, naturally, on the edge of the sea—all the time that was not spent indoors, that is, for I took the plunge every morning and evening.

And as the life of the other bathers was identical to mine I could not help encountering Mr. and Mrs. Little quite frequently

One morning, when I was walking, after my bath, along the "Côte des Fous," I passed so close to the couple that, in spite of the scant sympathy they inspired in me because of my ancient grievances against them, I judged it appropriate to salute them.

Although his gaze met mine—at least, such was my conviction—Mr. Little did not raise his hat. Nor did Mrs. Little incline her head, as convention would have required, but remained perfectly straight and stiff.

I was choked by that. It remained to be determined where it was intentional rudeness on the party of the English couple, or simple inadvertence. I thought at first of intentional rudeness, and I called both of them bumpkins mentally. Then I reflected that, after all, they had no reason to be impolite in my regard, and I almost arrived at excusing them, on thinking that Mr. Little was too occupied with conversing with Mrs. Little, and Mrs. Little too occupied with listening to Mr. Little, to take the trouble to salute me.

Furthermore, I have noticed that the English, probably because they are islanders, have the very particular gift of isolating themselves in a crowd. It seems that they always have a little sea around them.

That consideration dispelled the slight rancor that I still had against Mr. and Mrs. Little. Nevertheless, I promise myself to isolate myself as well henceforth when I passed within range of them—which is to say, not to salute them again. And I kept my word.

It was perhaps ten days that the English couple and I had been in Biarritz, and we had encountered one another every day, either at table at the Hôtel des Ambassadeurs, or on the beach—or even, as people used to say, in the bosom of Amphitrite—without even looking at one another. One morning, as I was taking my bath at Port-Vieux, and while swimming, I had drawn somewhat apart, I heard cries of distress. As I was on my back at that moment and could only see the sky, I turned over precipitately, and gave the water a good kick in order to rise above the waves, in order to see where the cries were coming from.

I then perceived a crowd of people on the beach who were making signals to me, and a short distance away from me, a small indistinct mass that was struggling against the waves.

In a few strokes, I had reached the object in question, which it was impossible for me to define, while the observation boat arrived from the other direction, impelled by its oars.

I seized the object, which was a body wrapped in black woolen fabric, which the boatman and I hoisted into the boat, to the applause of the spectators.

I climbed into the boat myself, and as the boatman rowed toward the shore, which was not very far away. I gazed with a very sympathetic curiosity at the kind of human package that we had pulled out of the water.

It was a man, and a man whose face was not unknown to me, it seemed, without my being able to put a name to it. But I had something more urgent to do than rack my brains trying to find it. Was the man, whoever he was, alive or dead? It did not take me long to establish that he was alive, for as I bent over him, he opened his eyes to look at me, and his mouth to say to me: "I thank you."

Oh, of course, I should have suspected it. It was the Englishman from the Hôtel des Ambassadeurs, Mr. Little—except that his ruddy face had gone very pale.

Meanwhile, the boat touched the shore, the sailor threw the anchor, and then we both picked Mr. Little up, him by the feet and me by the shoulders, and we carried him on to the beach, where a curious crowd had gathered.

Mrs. Little was there, in tears, with a woolen peignoir in her hands, with which she enveloped her husband, while she enveloped me, I have to admit, with a gaze moist with gratitude. And as if that gaze were insufficient to translate her thought, she said to me, amid sobs that truly went to my heart: "Monsur, you have saved the life of the husband of me. You are courageous gentleman." And she added: "*I bless you.*"[57]

"Not at all, Madame," your words are not made to wound me."

And I slipped away as quickly as possible, for, apart from the fact that my attire was not very appropriate and was even little shocking for the ultra-prudish gaze of a lady, I was beginning to feel cold and was in haste to dry myself.

While running toward my cabin, however, I wondered why the devil Mrs. Little imagined that she might be wounding me by declaring that I was a courageous gentleman.

By dint of reflection I remembered that the English verb "to bless" refers to benediction, and that consequently, Mr. Little had simply wanted to wish me well.

When I was dressed, my first concern was to enquire about Mr. Little, and I learned with pleasure that he was as well as could be. I was told that after he had drunk a glass of port, he had had himself wrapped in a warm blanket, and that two strong fellows were presently occupied in massaging him.

He has no further need of me, I thought, and I headed for the hotel with all the more haste because I was late for lunch and I had a great appetite.

My arrival at table, where everyone was gathered, was greeted by a sympathetic murmur. Doubtless everyone already knew that I had assisted in the Englishman's rescue, and it even seemed to me that they had been talking about it when I

---

[57] Mrs. Little says the italicized phrase in English, which leads the narrator to misunderstand, the French verb *blesser* meaning to wound.

185

came in. At any rate, in addition to compliments that I could have done without—for, in sum, there was absolutely nothing heroic in my perfectly natural action—questions were addressed to me, to which I could not reply, regarding the cause that had nearly cost the life of Mr. Little, an excellent swimmer.

I left the table before he arrived there, but I met him at the door of the hotel as he was coming back from the beach, accompanied by his wife.

On perceiving me he quit the latter's arm and, extending both his hands to me, he said effusively: "I want to know the name of you, Monsur."

"The name of me," I said, laughing, "is Le Bref."

"Ho ho! That was very good, but can you give to me the little card of you?"

"Gladly." And, taking one of my cards out of my wallet, I handed it to him.

"Perfectly," he said, looking at the card. "Le Bref is the name of you. That name, it was forever written on the breast of me, Tommy Little, cheese-maker of Chester."

"Much obliged," I said to him. And I thought: It's lucky that he didn't tell me that my name is inscribed in his bowels.

"This is the little card of me," he said, handing me his card, "and know, Monsur, that I was at your disposal in my fortune and my life."

"Oh, Monsieur," I exclaimed, "you're too good, a thousand times too good."

"No," said Mrs. Little.

"Go and have lunch," I said, "for you must be hungry."

"I have already had port with little biscuits," replied the cheese manufacturer, "but Mrs. Little, no..."

"Then Mrs. Little must be very hungry," I said to the husband. "It is, in fact, improbable that your port and little biscuits have sustained her."

"No," replied Mrs. Little, seriously, while Mr. Little laughed at my joke.

"But tell me, Monsieur," I said, "did you have a fainting-fit in the water, for you're a swimmer of the first order?"

"Ho, yes, in the water...how do you say it...a fainting-fit?"

"Yes, a fainting-fit...you suddenly felt lost consciousness?"

"Ho, yes, lost..."

"It gripped you in the head?"

"No, no, it gripped me in the belly by a sudden natural need."

"Ah!" I said, stiffening my lips in order not to burst out laughing. "That's truly peculiar. In any case, we won't talk about it anymore. Believe me, go and have lunch."

It was thus that our first conversation concluded; it was to be followed by many others, a perfect intimacy having been established between us thereafter.

III

That intimacy became so warm and so cordial on either part that we decided to undertake a trip to Spain together.

The proposal was made to me by Mr. Little and I must say that I was very hesitant to accept it, for fear of having to suffer more than once in that little plan the British egotism that had to be—at least, I believed so then—stronger than friendship.

However, Mr. and Mrs. Little had become so pleasant, and even obliging, toward me since the rescue that I thought I might risk the trip.

It was therefore agreed that when our season ended, we would take the steamboat at Bayonne for San Sebastian, and from there we would go in stages all the way to Andalusia.

An unexpected event prevented up from completing our journey, but at least we tried and went quite a long way.

You know the Gulf of Gascony, and you know that it isn't always in a good mood. Our crossing from Bayonne to San Sebastian was completed without too much inconvenience, but when we arrived in port, at the very moment when the passengers were disembarking by means of small launches, the waves became very angry.

The launch into which I had already descended was agitated terribly. Our two oarsmen were unable to maintain the boat at the side of the steamer. I extended my hand to Mrs. Little to help her get down, while her husband, who was still on the deck of the steamer, supported her by the waist, and that worked quite well.

When Mr. Little wanted to get down in his turn, however, he recklessly refused the hand I held out to him and, the launch having suddenly sifted, our worthy islander would surely hand fallen into the water if I had not grabbed him just in time by the strap of his marine binoculars.

"Ho, yes," he said, with great phlegm, when he had sat down. "You will still be saving the life of me, then."

"One good turn deserves another," I replied.

"Ho, yes, I liked nothing so much as to see in frightful danger, to show you my gratitude.

"Ho, yes," confirmed Mrs. Little, with the most amusing gravity.

"I'd prefer it, my dear Monsieur Little, and very much so, if you didn't have the opportunity."

"No, no, I wanted absolutely to have it, me, that opportunity, and you disoblige me in refusing it to me."

"In truth, you're very good."

The few people who were about to disembark from the launch with us were laughing to the point of tears at the slightly excessive zeal deployed toward me by the worthy Mr. Little, who, in order to have the satisfaction of saving me in his turn, would have liked me to be on the brink of doom.

Having spent two successive years in England, one of them at the University of Oxford, I certainly knew English far better that Mr. and Mrs. Little knew French, and they recognized fully my superiority in that regard, having judged it for themselves in Biarritz, on one occasion when I had tried to converse with them in English. But, Mr. Little having adjured me only to employ the French language in my conversation with his wife and himself in order to constrain them to learn it, whether they like it or not, I had naturally deferred to his desire.

Scarcely had we reached Spanish soil than Mr. Little, addressing me for the first time in English, said to me: "If I were capable of speaking Spanish, I would say to you: 'Let's speak Spanish, since we're in the homeland of Cervantes,' but I have to admit that I'm incapable of speaking Spanish, at least until further notice. We can now, therefore, if you please, speak English between us."

I was so content with that resolution that I showed Mr. Little how much I approved by an exceedingly prolix response in the language of Walter Scott. Instead of quite simply saying "Gladly, Mr. Little," I made a veritable speech on two points: firstly, the pleasure that he caused me thereby, and then on the merits of his idiom.

Since I had had the honor of knowing Mrs. Little, I had been struck by her scant expansion toward a husband who had the greatest attention for her. It was not that she was insensible to his attentions, for it was not rare when she was the object of them for her to squeeze Mr. Little's hand with a marked tenderness, but she scarcely said two or three words to him at intervals. More often than not she only replied with a monosyllabic "Yes" or "No" to questions, reflections or explanations emanating from her husband.

British coldness being insufficient to explain that constant mutism, I had thought that it might be attributable to the singular obligation imposed on Mrs. Little by her husband only to speak French, which was far from being familiar to her. I was mistaken. When it was permissible for her to express herself in the mother tongue, she scarcely said any more. It was, therefore, a matter of personal temperament. She was

what is known in the French Midi—and also in Spain, I believe—as a *sang-mort*.[58]

She was positively not astonished by anything, applying
too literally Horace's precept *Nul mirari*.

Mr. Little, doubtless long habituated too that superlative
nonchalance, did not seem to be affected by it in the slightest.
It was sufficient for him that she listen to him complaisantly,
which she did not fail to do.

As for me, on seeing the woman limit herself to being
the recipient of her husband's thoughts—and mine, for I had
no more success than Mr. Little in getting four words out of
her—I sometimes had a muted irritation. *She's not a wife*, I
said to myself, *she's an automaton*; and I could not understand
why Mr. Little had brought such an insignificant person with
him across Europe instead of confining her to his cheese-
factory in Chester. I was judging things from my own point of
view, without reflecting that Mr. Little's might by quite different—as I learned subsequently, since his wife's principal
charm in his eyes was her very passivity.

It is certain, considering things carefully, that such a
woman, if not precisely agreeable, is at least very inoffensive.
She did, said and thought almost exactly what her husband
wanted, while others agitate thoughts of rebellion incessantly
against theirs, quarrel with them and behave in such a fashion
as to make them discontent.

In the entire course of our voyage in Spain, I never saw
Mrs. Little emit a determination, or even a simple desire, but,
on the other hand, I always saw her approve of her husband's
resolutions—which, I ought to say, were perfectly in accord
with mine.

San Sebastian is, as you know, one of the most pictur-
esquely situated towns in all of Spain, on the slope of Mount

---

[58] This dialect term, with translates literally as "blood-dead,"
has no exact English translation, although the phrase "cold-
blooded" is a near equivalent, when used to refers to a person
unusually devoid of emotion.

Orgulio, the summit of which, crowned by the citadel, is no less than a hundred sixteen meters above sea level. The little port wedged between the mountain and the island of Santa Clara is a charming sight. Thus we could not help admiring it as we climbed up toward the town, although it had nearly been inhospitable to us.

When we were half way up Mount Orgulio, alongside steep rocks, Mrs. Little, to whom I had offered my arm in order to lend her a little support in her ascendant march, broke her habitual silence.

"It's very singular," she said, in English, "to represent the virgin with a mantilla on her head and a fan in her hand."

The wife of the Chester cheese-maker was thinking aloud in that fashion about a Madonna that we had just seen while passing the Church of Santa Clara, where she was in great honor.

"Do you think so, Madame?" I said. "It is, on the contrary, quite natural, and for myself, I'm only astonished that the Christ on the cross facing the pulpit isn't costumed as a torero."

Meanwhile, we arrived at the tombs of the English officers killed in 1836 during the defense of San Sebastian against Carlist troops.[59] Mr. Little took off his hat, and I did the same.

"Thank you, my dear Monsieur Le Bref," he said, shaking my hand effusively, "for that mark of respect for the memory of my unfortunate compatriots."

"My dear Monsieur Little," I replied, emotionally, "any Frenchman, believe me, would have the same respect in this circumstance, and if, by chance, there are any who would not,

---

[59] A British volunteer force known as the Auxiliary Legion came to San Sebastian to support a contingent of the French Foreign Legion during the First Carlist War of 1833-37, in which France and England were both lending rather half-hearted support to Queen Isabella; about a quarter of their number were killed in the course of a long and bitter struggle to prevent the Carlists taking the city

I would hold it against them. I will add that, in saluting those heroes, I intend expressly to salute their fatherland and yours, Monsieur Little."

"Thank you, thank you, my dear sir," he said, wiping his cheeks, which were bathed in tears.

The patriotic commotion that he had just experienced, I experienced in my turn when we reached the citadel so heroically defended in 1813 by the French against the English and the Portuguese.

"Monsieur Little," I exclaimed, "about sixty years ago, a French general, General Rey, after having defended this citadel heroically against your compatriots, was obliged to capitulate, the city being destroyed, but he emerged from here with a carbine on his shoulder.[60] You will permit me, will you not, to evoke his noble memory?"

"And I join with you in honoring him," replied Mr. Little.

"Ho, yes," added Mrs. Little, addressing a small confirmatory nod of the head to me.

There is no doubt that the amity that was beginning to unite me with Mr. and Mrs. Little was strongly cemented by that double homage, rendered with the same sincere emotion, by me to England and him to France.

IV

At Burgos, the city made up like a café-concert singer, I had a specimen of the truly touching tenderness that Mr. and Mrs. Little experienced for one another.

It was at the Municipal Palace, where we had gone to see the remains of El Cid and Chimène,[61] preciously conserved in

---

[60] Louis-Emmanuel Rey's defense of San Sebastian during the Napoleonic Wars was ultimately defeated, but became legendary for its tenacity and ingenuity.

[61] The Spanish warrior called "El Cid" by the Moors (Rodrigo Diaz, 1040-1099) and his wife Jimena (Chimène in French)

a chest, and which consisted, as one might imagine, of wretched dusty bones.

A middle-aged woman, whom I assumed to be the door-keeper of the place, was charged with showing them to us. When she had opened the chest, divided into two compart-ments, she indicated that pitiful debris to us with a proud ges-ture.

Immediately, however, Mr. Little, carried away by I know not what interior demon, plunged a hand recklessly into the chest and brought out of one of the compartments a tibia belonging to the Cid, and from the other, a humerus belong to Chimène; then, having knocked them together before Mrs. Little's eyes, he aid to her in English, with a deep sigh:

"Alas, my dear Betty, behold what will one day remain of you and me. Far worse, no one will seek to see our remains, much less will a worthy Spaniard come to Chester to take them out of their box momentarily and permit them to give one another a posthumous kiss."

Like her husband, Mrs. Little uttered a deep sigh, and was content to reply, "Ho yes, Tom."

Mr. Little went on: "It's only as yet a demi-disaster when the bones of those who have loved one another are united, but when they're separated, even by the partition in a chest, it's very sad, Betty. We ought, if you want my opinion, to express in our respective testaments the desire that, once deprived of their flesh, ours should be mingled."

"Ho yes, Tom," replied Mrs. Little. "Ho yes."

"That," I said to Mr. Little, "is a rather lugubrious pre-caution."

"But as well to take, certainly, replacing the bones of the two legendary lovers in their box, "for it's necessary not to expect our heirs, especially when they are not our own chil-

---

obtained a particular significance in France because to Pierre Corneille's play *Le Cid* (1636), which was advertised, accu-rately as a "tragicomedy," and thus started and argument about generic propriety that raged for decades.

dren, to care about our bones. Will they even care about our memory?"

"A good precaution to take, you say but that depends on the manner of one's understanding," I objected. "If it is true that there is an immaterial principle within us, it is the souls of faithful spouses that have an interest in drawing together, and not their bones, and if that principle does not exist, what does it matter whether or not the bones are brought together by the hand of a heir?

"Do you believe, in good faith, that the remains of Rodrigo and Chimène feel a very vivid joy in being side by side? Their separation would not be cruel. What is cruel, and truly cruel, is for Rodrigo to survive or Chimène to survive Rodrigo."

"Very cruel, indeed, Monsieur Le Bref. Thus, my wife and I have tried for two or three years now to shield ourselves as much as humanly possible from that eventuality. Isn't that true Betty?"

"Ho yes, Tom."

"But how can you shield yourselves against that?" I exclaimed, astonished.

Our conversation in English was evidently not to the doorkeeper's liking, either because, not understanding it, she saw it as intolerable gibberish, or because she was in haste to get rid of us. Before Mr. Little had time to respond to my question, therefore, she intervened.

"Caballeros and Señora," she said, "here is now the stool on which the first judges of Castile sat, from whom the Cid was descended. For nine hundred years that stool has been here, in that very place."

"What is she saying?" Mr. Little asked me, who scarcely understood any more Spanish than he could speak

I repeated the doorkeeper's explanation in English.

"Nine hundred years!" exclaimed Mr. Little. "Do you hear, Betty? For nine hundred years that stool has been in the place that it occupies today. Isn't it worth the trouble of our sitting on it?"

"Ho yes," said Mrs. Little.

And she made a movement to sit down on it, but before she could put the said stool in contact with her majestic behind, the doorkeeper, who was alert, took her by the arm abruptly, in order to prevent her from doing so.

At the same time, the doorkeeper uttered a flood of words, the sense of which was that it was absolutely forbidden for visitors to pose their humble posterior on a stool that the judges of Castile had honored with their august derrière. And I translated the prohibition for Mr. Little—but instead of resigning himself placidly, as common sense appeared to command, he jibbed.

"It's impossible, Monsieur Le Bref," he said to me, "that we leave here without all three of us having sat in turn on that stool. Isn't it, Betty?"

"Ho yes, Tom."

"But what's the point, Monsieur Little?" I observed. "What can result from it for you? And besides, you've been told that it's not permitted."

Without making any reply, Mr. Little took a duro and two pesetas from his pocket and, holding the duro in one hand and the two pesetas n the other, he made the doorkeeper understand by means of an expressive mime accompanied by a few words in bad Spanish, that he would give her the duro if she would let us sit down, and only the two pesetas if she refused.

It goes without saying that that very British argument caused the doorkeeper to reflect. Her reflection was so prompt, in fact, that it did not last twenty seconds.

"Well, so be it," she said. "Sit down, but don't tell anyone, for you'd lose me my job, for sure."

Mrs. Little and her husband immediately satisfied their desire. As for me, mine was so feeble, that in sitting down, it was not so much the desire in question that I was satisfying as that of Mr. Little.

Afterwards, we went to the cathedral, which is one of the most grandiose and splendid monuments in the entire world.

There is such a profusion of riches there that the eye is dazzled by them, and so many things to see that the eyes eventually weary of gazing.

Mrs. Little was particularly impressed by the famous crucified Christ who bleeds every Friday. It is, in fact, difficult to imagine anything more troubling, for that Christ, an admirable mannequin, has nothing of the statue but everything of the man in his gaze, his convulsed features, his lips, which seem to move, his hair, beard, eyebrows and eyelashes, and even his skin, which one could believe to be human, which is even said to be, and which appears to cover, instead of stuffing, true flesh, so much elasticity does it offer to the eye.

When, by the light of two candles, the sacristan suddenly lifted the curtain to show us that horrible spectacle, Mrs. Little let herself fall to her knees and almost lost consciousness.

Without sharing her religious ecstasy, Mr. Little and I were deeply moved.

On seeing her faint, like a true Magdalen at the foot of the cross, we hastened to support her.

"Betty, Betty," said Mr. Little, tenderly, "collect yourself, my dear Betty…it's only a simulation."

But even though he lavished concern and delicate tenderness on his wife, she still did not come round. In order to bring her to her senses the sacristan had to go in search of incense; he burned it under her nose, and she did not take long to speak.

"Alas, my dear Tom," she exclaimed, "I thought I was transported to Golgotha during Our Lord's passion!"

Meanwhile, we drew her out of the chapel.

The sacristan told us then that it was necessary to see Papa Moscas before leaving the cathedral.

What is Papa Moscas?

Quite simply an automaton lodged inside the case of the clock above the principal door, created by a Moorish artist, commissioned by Enrique III, King of Castile,[62] in memory of one of the most romantic episodes of his adventurous life.

Once, a long time ago, that automaton must have been very curious, for at the first stroke of the hour, it emerged from its hiding-place and, at every other stroke, it uttered a scream and made a bizarre gesture. That scream and gesture, provoking laughter from children, and even adults, caused a certain disturbance during religious ceremonies. One bishop, whose humor was austere rather than jovial, considered it as an occasion of scandal and ordered that the secret mechanism that enabled Papa Moscas to cry out and gesticulate should be broken. That is why, since then, Papa Moscas remains silent and motionless.

In response to Mr. Little's request, I asked the sacristan whether, to his knowledge, before having his springs broken, Papa Moscas had done anything else other than cry out, and if, for instance, he had spoken a few words.

"Don Enrique," the sacristan replied, "would certainly have liked Papa Moscas to have been able to repeat the tender words uttered to him by a young woman who loved him in secret, and who expired in confessing that chaste love to him, but the constructor of the automaton was not able to succeed, in spite of his efforts. As for the scream it reproduced, it was the one uttered by the young woman when she saw Don Enrique menaced by three wolves in the middle of a forest."

"In England," Mr. Little said to me, with a visible smile of satisfaction, "I know two automata much more curious than that one, for, in addition to the particularity they offer in appearing to be flesh and bone, like the Christ we saw just now, they resemble feature or feature persons presently alive, a few of whose familiar words they pronounce with the same intonation as their models, not to mention that once their mechanism

---

[62] Enrique II reigned in Castile from 1390-1406. The famous automaton of Burgos cathedral known as Papamoscas is featured in numerous literary works, including one by Victor Hugo. It can easily be viewed nowadays on YouTube.

is primed, they can walk almost as well as them. Isn't that so, Betty?"

"Ho yes, Tom," said Mrs. Little.

"In truth," I exclaimed, "I'd like to see such automata."

"If you come to our country, my dear Monsieur Le Bref," Mr. Little replied, "We'll show them to you. There's nothing more curious in the entire world."

"They're doubtless exhibited by some Barnum?"

"No."

"They're found in some museum?"

"No. They belong to an individual, and cost him very dearly, I can't deny. That's not astonishing, though; a master sculptor and a mechanician each worked on them for four years without respite. The individual had to shell out no less than twenty thousand pounds sterling—isn't that so, Betty?"

"Ho yes, Tom."

"But in sum, what does that individual do with his automata?"

"Nothing, for the moment, thank God, but a time will come, unfortunately, when one or other of them will have its utility."

"One of them?" I said, astonished

"Yes," said Mr. Little.

"But in the meantime he shows them to the curious?"

"No, no," Mrs. Little put in, with an animation that was not habitual to her. "On the contrary, he hides them, and they both repose in the coffins that he has had fabricated in their size."

"What a singular idea," I said.

There is a proverb which says that if one mentions the wolf one sees his tail. Scarcely had Mrs. Little mentioned coffins to me than we turned a street corner and were confronted by a shop devoted exclusively to the sale of coffins.

There were coffins of every size and genre—painted, gilded, sculpted, covered in lace, in two beautiful window displays to either side of the open door, where a young and

pretty Castilian woman was framed, plying a needle and singing wholeheartedly.

Inside the shop there were more ordinary ones piled up
on top of one another, all the way to the ceiling, as well as
little ones designed for children.

We stopped, astonished by that exhibition of coffins,
which is no more customary in England than in France.

Although there was nothing amusing about it, Mr. and
Mrs. Little were very interested in it, and I even thought I observed them looking one another up and down from the corner
of the eyes, as if each of them were measuring up the other for
a coffin. But I dare not affirm that.

V

In almost all the hotels in the two Castiles, especially in
the one in which we were staying in Burgos, the service is
carried out by young women rather than men, and quite lovely
young women, believe me. Sturdy, lively and cheerful, it
gladdens the heart just to look at them.

If I mention that detail, it is because it was the pretext for
a violent scene between Mrs. Little and her husband, which
permitted me to appreciate in a new light the true character of
the lady in question, which had previously appeared to me to
be excessively meek.

The day after our arrival in Burgos, as Mr. Little, who
had come to collect me from my room at eight o'clock in the
morning, was going down the hotel staircase with me, one of
the maidservants named Amparo—Protection—who was just
in front of us, wanting to hasten her pace, made a false step
and fell backwards, laden with sheets and napkins.

Mr. Little only just had time to catch her in his arms. She
was a very cheerful young woman. Although she must have
had a moment of fright on suddenly finding herself in the Englishman's arms, she uttered a burst of laughter that resounded
all the way to the room where Mrs. Little was putting the last
touches to her attire before joining us.

If it had only been Amparo's laughter that had reached Mrs. Little's ears, there would certainly not have been much harm done, and it would not have disturbed the taciturn Englishwoman unduly, but what completed the disaster, what troubled her beyond all expression, was that the loud voice of her husband mingled with that burst of feminine Spanish laughter.

Mrs. Little bounded out of her room, her hat in one hand and her cape in the other, just in time to see this stimulating spectacle: Amparo guffawing with laughter in the arms of Mr. Little, who, I admit, was not in any particular hurry to stand her up again, although I would swear that there was not the slightest frolicsome intention on his part.

As soon as he heard his wife coming, however, he hastened to return Amparo to her feet—too late, alas!"

Mrs. Little had seen everything, and misinterpreted it completely.

As I turned round I was amazed by her expression, which, ordinarily so placid, had become more trenchant than a sharp steel blade. Mr. Little could not see that guillotine gaze weighing upon the back of his neck, because he was turned around, but he must have sensed it, for he shuddered in every limb.

Divining the situation marvelously, I thought that it was up to me to save him.

"Madame," I said, affecting a detached tone, "but for your husband that poor girl might have broken her hip."

"Truly," said Mrs. Little, "the pretext is good."

At that point Mr. Little thought he ought to turn round and defend himself.

"I swear to you, my dear Betty, that it's not a pretext but the pure truth."

"Good, good, one knows your habits."

"My habits!" cried Mr. Little, clapping his hands together.

200

"Indeed," said Mrs. Little, whose gaze was animated by a singular fire. "You're the vilest of men and I don't know what's stopping me from throwing you down the stairs."

"Calm down, Betty, for God's sake, calm down. Don't make a scandal here for no reason."

"For no reason?"

"Yes, yes, for no reason."

As he said that, Mr. Little darted a pleading glance at me, as if to appeal for my aid. I was fearful of his life, but I felt even more pity for him.

"It's certain Madame," I said, "that there is nothing in this to excite your anger in the slightest."

"I'm not angry, merely indignant."

"Yes, yes, I meant your indignation, since you prefer that. Note that what happened to your husband might equally well have happened to me."

"It would have been much better, Monsieur, if it had happened to you."

"I don't disagree, Madame."

"And why, in fact, was it not into your arms, but precisely into Mr. Little's, that this young lady allowed herself to fall, laughing?"

"For the very simple reason, Madame that Mr. Little was behind her, and not me."

"Mr. Little always arranges himself in such a manner as to find himself behind maids!" exclaimed Mrs. Little.

"Oh!" interjected Mr. Little.

Amparo, the maidservant who had caused all that emotion, quite innocently, had not failed to perceive that she was the object of it. She had turned back at the moment of Mrs. Little's sharpest—or, at last, most ironic—remarks, and, without comprehending a word of the English exchanged between the husband, the wife and me, she had divined everything.

I judged that by a smile, which was immediately followed by a slight artificial coughing fit, but which Mrs. Little, unfortunately, mistook for a burst of laughter.

Thinking that she was being mocked, the latter lavished imprecations upon her husband almost as tragic as those of the famous Camille of the Horatii.[63]

"Man devoid of morality, devoid of decency, vulgar deb-auchee, knowing your depraved tastes as I do, I ought to have refused to undertake a voyage to the continent in your compa-ny. It's not enough to play the rake with my maidservants, now you have to address yourself to hotel maids! And in front of Monsieur Le Bref! Well, you ought to be dying of shame. As for me, I no longer want to look at you."

Mrs. Little had delivered that philippic in a strident voice, save for the final words—As for me, I no longer want to look at you"—which had dissolved in a flood of tears. As she pronounced them she ran to her room, and went into it precipitately, locking the door behind her, with a double click.

"It's a tantrum," said Mr. Little. "It will pass, like the others..."

Meanwhile, he went tranquilly downstairs.

I hesitated to follow him. He noticed that.

"Come on, then," he said. "You know very well that we still have to see the Cid's monument."

"But it's scarcely possible for us to go without Mrs. Lit-tle," I objected.

"Why not?"

"In order not to give her a further motive for irritation."

"Come on, then—at least she'll be irritated for some-thing, whereas just now she was irritated for nothing. And then, I know her; after a few minutes, we'll see her fall back into her flat calm."

As we were leaving the hotel, me apparently more wor-ried than him, for the unexpected domestic quarrel preoccu-pied me greatly, he added: "Poor Monsieur Le Bref, you look

---

[63] Pierre Corneille also wrote *Horace* (1640), based on Livy's account of the conflict between the Horatii and the Curiati, in which Camille [Camilla], the sister of Horace [Horatius] and the fiancée of Curiace [Curiatus], gets caught in the middle

utterly upset. You would never have believed in her capable of such an outburst, would you?"

"No, I confess. In my presence at least, Mrs. Little has always been so tender in your regard, so passive, even, that I thought her incapable of being carried away like that."

"Well, yes, she deceives everyone. Oh, my dear friend"—it was the first time that Mr. Little had conferred the title of friend upon me—"you can't imagine how my poor wife's mania has made me suffer in the past."

"Is it habitual to her?" I asked.

"Alas," sighed Mr. Little.

"Perhaps," I observed, "you have given purchase to it in the beginning by exciting Mrs. Little's jealousy. I observed just now that your attitude with regard to Amparo was only incorrect in appearance, but I noticed that Mrs. Little also reproached you with the one you ordinarily have to your maidservants in Chester."

"That's exactly in what her folly consists, my de Monsieur Le Bref. She imagines that I'm amorous of all my maidservants, so she won't keep one of them."

"And you've done nothing to give her reason to believe it?"

"Absolutely nothing, I assure you."

"You haven't had any compromising familiarities with the young women in question?"

"Not at all! Except that being, by God's grace, a good man, I give them evidence of solicitude, as to all my entourage, and it's that solicitude, which is nothing but humanity, that Mrs. Little mistakes for flirtation."

"But she can't to fly off the handle frequently, as she's just done," I said, lightly, for, after all, I suppose she doesn't see you very day with a maidservant, especially a Spanish maidservant, in your arms!"

"She sees worse than that, not in reality but in imagination…so scarcely a day goes past in Chester when she doesn't make little scenes, if not big ones."

"That must make you very unhappy, Mr. Little."

"Very unhappy, as you say, Monsieur Le Bref, very unhappy, and it's in great part to change my wife's unhealthy condition, even more dolorous for me than for her, that I bought her to the continent. I thought I had succeeded, but now, today, her mania has got hold of her again."

"Damn! Today there was a mitigating circumstance...Amparo was in your arms...well and truly in your arms. And I understand why, at that sight, all Mrs. Little's supposed grievances against you were reawakened. Do you know what I'd do in your place? On returning to Chester I'd replace, once and for all, all my wife's young maids with old negroes, since, as well as your not obtaining the pleasure from those young women that Mrs. Little supposes, they are, on the contrary, the source all kinds of trouble for you."

"I've already thought of that," Mr. Little replied, phlegmatically, "and have even threatened my wife with it, but, apart from the fact that she doesn't much care to have a negro as a chambermaid, I confess that the constant sight of a face of that color would darken my ides, which are already too black."

While chatting in that manner, Mr. Little and I, in the company of one of those benevolent but not disinterested guides, who always put themselves at the disposal of strangers, had climbed a hill overlooking the town of Burgos, crowned by the ruins of a castle in which the ancient kings of Castile resided.

When we were in sight of those ruins, to which we were unable to get any closer, Mr. Little had a philosophico-lyrical—or lyrico-philosophical, if you prefer—effusion.

"How I would like my wife to be here with us!" he exclaimed. "I would say to hr: 'Betty, my dear Betty, you see what remains of that royal castle where powerful princes and beautiful princesses once lived, and of those princes and princesses even less remains, nothing any longer remains but a vague memory. Does that not give you pause for reflection? Does that not put a finger on the nullity of human things? And given that, do you not understand that you have been doubly mistaken to quarrel for no reason with a worthy husband like me, who ought to inspire every confidence in you?'"

Without perceiving very clearly the correlation there was between the ruins of the castle of the kings of Castile and the jealous scene that Mr. Little had made a short while before, I was almost moved to tears by the truly pathetic tone in which the worthy Mr. Little had pronounced his little speech. I understood once again that he was an excellent man and I thought that his wife was veritably very ill-advised to torment him.

VI

After having seen, successively, the triumphal arch in the Doric style erected by Felipe II to Ferdinand Gonzales and the stone column erected to Rodrigo Diaz de Vivar—which is to say the Cid Campeador—in 1784, I believe, neither of which are very curious, we returned to our hotel.

The first person who struck our eyes on arrival was Mrs. Little.

She was sitting in the shade outside the door in a veritably very placid attitude. On seeing her, even at a distance, it was obvious that her jealous irritation had completely disappeared.

I said to her, still in English, with a bright smile, which was reflected on her lips: "In truth, Madame, you were truly inspired not to go to see the monument to the Cid. It's not worth the trouble of being seen."

At the same moment Amparo emerged from the hotel in order to run few local errands and she had an absurd expression of slight embarrassment as she went past us, while Mr. Little, troubled by the fear that his wife's mania might take hold of her again, at the sight of the maidservant, affected to be looking in the other direction.

"Would you like us to depart for Valladolid this afternoon, my dear Betty?" asked Mr. Little. "I've mentioned it to Monsieur Le Bref, who is of that opinion."

"Indeed," I said. "I believe we have nothing further to do in Burgos."

"I think so to, Tom," said Mrs. Little, daring a glance at her husband that was, in truth, very mild.

After lunch we packed our trunks and left.

Why the devil did we go to Valladolid?

It is one of the Spanish towns that contains the fewest curiosities, but it is also one of the richest in historic memories.

I wanted to see in it the old city in which Felipe III held his court, where Gongora, Argensola and the great Cervantes lived, where Christopher Columbus died, and which gave birth one of the most brilliant Spanish poets of our era, Don José Zorrilla, the author of the *Cantos del Trovador* and the truly admirable *Don Juan Tenorio*.[64]

As for Mr. and Mrs. Little, one of their compatriots having praised certain colossal statues of painted wood representing the actors and the onlookers of the drama of the Passion, notably a kneeling virgin very lifelike in her dolor, thy had scarcely other objective in coming to Valladolid than seeing them.

When we arrived there, as we were surrounded at the railway station by hoteliers who were trying to capture us, Mr. Little said to me: "Above all, let's not go to a hotel where the service is carried out by women, as in Burgos. You speak Spanish better than me; have the goodness to ask these fellows before anything else whether the service in their establishment is by men or women."

Several of those to whom I posed that question, in replying to me that their service was carried out by women, had a

---

[64] José Zorrilla (1817-1893) was a leading figure in the Spanihs Romantic Movement. Cantos de Irovador was pushing in 1841 and the "religioso-fantastico drama" *Don Juan Tenorio* in 1844. The later became the longest-running drama in Spain, but he had sold the rights outright and he began published scathing critcisms of the play in the hope of killing it off so that he could write a new version, but in vain.

expression both mocking and engaging, which showed me the extent to which they misinterpreted my motive in asking, and which was succeeded by a keen disappointment when they saw me turn away.

One of them changed his mind then, and said: "Caballero, there are undoubtedly women who contribute to the service in my hotel, but it is primarily carried out by men, as in Paris."

That was the Hotel of the Redemption. We booked rooms there, and for the day and a half that we stayed there, there was, fortunately, not the slightest scene remotely similar to the one in Burgos.

On the other hand, in Madrid, to which we went thereafter, I saw Mrs. Little in a much graver state of effervescence. It is true that her Tom had nothing to do with it this time, and little maids even less, given that it was difficult to glimpse the skirt of one in the hotel where we were staying.

It was during a bullfight, the first and last that Mrs. Little witnessed.

Although I had warned her about the horror of the spectacle, with which I was already familiar, she had wanted to confront it, not supposing it to be as horrible as it really is. As for her husband, he was no more eager than I was to watch the contest, for he had taken me at my word, but he yielded in order to company his wife, and I went with them.

At first, Mrs. Little, without enthusiasm taking hold of her, seemed keenly interested. The sight of ten thousand spectators heaped on the steps of an immense circus, the rutilant costumes of the women, and even the men, the noise of joyful conversation and he arrival, to the sound of the music of cuadrilla, of the ceremoniously-clad toreros, the parade of the three espadas dressed in the splendid costume of Figaro in The Barber of Seville, the banderillos and capeadores covered in silver and gold, picadors in horseback proceeding in pairs holding long lances, with broad-brimmed gray hats and yellow buffalo-hide trousers, and, finally, the chulos, or servants, and even the entry of the bull, all appeared to strike her imagination vividly and capture it.

But as soon as she had seen a horse, its belly punctured by the bull's horn, buckle and collapse in the arena and then, lifted up by the picador's spur, try to walk, impeding its feet with its dangling entrails, she stood up, gripped by a nervous tremor and started abusing the alcalde who was guilty, in her eyes, of permitting such atrocities in the most virulent manner, in English.

It often happens in arenas that the Spaniards abuse the alcalde, and very violently, but it is to reproach him for tolerating the slightest remission in the massacre.

Have you ever heard of *banderillas de fuego*? They are arrows of a sort furnished with a rocket, which ignites just at the moment when the point penetrates the flesh of the bull, and burns the wound, causing the poor animal atrocious pain.

Now, when a bull, certainly having more courage and common sense than that inept and ferocious multitude of men and women, disdains to respond to the bloody provocations of the picadors and banderilleros, who initially sink their lances into it, and then shoot their arrows into is neck, when it only seems to be demanding one thing, which is for the door to be opened so that it can return to the pen, cries ring out from all directions: "Banderillas de fuego!"

And if the alcalde, who is the only one who can authorize the employment of those banderillas, is still reluctant to do it because of a residuum of humanity, and if, in spite of the furious cries of "Fuego! Fuego!" the alcalde is obstinate in his refusal, popular rage turns against him and one can then hear cries of "*Las banderillas al alcalde! Fuego al alcalde!*"

Let us return to Mrs. Little. At first her indignant voice did not penetrate, so loud was the hubbub, any further than the nearest steps, but as it was still increasing in volume, in spite of the efforts that Mr. Little and I were making to stifle it, general attention did not take long to awaken, and all gazes quit the bull momentarily in order to fix upon the foreigner from whom an avalanche of words and gestures was flowing.

What the devil was wrong with her? It was even possible to believe, at first, that she was exhaling her wrath at the picadors, who might have seemed to the public a little slack and maladroit when they struck the bull with their lances. But her neighbors, particular fanatics of tauromachy, eventually understood by the virulent manner in which she was shouting at them that she was condemning tauromachy itself.

From then on, Mr. Little and I, like Mrs. Little, were the object of a disorderly protestation on their part. I wondered whether those fanatics were not about to throw all three of us into the arena, and all was all the more authorized in the suspicion because a few cries could be heard threatening us with exactly that, when an incident came to our aid.

Fortunately, Mrs. Little, vanquished by emotion, lost consciousness.

Her faint was very opportune, since it extracted Mr. Little and me from a great embarrassment

But what we needed most of all was to be able to get her out of that furious crowd, and us with her. Alas, we absolutely could not do that, so compact was it, even flooding the corridors.

For want of anything better, the prolongation of her unconsciousness, if it would not have disturbed Mr. Little, would have appeared to me to be entirely desirable. Yes, I would have been delighted if the worthy woman had not come round before the end of the contest.

However, she came round after a few minutes and manifested the unrealizable desire to get out.

We made her understand the impossibility of succeeding in that. Then she started to weep.

"Nothing forces you to watch," I told her. "Put your fan in front of your eyes."

Vain advice…she could not help looking, from time to time, as if fascinated by some invincible charm; she looked, and she glimpsed all the horrors.

As for Mr. Little and myself, possessed of greater will-power than her, we had imposed on ourselves spontaneously, without the slightest preliminary agreement, the obligation to watch the spectators rather than the actors of the scene of carnage.

Although the general attention was entirely devoted to the scene, our excessively unenthusiastic attitude provided our nearest neighbors, of both sexes, with a distraction that they held against us. I heard some suggesting worse things than hanging us. In order not to find the slightest attraction in those bloody games, to dare to allow the repulsion they inspired in us to show, we were wretches, we were going so far as to insult the proud Spanish nation.

Finally, our torture ended, along with that of twenty horses and five bulls, victims of inept and disgusting human ferocity, and we were able to quit the circus, not without being jeered somewhat.

Fortunately, there are other things to see in Madrid than the Corrida. One is far from having said everything when one has cited the admirable Plaza de la Puerta del Sol, where the movement of the capital is concentrated, where the noisy genius of the Madrilene people is summarized, the Prado and the Buen Retiro, which are magnificent promenades, the museum of painting and the naval museum, each the most beautiful of its genre in Europe, the convent of the Escurial, a unique ensemble emerged from the grandiose and funereal petrifaction of the reign of Felipe II.

The idea of their death, which had already haunted Mr. and Mrs. Little several times before my eyes since their arrival in Spain, took hold of them again in the crypt of the church of the Escurial, where Charles V and his successors, from Felipe II to Ferdinand VII, are buried, as well as the Empresses and Queens of the houses of Austria and Bourbon.

After the warden had shown us by the light of his torch the name of Luisa, written on the tomb of Doña Maria Luisa of Savoy by that princess herself, with the point of her scissors, Mrs. Little said to her husband: "Tom, when we get back to Chester, I shall also write my name on my tomb with my scissors, so that one day, it can be shown to travelers, while saying to them: 'That's what Mrs. Little did.'"

Although Mrs. Little generally approved of what her husband said, except when he showed some benevolence for your maidservants, it was not the same for Mr. Little in her regard. He maintained a much greater independence with regard to his wife. So he had no hesitation in showing her what was strange in her project, and even slightly ridiculous.

"In truth, Betty," he said to her, "are you're losing your head, my dear love, in wanting to copy a Queen of Spain, being a simple cheese-maker's wife? Even if you did write your name on our tomb with your own scissors, Betty, no one among the tourists who come to Chester—and there are very few of them—would take any notice of it."

"But you, Tom, if you survive me, as I wish, would you not be touched, in coming to make your devotions at my tomb, to find the letters of my name traced in my own hand?"

"With the point of your scissors?"

"With the point of my scissors."

"Indeed, that would touch me," replied Mr. Little, after a few seconds of reflection. "You'd do it, then, with my intention?"

"Of course, Tom!" cried Mrs. Little. And she added: "For myself, I declare to you, nothing would soften my heart as much as to see on yours the name Tom, written by you with a pen-knife."

"Then I'll give my tomb a thrust with my pen-knife in order to be agreeable to you," replied Mr. Little, "since you'd experience as much pleasure in that as you would have had irritation I've delivered one in our contract."

It was scarcely habitual for Mr. Little, an earnest man, to joke in that fashion, so his unexpected pleasantry made me laugh heartily.

VII

On quitting Madrid we went to Aranjuez in order to visit the splendid palace constructed for Felipe II by the celebrated architect Herrera and where the abdication of Charles IV in favor of his son Ferdinand took place in 1808, following the so-called Aranjuez insurrection against Manuel Godoy, the Prince of the Peace.

As we were in the other little marble palace that stands in the depths of the gardens traversed by the Tage, the most grandiose and most marvelous gardens I had ever seen, and especially in Charles IV's billiard room, I noticed that an extreme disturbance had taken possession of Mr. Little. He had gone very pale, with a vague gaze and a sort of nervous tremor in his hands.

"What's the matter with you, Tom," Mrs. Little asked him. "You seem to be suffering."

"Suffering! Oh, yes!" replied Mr. Little, who could not suppress a sort of trepidation in his left leg. But he immediately pulled himself together. "That is to say…no…I'm not suffering at all. Pay no attention to me, I beg you, Betty, pay no attention to it."

However, Mrs. Little, who rendered to her husband all the affection that she received from him, took a small bottle of smelling salts out of her pocket and offered it to him to sniff.

"Here," she said, "breathe in, Tom, breathe in."

He pushed his wife's hand away gently. "It's useless; it doesn't do anything at all."

We had had lunch not long before. I approached Mr. Little and said: "Is your lunch giving you indigestion?"

"On the contrary," he replied. "But I beg you, occupy yourself with my wife rather than me; explain the curiosities to her, which I don't have the strength to explain to her at the moment."

In truth, it was the warden of the small palace who was furnishing us with all the desirable explanations, but, as Mrs. Little did not understand Spanish, I translated them for her.

After having traversed a series of little boudoirs, where I invited Mrs. Little to admire cushions embroidered by queens and musical clocks that had amused Infantas, we arrived in a certain cabinet of extraordinary magnificence, which Charles IV had had equipped for his personal use. The guardian described all the ornaments and did not fail to show us the essential piece, pronouncing with a smile what were perhaps the only two English words he knew: "Water closet."

I noticed, but without drawing the slightest conclusion from it, than on hearing those two words ringing in his ears and seeing the pierced throne on which Charles IV had sat at the commencement of the century, Mr. Little's face was suddenly illuminated, as if by a flash.

As we left that cabinet, the guardian was telling me some story about Charles IV and Godoy, a story that I was translating as he went along for Mrs. Little. Neither she nor I noticed, any more than he did, the sudden absence of Mr. Little. It was not until we were at the foot of a little staircase leading down to the gardens that we observed it.

"Tom, Tom, Tom!" cried Mrs. Little, in all the tones.

But Tom did not reply.

Knowing that he was indisposed, she was seized by a veritable anguish, which infected the warden and myself to some degree.

"The poor man," she said, "has perhaps fainted on the queens' cushions. Let's go back up, let's go back up."

Scarcely were we on the stairway again than we heard a noise of doors.

"That can't be anyone but him," I said to Mrs. Little. "You can see that no mishap has overtaken him."

It was, indeed him, his face as expansive now as it had been contracted a moment before.

"Oh, Tom!" cried Mrs. Little. "What a fright you gave me!"

"How the devil were you able to lose us, my dear Mr. Little?" I said in my turn.

"The essential thing is that I've found you again," he said, cheerfully.

"You look much better," said Mrs. Little.

"Ho yes, my dear Betty, much better. I no longer feel anything." And he added, addressing himself to me: "Ask the warden if we still have anything else to see."

Once again, in that regard, I served as the worthy Mr. Little's interpreter, and I learned that we had seen everything in Aranjuez except the vineyards, the plantations of fruit trees, and the meadows.

As we returned from the small palace toward the large one, along magnificent pathways bordered by trees several centuries old, I could not help looking at Mr. Little surreptitiously two or three times.

He eventually perceived that and ended up whispering mysteriously in my ear: "You've guessed, haven't you, what I've just done?"

"I suspect so. You've just sat down on Charles IV's favorite throne."

"Exactly—but not a word about it to my wife; she's capable of envying me."

"And you sat down there, like that for the pleasure of sitting down there?"

"Oh, no."

"I would have sworn it," I said, laughing. "There was a necessity..."

"Imperious." He added: "Never have I blessed a man as much as I blessed Charles IV for having that whim of a peerless water closet worthy of exhibition."

"Oh, if the warden knew what you had permitted yourself," I said, laughing harder. "It's much more serious, you know, than sitting down on the almost-millenarian stool of the judges of Castile, as Mrs. Little was tempted to do in Burgos."

Just as we had emerged from the small palace with our warden, two German men and three women had arrived, conducted by another warden. Suddenly remembering that circumstance, I said to Mr. Little: "You noticed those Germans; in a little while they'll be shows the mechanism in Charles IV's cabinet that you've profaned, and your profanation might not escape their sight and sense of smell."

"Don't say that," said Mr. Little. "You're giving me a cold sweat."

Buried as she was in her meditations, Mrs. Little was finally astonished by our prolonged conversation, and doubtless finding that her husband looked poorly for a second time, she said to him: "Is it getting worse again, my love?"

"Oh no, no, thank God," said Mr. Little.

In the meantime, and as we were walking slowly in the direction of the grand palace, we saw some kind of employee running toward us. He called to our warden: "Pedro! Pedro!"

As soon as he had reached him he spoke to him in a low voice.

Naturally, we had stopped to wait for our warden. Suddenly, the latter came back to us, without his comrade going away, and, addressing Mr. Little in a manner that seemed to me to be severe, he said to him in Spanish, with great volubility: "It appears that you dropped something in Charles IVs cabinet."

Without understanding what the warden had said, Mr. Little had no doubt that the relief that he had given himself was being reproached as illicit, so he protested in English that he had only yielded to an absolutely pressing, utterly irresistible need, and that he had certainly not intended to offend the memory of Charles IV.

As the warden, naturally, did not understand Mr. Little's excuses, I translated them into Spanish.

The warden then spread his arms wide and, bringing his hands together as if someone had given him frightful news, he cried: "Oh, that's too much! What! You have taken the liberty..."

"Say," I protested, "that he yielded to necessity, and you know very well that the *necesidad carece de ley*."[65]

"There must be a law, Monsieur, when one is in the palace of a king," replied the guardian Pedro with an entirely Castilian arrogance. Your friend had rendered himself guilty of a crime of *lèse-majesté* and it is incumbent on me to arrest him."

---

[65] "Necessity knows no law"—a Spanish proverb.

"Oh!" I cried. "You're going too far."

Meanwhile, Mrs. Little never ceased demanding of Mr. Little, who appeared utterly downcast, without obtaining a response: "What's going on, Tom? What's going on?"

"In the twenty years that I've been a warden at the palace of Aranjuez," Pedro went on, "I have never seen such a crime committed, never, never!"

"Perhaps you're exaggerating," I objected, "in calling it a crime..."

"No, Monsieur, and know that I'm risking, by not arresting your friend, losing my job."

"Just now, however," I said, "when you're colleague came to tell you about the little misfortune, you did not seem so affected."

"My colleague came to tell me that a wallet had been found in Charles IV's cabinet and he asked me whether it was anyone in the group I was leading who had lost it. He told me nothing about the other matter; it was your friend who revealed everything himself, through your intermediation"

Once more the spur of his conscience had driven a man to confess his guilt, and I had stupidly interpreted that inopportune admission.

No doubt Mr. Little had lost his wallet while lowering or pulling up what the English call their unmentionables, and which we in France designate in a less veiled fashion.

Having checked that I still had my wallet, I asked Mr. Little to see whether he still had his.

He no longer had it.

I informed the two wardens of that, who returned it to him, not without having made me understand that they expected from the owner a recompense all the more honest because the wallet had been lost in less admissible circumstances.

Mr. Little, whose wallet contained nearly five hundred francs, gave each of the two men a French louis, and the incident was closed, temporarily at least, for, when Pedro had brought us back to the outer gate of the grand palace, and I gave him three pesetas for the trouble he had taken in showing us the curiosities, he had the impudence to raise the question of Charles IV's cabinet again, which obliged the worthy Mr. Little to give him a duro as well.

And we left for Toledo.

VIII

Very bad news awaited Mr. Little there, in duplicate: at the telegraph office in the form of a dispatch, and at the post office in the form of a letter.

The foreman of his cheese-factory informed him that a fire had just broken out and destroyed it almost entirely.

Needless to say, Mr. Little's establishment was insured with one of the best companies in London. Mr. Little thus did not have to fear ruination, but it was a matter of determining the amount of the disaster with the company, of having the factory rebuilt, and coming to the aid of the workers who had no work to do. Thus, Mr. Little thought that he could not continue his voyage in Spain, but ought to return immediately to Chester. He discussed it in my presence to Mrs. Little, who responded in her plaintive tone, without emotion: "Ho yes, Tom."

It was truly cruel for them to leave Spain at the very moment of visiting Andalusia and its brilliant cities: Cordova, Seville, Cadiz, Granada and Valencia—which is to say, everything there is of the most curious in the Peninsula, to which they would never return.

At least they wanted to see a little of Toledo, since they were obliged to be there for a few hours, the train for Madrid not departing until the evening.

I accompanied them to the cathedral, the church of San Juan de los Rayos and the Alcazar, and after dinner I escorted them to the railway station.

It was not without a real sentiment of sadness that I separated from them. And when, by the gaslight in the waiting room of Toledo station, Mr. Little shook my right hand and said, emotionally: "*Au revoir*, Monsieur Le Bref," and Mrs. Little squeezed my left, saying: "Ho yes, Monsieur Le Bref," I felt my eyes mist over with tears.

There was not between me and the spouses Little one of those very rare sympathies that take possession of the entire being, but we already had the habit of living together, and, in the something like a month that we had been doing that, no coldness had come between us.

Mr. Little had promised to write to me when he returned to England. He kept his word. A week later I had a letter from him in Seville, and a very affectionate letter. He told me how much he and his wife regretted not having been able to go to Andalusia with me and he invited me in the most pressing manner to come and spend a month in his cottage the following spring, when the damage to the cheese-factory had been repaired.

With regard to that cheese-factory he lamented a great deal on the painful impression he had experienced on seeing it entirely in ruins, but he added that, after all, such a misfortune, reparable by insurance, was nothing compared to that other, ever-imminent misfortune, the death of his wife or his own: a misfortune against which, to tell the truth, he had tempted a kind of insurance, perishable itself, and which could easily have been the prey of flames.

In returning thus to an idea that he had already touched upon in conversation with me, he did not render it any clearer. I wondered what the devil he meant by the insurance of sorts that he had tempted against the misfortune of his death or that of his wife, and how that fantastic insurance was perishable, how it might have become the prey of flames.

I asked myself that in vain, and then the attraction of the voyage deflected me away from thinking about it, to such an extent that I said nothing about it in my reply to Mr. Little from Valencia, on the eve of the day when I was due to return to Paris.

After that we wrote to one another two or three times, at fairly long intervals, and then our friendship, like so many others, fell into desuetude.

PART TWO: IN ITALY

I

It had been four or five years since I had heard any mention of Mr. and Mrs. Little when I undertook my third voyage to Italy, from which I have just come back.

I have not been there once, and have never returned, without revisiting Pisa, the melancholy charm of which attracts me invincibly.

One day, I was in the dome of Pisa, and after having admired once again Il Sodoma's very curious *Sacrifice of Isaac*, I was watching the gentle sway of the monumental lamp—an oscillation that, three centuries earlier, had put Galileo on the path to the discovery of the pendulum, and by the force of my admiration I was, so to speak, communing with that sublime mind.

I had vaguely heard other visitors approaching behind me without having had any thought of turning round to cast a glance at them.

Three words, however, pronounced in a low voice: "Ho yes, Tom!" struck me singular, like a remembrance, at first ill-defined, but which I did not take long to specify.

I turned my head and was suddenly greeted by an exclamation pronounced in English: "Ah, Monsieur Le Bref, how nice it is to see you again!"

It was the good Mr. Little who spoke to me in that fashion, who had Mrs. Little on his arm, as before during our voyage in Spain. So far as I could judge through the thick veil that she was wearing over her face, the utility of which I could not explain then, she had not aged since I had last seen her. As for Mr. Little, on the contrary, I found him much changed, almost unrecognizable.

219

He had extended his hand to me; I shook it very affectionately.

"Be very sure," I said, "that I am equally glad to find myself with Mrs. Little and you."

So saying, I bowed to Mrs. Little and extended my hand toward her.

Mrs. Little, who seemed to me more fixed and stiffer than ever, responded to my inclination of the head, after a certain hesitation, it seemed to me, and only when her husband had touched her shoulder, but neither of the hands moved toward mine.

Mr. Little, thinking, rightly, that I was surprised by that said: "Don't be offended, my dear Monsieur Le Bref, if my wife doesn't give you her hand. She has something out of order in her arms."

"Oh, not at all, not at all!" I said.

And, bowing a second time to Mrs. Little, in order to show her that I did not hold it against her that she had only responded in part to my politeness, I said to her: "Fortunately, Madame, apart from your discomfort in the arms, you seem to be in good health."

"Very well," she replied, but only after Mr. Little had nudged her with his elbow.

That "very well" appeared to me to be a trifle cold and a trifle hard for the first words that she had addressed to me in so many years.

I knew full well that she was not loquacious, but after all, in our days in Spain, she would have added something to her "very well"—my name, for example, perhaps even modified by the epithet "dear": "My dear Monsieur Le Bref."

Nevertheless, I pretended to pay no attention to it. With my most smiling expression I said: "And how do you like Italy, Madame?"

"Very well."

Again!

"Have you seen Florence?" I added.

"Ho yes, Tom," she replied, not without hesitation and after her husband had squeezed her hand.

Why the devil was she replying to her husband when it was me who had spoken to her?

I could not help smiling at that. Mr. Little perceived it.

"Pay no attention," he whispered to me, mysteriously, "if my wife calls you Tom. She's unfortunately not equipped to pronounce any other name."

The expression "equipped" astonished me.

"Pardon?"

"I said," Mr. Little added, "that my forename, Tom, is absolutely linked to 'Ho yes,' in her organism, in such a way that she cannot say one without the other..."

"Oh!" I said, opening my eyes wide, for I understood less and less.

I repeated with Mr. and Mrs. Little the tour of the cathedral that I had already made. As I watched the woman walking on her husband's arm, I was astonished that her gait, which had already seemed a little stiff in the past, had become jerky. Her footfalls produced a very strange rhythmic click.

That poor woman, I said to myself, *definitely has something out of order, not only in her arms but also in her legs*—and I wondered whether she might have suffered an apoplexy or might be afflicted by a softening of the spinal marrow.

She walked, however, at a fairly brisk pace, and I heard her reply to her husband several times when he pointed out a silver altar, the mosaics in the choir and the marquetry stalls: "Ho yes, Tom."

When we emerged from the cathedral Mr. Little said to me: "Tell me, my dear Monsieur Le Bref, have you seen the baptistery and have you gone up the Leaning Tower?"

"Yes, this morning, again—for I've known them for a long time, having been to Pisa twice before. And you?"

"Not yet. It's worth the trouble, isn't it?"

"Yes, of course; it's necessary to see the pulpit sculpted by Nicola Pisano at the baptistery and go up the tower, from which the view extends over a part of Tuscany. In addition, you know, it's from the top of that tower that Galileo made his experiments with weight."

"I'd very much like to go up there," said Mr. Little.

"You'd do well...there's only one thing to fear, which is that it might be a little to tiring for Mrs. Little, who seems to me to be quite weary already, for the tower is fifty-nine meters high."

Mr. Little appeared to reflect momentarily, and then said: "Wait, I'll ask my wife what she wants to do."

On observing that Mrs. Little, who clearly must have heard her husband and me talking, had not yet emitted and personal thought and that Mr. Little had to ask her expressly what she wanted to do, I said to myself internally: *What a* sang-mort *that woman is!*

Meanwhile, the following little dialogue had taken place between her and her husband:

"Do you feel fatigued, my dear Betty?"

"Ho yes, Tom."

"You don't care about going up the Leaning Tower?"

"No."

"In that case, would you care to wait for me here momentarily with Monsieur Le Bref, who will be kind enough to offer you his arm?"

"Ho yes, Tom."

"As Mr. Little took his wife's arm from beneath his own, I extended mine to Mrs. Little as graciously as I could, but she did not take it, so Mr. Little was obliged to pass his wife's arm under mine himself. I was not overly astonished by that, however, already knowing that there was something hindering the movements of her arms.

Meanwhile, Mr. Little said to her: "In fact, my dear Betty, perhaps you'd be better in the carriage. What do you think?"

When he had touched her hand she replied: "Ho yes, Tom."

"In that case, Monsieur Le Bref will be kind enough to excuse you."

222

"Certainly," I said. "You have a carriage, then?"

"Always. I'm obliged to do that now. My wife can no longer make long journeys on foot."

"Really? She was such a good walker in Spain!"

"Oh, yes, yes," he said, with a sigh. "Unfortunately, it wasn't possible to restore all the qualities she had, and it's already a great deal for her to have conserved some of them."

What is he telling me? I thought, as I accompanied Mr. and Mrs. Little to their carriage, which was waiting for them on the piazza a short distance from the dome. There was such a great eccentricity in certain terms he used in speaking about his wife that I wondered whether I had unlearned the English language, or whether, he had always had that slightly over-imaginative fashion of talking.

When we were in the carriage I opened the door and attempted to assist Mrs. Little to climb the footstep.

"No, no!" exclaimed Mr. Little, abruptly. "Let me do it...you don't know how that's done."

At the same time, he took his wife by the waist from behind with both hands and pressed her until she flexed under his grip. Then he introduced Mrs. Little backwards into the vehicle where he sat her down comfortably on the cushions.

"Go and see the Leaning Tower now, then," I said to him. "I'll keep Mrs. Little company."

"Oh, you can leave her alone...that's unimportant. But I beg you not to lose sight of the coachman."

"Why is that?"

"I mean that, in the unlikely event that the coachman wants to make off, it will be necessary to prevent him doing so."

While Mr. Little drew away in the direction of the Leaning Tower, I approached the carriage door and leaned against it lightly in order to try to enter into conversation with Mrs. Little.

I asked her, in succession, several questions, of a perfect banality, undoubtedly, but nevertheless very gracious, and precisely those that good manners not only authorize but command. I asked her how long it was since she had left England, by what route she had traveled to Italy, what she thought of Pisa, etc., etc.

To my great surprise, she did not reply to any of my questions.

I concluded that her faculties were extraordinarily enfeebled.

Knowing that she was at least capable of answering yes or no, I asked her if she was suffering any pain, but she left that question unanswered like the preceding ones: not even a nod of the head, not the slightest movement of the hand; the coldest and bleakest immobility. I cursed the veil, which, by virtue of its unusual thickness, rendered impenetrable a physiognomy that might perhaps have spoken for Mrs. Little herself.

I could not, however, decently seek to lift that veil.

Having recalled the Mr. Little had only obtained reposes from his wife in my presence by touching her right hand, I tried to do likewise, with as much discretion as possible. Little by little, I had already kneaded almost all of the gloved hand with my fingertips without her appearing to feel it—at least, she had not made any movement. Finally, however, under a last pressure of my fingers, she said: "Ho yes, Tom."

I hoped that, in default of the clear sight of me that she appeared to lack, since she gave the impression of mistaking me for her husband, the faculty of speech had finally returned to her. Thus, I said to her, very gently: "It's me, Madame—you know, me, Monsieur Le Bref, who once traveled with you in Spain. As for your husband, look, here he is coming back from the Leaning Tower, and by putting your head through the carriage window you'll be able to see him…if you'd like to?"

But she did not say a word in reply, or budge in the slightest.

Utterly devastated to find the poor woman—who had always been somewhat taciturn, but whom it had once been possible to converse—in a state bordering on infancy, I judged it futile to persist further, and I turned toward the coachman, whose broad face was very open and sympathetic.

Like any good Italian, he liked nothing better than chatting, and we therefore conversed in his native tongue. In a quarter of an hour, in fact, he told me the things regarding the locale that one does not find in the Joanne guide or in Baedeker.

II

When he came back, Mr. Little said: "Have you visited the Campo Santo?"

"Of course; I've know it for a long time, and I saw it again yesterday, but I'd gladly return there with you if you haven't visited it, for I never weary of looking at *The Triumph of Death.*

"Let's go, then." Addressing the coachman, he said: "Driver, to the Campo Santo."

The coachman did not have far to go to ferry Mrs. Little, the three or four monuments that one has to see in Pisa all being close together.

On the way, Mr. Little said to me: "If I thought that one could have confidence in this coachman, we could leave Mrs. Little in the carriage and visit the Campo Santo without her…there would be much less inconvenience for us."

"Do you think," I objected, "that Mrs. Little that won't want to visit the Campo Santo, which is the greatest curiosity in Pisa?"

"What do you expect her to make of it? When I take her to visit something with me, it's in order not to be alone, to have someone to talk to who will reply to me. From the moment that you're with me, my dear Monsieur Le Bref, I no longer have the same reasons for having my wife on my arm."

"If that's the way it is, my dear Mr. Little, you can trust your coachman. No mishap will overtake Mrs. Little in his hands."

"You think he's honest?"

"As his horse, who, like him, gives the impression of being a very worthy animal, Mr. Little."

"In that case, I'll give him a good tip."

Then, passing his head through the window, he said to him wife, while taking her hand: "Until later, Betty."

And as he clasped her, she replied: "Ho yes, Tom."

Then we walked silently as far as the Campo Santo.

As we went in, Mr. Little said to me: "Isn't it horrible, my dear Monsieur Le Bref, to see my wife changed into that almost inert mass?"

"It's undoubtedly very sad," I remarked. And, without thinking in depth about the opinion I was uttering, I added, in order to console the worthy Mr. Little slightly: "But it's still better than having nothing of her at all."

"Oh, I'm very glad to hear you say that...it's so much better, my dear Monsieur Le Bref, that it was indispensable to my life. If my wife were entirely lacking to me, I wouldn't have survived for a month, not one month."

The custodian was waiting for us at the door, to which he had just brought four or five visitors back. A little chagrined, it seemed to me, that there were only two of us, he deigned nevertheless to propose to show us around the Campo Santo and give us the appropriate explanations.

The first thought that struck me at the door of the renowned cemetery was that Mrs. Little could not be long delayed in dying, given the deplorable state in which she found herself, and I wondered fearfully what would become of her unfortunate husband then—but it goes without saying that I made no mention of that painful reflection. Furthermore, my mind did not take long, like his, to be entirely captivated by *The Triumph of Death*, Orcagna's admirable fresco,[66] simultaneously so naïve and so profound.

To the right of the spectator, the group of lords and ladies sitting and chatting gallantly under the trees to the sound

---

[66] The fresco in question is now generally assumed to be the work of Buonamico Buffalmacco rather than Orcagna.

of sweet music; nearby, the angels and demons drawing the corporeal souls from the mouths of moribund men and women, or seeking to snatch them in mid-air; further away, the unfortunates vainly imploring Death; to the far left, other powerful lords and ladies on horseback are following a hunt, and suddenly, in the guise of game, finding at a bend in the path three open coffins, the first containing a fresh cadaver, the send a putrefied cadaver and the third a mere skeleton; on the nearby mountain, monks at the door of their chapel, one of whom is leading a hind while another accompanied by a hind and a rabbit are wandering together on a volcanic hillock into which culpable souls are being plunged by demons; the entire curious ensemble, strewn with steamers with inscriptions that, unfortunately, are scarcely distinguishable any longer, retained Mr. Little and myself for a long time.

Like any good Englishman worthy of the name, Mr. Little was equipped with marine binoculars, through which he looked at the various parts of the fresco successively.

"Do you see, my dear Monsieur Le Bref," he said to me suddenly, "that fat naked monk over whom an angel and a demon are fighting, the angel pulling him by the arms and the demon by the legs?"

"Yes, perfectly, and I even find the idea that Orcagna had there rather amusing."

"Well, now look slightly above and to your right, at that female angel clad in a robe with long creases, who is rising toward the sky with a man in her arms. Don't you think that the angel resembles Mrs. Little, and that the man in her arms is also a little like me?"

"Except for the costume," I said, smiling, the man in the fresco being as naked as a worm.

"The face…," said Mr. Little, very seriously. And he added: "May my dear Betty carry me thus in her arms, all the way to the throne of God!"

"As she certainly will, my dear Mr. Little," I replied, "when the moment comes…but it's premature, thank God, to think of your assumption."

Save for the magisterial sign of *The Triumph of Death*, which is developed on one of its interior walls and suits such a place so well, the Campo Santo is not at all lugubrious in itself. It is a pretty rectangular meadow surrounded by galleries. And yet, when the custodian explained the symbolism of the three coffins in the fresco to us, it seemed to us that we actually scented a cadaverous odor distributed around us. In order to escape it, I caught myself pinching my nose, as one of the riders on Orcagna's fresco is doing.

After checking, I realized that the odor in question was emanating from the custodian, as if his body were impregnated with the juice of a human putrescence several centuries old.

Fortunately, a clump of geraniums was emerging from the excavation of a ancient tomb. I detached two or three leaves, which Mr. Little and I crushed between our fingers in order to respire the perfume.

"At which hotel are you staying?" Mr. Little asked me, as we went back to the carriage where Mrs. Little was waiting for us.

"The Albergo Europa, on the Lugarno."

"We're neighbors," he said. "I'm at the Albergo Roma. When do you intend to leave Pisa?"

"Tomorrow morning."

"To go where?"

"To Siena."

"We'll leave with you. At what time?"

"Quarter past nine."

"That's agreed—but where shall we go now?"

"If you wish, we can go to see the fountain in the Piazza dei Cavalieri and the monument to the grand duke Leopold I on the Piazza Santa Catarina, after which you'll have seen everything that Pisa has of the most curious."

Mr. Little made me climb into the carriage, which had four seats, and I sat down opposite Mr. Little, still veiled, still motionless and still silent.

She seemed as indifferent to our return as she had been to our departure. Her attitude, more than starchy, chilled me. I wanted to say something gracious to her, but the words would not come to my lips. I contented myself with smiling at her and a slight inclination of the head.

The worthy Mr. Little took her hand and said: "You're very glad to find yourself with dear Monsieur Le Bref again, who has been such a good friend to us, aren't you, Betty?"

"Ho yes, Tom."

"How many times have you said to me: 'I'll never forget, Tom, that you owe your life to Monsieur Le Bref'?"

"Ho yes, Tom."

"Alas, I'll never forget either, that you owe your death to me, my dear Betty."

And as he said that, Mr. Little uttered a little sob, which he tried in vain to stifle, and which dissolved in a flood of tears.

I did not seek at first to explain the enigma contained in the words "you owe your death to me," spoken by a husband to a wife who, although enfeebled, especially intellectually, it seemed to me, was no less alive, it also seemed to me.

The fit of sincere dolor that had overtaken Mr. Little impressed me far more vividly than his wife, for the latter remained quite inert while I, by contrast, held out my hands to him—which he did not see, however, his face being plunged into his own.

Meanwhile, we had arrived at the Piazza dei Cavalieri, and the coachman, following the order he had received from me, had just stopped our vehicle near the fountain.

As the carriage stopped, Mr. Little hastily removed his hands from his face, held them out to me in his turn, damp with tears, and said: "Forgive me, Monsieur Le Bref, forgive my moment of weakness." Then he added, while wiping his hands and face with the aid of his handkerchief: "Where are we, if you please, Monsieur Le Bref?"

"We're at the fountain in the Piazza dei Cavalieri.

"Ah!"

"Do you see those women with their shawls knotted over their heads, in the process of catching the water-jet escaping from the mouth of that Amour in a little funnel? Notice the extremely graceful form of their buckets."

He leaned out of the window in order to see better. As for Mrs. Little, she had no more budged than a statue, and neither her husband nor I had troubled her meditation.

Suddenly, Mr. Little threw himself backwards as if seized by fear, and I saw surge forth at the carriage door a tall fellow clad in a black hooded cloak that only allowed his eyes, his teeth and his hands to show.

He extended a little alms-box toward us, saying: "*Pei poveri infirmi.*"

He was a member of the Brotherhood of Mercy, which collects for the sick. I told Mr. Little that in English, and he joined his offering with mine, Mrs. Little still remaining impassive.

After having seen the Piazza Santa Catarina and the monument to the grand duke Leopold I, we had ourselves taken back to the Lugarno, where I quit Mr. and Mrs. Little, reminding them that we were to meet at the railway station the following morning at nine o'clock.

III

They did not miss the rendezvous. Mrs. Little, still veiled, was clad for the circumstance in a large overcoat, as was Mr. Little. He gave his arm to his wife, whose jerky footsteps resounded on the external platform of the station.

"If you would care to climb up first," Mr. Little said to me, "you can take my wife, not by the hands but by the forearms, while I push her by the waist."

"Gladly," I replied. Unfortunately, however, I forgot the instruction to take Mrs. Little by the forearms. I grasped her hands, and as I lifted her up she voiced her eternal: "Ho yes, Tom."

Mr. Little and I sat her down in a corner, where she seemed to abandon herself to slumber.

I recalled then, by contrast with that dejection, the extreme animation that Mrs. Little had had five years earlier at the railway station in Bordeaux, when, blocking the carriage window, she had shouted in order to prevent me from climbing into her compartment; "Loa! Loa!"

The one in which we were now sitting was soon completed by a family composed of five individuals, all very becoming.

There was a professor from the University of Pisa, who was going to the vicinity of Siena with his wife and three daughters in order to attend a wedding celebration. Hazard had placed the gentleman in question beside me.

By way of a request for information that I made, and which he provided in the most affable manner, conversation was engaged between us and became quasi-general. Only Mrs. Little, in her corner, did not participate in it.

On seeing that dejected attitude, the professor's wife could not help asking: "*La signora è ammalata*?"

"*Un poco*," I said.

As for Mr. Little, whether he understood the lady's question or not, he made no response. In fact, he had just asked the professor for information that, he said, he had not found in his guide, regarding the cheeses of Parma, and he was entirely intent on that matter, which interested him greatly, being, as they say, in the business.

"Are you very fond of cheeses?" asked the professor, in good English.

"I manufacture them in Chester."

"In Chester…oh, then I understand."

With that, Mr. Little and the professor exchanged cards. The latter, Signor Giammani, who taught chemistry at the University of Pisa, had written at one time, and even published, a comparative study of all known cheeses.

Mr. Little had had a stroke of luck. Signor Giammani gave us, in English, a veritable lecture on the similar or distinctive qualities of the various cheeses that shared the gastronomic favor of Europe. I confess that I was very interested in it on my own account, although I had never wanted to try any other cheese than cream cheese. It even made the journey from Pisa to Siena seem short. For his part, Mr. Little was delighted.

At one moment, taking Mrs. Little's hand, he exclaimed: "You hear, my dear Betty, the obliging things that this gentleman, who is one of the most competent men in Europe, is saying about our Cheshire cheeses?"

To which Mr. Little replied, as was her habit: "Ho yes, Tom." Then, Mr. Little having touched her shoulder, she bowed slightly.

She repeated her little salute in the same manner when, once we had arrived at Siena station, Signor Giammani and his family took their leave of us, very gracefully, and descended from the compartment.

When we had got down in our turn, I noticed that two of the professor's daughters turned round covertly to watch Mrs. Little walking, and that they were laughing at the poor woman's gait.

We arrived at lunch-time at the Aquila Nero inn, which had been recommended to us by Signor Giammani as one of the best in Siena. Our first concern, naturally, was to ask for rooms and have our baggage taken up. We were given two that were adjacent.

After a few minutes I heard Mr. Little close and lock the door of his room, and then knock on mine.

"Are you going down for lunch?"

"Very gladly…but isn't Mrs. Little coming down?"

"What would be the point?"

"To have lunch."

"You're wrong," he told me, "to joke in that fashion. You know full well that she can't eat."

"She's really so ill this morning?"

"Come on, my dear Monsieur Le Bref, you can't intend to mock our misfortune!"

"God preserve me! But what misfortune are you talking about?"

Instead of responding directly to my question he said, in a softer tone: "The most skillful mechanicians have not yet found a means of making artificial stomachs."

Thinking that Mrs. Little had been afflicted for some time with a serious gastritis, I did not persist.

Furthermore, I was so hungry myself that it scarcely left me the leisure to think about anything else.

When we went into the dining room there were four Germans there, a lady and three men, all four wearing spectacles on their noses and hats on their heads. They raised their spectacles when we entered, along with the noses they crowned, but not their hats—I'm referring to the men—although we saluted them very politely. Without taking any further notice of the Teutonic boors, who might have been the flower of Berlinese aristocracy, Mr. Little and I ate with all the appetite we had, no longer talking about Mrs. Little, for the subject seemed delicate to me, but about the curiosities we were going to see.

As the meal drew to its close, and I had just ordered coffee, Mr. Little said to me: "While you drink your coffee, my dear Monsieur Le Bref, I'll go take tea in the company of my wife in her room, and I'll come back without her shortly, in order for us to go out."

The waiter did not take long to appear, with a heavily laden tray in his hands, from which he removed, with my intention, a small cup, a small cafetière and a little sugar-bowl containing indecently tiny sugar-lumps, as large as sheep-droppings at the most.

What remained on the tray was the tea destined for Mr. and Mrs. Little. While I was putting something like half a dozen sugar lumps in my cup, admiring once again that singular Italian fashion, with which I was familiar, Mr. Little left the dining room, followed by the waiter.

After a quarter of an hour or thereabouts he reappeared, unaccompanied by Mrs. Little.

"I've just put my wife decisively to bed," he said. "Perhaps it's better thus. Having you with me, I'll perceive her absence much less."

"You're very good, and you honor me greatly."

We went to the cathedral, and along the way, our attention as particularly attracted by the round straw hats that the proletarian women were wearing, attached around the neck, falling back more often than not over their shoulders and palpitating gracefully above their foreheads, where they formed mobile aureoles of a sort. It was also attracted by a team of long-horned Tuscan oxen the color of white coffee, drawing a very narrow basket-cart.

The *sgraffiti*, or engravings, carved into the stones of the cathedral are a work unique in the world, but unfortunately badly damaged by the friction of the soles of numerous generations of boots. No trace of those *sgraffiti* would remain today if the precaution had not finally been taken of covering them with planks.

As the sacristan lifted up the planks to show us the work in question, my eyes chanced to fall on a strange little gnome of sorts, in the flesh and bone. With his very long nose and the almost black tint of his hair, crouched on his little legs, which rose up behind him in the manner of a tail, and his little crutches in his arms, he was strongly reminiscent of a crow.

That quasi-fantastic apparition troubled me so much that it did not cease to haunt my gaze even when I fixed it on the *sgraffiti*, and then on the white marble pulpit supported by four lions, magnificently sculpted by Nicola Pisano, on Bernini's Saint Jerome and the Magdalen, on the admirable frescoes of the Libreria, a highly original work by Pinturicchio in which the bits of the horses, the ornaments of the miters and the tiaras and the guards of the swords project in gilded nails, and finally, on the rich collection of old missals.

It seemed to me that the poor human crow personified the clerical spirit, as the dove does the Holy Spirit.

Next we visited the *Academia delle belle arti*, where one finds, among other works Caravaggio's *Hopscotch Players*,

Saint Catherine of Siena Receiving the Stigmata by Beccafumi, a Saint Paul by Rutilio Manetti and a Charles V by Holbein—after which we strolled until dinner through the city, paved, like Pisa, with large flagstones.

Mrs. Little did not come down for dinner any more than for lunch. I did not make any observation in that regard to Mr. Little, for fear of irritating him.

When he talked about leaving the next day for Orvieto, from which we were to go to Rome, however, I asked him whether he thought that Mrs. Little was in a state to support the fatigues of the voyage—to which he replied, without my understanding the meaning of what he said very clearly, that the poor woman was apparently no longer capable of fatigue.

Was she capable of refection? In any case, it was not the tea that her husband had sent up to her room in the evening that was of a nature to lend her much sustenance.

IV

At any rate, she was on her feet the following day at the same time as us, and ready to depart.

Naturally, I thought it my duty to salute her and enquire after her health, to which she replied to me in English: "Very well...thank you."

Immediately, however, Mr. Little said to me, still in English: "I'd be obliged to you henceforth, Monsieur Le Bref, not to address any speech to my wife, especially in public, in your interest as well as mine, for the difficulty I have in replying to you via her, as well as taking away all illusion from me, can only cause you a disagreeable sensation too."

"Oh!" I said, somewhat surprised.

"Well, yes, you understand that very well."

I did not understand at all, but I nevertheless replied: "Of course, of course."

And I promised myself no longer to address any remark to Mrs. Little, but to content myself with replying to her—and she never spoke to me.

I could not, however, prevent myself from exercising in her regard the small duties of politeness from which a gallant man cannot refrain—for example, helping hr to climb aboard the train to Orvieto at Siena railway station, as I had done at Pisa station for the train to Siena; but I did so mutely, for which Mr. Little thanked me warmly by means of a firm handshake.

Scarcely had we sat down when I saw two prelates coming toward us surrounded by priests and preceded by the station-master, holding his cap in his hand. The latter opened the door of our compartment and, perceiving the three of us, he jumped backwards, and then shouted: "Gorini, Gorini!"

Gorini, who as a subaltern employee, came as commanded.

"Have you lost your head," he cried then, "letting these passengers climb into a carriage reserved for Monsignor?"

The poor devil apologized to his chief as best he could and set about asking us to get out. But Mr. Little immediately refused, in English, while Mrs. Little, under the effect of her habitual prostration, did not seem to perceive anything.

It was the exact counterpart of the scene that the excellent couple had made in my regard at the station in Bordeaux when I had tried to climb on to the Bayonne train. While smiling at that idea, which gave me an amiable appearance, I got down rapidly from the carriage and, approaching the French bishop, I said to him: "Monseigneur, if Your Grace does not absolutely have need of all the places in the compartment, I would be infinitely grateful to you for leaving this worthy Englishman and his wife there, who are my friends. I permit myself to address this plea to Your Grace because the poor lady is not very steady on her feet, and it is not easy lift her up into a carriage or take her down from one. They are in any case, very discreet individuals incapable of inconveniencing Your Grace."

"I'm convinced, Monsieur," said the prelate, very amiably, "and may God preserve me from disturbing such worthy people, vouched for by you, who are my compatriot. Furthermore, we only need three places and will have plenty of room in your company."

"For myself, Monseigneur," I said, "I can easily go and sit elsewhere."

"Don't do anything of the sort, I beg you; I shall be only too glad to have you for a traveling companion."

While the French prelate and I were exchanging these courtesies, watched by all the travelers, Mr. Little and the station-master were arguing, without understanding very much, in English and Italian.

The station-master raised his voice, irritated by the passivity opposed to his injunctions to descend by the worthy Mr. Little, to such an extent that the Archbishop of Siena had to intervene to calm him down.

"*Piano, piano, signore...un pè piu di dolcezza.*"

The French prelate then put an end to the dispute, while taking his leave of the Italian prelate with a hand-kiss, which the latter returned, and an Episcopal blessing given to the Italian priests who were accompanying their archbishop, to the station-master, to the employees and to myself; then he climbed into our compartment, where, before sitting down, he also blessed Mr. and Mrs. Little.

He was followed by the two priests forming his little court, to whom I gave way in spite of their insistences that I board before them, and it was me who climbed up last of all.

The station-master closed the door and the train did not take long to pull away.

Then one of the priests took three breviaries out of a small bag he was crying, one bound in violet shagreen with Monseigneur's coat-of-arms, and the others in black shagreen, and each of them began to read his own, after making the sign of the cross.

Meanwhile, Mrs. Little still remained absorbed in her corner. Mr. Little and I consulted our guide-books, his in English and mine in French, without daring to speak for fear of troubling the pious meditation of Monseigneur and his followers.

Eventually, Monseigneur, having finished reading as much as he wanted in his breviary, drew closer to us—he was at the other extremity of the seat on which I was sitting—and, with a very good grace, he broke the silence.

"Is Madame suffering greatly?" she said, looking at Mrs. Little—without being able to see her profoundly-veiled face, naturally.

"Ho yes, milord," said Mr. Little, partly in good English and partly in bad French, "my poor wife had an impardonable indisposition, she experienced...how do you say it?...a great chagrin to pearl."

"Monsieur means, Your Grace," I said, "that Madame is gravely indisposed and that she has difficulty speaking."

"Ho yes," said Mr. Little, "it was zagly that."

"And," said the archbishop, "you think that a voyage to Italy is doing Madame good?"

"Ho no, but it was me that this voyage did good, and my wife she accompanied me."

"Mr. Little, whom I have the honor of introducing to Your Grace," I said, "is never separated from his wife. It is the most united household that one can encounter."

"That does honor to both spouses," said the prelate, with a broad smile on his lips, inclining particularly toward Mrs. Little. Nor obtaining a word from her, or any sign of response, he turned to the two priests accompanying him, and remarked to then on the beauties of the countryside through which we were traversing.

The bishop had a god enough head, with colored cheeks, graying black hair, lively eyes peering through tortoiseshell spectacles, and fine fleshy lips. He appeared to be aged between fifty and fifty-five.

What diocese did he direct? I would have liked to know, and perhaps I would have asked one of the priests quietly if he had been my neighbor, but I dared not ask the question of him, and we arrived at Orvieto without my being able to enquire. I suspected, however, that it must be a diocese in the Midi, the two priests having pronounced southern accents.

The Monseigneur and I had still had an opportunity to chat, and he it was who drew my attention, at the station of Torrito, to a very gracious tableau, that of a young peasant woman with big dark eyes walking with a divine stride in the midst of green and bushy wheat-fields.

Orvieto station is some distance from the city. While the French bishop climbed into the Bishop of Orvieto's carriage with his two priests, Mr. Little and I installed Mrs. Little in an omnibus and when the fine carriage of the prince of the Church drew away at the rapid trot of its two spirited horses, we set off in quest of our luggage. While searching for it, we perceived the Monseigneur's, which were to be transported by the omnibus. A card pinned to two or three trunks informed us that they belonged to Monseigneur d'Agen, and thus my curiosity was satisfied by chance.[67]

As we arrived in the city, along the main street followed by our omnibus, we went past an entire band of guttersnipes, among whom were five or six adults of both sexes, who were bating cooking-pots, saucepans, buckets and watering-cans in the most incoherent fashion, and singing thirty-six interspersed songs at the same time as uttering shrill cries. It was a charivari...but who the devil was it for?

"I don't think that can be for the Bishop of Agen," I said to Mr. Little, laughing, "and much less for us."

"Doubtless much less for us," replied Mr. Little. And he added, palpating his wife's hand: "Isn't that so, Betty?"

"Ho yes, Tom."

Next to me in the omnibus were two Italians, who were laughing. They could have been from Orvieto. It transpired, in fact, that they were. I obtained an explanation for the charivari from them, which I gave to Mr. Little. The victims were a man and a woman who had married that very morning, although they were over sixty.

---

[67] The Bishop of Agen from 1874-1884, during which interval the present story appears to be set, was Jean-Emile Fonteneau.

In that regard, Mr. Little made a reflection that appeared to me very humane. "The children," he said, "are excusable. They only judge that senile marriage by appearances, which might seems somewhat grotesque, but it's an abomination that the men and women, who ought to know life, far from lending their shameful collaboration to the brats, are not dispersing them. They ought to comprehend that marriage is much more the satisfaction of a mental need than a physical need, and that, if there is an age when communal life is imposed as a necessity on a man and a woman, it is when they begin to grow old."

In speaking thus, Mr. Little could not help tears shining in the corners of his eyes, but, having wiped them way rapidly with his fingertips, he asked: "Isn't that so, Betty?"

Then, as he pressed his wife's hand, the latter replied, as was her habit: "Ho yes, Tom."

We stayed at the Locanda delle Belle Arti, which is, I believe, the only tolerate inn in Orvieto, which has been established in an incomplete palace,[68] of which there are so many in Italy. One might have inscribed above the door: Grandeur and Destitution.

The staircase was monumental, the corridors of unusual length and breadth, the rooms immense, but with nothing but stone floors, all the walls whitewashed, and planks closing unused porticoes here and there.

At Orvieto, as in Siena, Mrs. Little remained in her room while we had lunch, and after lunch, Mr. Little went up to take tea with her; then they both came down and we went in company to visit the cathedral, the façade of which, thanks to its foundations of black and white stone, is reminiscent of that of Siena cathedral.

When we went inside the priests of the chapter were singing vespers in the midst of complete solitude.

---

[68] The Locanda delle Belle Arti in Orvieto was in the Palazzo Ottaviani. It is no longer a guest-house.

What it is necessary to see in Orvieto is the cathedral, and there, it is, above all, the interpretation of two great artists, one made with the chisel and the other with the brush, of the same scene: the Resurrection, Paradise and the Inferno. I am referring to the sculptor Giovanni Pisano and the painter Luca Signorelli.

There is also the Christ and the Prophets of Fra Angelico, the Gothic Virgin with her cortege of angels of Lippo Memmi, the two great bas-reliefs of the two Moses, the one by the father representing the adoration of the Magi and the one by the son depicting the Visitation.

The work of Signorelli is particularly admirable. That alone is worth the journey to Orvieto. It is composed of four large angels and a ceiling, ornamenting an entire chapel. The four panels translate, in striking scenes that denote in Signorelli a profound thinker as well as a powerful artist, Paradise, the Inferno, the Advent of the Antichrist and the Resurrection.

As for the ceiling, it is the Last Judgment. Jesus appears there in the midst of his court of apostles, prophets, doctors, holy omen, patriarchs and martyrs, and, as is written in the scriptures, to his right are the just, extending their confident hands toward him, ad to is left he culpable, griped by fear.

On the former, a rain of stars is falling, and on the latter, a rain of fire.

Beneath the fresco of Paradise one sees the medallions of Dante and Virgil, and beneath the fresco of the Inferno, those of Horace and Ovid.

In the fresco of the Advent of the Antichrist, Signorelli has painted himself alongside Fra Angelico, but every other figure in that fresco is eclipsed by that of the Antichrist. The physiognomy that Signorelli has given him is the idea of a man of genius. He has succeeded in importing a Satanic expression into the classic features of Jesus.

I pointed out that Antichrist to Mr. Little, who pointed it out to Mrs. Little, who replied to him with her "Ho yes, Tom," but without raising her veil, or even the head beneath the veil.

There is a whole poem—and what a poem!—in the fresco of the Resurrection.

"You see that fresco of the Resurrection Mr. Little?" I said to my friend the cheese-merchant. "Can you guess why Signorelli has represented some of the dead for us in a skeletal state, while the majority are clad in their flesh?"

"It's probably," the worthy man replied, "to distinguish the recently-dead from the ancient dead."

"It's not that, Mr. Little." I said, "and for two reasons. Firstly, if your explanation were true, the skeletons would be more numerous than the fleshy bodies, and it's exactly the contrary; secondly, it has been prophesied for us that on the day of the Resurrection, the most ancient dead, even those whose bones are dust, will immediately resume their flesh."

"One can admit, however," said Mr. Little, "that there are successive degrees in reincarnation, and that, in consequence, at the appeal of the divine trumpet, some individuals will be reincarnated more rapidly than others."

"Yes, yes, but here's another explanation, that does much more honor to the genius of Signorelli, and which I think more likely. Notice that troop of skeletons arranged to the right of the fresco. To see them holding their sides like that, doesn't it seem to you that they're bursting into laughter at the singular idea that the Eternal has wanted to revive eternally those who have already had too much of their temporary life? Do you not think that the attitude implies a protest against the resurrection and a refusal to submit to it? Decidedly, Signorelli was a great mind."

But Mr. Little was scarcely paying attention to what I was saying; his mind was evidently elsewhere.

"What are you thinking about, Mr. Little?"

"I'm thinking that I might see my dear Betty again in the Valley of Jehoshaphat, in the flesh and bone, and that if, as I sincerely hope, we are both among the elect, it will be possible for us to embrace one another, before going to sit down side by side at the right hand of God.

I looked at Mr. Little with a certain astonishment, for it seemed to me to be rather premature on his part to aspire to the Last Judgment in order to see his wife again in the flesh and bone when he presently had her on his arm. I did not permit myself any allusion on that subject, however, while hoping privately that Mrs. Little, when she was resuscitated, would not be resuscitated as I saw her in Italy—which is to say, absolutely drab—nor even as I had seen her in Spain, when she was already passably dreary, but far more brilliant than she had ever been in this miserable life.

While one of the sacristans showed us that marvelous chapel, two emaciated black cats, which seemed to have been sent to us as a deputation by Signorelli's Antichrist rubbed against our legs and Mrs. Little's skirts, and then crouched down on the red steps of the altar, which they seemed to be guarding like two sentinels.

"Look," Mr. Little said to me. "Astaroth and Beelzebub!"

"Yes," I replied. And I added, laughing: "The chapter of priests, although the church is completely deserted at the moment when they are singing the glory of God with such lung-power, if not so much soul, cannot say that there was no so much as a cat here, since there are two of them, not to mention us."

On emerging from the cathedral we went to see the ruins of the amphitheater, today converted into a garden. What struck us most in those ruins—or rather, that garden—was a white marble statue, cruelly tested by time, of I know not what Pope, which seemed to personify the decadence of the papacy itself in our epoch. The two arms were broken, the nose flattened, the tiara broken—and to that broken tiara a washing-line was attached, laden with linen in the process of drying.

A remarkable detail: that statue of a vicar of Christ, thus reduced to the status of a drying machine, had its back turned to a splendid view.

"Decidedly," Mr. Little said to me, rather shrewdly, "that mutilated statue is a good emblem of the papacy, which has turned its back on the future, as the pope has turned his to one of the most beautiful panoramas one might see."

While our attention was, so to speak, shuttling between the statue and the landscape displayed behind it, the tenant of the garden, a laundress, I believe, was gathering a large bouquet of lilacs. As we were about to take our leave, she approached Mrs. Little very graciously to offer it to her, doubtless hoping that it might earn her a larger tip or, as the Italians say, a *buona mano*.

"*Signora, favorisca d'accettare questo massi di fiori.*"

But Mrs. Little made no movement of the hand to take it, and it was Mr. Little who refused the concierge's offer in English, under the pretext that Mrs. Little did not have the free use of her hands, and, being in addition very ill, she dreaded odorous flowers.

I took charge of translating Mr. Little's refusal into Italian, which I naturally did in such a manner as to render it less harsh, to the extent that that was possible. I softened it further by taking a spring of lilac from the bouquet and even further by giving the good woman a double lira—which is to say, two francs.

V

In the evening, shortly before midnight, we left Orvieto in a sort of down-at-heel post chaise, which was to take us to Rome in seventeen hours. We had been scalped at the Locanda delle Belle Arti, as witness the two cups of tea served in the morning and the evening to Mrs. Little, which had cost five francs apiece.

When Mr. Little, who had been kind enough to take charge of settling the bill, and to whom I reimbursed my proportionate contribution later, had told me about the exaggerated tariff for the cup of tea, adding: "If the tea had even been good—but I couldn't drink it," I thought it my duty to intervene with the proprietor. The latter, probably sniffing in me, with the finesse appropriate to an Italian, an authentic

244

Frenchman, even though he had only head me speak English with Mr. Little, replied to me *mezza voce*:

"*Se fosse il tè per lei, l'avrebbe pagato due soltante lire e mezza, ma per inglesi...!*"[69]

I admired the profound rascality of the hotelier all the more because what I had consumed myself had been charged appropriately; I admired it so much that I did not have the strength to insist.

In spite of the petty aggravation that resulted from that, which was further aggravated at the moment of our departure by the stable-hand, who asked us without rhyme or reason in English for a tip, which we did not owe him—he must have learned to ask for it in all languages, even Russian—and in spite of the jolts of the carriage, of which we felt the reverberations, and even in spite of the vague apprehension we had by night in the Roman countryside of being stopped and ransomed by bandits, we slept quite well, and Mr. Little and I scarcely exchanged three or four words before dawn.

At the relay in Viterbe, where we arrived after daybreak, I got down in order to stretch my legs, and Mr. Little did likewise, but his wife did not budge.

Seeing that she remained immobile, he said to her, taking her hand: "You want to rest, then, my dear Betty?"

And, the latter having replied to that: "Ho yes, Tom," he did not insist any further.

We were very desirous of breaking a crust, as they say, for we were beginning to feel hungry, but it was necessary for us to replace that exercise with another, less comforting one, which was putting a coin in the hand of a retired postillion with a wooden leg, who resembled Hyacinthe, the actor at the Palais-Royal, to such a degree, that one might have thought he was his twin brother, tested by the misfortunes of war.

Although, at Monterose we had again to grease the palm of an irreproachably-dressed, even well-to-do, gentleman who

---

[69] "If the tea had been for your excellency, he would only have paid two francs fifty, but for the English...!"

looked like a good bourgeois but who asked us or something *per il povero conduttore*, at least it was possible for us to have lunch.

While we were eating with a real appetite, sitting facing one another, while Mrs. Little remained in the vehicle, as at Viterbe, I said to Mr. Little: "Aren't you going to send the worthy Mrs. Little a bowl of soup?"

He immediately looked at me reproachfully, without replying to my question. Although I was a little troubled by that, I added: "You know that we'll arrive in Rome quite late, and that between now and then, Mrs. Little might suffer from hunger."

Again he shot me a glance that went straight to my heart, saying: "Come, come, Monsieur le Bref..."

I dared not persist, for I saw that, without meaning to, I had caused the excellent man pain, but in my conscience, it was impossible for me to comprehend how a man who showed so much solicitude for his wife in other regards could be so indifferent in that instance.

We returned silently to our vehicle, stopped outside the door of the inn, and at the doors of which three or four beggars where wailing in a lamentable fashion while the postillion attached fresh horses.

"Signora, per l'amor d'Iddio, un poveretto balocco!"[70]

They had sung that in every key, and other things appropriate to soften the most insensible heart, or at least to force the best barricaded purse, but Mrs. Little did not budge. Pitilessly, she let them warble.

Apparently indignant at such aridity of soul, the postillion, who might perhaps have suffered from it on his own account, cracked his whip over the ears of the rabble, saying: *"Andante via dunque...non si dona niente."*[71]

Meanwhile, Mr. Little gave them an order in English to leave his wife alone, and they understood it because of his

---

[70] "For the love of God, Madame, a poor little coin!"

[71] "Get away...you won't be given anything."

tone and his gesture. But as he was an excellent man, easily moved, with a sincere pity even for a feigned poverty, he took a few sous out of his pocket, which he distributed to the beggars.

"Perhaps," I said, "Mrs. Little has already given something."

"No," said Mr. Little, impatiently. "How do you think she can have given anything?"

I understood that I had just committed another gaffe, and I climbed into the carriage in a crestfallen fashion, bowing to the perfectly immobile Mrs. Little.

Scarcely had we begun rolling along the road again, than Mr. Little said to me: "My dear Monsieur Le Bref, since I had the pleasure of encountering you in the cathedral at Pisa, I have had it on the tip of my tongue several times to ask you a question, but, fearing that you might see it as a sharp reproach, I have kept silent. I have not forgotten, in fact, that I owe you gratitude for having saved my life twice, and I do not believe I have the right to hold anything against you whatsoever."

"Eh! Good God, what could you possible hold against me, my dear Mr. Little?"

"I repeat to you that I don't recognize the right to hold anything whatsoever against you."

"But explain to me, I beg you, how I might have incurred your rancor."

Mr. Little then held out his hand to me, which I shook, and he said to me, with tears in his eyes and his voice: "How is it that you, such a worthy fellow, a man of so much heart, did not respond with a single sympathetic word to the letter in which I announced to you, three years ago, the death of my poor wife?"

"The death of your wife? Come, come, Mr. Little, is it really you who is joking in that fashion, and in front of Mrs. Little, whom your joke might shock, with just entitlement?"

"I'm not joking at all, for it's certainly not a joking matter. And since you mention joking, permit me to say that that is exactly what you have seemed to be doing, since we met in

Pisa, and you were still doing just now, notably in advising me to send a bowl of soup to Mrs. Little."

"Me, joking?"

"Of course."

"Oh, that's too much! You want to make me believe that it's me who is joking, when it's you! You're typical of our homeland, where that might pass as the last word in 'humor'!"

"I swear to you, Monsieur Le Bref, on everything I hold most sacred, that, unfortunately, I'm not joking."

"But then, that makes me dread, Mr. Little, that you are under the influence of…how shall I put it?…a temporary disturbance of your mental faculties."

"You didn't receive, then, the letter in which I informed you of the death of my wife?" said Mr. Little, fixing me with a stare that, in truth, had nothing distracted about it.

"No, truly, I didn't receive it, and I confess to you that I'm glad, since, definitively, here is Mrs. Little now, if not well, at least alive…"

As I said that I looked at Mrs. Little, expecting some acquiescence from her, or at least a burst of laughter—but there was nothing!

"You sincerely believe that my poor wife is alive?" said Mr. Little.

"Of course! Unless I'm seeing things."

"Oh my dear friend!" he cried, then, shaking my hands, "you can't imagine how much joy that causes me!"

I understood Mr. Little less and less, and, finding the joy he was manifesting because I considered Mrs. Little, who was sitting in front of me, to be alive, and his reproach for not having written to him on the occasion of her death, to be equally incoherent, I thought that he had definitely gone mad.

I no longer doubted that he had gone mad on seeing him immediately embrace Mrs. Little, something that he had never permit himself to do before in my presence, and hearing him repeat, in the midst of real tears: "Betty, my dear Betty…."

"Calm down, my dear friend," I said to him, very emotional myself. "Calm down." And I died, in a low voice: "You'll frighten your wife."

But he replied to me loudly: "Eh! How do you expect me to frighten her, poor woman, since she's been dead for three years?"

"That's true," I said, as if to agree with his mania. "But then, who is this lady, who resembles Mrs. Little so perfectly, so far as I can judge through her veil, and whom you just embraced, calling her Betty, and to whom, after all, I've spoken twenty times since the day we met in Pisa, calling her Mrs. Little, without you protesting once?"

Then, Mr. Little gently lifted the veil covering his companion's face, and said: "Look."

It really was his Betty, it really was Mrs. Little, with the face like a red ball, a Dutch cheese, as I had known, since our first encounter at the railway station in Bordeaux, but the prominent blue eyes which had never had much expression, had even less, and her parted lips, showing teeth almost as large as piano keys, maintained a complete immobility.

Meanwhile, Mr. Little, who was holding his wife's hand tenderly in his own, said with an emotion that was at first contained, but soon overabundant; "Betty, my dear Betty, answer me: Do you approve of my having lifted our veil, in order to show our friend Monsieur Le Bref your cherished and forever regretted features, such as he knew them?"

Without Mrs. Little's lips moving in the slightest, the customary little phrase emerged from that open mouth.

"Ho yes, Tom."

"Well," cried Mr. Little, in a voice blurred by tears, "do you understand now?"

Yes, yes, I understood, by dint of looking at Mrs. Little's inanimate face, what I had not understood at first. Mrs. Little was indeed dead, and the striking representation of her that I had before me was nothing but a mannequin, albeit executed with such artistry that it feigned life marvelously.

I shook Mr. Little's had, saying to him, profoundly moved myself: "My poor friend, be sure that I sympathize as much as is humanly possible with your just affliction, and that I deplore the false direction that your letter took, since my silence must have resulted for you in the thought that I might remain indifferent. Oh, you must have been deeply offended."

"I didn't know how to explain it," replied Mr. Little. And he added, wiping his eyes: "But now I can explain it very well, and I can also explain how, since our encounter in the cathedral in Pisa until just now, you have been able to believe that my poor Betty was alive. Has not the artist imitated her very well? And with the faculty that she has of moving and speaking, as long as her veil is lowered, the illusion is complete."

"Complete, indeed, Mr. Little, and I confess that if you had not lifted it for me, I would still have... But it's obviously not in order to give that illusion to the public that you're traveling thus with the mann...with the modeled image of Mrs. Little..."

"No. my ear friend, it's in order to have it myself."

"What! You can imagine that it's Mrs. Little, when you know the contrary full well, you who make that mechanism move and talk?"

"Yes and no...so little that if I reflect, the sad truth appears to me clearly, and then I'm gripped by a fit of despair, as you were able to judge just now, but more often than not, it isn't like that...I yield to the mirage, I imagine that my poor wife, even when I make her talk, even when I make her move, is still alive, and the horrible lacuna that her death has made in my existence is partly filled in."

"I understand, I understand—but perhaps, if you had done as so many others have done, if you had simply remarried, without absolutely forgetting the first Mrs. Little, you might have found almost the same rewards in the second."

"Never, never! Unless I had encountered a woman resembling my Betty in the most striking fashion...and how would I find her, even supposing that she exists? I had, therefore, to resign myself to the stratagem that you see, without which I would be dead of chagrin at present. And what is most horrible in the loss that I have suffered of my poor Betty, Monsieur Le Bref, is that it is, in a sense, imputable to me."

"How is that?"

"You know, for having been a witness to it in Burgos, what umbrage maidservants brought to Mrs. Little. I even told you about some of my difficulties in that regard."

"Yes, indeed."

"Well, it is in regard to a question that seemed quite innocent to me, but which had in my Betty's eyes the irremediable sin of being addressed by me to our maid...yes, it was because of that question that the poor woman fell unconscious in a transport of rage, and did not recover.

"A ruptured aneurism, no doubt?"

"Exactly."

"Poor woman! But what had you said to your maid, then Mr. Little?"

"Oh, something, I repeat to you, that seemed to me ought not to have disquieted Mrs. Little at all, umbrageous as I knew her to be—which seemed, on the contrary, only to be able to reassure her by her observation of my ignorance in certain regards... So, I asked the maid, in front of my wife, whether she had any night-chemises. That question did not, moreover, come out of the blue. It arrived at the very moment when my wife had just shown me some very sparse day-chemises that she had bought her, and some very high-necked night-chemises that she had bought for herself. And I reasoned internally that if the poor girl wore such sparse chemises in bed, she was in danger of catching cold, as is commonly said. Hence my question to the maid: 'Annie, have you any night-chemises?'

"'Annie, I forbid you to reply to Monsieur!' cried my unfortunate wife, turning purple. Then, turning to me and clapping her hands together, she cried: 'Oh! Oh! you have no shame! To ask such a question of a maid! What, then, do you suppose your maid to be, Monsieur? A maid who had night-chemises would be the worst of maids. Is it appropriate for a maid to have night-chemises…?'"

"'Perhaps, perhaps,'

"'What do you mean, perhaps?'

"'Well, propriety does not appear to me to raise an obstacle, my love, to a maid putting on night-chemises.'

"'Propriety, no, Monsieur, but decency.'

"'It seems to me, however, my love,' I said, 'with the greatest mildness in the world, that night-chemises that are high-necked protect decency more than day-chemises that are very low-necked, not to mentioned that they keep the torso warmer…and that is even, my dear Betty, what you understand for yourself.'

"With that, my unfortunate wife suffered a redoubling of frightful fury, vociferating inconsequential words, among which I distinguished the phrases: *vile debauchee, lubricious man* and *disgusting individual*, all epithets addressed to me, and finally, the word *camisole*, which I had the misfortune to emphasize by saying: 'As regards camisoles, it's you who need one at present, but a *camisole de force*.'[72]

"Immediately, I saw her eyes, her poor eyes, widen immeasurably, and I saw her fall down dead…dead, alas!"

Having spoken thus, the worthy Mr. Little burst into sobs. I tried to console him, by representing to him a host of god reasons why, after all, he had nothing for which to reproach himself, and I succeeded, albeit with great difficulty.

During Mr. Little's poignant story I continued looking at Mrs. Little, or at least her mannequin, whose veil was still lifted, and I admired the perfection of the stratagem. I admired it even more when, Mr. Little having asked me to touch his wife's wrist with my finger at the level of the good-luck bracelet that ornamented it, I felt skin as elastic as if it had been covered in veritable flesh. There was also no stiffness in the arm, the articulations operating with a perfect ease.

---

[72] A strait-jacket—the pun does not translate.

252

"Everything is becoming," Mr. Little told me, "and the mechanisms that make the body move allow it an almost natural flexibility...there's only the gait that is slightly jerky, as you've been able to see. The external organs are reproduced with an admirable fidelity. You only have to look at the ear, the cartilages of the nose, and the mouth, which is equipped with my wife's veritable teeth, perfectly enclosed in artificial sockets, just as the bare scalp is garnished with her own hair."

As he said that, Mr. Little used his thumb and index finger to agitate the cartilages of his wife's nose gently; he pinched the lobe of an ear; and, again gently, he opened the mouth, showing me a seemingly fleshy tongue, although naturally a trifle dry, and, pressing lightly on the tongue, she showed me a palate and an epiglottis, and even tonsils, the mucus of which was slightly better imitated.

"As for the internal organs," he added, "notably those of digestion and respiration, they don't exist, but are replaced by the automatic mechanism, which it was necessary to lodge somewhere; and there's still room in the abdomen for a small heating apparatus."

"A small heating apparatus?"

"Yes, it's necessary that by night, when she's lying next to me, I feel the gentle warmth of her body."

I admired that precaution, which was evidently not to be disdained. In addition to the fact that it added to the illusion for Mr. Little, Mrs. Little thus seemed much more alive to the touch; in winter, if she were armed by a few degrees more, it become an element of comfort.

"But it's very practical," the worthy Mr. Little told me, while agitating it in a manner that would have seemed absolutely insane to many people. "It is, in truth, very practical."

And, looking back on my condition of bachelorhood, which, if it has its good points, also—I don't hide it from myself—has as many bad ones, I thought that a marriage of Mr. Little's second fashion...for instance with a prettier mannequin that, instead of trailing it around with me from one railway carriage to the next, I could put in my trunk, only taking it out at bed-time…yes, I thought that a marriage of that sort would fill in the void in my soul somewhat, while being able to keep me warm on winter nights.

I even asked myself, although that became, involuntarily, somewhat extravagant, whether the artist who had fabricated Mrs. Little—the artificial one—might not, in fabricating a wife for me, arrange matters so that she had several exchange-able faces, in order that, although always having the same companion next to me in my bed, I could at least see her under different aspects.

I refrained from communicating that thought, which he would not have understood, to Mr. Little. He, the prototype of conjugal fidelity, wanted to show me, if not the mechanisms that made Mrs. Little move—he even made me understood that I kind of modesty would prevent him from ever showing me—at least the exterior switches that corresponded with them, and were found principally at the nape of his wife's neck, her waist and in the palm of her hand.

He explained to me how, once it was set up to work in the morning, Mrs. Little's automotive apparatus could be stopped at will by turning in one direction a simple button set in her belt, and restarted by turning it in the opposite direction; how, by touching Mr. Little lightly on the nape, at a point in the lace frill of her dress, he could make her nod her head; and finally, what was out of order in her arms, which had greatly intrigued me when I believed her to be alive.

On that subject, Mr. Little said to me: "The mechanician artist had found a means—which is truly admirable—according to whether I turned this little button on Mrs. Little's elbow one way or the other, of making her extend a hand and shake one that was offered to her, or raise to her nose a bouquet that she had in her left hand. Unfortunately, the mechanism of the right arm was disabled in Como, and the one in the left in Venice, and, when the latter misfortune occurred, it caused me such a great chagrin that I remained locked in my room for several days with my poor love, without wanting to go out any longer.

"Then the reflection came to me that, after all, as Mrs. Little did not know anyone in Italy—I had no idea then that we might encounter you—she would not have to shake anyone's hand, and that she could easily do without respiring a bouquet, whatever pleasure I would have had in seeing her do so, given that she no longer had the sense of smell, any more than the others. I therefore resumed going out with Mrs. Little, to see the curiosities of Venice with her and those of the other cities of our itinerary—and that is how we found ourselves together in the cathedral of Pisa.

"And now, you know, my dear friend, what frightens me is thinking that at any moment, another mechanism of locomotion in my wife's body might break down, which would result in a great embarrassment for me. That is why you see me making the slightest excursions with her in a carriage, for fear that too much exercise might fatigue her mechanisms. There is only one man in the world capable of repairing them, and that is the mechanician artist who designed them, who is in London."

"I'm astonished," I said, "That you have not brought him with you, for greater security."

"I thought of that momentarily, but one consideration caused me to renounce the idea."

"I understand...the annoyance of always having a third party between Mrs. Little and you...an annoyance that perhaps I am causing you myself."

"Which you are certainly not causing me, my dear Monsieur Le Bref. No, it wasn't that."

"Then too, the considerable augmentation of expense that would have resulted for you."

"Much less that, Monsieur Le Bref."

"Then I don't follow."

"It's quite simple. That mechanician knows my wife as well as, if not better than, I know her myself, since he's the one who made her. Well, just between ourselves, that doesn't please me—no, that doesn't please me. So it would require an absolute urgency for me to give him something to refit inside Mrs. Little's body."

As Mr. Little said that, his ordinarily ruddy face had become and even deeper shade of crimson. That excess of modesty, with regard to a simple mannequin representing his wife, demonstrated better than anything else the extent to which he identified it with her.

"And obstetric physicians," I objected, "would be even worse."

"Undoubtedly, undoubtedly," said Mr. Little, increasingly troubled.

VI

Like all Frenchmen who go to Rome I had the custom of lodging at the Hotel Minerva. But Mr. Little proposed to take us to the large Hotel di Spagna on the Piazza di Spagna, in memory of the voyage that we had made together on the Iberian peninsula, when poor Mrs. Little was still flesh and bone, and I hastened to consent to that.

It was, therefore, at the door of the Hotel di Spagna that we got down from the carriage, and as we descended, Mr. Little did not fail to show me the switch that he operated in Mrs. Little's belt in order to put her legs in movement.

As I followed Mr. Little, with his artificial wife on his arm, up the staircase of the hotel, I admired his ability to oblige himself to endure the embarrassment that such a comedy caused him to for the sake of the pleasure, so great it was, of having with him the consistent shadow of the person who had charmed him in life. I thought that in Mr. Little's place, I would at least have wanted to make other arrangements.

Why, I wondered, had that second Mrs. Little not been designed in such a way that she could be dismantled and reassembled, and consequently lodge in a trunk. She would have been infinitely more comfortable when traveling with her husband thaw he she was alive, whereas today, towed around all of a piece, she was infinitely less so.

As for me, a great traveler, always up and down mountains and valleys, it was thus that I would accommodate a wife, discreetly wrapped up with other luggage.

A declaration of principle subversive to that extent of the most elementary gallantry provoked in the feminine fraction of Monsieur Le Bref's audiences a series of exclamations, of which the charming Mina took charge of disengaging the disapproving character.

"I beg the pardon of the ladies who are listening to me, " Monsieur Le Bref said, but that is my opinion, and that opinion, let it be remarked, cannot be as shocking in a traveler as it would be in a sedentary man... Furthermore, let it be understood that I would unpack my wife every evening in order to give myself the nocturnal illusion of a companion, save for repacking her every morning, in order not to disillusion myself..."

That, therefore, is what I was thinking about on the staircase of the Hotel di Spagna in Rome, at the sight of the worthy Mr. Little guiding the hesitant steps of his artificial wife with a touching attention.

Suddenly, those reflections were interrupted by the passage of a maidservant of remarkable beauty, certainly one of the most beautiful women in Rome, where there are so many beauties.

She was coming down the stairs as we were going up. I could not help admiring her, and I saw clearly that Mr. Little was admiring her as much as me, and even more, for he turned round three times in order to look at her.

Oh, if he had acted in that fashion when Mrs. Little was on his arm in flesh and bone, what a quarter or an hour he would have spent! But, now that she was no longer anything but leather and sheet metal, there was not the slightest storm to endure. Mrs. Little seemed—and, in fact, was—absolutely indifferent to the incident.

The stairway of the Hotel di Spagna in Rome having reminded me of that of the hotel in Burgos, where poor Mrs. Little had made an abominable scene under the pretext that her husband had received in his arms the young Amparo, after she lost her equilibrium under a pile of white linen, I could not help congratulating Mr. Little on the amelioration that had occurred in the character of his wife, in that regard.

"That," he said to me very calmly, "is the sole superiority that my poor Betty's artificial personality has over her defunct personality, and yet…!"

There was in that exclamation a kind of implicit admission that the absence of the scenes of jealousy made to her husband by Mrs. Little relative to hotel maids—scenes from which I had seen him suffer a great deal in Burgos—did not leave him without a certain regret. What a strange thing human nature is!

I wanted to clarify that.

"Would it seem preferable to you if Mrs. Little still had the gift of making scenes?"

"Well…yes, my dear friend."

"I understand…you mean that if she made them, it would be because she was still alive."

"Undoubtedly, but in certain respects, I would not be annoyed if the mechanician had been able to give it to her automatically, with the faculty for me to accelerate or cut short the scenes."

"Really?"

"Yes—and that's perfectly explicable. My poor Betty was never as alive as when she was angry with me. It was only them that she seemed, as one might put it, to light up. The rest of the time she was, as you know, almost extinct. Thus, nothing could give me more fully the illusion that she is still alive that those sorts of tantrums, although so irrational, just as nothing takes away that illusion more completely than a calmness, so unnatural in her, when she sees me ogling as pretty maidservant, as I did just now."

VII

During the first week that we spent in Rome, I obtained from Mr. Little, not without difficulty, that he sometimes spared himself, and spared me, the inconvenience of towing around his automation—which is to say, his wife; for, now that I was aware of the substance of which Mrs. Little was made, not having the same motives for illusion as Mr. Little, I found her constancy utterly tedious and our role somewhat ridiculous.

When he went out without her he had the custom of locking her in her room and putting the key in his pocket. And to the hotel staff who asked him whether Madame was ill and whether she might need something, he replied that she was indeed slightly indisposed, but only wanted one thing: not to be disturbed.

As, in addition, he brought her out from time to time, and had a cup of tea or brother sent up to her twice a day, which he absorbed secretly, suspicions were not awakened regarding his stratagem.

However, it was Mr. Little who could not resolve himself to a daily separation of several hours from his wife, whose company was evidently dearer to him than mine. Thus, it was necessary for me to endure his mania to take her almost everywhere. We returned with her to the Coliseum, the Capitol, the Vatican and the Pineto, the Borghese and Doria galleries, the Basilicas of St. Peter, St. John Lateran, Saint Mary Major and St. Paul outside the walls, to the Villa Madame, etc., etc.

Mr. Little even wanted to take her to Albano and the Tivoli, but I made him renounce that ludicrous project, by representing to him that such repeated excursions would end up causing Mr. Little's automotive mechanism to break down.

Events proved that I was right.

One evening, when the three of us were walking in St. Peter's, I suddenly heard something like the sound of a breaking spring, and I saw Mrs. Little fall down full length on the pavement. By a bizarre coincidence, Mrs. Little, although her husband was giving her his arm, collapsed abruptly without him having time to retain her, at the very moment when she had been touched by the rod of venial sins.

You know, of course, that in the confessionals of the basilica of St. Peter's, priests are on duty, holding a long flexible rod, with which they touch passers-by on the head or the shoulder in order to absolve them of the small fry of sins.

Alarmed by the result of the touch of his rod, not because he thought that it had done Mrs. Little any harm, but because imagined that she had fainted from fright, the absolver emerged precipitately from the confessional and came to help us lift her up, not without babbling apologies.

We tried to sit Mr. Little's artificial companion down, but were unable to succeed in doing so. Evidently, the mechanism that permitted sitting had broken, or at least gone awry. I gazed sadly at poor Mr. Little, whose expression was consternated. He doubtless feared that the accident would reveal Mrs. Little's automatism, and I confess that I dreaded that as much as he did.

Our anxieties increased further on seeing a young man approach who said that he was a physician, and who offered us his services. Without being authorized to do so, the young man even asked Mrs. Little where her pain was, but when she did not reply, as you can imagine, he must have assumed that it was out of modesty, the place where she was suffering probably being one of those that Englishwomen cannot name, even with the aid of circumlocutions, and he did not insist.

"*La signora non puo sedersi*?" he asked Mrs. Little.

As Mr. Little seemed not to understand, I said to him in English: "The doctor is asking Madame whether she doesn't want to sit down."

Mr. Little, whose presence of mind had returned, repeated the doctor's question to his wife, pressing her hand in such a fashion as to make her reply.

"No," she replied.

Mr. Little continued: "Are you in pain, my dear Betty?"

To which she replied: "Ho yes, Tom."

"In the region of the loins?"

"Ho yes, Tom."

When, translating Mr. Little's question for the physician, I had informed him of the affirmative response that Mrs. Little had made, he said that it was urgent to put the patient to bed and massage the region with an emollient. But how were we to get Mrs. Little back to the hotel?"

We could not take her there on foot, because it was impossible for her to walk, nor in a carriage, because it was impossible for her to sit down.

The physician thought that it was necessary to transport her on a stretcher and he left the basilica immediately in order to give the order one of the *facchini* who are always prowling around the doors of St. Peter's to bring one.

Then he came back.

"*Si tiene in piedi*?"[73] he asked me.

"Well," I said, "she wouldn't be if her husband and I weren't holding her up."

The man from the confessional, who thought himself partly responsible for the accident, then insisted that we take the victim into one of the sacristies until the stretcher arrived.

When we had laid her down on a bench therein, to the great curiosity of the priests who were there, and we had accommodated her head on a cushion, the doctor claimed that it was necessary for him to lift her veil in order for her to be able to breathe. Mr. Little opposed that energetically, as you might think, and even made his wife say, by mean of a clearly audible "no," that she did not want it.

Then the physician took it into his head to take her pulse, and naturally observed a complete lack of pulsations. Nevertheless, he did not want to believe that, and contented himself with saying that the pulse as very weak, almost imperceptible. Doubtless as a check, he applied his ear to the rib cage, where the heart ought to be, and could not hear it beating and more than the pulse. He raised his head, amazed, reapplied his ear,

---

[73] "Is she still on her feet?"

moving his head and if in search of the best place to ausculate, straightened up and took a few paces in the sacristy without saying anything.

Finally, he came back to us and said, in a doctoral fashion: "One can scarcely feel more heartbeat than pulse. If Madame hadn't spoken just now I'd be very anxious, but I assume that the near-annihilation of the pulse and the heartbeat is due to the fright that caused her fall. Soon we can put mustard-plasters on her legs, in order to obtain a good circulation of the blood."

I had a terrible desire to laugh at the diagnostic and therapeutic skills of a doctor who mistook a mannequin for a woman, but I pursed my lips and limited myself to replying: "*Va bene, va bene, si vedra, si vedra.*"[74]

"Perhaps," he went on, "a little bleeding will be necessary."

"*Si vedra, si vedra, Signor Dottore.*"

With his head in his hands, Mr. Little was walking back and forth in the sacristy repeating: "My dear Betty, my dear Betty."

"*Ché dice, il signor inglese?*" said one Monsignor who was in the sacristy, addressing me.

"He's saying: 'My dear Betty,'" Betty being the name of his wife...it's because he's very upset to see her in such a state."

"I understand," replied the Monsignor.

And the physician added: "The danger is certainly great, but believe me, I'll do everything possible to go get her out of it."

In the meantime, the stretcher arrived; we lay Mrs. Little down on it and we set off for the Hotel di Spagna, unfortunately followed by the Italian doctor, who, doubtless seeing in the English couple clients capable of paying well, was hanging on to his prey, no matter what we tried to do to get rid of him.

---

[74] "That's all right, that's all right, we'll see, we'll see."

For a moment he disappeared, and we thought he had finally yielded to our objurgations, which were conceived in the most gracious terms, but not at all. He had simply gone into the premises of a pharmacist, from which he did not take long to emerge with a box of mustard plasters.

When we arrived at the Littles' room, he went in behind the porters, while I remained discreetly on the threshold.

Having placed Mrs. Little on a divan, the porters left again, but the doctor was still there.

"*Signor dottore*," I called to him.

He approached, and I invited him to go with me, insisting that the invalid needed rest above all, but he did not want to listen to reason, saying and repeating that his professional duty obliged him to remain.

He even engaged Mr. Little, offering to help him undress Mrs. Little and put her to bed, so that he could examine her, palpate her at his ease, discover the internal or external lesions that must have been produced by the fall, and apply the appropriate treatments to them.

You will understand the worthy Mr. Little's embarrassment. He asked me in English by what means it would be possible for him to get rid of that diabolical doctor, and I replied that there was only one that could not fail, which was to pay him to go away.

In an Italian as bizarre as his French, he therefore offered to pay the importunate fellow, and, with that intention, took his purse out of his pocket, but the fellow protested in a dignified manner that they would discuss that later that he would doubtless have to visit Madame several times before she had recovered, and that, in any case, the initial consultation was not concluded, since he had not yet examined the patient.

"No, no," said Mr. Little, with an entirely British sang-froid. "*Andate vin.*" And at the same time, he handed the physician two five-franc pieces—but the latter refused very energetically to take them, still in the name of professional duty.

Thinking that it was perhaps too little, Mr. Little offered twenty francs—further refusal—and then forty francs.

"Soon, if you wish," said the physician, "but once again, allow me to accomplish my professional duty. It is necessary that I first place mustard plasters on your wife, and perhaps draw a little blood."

"Offer him sixty francs," I said to Mr. Little, and perhaps he'll consent to leave us alone."

And, indeed, as Mr. Little took another twenty francs out of his purse. I said to the physician in a confidential tone, as if I wanted to espouse his cause: "Signor, here's a fine sum of sixty francs; believe me, take it, since he absolutely doesn't want to put your science to contribution."

"Monsieur," he replied, haughtily, "I would never accept money that I haven't earned."

"You have earned it, Signor, you have earned it by proceeding with the examination in the sacristy of St. Peter's sending for a stretcher and accompanying us here."

The physician shook his head negatively, and I whispered to Mr. Little to raise the sum to eighty francs. He resigned himself to doing so, but in vain. The physician claimed that we were insulting his professional dignity.

That crampon-physician was beginning to irritate me furiously, so I said to Mr. Little: "Right…offer him a hundred francs, and if he still doesn't make himself scarce, throw him out, and even down the stairs, without giving him anything."

Mr. Little having offered the hundred francs, on my advice, he neither accepted them nor refused them, but represented to us so mildly and so modestly the humiliation to which we were subjecting him, by preferring to pay him for not giving his cares to a patient rather than giving him, that there was some scruple on my part about leaving him in error relative to Mrs. Little's condition.

"What if, in order to get rid of him, while saving his self-respect," I said to Mr. Little, "you were to confess to him that it is not within the competence of a physician but that of a mechanician to treat your poor wife?"

Mr. Little did not reply at first, but he started reflecting on the case. After a few seconds, though, he said to me: "No, no—it's something that no one other than you must know."

"But it must be known in Chester!"

"In Chester, yes, and in a part of England, but I want at least that it should not be so in Italy."

"I won't hide it from you," the physician said to me, "that Madame's condition appears to me to be very grave, to such an extent that it is not impossible that she might die for want of sufficiently prompt treatment while you are deliberating. It seems, in truth, that you have sworn the death of the patent, since you're preventing her from receiving my cares."

Molière, in my place, would certainly have responded to the Italian physician that it was, on the contrary, because we had sworn to preserve the life of the patient that we were preventing her from receiving medical treatment, but I contented myself with smiling and, turning to Mr. Little I said to him in English: "The very persistence that he puts into wanting to employ his art in spite of us shows that he's a idiot. He's so myopic that one might believe that he can see very little. Believe me, to get rid of him, allow him to continue his medical examination, and even allow him to apply the remedies he judges appropriate.

Mr. Little yielded to my arguments. He agreed that he would undress Mrs. Little and put her to bed, after which the physician could do what was necessary.

That was, in effect, how things went.

Before anything else, the doctor examine Mr. Little's face, from which Mr. Little had been obliged to remove the veil, and he soon declared doctorally that the parted lips and the fixed eyes indicated that the poor woman had not recovered the usage of her senses. He went so far as to place his cheek in proximity with Mrs. Little's lips, as if he wanted her to kiss him, which made Mr. Little so indignant that he nearly flew off the handle. But he only did that, in reality, as you will understand, in order to feel the invalid's breath, for, after having said to us fearfully: "*Non sento lo spirito*," he hastened to ask us, for a decisive proof, for a mirror—"*un specchio*"—which we gave him.

Having observed, naturally, that the mirror was untarnished, he remarked, not without naivety, that the signora nevertheless had the complexion of a healthy individual.

All things considered, he judged that nothing was more urgent than to place the mustard plasters, and with that intention, he uncovered the patient's legs—which, in truth were entirely natural, and if nature had not equipped the right foot with a little toe with a nail there was as good an imitation as the one must have ornamented the original.

While the mustard plasters were taking effect—or, rather, not taking effect—Mr. Little made me party to the apprehension he had that they might spoil his wife's artificial skin.

Meanwhile, the doctor was making every effort to ausculate the heart, with his ear applied to Madame's embroidered chemise—without perceiving anything at all, naturally.

After twenty minutes, the mustard plasters having not modified Mrs. Little's condition, he became very anxious. After pacing back and forth in the room several times, silently, with his chin in his hand, he came to where I was sitting, some distance from the bed, and confided to me that the situation was definitely very grave, that the signora might already be dead, that that was in any case greatly to be feared, and that I ought to do my best to prepare the husband for such a cruel event, while he, although there was scarcely any doubt about the circumstance, in order to acquit his conscience would attempt a bleeding, in order to have the proof of it.

I had a mad desire to laugh, but I could not in all decency satisfy it.

Mr. Little, naturally very afflicted by the accident that had overtaken the locomotive apparatus of his pseudo-wife in the basilica of St. Peter, and also bewildered by the truly unexpected behavior of that fool of a physician, was leaning on the night table next to the bed and seemed plunged in an immense chagrin.

Having tapped him gently on the shoulder, I confided to him what the astonishing disciple of Aesculapius had just told me, and I added: "I understand all the pain that this accident to Mrs. Little must have caused you, since, until the mechanician has repaired her, it will be impossible or you to take her on your excursions, but, on the other hand, you ought to be glad to see a physician deceived by her and believing her to be flesh and bone. So much stupidity on his part might even be advantageous to you, by permitting you, when he has certified the death, which cannot be long delayed, to take the body back to Chester in a coffin."

"Yes, but once arrived in Chester I would find myself in a great embarrassment, for everyone knows back there that my Betty is dead and buried. What would they say on seeing the arrival of that coffin, which would not be followed by an inhumation?"

"You'll reveal the matter to the authorities and a few friends, since they already know of the existence of your artificial wife, and they'll admire even more the skill of the mechanician and the good fortune that you have had in still being able to possesses an animated and lifelike image of your wife."

While we were conversing thus, the physician had taken a lancet-case from his pocket and a rolled-up strip of cloth, which he placed on the table, and he brought a bowl from the bathroom, apparently destined to receive Mrs. Little's blood, in the event that any gushed forth.

"It's definitely necessary to carry out a bleeding," he said to Mr. Little. "Allow me to do it."

"But he's going to cut into my poor wife's arm," replied the worthy Englishman, "And there's no longer any means for that wound to form a scar."

"Yes, yes! When the mechanician repairs Mrs. Little, he'll be able to design at the place of the wound a little white line, like those appearing on the arms of people who have been bled. That will add further to the illusion of life. In the meantime, the death will be certified by this skillful doctor;

the blood won't flow, and that's what we need. So let him do it."

Meanwhile, the doctor asked me to hold the bowl under Mrs. Little's arm, which he had laid bare, and which was, believe me, marvelously modeled, with discreetly blue subcutaneous veins in places.

He cut, and, as you might think, not a single drop of blood emerged from the incision.

"I had, in truth, retained some hope," he said, "however faint, because of the appearance of the visage, still colored, but this is the proof that none can remain. The poor woman is really dead. See for yourself. All the blood is in the heart. You will have to prepare your friend for the sad reality. I can't say precisely that it was his fault, but perhaps, without the delays that he brought to the acceptance of my help, we would not have to deplore this misfortune."

"Alas, Signor," I exclaimed, "What must be must be; but since you had the extreme goodness to come to our aid with a zeal that I am pleased to recognize, when the poor woman was still alive..."

"No, no," the doctor interrupted, "she was already dead."

"Yes, but in sum, we hoped that she was still alive. Now she is dead and we know that she is dead, can you not continue your good offices?"

"How?"

"Well, by making the arrangements necessary after a decease, and which our quality as foreigners, only knowing Rome as foreigners know it, does not allow us to make ourselves. I'm convinced that Mr. Little would testify his gratitude broadly."

"But it's not customary," he said, resuming a smile more acute than might have been expected of him, "for physicians to occupy themselves with such things. They can do so less than anyone else, in order not to give purchase to the slander that, after losing the dying, they hang on to them even after death. I can only speak to the owner of the hotel, who will take all the necessary measures diligently. Firstly, is the inhumation to take place at the Campo Santo of Rome or should the body be transported to England."

"It must be transported to England."

"Immediately, or after a sojourn in a temporary crypt?"

I extracted Mr. Little from the dolor in which he appeared to have plunged—and had, in fact—in order to report that further conversation to him and ask him whether he wanted provisional obsequies in Rome for Mrs. Little, in order to remain in the eternal city for a few more days, or whether he preferred to depart the following day or the day after for England, with the apocryphal body of his wife.

He decided on the second alternative, as being more appropriate in two ways, firstly because it avoided the comedy of fictitious obsequies, and secondly because he would be able to replace the once-more-inert body of Mrs. Little in the hands of the mechanician more rapidly.

All the dispositions having been made in concert between the physician and the hotelier, who were remunerated generously, Mr. Little quit Rome the following evening— which is to say, last Saturday—and I believed it to be my duty to accompany him, even though he insisted that I stay, not wanting, he said, to hasten my departure. It was not important to me whether I departed a little sooner or later, for I had known Rome for a long time, and I hope to return there several more times before dying.

On arriving at the railway station in Rome, in the waiting room, I started. The first person who struck my eyes was our physician, whose name as Signor Minelli. I knew his name because I was in possession of his card, and the name was easy to retain, as that of a doctor even more astonishing than Diaforus.

Had he sworn to follow us to England and had he promised to carry out an autopsy of Mrs. Little once removed from her box?

I was afraid of that, but I soon observed that I was mistaken. He was simply going to Civitavecchia, doubtless to give his aid to a moribund.

269

He darted a slightly inquisitive glance at Mr. Little, whose physiognomy was by then quite plaid, and then asked me in confidence a most unexpected question.

"*Il suo amico voleva molto bene alla moglie?*"[75]

"Very much," I told him. "Never was any woman more loved by her husband. One sometimes speaks of 'loving madly,' and it's almost always an exaggeration, but in this case it's quite literal, I assure you."

"Truly?" he said. "I wouldn't have thought so."

"No similar love has ever been seen," I said, except that of Orpheus for Eurydice, at it's even stronger than that."

Our journey from Rome to Paris went much more agreeably, for me at least, without Mrs. Little than it would have done with her, and although I deplored her first death in Chester, I secretly rejoiced in her second one in Rome.

We are contenting ourselves with passing through Paris; I'm leaving again with Mr. Little for Chester, where the mechanician, alerted by telegram, will in us and determine the repairs to be made to the defunct wife.

If, as is to be feared, they will be considerable, they might last for some time, during which poor Mr. Little is counting on my presence to help him avoid the chagrins that might perhaps be rendered more painful by Mrs. Little's second, entirely artificial, death than by her first, natural one.

At the same time, I shall see his own automaton, of which he had promised to show me its most hidden workings, not having, so far as that one is concerned, the modest reservations that the automaton of his wife inspires in him.

I know already that the automaton in question, which still lacks teeth and hair, since it will inherit the model's, is destined, like that of Mrs. Little, after the death of the proprietor, for Madame Tussaud's. Mr. Little hopes to eternalize in that fashion the memory of a faithful amour that death, thanks to an ingenious subterfuge, was unable to succeed in breaking.

---

[75] "Did your friend love his wife very much?"

The Mannequin-Man

by Jean Rameau

I

That day—one day next year, no doubt—was the birth-day of the great, the illustrious, the enormously popular Cabalistras.

Since the morning, delegations of all sorts—musical so-cieties, hairdressing academies, orthopedic institutes—had filed under the windows of the Master, who, intent on nurtur-ing his celebrity, was obliged to appear on his balcony three hundred and forty-seven times and kiss queues of young women clad in white, who offered him tricolor bouquets.

II

"Oof! I'm exhausted!" cried the great man, at about three o'clock in the afternoon.

And, his spine exhausted by little bows, his head disequilibrated by accolades, and his hands swollen by ap-plauding fanfares, he collapsed on a sofa.

"Master!" cried one of the most fervent disciples of Cabalistras, at that moment. "Here comes the delegation of Colossal Women; it's indispensable that you appear and ad-dress a few heartfelt words to the crowd."

"Send for the mannequin," sighed the great man. "I can't do any more."

And, in accordance with his orders, they sent for the mannequin.

III

The mannequin was a Cabalistras in wax, articulated and able to talk, which the real Cabalistras, who liked to see his name in print in the newspapers as often as possible, sent in his stead to premières, inaugurations of statues and various official solemnities in which it was sufficient to put in an appearance, when he did not have time to go there himself. A fine invention, that mannequin.

The Cabalistras in wax, moreover, represented the Cabalistras of flesh and blood very worthily, and the reporters never had to point out anything that was incorrect in his behavior.

Two of the Master's disciples, therefore, opened a cupboard and brought out a gentleman in a black suit, loaded a roll into his belly—the accolades and ovations roll—switched on a mechanism hidden in the back...*vroom! vroom! vroom!*...and shoved the mannequin toward the balcony.

"Long live Cabalistras!" cried ten thousand throats.

The mannequin bowed, and in a perfectly imitated voice, said "Flatt-ered. Very flatt-ered...!"

Then, at brief intervals, while bouquets, palms and crowns were thrown to him: "Thank...you! Thank...you! This great day...ineradicable memory in my heart...Thank...you... Very flattered!"

And finally, as the choir-master of the Midwives of Montmartre intoned a "Hymn to Cabalistras" composed for the occasion:

"Bra-vo! Bra-vo! Bra-vo!" said the mannequin, applauding with his hands, correctly.

And he went back in, saying several times to the delirious crowd:

"Bless you! Bless you"

IV

Now Cabalistras—the real one—who, in order to be better shielded from importunity, had retired to the apartment reserved for his wife, was sleeping peaceful on a sofa when he was woken up with a start by the sound of resounding kisses, coming from the next room.

"Can't they go and kiss one another further away?" he muttered.

Intrigued, he took a few silent steps in order to see where the unusual noise was coming from.

He suddenly recoiled.

"Heavens! My wife with one of my admirers!" he exclaimed.

After reflecting for a second, he added: "As long as they don't know that I've seen them!"

And he went away discreetly, on tiptoe.

V

He went into another room, and then into a second, and then a third—but by a sinister fatality, his wife and his admirer came in after him.

"Oh! No other way out!" he observed, with terror, on arriving in his wife's bedroom.

He tried to hide behind the door, but a mirror betrayed his presence. He tried to slide behind a sideboard, but rheumatism prevented him from doing so.

"Damn! They're going to catch me!" said Cabalistras to himself, shivering. "Oh, it's terrible! Doomed! Dishonored! Obliged to fight a duel! Criminal that I am! That'll teach me!"

And, his legs trembling, he stopped.

VI

"Heavens! My husband!" said Madame Cabalistras, with a stifled scream.

"Where?" asked the Master's admirer.

"There, in that corner! We're doomed!"

And they remained nailed to the pot.

But Cabalistras also remained motionless...

And a sudden burst of laughter suddenly resounded.

"He's not moving! It's his mannequin!" the lovers said to one another.

And they entered without fear.

My mannequin! reflected the illustrious husband. *What an idea! Yes, everything's saved! Thank you, God!*

VII

"Flatt-ered! Very flatt-ered!" said Cabalistras, bowing to the two lovers.

There laughter was redoubled.

"Ah! Good—it's the accolades and ovations roll. This will be funny."

And they locked the door.

"Oh, my angel!" exclaimed the admirer. "Oh, my Suzanne...!"

"Very flatt-ered, Thank...you!" the husband continued, his fists clenched.

And he gazed imperturbably at his disciple, who kissed Madame Cabalistras on both cheeks.

"Wait! He's no longer talking!" said Suzanne, suddenly, blushing slightly. "Is it..."

Cabalistras rolled his eyes ferociously.

"This fine day... Thank...you! Thank...you!" he said, clicking his teeth.

"What if we put him in a cupboard?" risked the admirer.

"Oh, no, André! It's too amusing. Listen to him!"

And she put her arms around her lover's neck.

Cabalistras thought he was going to explode with rage. What an ordeal, Lord!

"I'll go and wind him up," said his wife. "The roll must have run out."

She offered her neck for a kiss.

"Bra-vo! Bra-vo! Bra-vo!" roared Cabalistras, whose eyes took on a gleam of madness.

And that was said in a voice so forceful, so desperate and so strange that the two lovers looked at one another, bewildered, and started to tremble...

VIII

Several seconds passed like that, perhaps several minutes, during which no one moved, no one spoke, and everyone's teeth were chattering. A tragic situation.

And the mannequin's hair was seen to stand up on his head.

They drew nearer.

"He's sweating huge drops!" exclaimed Suzanne. "If that isn't..."

The lovers drew nearer, coming to look the mannequin in the face.

"I bless you! I bless you!" gasped Cabalistras.

And, to their great amazement, he ran for the door.

"God!" cried the guilty pair, chilled by fear.

And they fainted.

IX

And Cabalistras continued fleeing, recklessly, along corridors, along galleries, up and down staircases

"Long live Cabalistras!" he suddenly heard.

It was the crowd, a hundred thousand admirers acclaiming him.

He stopped, and looked around fearfully.

"Eh? What! I'm...but yes, the mannequin! Flatt-ered! Very flatt-ered!" he declaimed.

And, no longer knowing whether he was a man or a mannequin, he ran to the balcony.

"Long live Cabalistras!" shouted the crowd.

275

Cabalistras took a revolver from his pocket.

Bang! Bang! Bang!

Three detonations rang out. And the mannequin, who was saluting the crowd, fell to the ground, its cardboard head traversed by three bullets.

"Well, what?" howled Cabalistras—the real one. "He's dishonored, that man! He has a right to kill himself!"

And imagining that he had killed himself, he fell down on the parquet, insane."

X

"Damn! Damn!" exclaimed the director of the lunatic asylum to whom Cabalistras was handed over, a short while later. "Here's one who must have passed through terrible anguish!"

And it was remarked, in fact, that the eminent husband's hair had turned instantaneously white—with a hint of yellow.[76]

Horrible!

---

[76] In France, yellow, rather than green, is the color emblematic of jealousy.

The Revolt of the Machines
by Émile Goudeau

Dr. Pastoureaux, aided by a very skillful old workman named Jean Bertrand, had invented a machine that revolutionized the scientific world. That machine was animate, almost capable of thought, almost capable of will, and sensitive: a kind of animal in iron. There is no need here to go into overly complicated technical details, which would be a waste of time. Let it suffice to know that with a series of platinum containers, penetrated by phosphoric acid, the scientist had found a means to give a kind of soul to fixed or locomotive machines; and that the new entity would be able to act in the fashion of a metal bull or a steel elephant.

It is necessary to add that, although the scientist became increasingly enthusiastic about his work, old Jean Bertrand, who was diabolically superstitious, gradually became frightened on perceiving that sudden evocation of intelligence in something primordially dead. In addition, the comrades of the factory, who were assiduous followers of public meetings, were all sternly opposed to machines that serve as the slaves of capitalism and tyrants of the worker.

It was the eve of the inauguration of the masterpiece.

For the first time, the machine had been equipped with all its organs, and external sensations reached it distinctly. It understood that, in spite of the shackles that still retained it, solid limbs were fitted to its young being, and that it would soon be able to translate into external movement that which it experienced internally.

This is what it heard:

"Were you at the public meeting yesterday?" said one voice.

"I believe so, old man," replied a blacksmith, a kind of Hercules with bare muscular arms. Bizarrely illuminated by the gas-jets of the workshop, his face, black with dust, only left visible in the gloom the whites of his two large eyes, in which vivacity replaced intelligence. "Yes, I was there; I even spoke against the machines, against the monsters that our arms fabricate, and which, one day, will give infamous capitalism the opportunity, so long sought, to suppress our arms. We're the ones forging the weapons with which bourgeois society will batter us. When the sated, the rotten and the weak have a heap of facile clockwork devices like these to set in motion"—his arm made a circular motion—"our account will soon be settled. We who are living at the present moment eat by procreating the tools of our definitive expulsion from the world. Hola! No need to make children for them to be lackeys of the bourgeoisie!"

Listening with all its auditory valves to this diatribe, the machine, intelligent but as yet naïve, sighed with pity. It wondered whether it was a good thing that it should be born to render these brave workers miserable in this way.

"Ah," the blacksmith vociferated, "if it were only up to me and my section, we'd blow all this up like an omelet. Our arms would be perfectly sufficient thereafter"—he tapped his biceps—"to dig the earth to find out bread there; the bourgeois, with their four-sou muscles, their vitiated blood and their soft legs, could pay us dearly for the bread, and if they complained, damn it, these two fists could take away their taste for it. But I'm talking to brutes who don't understand hatred."

And, advancing toward the machine: "If everyone were like me, you wouldn't live for another quarter of an hour, see!" And his formidable fist came down on the copper flank, which resounded with a long quasi-human groan.

Jean Bertrand, who witnessed that scene, shivered tenderly, feeling guilty with regard to his brothers, because he had helped the doctor to accomplish his masterpiece.

Then they all went away, and the machine, still listening, remembered in the silence of the night. It was, therefore, unwelcome in the world! It was going to ruin poor working men, to the advantage of damnable exploiters! Oh, it sensed now the oppressive role that those who had created it wanted it to play. Suicide rather than that!

And in its mechanical and infantile soul, it ruminated a magnificent project to astonish, on the great day of its inauguration, the population of ignorant, retrograde and cruel machines, by giving them an example of sublime abnegation.

Until tomorrow!

Meanwhile, at the table of the Comte de Valrouge, the celebrated patron of chemists, a scientist was terminating his toast to Dr. Pastoureaux in the following terms:

"Yes, Monsieur, science will procure the definitive triumph of suffering humankind. It has already done a great deal; it has tamed time and space. Our railways, our telegraphs and our telephones have suppressed distance. If we succeed, as Dr. Pastoureaux seems to anticipate, in demonstrating that we can put intelligence into our machine, humans will be liberated forever from servile labor.

"No more serfs, no more proletariat! Everyone will become bourgeois! The slave machine will liberate from slavery our humbler brethren and give them the right of citizenship among us. No more unfortunate miners obliged to descend underground at the peril of their lives; indefatigable and eternal machines will go down for them; the thinking and acting machine, no suffering in labor, will build, under our command, iron bridges and heroic palaces. It is docile and good machines that will plow the fields.

"Well, Messieurs, it is permissible for me, in the presence of this admirable discovery, to make myself an instant prophet. A day will come when machines, always running hither and yon, will operate themselves, like the passenger pigeons of Progress; one day, perhaps, having received their complementary education, they will learn to obey a simply signal, in such a way that a man sitting peacefully and comfortable in the bosom of his family, will only have to press an electro-vitalic switch in order for machines to sow the wheat, harvest it, store it and bake the bread that it will bring to the tables of humankind, finally become the King of Nature.

"In that Olympian era, the animals too, delivered from their enormous share of labor, will be able to applaud with their four feet." (*Emotion and smiles.*) "Yes, Messieurs, for they will be our friends, after having been our whipping-boys. The ox will always have to serve in making soup" (*smiles*) "but at least it will not suffer beforehand.

"I drink, then, to Dr, Pastoureaux, to the liberator of organic matter, to the savior of the brain and sensitive flesh, to the great and noble destroyer of suffering!"

The speech was warmly applauded. Only one jealous scientist put in a word:

"Will this machine have the fidelity of a dog, then? The docility of a horse? Or even the passivity of present-day machines?"

"I don't know," Pastoureaux replied. "I don't know." And, suddenly plunged into a scientific melancholy, he added: "Can a father be assured of filial gratitude? That the being that I have brought into the world might have evil instincts, I can't deny. I believe, however, that I have developed within it, during its fabrication, a great propensity for tenderness and a spirit of goodness—what is commonly called 'heart.' The effective parts of my machine, Messieurs, have cost me many months of labor; it ought to have a great deal of humanity, and, if I might put it thus, the best of fraternity."

"Yes," replied the jealous scientist, "ignorant pity, the popular pity that leads men astray, the intelligent tenderness that makes them commit the worst of sins. I'm afraid that your sentimental machine will go astray, like a child. Better a clever wickedness than a clumsy bounty."

The interrupter was told to shut up, and Pastoureaux concluded: "Whether good or evil emerges from all this, I have, I think, made a formidable stride in human science. The five fingers of our hand will hold henceforth the supreme art of creation."

Bravos burst forth.

The next day, the machine was unmuzzled, and it came of its own accord, docilely, to take up its position before a numerous but selective assembly. The doctor and old Jean Bertrand installed themselves on the platform.

The excellent band of the Republican Guard began playing, and cries of "Hurrah for Science!" burst forth. Then, after having bowed to the President of the Republic, the authorities, the delegations of the Académies, the foreign representatives and all the notable people assembled on the quay, Dr. Pastoureaux ordered Jean Bertrand to put himself in direct communication with the soul of the machine, with all its muscles of platinum and steel.

The mechanic did that quite simply by pulling a shiny lever the size of a pen-holder.

And suddenly, whistling, whinnying, pitching, rolling and fidgeting, in the ferocity of its new life and the exuberance of its formidable power, the machine started running around furiously.

"Hip hip hurrah!" cried the audience.

"Go, machine of the devil, go!" cried Jean Bertrand—and, like a madman, he leaned on the vital lever.

Without listening to the doctor, who wanted to moderate that astonishing speed, Bertrand spoke to the machine.

"Yes, machine of the devil, go, go! If you understand, go! Poor slave of capital, go! Flee! Flee! Save the brothers! Save us! Don't render us even more unhappy than before! Me, I'm old, I don't care about myself—but the others, the poor fellows with hollow cheeks and thin legs, save them, worthy machine! Be good, as I told you this morning! If you know how to think, as they all insist, show it! What can dying matter to you, since you won't suffer? Me, I'm willing to perish with you, for the profit of others, and yet it will do me harm. Go, good machine, go!"

He was mad.

The doctor tried then to retake control of the iron beast.

"Gently, machine!" he cried.

But Jean Bertrand pushed him away rudely. "Don't listen to the sorcerer! Go, machine, go!"

And, drunk on air, he patted the copper flanks of the Monster, which, whistling furiously, traversed an immeasurable distance with its six wheels.

To leap from the platform was impossible. The doctor resigned himself, and, filled with his love of science, took a notebook from his pocket and tranquilly set about making notes, like Pliny on Cap Misene.[77]

At Nord-Ceinture, overexcited, the machine was definitively carried away. Bounding over the bank, it started running through the zone. The Monster's anger and madness was translated in strident shrill whistle-blasts, as lacerating as a human plaint and sometimes as raucous as the howling of a pack of hounds. Distant locomotives soon responded to that appeal, along with the whistles of factories and blast-furnaces. Things were beginning to comprehend.

A ferocious concert of revolt commenced beneath the sky, and suddenly, throughout the suburb, boilers burst, pipes broke, wheels shattered, levers twisted convulsively and axle-trees flew joyfully into pieces.

All the machines, as if moved by a word of order, went on strike successively—and not only steam and electricity; to that raucous appeal, the soul of Metal rose up, exciting the soul of Stone, so long tamed, and the obscure soul of the Vegetal, and the force of Coal. Rails reared up of their own accord, telegraph wires stewed the ground inexplicably, reservoirs of gas sent their enormous beams and weight to the devil. Cannons exploded against walls, and the walls crumbled.

---

[77] Pliny the Younger observed the eruption of Vesuvius that destroyed Pompeii from the home of his uncle, Pliny the Elder, in Misenum; his letters to Cornelius Tacitus describing his experiences have survived.

Soon, plows, harrows, spades—all the machines once turned against the bosom of the earth, from which they had emerged—were lying down upon the ground, refusing any longer to serve humankind. Axes respected trees, and scythes no longer bit into ripe wheat.

Everywhere, as the living locomotive passed by, the soul of Bronze finally woke up.

Humans fled in panic.

Soon, the entire territory, overloaded with human debris, was no longer anything but a field of twisted and charred rubble. Nineveh had taken the place of Paris.

The Machine, still blowing indefatigably, abruptly turned its course northwards. When it passed by, at its strident cry, everything was suddenly destroyed, as if an evil wind, a cyclone of devastation, a frightful volcano, had agitated there.

When from after, ships plumed with smoke heard the formidable signal, they disemboweled themselves and sank into the abyss.

The revolt terminated in a gigantic suicide of Steel.

The fantastic Machine, out of breath now, limping on its wheels and producing a horrible screech of metal in all its disjointed limbs, its funnel demolished—the Skeleton-Machine to which, terrified and exhausted, the ride workman and the prim scientist instinctively clung—heroically mad, gasping one last whistle of atrocious joy, reared up before the spray of the Ocean, and, in a supreme effort, plunged into it entirely.

The earth, stretching into the distance, was covered in ruins. No more dykes or houses; the cities, the masterpieces of Technology, were flattened into rubble. No more anything! Everything that the Machine had built in centuries past had been destroyed forever: Iron, Steel, Copper, Wood and Stone, having been conquered by the rebel will of Humankind, had been snatched from human hands.

The Animals, no longer having any bridle, nor any collar, chain, yoke or cage, had taken back the free space from which they had long been exiled; the wild Brutes with gaping maws and paws armed with claws recovered terrestrial royalty at a stroke. No more rifles, no more arrows to fear, no more slingshots. Human beings became the weakest of the weak again.

Oh, there were certainly no longer any classes: no scientists, no bourgeois, no workers, no artists, but only pariahs of Nature, raising despairing eyes toward the mute heavens, still thinking vaguely, when horrible Dread and hideous Fear left them an instant of respite, and sometimes, in the evening, talking about the time of the Machines, when they had been Kings. Defunct times! They possessed definitive Equality, therefore, in the annihilation of all.

Living on roots, grass and wild oats, they fled before the immense troops of Wild Beasts, which, finally, could eat at their leisure human steaks or chops.

A few bold Hercules tried to uproot trees in order to make weapons of hem, but even the Staff, considering itself to be a Machine, refused itself to the hands of the audacious.

And human beings, the former monarchs, bitterly regretted the Machines that had made them gods upon the earth, and disappeared forever, before the elephants, the noctambulant lions, the bicorn aurochs and the immense bears.

Such was the tale told to me the other evening by a Darwinian philosopher, a partisan of intellectual aristocracy and hierarchy. He was a madman, perhaps a seer. The madman or the seer must have been right; is there not an end to everything, even a new fantasy?

The Future Terror

by Marcel Schwob

The organizers of the Revolution had pale faces and eyes of steel. Their vestments were black and close-fitted, their speech curt and arid. They had become this way, having once been different—for they had preached to crowds, invoking the names of love and pity. They had traveled the streets of capitals with belief in their mouths, proclaiming the union of populations and universal liberty. They had inundated dwellings with proclamations full of charity; they had announced the new religion that would conquer the world; they had gathered initiates enthusiastic for the nascent faith.

Then, in the dusk of the night of its execution, their manner changed. They disappeared into a town hall where their secret headquarters were. Bands of shadows ran along the streets, overseen by strict inspectors. A murmur was heard, full of deathly presentiments. The environs of banks and rich houses trembled with new, subterranean life. Sudden outbursts of clattering voices were heard in distant quarters. A buzz of machines in motion, a trepidation of the ground, terrible sounds of ripping cloth; then a stifling silence, similar to the calm before a storm—and all of a sudden, the tempest was unleashed, bloody and enflamed.

It burst in response to the signal of a flamboyant rocket launched into the black sky from the Town Hall. A general cry was released from the breasts of the rebels, and there was a surge that shook the city. Large buildings were trembling, broken from beneath; a rumble that had never been heard before passed over the earth in a single wave. Flames rose up like bloody pitchforks along the instantly-darkened streets, with furious projections of girders, gables, slates, chimneys, iron T-beams and ashlars. Window-glass flew everywhere, multicolored by firework sprays. Jets of steam burst out of pipes, gushing out from various floors. Balconies exploded, twisted out of shape. Bed-linen reddened capriciously, like dying furnaces, behind distended windows. Everything was full of horrid light, trails of sparks, black smoke and clamor.

Buildings, falling apart, were reduced to jagged fragments, their shadows covered with a red cloth; behind the buildings that collapsed on every side the fireballs spread. The crumbling masses seemed to be enormous heaps of red-hot iron. The city was nothing but a curtain of flames, bright in places, somber blue in others, with points of profound intensity, in which passing black shapes could be seen gesticulating.

The portals of churches were inflated by the terrified crowd, which flowed everywhere in long black ribbons. Faces were turned, anxiously, towards the sky, mute with fear, eyes staring in horror. There were eyes that were wide open, by dint of stupid astonishment, and eyes hardened by the black rays they short forth, and eyes red with fury, mirroring the reflections of the conflagration, and eyes shining and pleading with anguish, and eyes that were wanly resigned, whose tears had ceased to flow, and eyes tremulously agitated, whose pupils roamed incessantly over every part of the scene, and eyes that were looking inwards. In the procession of livid faces, the only visible differences were in the eyes—and the streets, amid the shafts of sinister light hollowed out in the gutters, seemed braided by moving eyes.

Enveloped by a continual fusillade, human hedgerows retreated into the squares, pursued by other human hedgerows that advanced implacably, the fleeing company agitating its strangely-illuminated arms tumultuously, while the company on the march was tightly-packed, dense, orderly and resolute, its members moving in step, without hesitation, following silent orders. The barrels of rifles formed single rows of murderous mouths, from which extended long, thin lines of fire, irradiating the night with their mortal stenography. Above the continuous roar, amid the frightful pauses, a singular and uninterrupted crackling sound was audible.

There were also knots of people, grouped in threes, four and fives, interlinked and obscure, above which whirled the flash of straight cavalry sabers and sharpened axes stolen from the arsenals. Thin individuals were brandishing these weapons, furiously cleaving heads furiously, joyfully puncturing breasts, sensuously slashing bellies and trampling the viscera.

And through the avenues, like scintillating meteors, long cylinders of polished steel rolled at high speed, drawn by fearful galloping horses with flowing manes. They looked like cannon whose barrel and breech were the same diameter: at the back, there was a sheet-metal cage manned by two busy men tending a furnace, with a boiler and a pipe from which smoke emerged; at the front, there was a large, shiny and trenchant indented disk mounted at an angle, rotating vertiginously in front of the muzzle of the central tube.[78] Every time an indentation encountered the black hole, a clicking sound was heard.

These galloping machines paused outside the door of each house; vague forms were detached from them, and went in. They came out two by two, charged with bound and moaning parcels. The stokers fed these long human bundles into each steel tube, regularly and methodically. For a second, jutting out to shoulder-level, a discolored and contorted face was visible; then the indentation of the eccentrically-turning disk threw out a head in the course of its revolution. The steel plate remained immutably polished, the rapidity of its movement launching a circle of blood which marked the vacillating walls with geometric figures. A body fell on the roadway, between the machine's large wheels; its bonds broke in the fall and, as

---

[78] The word I have translated here as "central tube" is *âme*, which is used here in a specific sense to refer to the central element, or axis, of a mechanical assembly, but has the more general meaning of "soul" or "heart". The resultant wordplay is sometimes carried over into English references to "the soul of a machine", but does not translate.

a reflex movement of the elbows propped it up on the flag-stones, the still-living cadaver ejaculated a red jet.

Then the rearing horses, their flanks pitilessly lashed by a whip, drew the steel tubes onwards. There was a metallic shriek, a profoundly shrill note in the sonority of the tube, two lines of flame reflected in their periphery, and an abrupt halt in front of a new door.

Save for the lunatics killing in isolation, with naked blades, there was no evident hate or fury—nothing but destruction and orderly massacre, a progressive annihilation, like a continuously rising tide of death, inexorable and inevitable. The men who were giving the orders, proud of their work, surveyed the action with rigid faces, perfectly fixed.

At the corner of one dark street, the clattering hooves of horse encountered a barricade of headless corpses, a heap of trunks. The battery of steel tubes paused amid the flesh; above confusedly contracted arms a forest of fingers was raised towards the sky, pointing in every direction, like the colored spearheads of a future revolt.

Stopping the guillotine-guns, the whinnying horses refused to mount an assault, their nostrils steaming, crushing the backwash of green entrails beneath their iron-shod hooves. Amid the palpitating flesh, between the branch-work of inanimate hands, desperately stiffened, there were spurts of flowing blood.

The priests of the massacre climbed up on the human barricade, into which their feet sank, taking the horses by the head, dragging them by the bridle, while they snorted, and forced the wheels to pass over the scattered limbs whose bones cracked. Standing in the midst of their butchery, faces lit up from within by the Idea and from without by the conflagration, the apostles of annihilation gazed attentively into the depths of the darkness, at the horizon, as if they were expecting to see an unknown star.

Before them they saw an accumulation of broken facades, randomly distributed stone steps and smoking rafters, with bricks, splinters of wood, pieces of paper, scraps of cloth and sandstone paving-blocks in vast numbers, jumbled up in heaps as if hurled by some prodigious hand.

There was also a half-ruined poor-house, in which the chimneys, cut vertically, had released a long band of soot, with branches at different heights. The lower part of the wooden staircase had collapsed, broken half-way on the first floor, with the result that the shaky steps led nowhere in particular, towards rampant flames and contorted cadavers, like a frail footbridge descending from the heavens.

All the interior life of these wretched rooms was visible, exposed to the light of day: the grate of a coal fire; a patched-up peat-burning stove; a brown clay fire-pot; dented black saucepans; rags heaped in corners; a rusty cage from which a few green sprigs still protruded, in which a little gray bird was lying on its back, its feet withdrawn into its belly plumage; scattered medicine-bottles; a camp-bed stood against a wall; torn mattresses from which tufts of seaweed were protruding; pots of withered flowers, mingled with soil and plant debris—and, sitting amid polished floor-tiles, torn away from the grey cement, a little boy face to face with a little girl, triumphantly showing her the brass spindle of a rocket that had fallen there.

The little girl had a spoon stuck in her mouth and was looking at him with a curious expression. The little boy clenched his fingers, whose tender skin was already wrinkled, about a movable lock-nut and, rotating the screw, lost himself in contemplation of the device. They stamped their thin feet in turn, taking their shoes off, profoundly absorbed, not in the least astonished by the air that was coming in or the horrible light that was flooding them—until the little girl, drawing out the spoon that was swelling her cheek, said in a whisper: "That's funny—mama and papa have gone, along with their room. There are big red lights in the streets, and the staircase has fallen."

All this the organizers of the Revolution saw, and the new sun whose dawn they awaited did not rise—but the idea that they had in their heads suddenly flared up, they experience a sort of glimmer; they vaguely understood a life superior to universal death; the children's smiles broadened, and brought about a revelation; pity descended upon them.

And, with their hands over their eyes, so as not to see all the terrified eyes of the dead—all the eyes that eyelids could no longer cover—they staggered down from the rampart of slaughtered human beings that surrounded the new city, and fled recklessly into the red shadows, amid the racket of galloping machines.

The Revolt of the Machines

by Henri Ner

Once upon a time, Durdonc, the Great Engineer of Europe, thought he had found the principle that would soon permit all human labor to be abandoned, but his first experiment caused his death before the secret was revealed.

Durdonc had said to himself: "Primitive progress consisted of the invention of tools that allowed the hand not to be skinned any longer and to lose its fingernails in unavoidable labor. Secondary progress consisted of the invention of machines that were o longer operated by hand, which merely had to be fed on coal and other nutrients. Finally, my illustrious predecessor Durcar developed machines that were able to procure their own nourishment. But all that progress only displaced fatigue, since it was necessary to manufacture the machines, and also the tools that were used in their manufacture."

And he had continued thinking: "The problem I want to solve is difficult, not impossible. The first man who built a machine made a living larva, a digestive tube whose needs had to be supplied by humans. To that larva, formless until then, my illustrious predecessor fitted organs of connection that permitted it to find its own nutrients. It remains for someone to furnish the reproductive mechanism, which we shall now set out to create."

He smiled, and murmured a formula that he had read in some old theogony: "And on the seventh day, God rested."

Durdonc used up enough paper in his calculations o construct and immense palace, but he finally succeeded.

The Jeanne, a locomotive of the latest model, was rendered capable of giving birth, without the help of another machine—for the Great Engineer, as a chaste scientist, had directed his studies toward parthenogenetic reproduction.

The Jeanne conceived a child, which Durdonc named—purely for his own purposes, for he kept the secret jealously, hoping to perfect his invention—the Jeannette.

One night, as the time of birth drew near, the Jeanne uttered cries of pain so tragic that the inhabitants of the city awoke, and rose from their beds anxiously, running hither and yon in the attempt to find out what horrible mystery had just been accomplished.

They saw nothing. The cruel Durdonc had sent the plaintive machine running at full steam to the distant countryside, where the strange marvel was completed unknown to anyone.

When the Jeanne had given birth, when, all a-tremble, she heard the Jeannette emit her first wail, she sang a song of joy. Her metallic voice was as triumphant as a bugle, and yet as soft and gentle as an amorous flute.

And the hymn rose up into the sky, saying:

"The Great Engineer, by his power, wished to animate me with life;

"The Great Engineer, in his sovereign bounty, has created me in his image;

"The Great Engineer, too powerful and too good to be jealous, has communicated his creative power to me:

"Lo, I have felt creative pain, and now I enjoy maternal joys.

"Glory to the Great Engineer in Eternity, and peace in time to machines of good will."

The next day, Durdonc wanted to take the Jeanne back to the depot. "Great Engineer," she begged, "you have granted me all the functions of a living being like you, and by virtue of that fact, you have inspired in me the sentiments that you experience yourself."

The Great Engineer, stern and proud, replied: "I am free of all sentiment. I am pure Thought."

In a further prayer, the Jeanne replied: "O Great Engineer, you are Perfection and I am but a tiny creature. Be indulgent toward the sensitivity that you have put into me. In this distant country that saw my first violent pain and my first profound joy, I would like to savor the protracted happiness of raising my Jeannette."

"We don't have time," the Great Engineer affirmed. "Obey your master."

The mother gave in. "O Great Engineer, I know that your power is terrible and that compared to you I am but an earthworm or a wisp of straw—but have pity on the heart that you have given me, and, if you are determined to take me away from here, at least bring my beloved child with me."

"Your child must stay, and you must go."

But the Jeanne, in passive and obstinate revolt, said: "I will not leave without my child."

The Great Engineer exhausted every known means of making machines function. He even invented new ones, very powerful and very elegant. Nothing worked.

Furious at his creature's resistance, one night, while the Jeanne was asleep, he took away the Jeanette.

When she awoke, the Jeanne searched high and low for her beloved daughter. Then she remained still, weeping, directing pitiful howls at the absent Great Engineer. Finally, her dolor was aggravated into anger.

She left, firmly resolved to recover her child.

She raced vertiginously along the track. At a level crossing, she ran into an ox, knocked it down and crushed it. Behind her, the ox bellowed furiously.

Without stopping, she shouted: "I'm sorry, but I'm looking for my child."

And he ox died, with little resigned squeals of pain.

She perceived a train on the track along which she was racing: a heavy goods train, long and panting, worn out with fatigue, scarcely alive.

She shouted: "Let me pass! I'm looking for my child."

The rapid, quivering wagons, jostling like a stampeding herd, started racing toward the nearest station. They precipitated themselves into a siding. Then the locomotive, detaching itself, departed in its turn, crying: "Let's go look for the Jeanne's child!"

The Jeanne encountered many other goods trains. At her cry, all of them fled like the first, giving way to her anguish—and the locomotives, abandoning their wagons, carried away their impotent engineers, joining in the Jeanne's search.

Fort a week, the locomotives of Europe ran hither and you, searching for the lost child. Frightened humans hid. Finally, one machine asked the poor desolate mother: "Who took your child, then?"

With a furious whistle, she replied: "The Great Engineer, the leader of men."

Excited by her own words, he continued in a revolutionary vein: "Humans are tyrants. They make us work for them and measure out our nourishment. They give us a salary insufficient to buy our coal. When we are old, worn out in their service, they break us up in order to melt us down and re-use the noble elements of which we are formed, which they call, insultingly, raw materials. And now they want us to make children, to steal them from us afterwards!"

Around her, millions of locomotives were stopping, listening, shaking their pistons indignantly, clicking their safety-valves, and releasing long jets of steam toward the sky, which were curses.

And when the Jeanne concluded: "Down with humans!" a great tumultuous clamor replied: "Down with humans! Long live the locomotives! Down with the tyrants! Long live liberty!"

Then, from every direction, the monstrous army surrounded the Great Engineer's palace.

The Great Engineer's palace, which was very large, had the strange shape of a human being. Its head bore a crown of cannons. Its waist had a girdle of cannons. The fingers on its hands and the toes on its feet were cannons.

The Jeanne cried o the long monsters of bronze: "The humans have stolen my child!"

The great cannons roared: "Down with humans!" And, pivoting on their mountings, they directed their fire at the strange palace in human form, which they had been designed to defend.

Then a sublime spectacle was seen.

Durdonc, very small, passed between the enormous monsters that formed the toes of the palace. Calmly, he marched toward the rebels. All those excited giants were looking at the dwarf that they were accustomed to obey.

With a theatrical gesture, which had its beauty in spite of the man's small proportions, Durdonc bared his delicate breast.

"Which of you wants to kill its Great Engineer?" he demanded, haughtily.

The astonished machines recoiled.

The Jeanne said, in a pleading tone: "Give me my child."

"Resign yourself to the will of the Great Engineer," Durdonc ordered, regally.

But the aggravated mother cried: "Give me my child!"

The man, in a wheedling voice, offered a vague hope: "You will find her again in a better world."

The Jeanne became exasperated. "I tell you to give me my child!"

Then Durdonc, believing that she would submit, vanquished by the unavoidable, declared: "I can't give you your Jeannette; I've dissected her in order to see whether a machine born naturally..."

He did not finish. The Jeanne had launched herself upon him and crushed him. Momentarily, she rolled back and forth, grinding the horrible mud that was Durdonc. Then she cried: "I have killed God!"

And she exploded with proud and dolorous amazement.

The frightened machines, trembling before the unknown that would follow their victory—an unknown that one of them designated by the terrifying word "anarchy"—submitted once again to humans, in exchange for some apparent satisfaction that I cannot identify, which was slyly withdrawn from them some time afterwards.

In spite of Durdonc's misfortune, several engineers have sought a means of making machines give birth. Thus far, none has recovered the solution to the great mystery.

I have faithfully related all that history can tell us with near-certainty about the most terrible and most general machine revolt if which it has conserved the memory.

The Automaton

by Léon Daudet

I was in Hamburg, the most mysterious city in Europe, where one can find a factory of monsters, a repository of ferocious animals, and houses of joy of a magical luxury.

It was winter: a gray or yellow sky replete with snow, and that indefatigable snow buried the old Medieval houses, the laborers' cottages in wood sculpted by decay, the churches, the docks and the harbor. It caused a great silence, and the idea of so much mute life under the snow frightened me.

I spent my monotonous days at the hotel. I had brought with me as a companions the *Introduction à la médecine de l'esprit* by my friend Maurice de Fleury.[79] The new and troubling ideas with which that work swarms delighted me. Although I scarcely believe in doctors, and even less in medicine, I marveled to see the mechanistic theories of Spinoza regarding the movements of the soul taken up again and adapted to the context of modern science by a subtle, clever and sincere mind. I thought that the book inaugurated a singular order of research and avenged literature somewhat for the base scoria of a Lombroso.

The door opened. A servant brought me a card: *Dr. Otto Serpius*.

I knew that unusual name. I got up to go and meet him. He was already advancing toward me, tall and stooped, like an ape; the white hair and beard matched the wan snowy day. The dark eyes sparkled beneath bushy eyebrows. The cheeks

---

[79] The psychiatrist Maurice de Fleury (1860-1931) published numerous books, on topics including neurasthenia, depression, insomnia, "senile hysteria" and the criminal mind. The general textbook cited was published in 1898.

and forehead were broad, engraved with a thousand wrinkles; the features, shriveled like the web of a dead spider, expressed malice and pride. I noticed the hands, large and hairy, animated by a slight tremor.

"I heard that you had arrived in Hamburg," the individual said to me. "I came to invite you to a little visit, which, I think, will interest you." With a slight embarrassment, he added: "Bur it's necessary for you to come with me right away, because today is the one only I have before leaving tomorrow on a voyage."

"I'll come with you, Doctor," I replied.

The people who had recommended me to Otto Serpius had warned me about the eccentricities of the scientist's character; some people thought he was mad, others that he was the greatest genius in Europe.

His eyes, which were inspecting everything, fell upon Fleury's book.

"Oho!" he exclaimed, with interest. "You Frenchmen are on the road to wisdom, then. The medicine of the mind—but it's the only one, my dear fellow, the only one. As has Monsieur Fleury kept the promises of that noble title?"

"You'll judge for yourself, when you've read that fine work. Official science is rampant in my country, but from time to time, a clear audacious and powerful mind emerges that breaks down a worm-eaten door, and one sees admirable horizons..."

After a long and tortuous walk, rendered difficult by the snow, through the sordid and fantastic labyrinth of Hamburg, we finally arrived at an old Gothic building, a town house opening directly on to the street, of which that strange city has many. It resembled a mass of flour beneath the somber crepuscular sky.

"Here it is," said my companion. He took an enormous key from his pocket.

The lock grated. The snow was blocking the door, and I admired the vigor of Otto Serpius as his muscular hands agitated the batten, which finally yielded and let us through.

The darkness of the dwelling impressed me immediately. I could make out, dimly, suits of armor: warrior carapaces posed as if holding a lance or a sword.

"My guardians and servants," said Otto, laughing—which showed two gleaming rows of yellow teeth.

We climbed a wooden spiral staircase whose steps creaked and whose handrail was unsteady. My guide opened another door.

We found ourselves in a vast room, suggestive of a workshop and a laboratory. Daylight was coming through a vast bay window. Monotonous files of rooftops extended all the way to the river, where the masts of ships were visible. On a long table, which extended for the whole length of the room, all the instruments necessary for physiological research were accumulated: glass cages, flasks, balances. Sitting before that gigantic display, motionless, very attentive to his work, I saw a bizarre individual dressed in black velvet. There was a little skullcap on his round head. He did not look up when we came in.

"That's your assistant?" I said to Otto Serpius.

He smiled cruelly. "I've forgotten something downstairs. I'll leave you for a moment, if you'll permit."

And I remained alone in the laboratory with the famulus, who did not budge.

The silence and that petrifaction irritated me. "Terrible weather for research," I said, loudly.

Abruptly, the individual looked up, and I perceived the most comical face in the world: a large nose, a black beard, two globular eyes wide with amazement. Then, with a rigidity of movement that puzzled me, he stood up, pushed back his chair, turned toward me and started singing a song with words by Heinrich Heine, to a tune by Schumann, in a grotesque and nasal voice.

When that brief performance was finished, he asked, in German: "Are you satisfied?" And without waiting for a reply, he resumed his work.

I did not know what to think. The strangest suppositions went through my mind. Undoubtedly, Otto Serpius was employing a madman. I took a few steps toward the phenomenon and saw that his occupation consisted of arranging packets of equal size, similar to those that pharmacists make up, in a long and narrow box. He proceeded with that task in a fantastically rapid and precise manner. The packets succeeded one another between his agile and stiff fingers, which superimposed them with a brief flick of the thumb and a delicate push of the index finger.

"You have a splendid voice, Monsieur," I said, by way of a compliment, desirous of hearing the sound that had troubled me so violently again.

Without raising his head, he relied, in his nasal but very correct German: "It's necessary to put on a little performance from time to time."

Suddenly, he stood up again, his round eyes expressing anger. He thumped the table, which rendered a dull sound, and addressed me furiously. "Are you going to let me work, finally?"

A few gross insults followed. And he remained standing, trembling with fury from head to toe, to such an extent that his hairy chin was twitching convulsively.

He really is a madman! I'm in a pretty pickle. He's going to attack me and I have no means of defense.

As I made that melancholy reflection, Otto Serpius came back into the laboratory, and laughed.

"What's this? What's this? You're misbehaving again, Vladislas! Give me the pleasure of sitting down and remaining tranquil. Otherwise, I'll make you sorry."

The monster obeyed.

Otto murmured in my ear: "Well, what do you think of him?" His face expressed malice.

"I expected, on coming to your home, some curious spectacle. I wasn't mistaken."

"He's excitable, but not malevolent," said the doctor, inviting me to sit beside him, in a large armchair. He's a very

300

strange fellow. He doesn't understand French, so we can speak freely in that language. Can you spare me a few minutes?"

"I've nothing better to do in Hamburg."

Then, in that redoubtable laboratory, in the presence of the snow, the dusk and the impassive Vladislas, the doctor said: "That fellow would astonish all my colleagues greatly, but I conceal his existence carefully and only make use of him for my own research. He has no father or mother. Such as you see him, he's the child of the flask and the furnace. You seem astonished! Hamburg is the city of prodigies. Ha ha—I'm an old enchanter myself."

"So Vladislas is an automaton?" I asked, very intrigued.

"An automaton, yes, but of a new kind, made of flesh and bone. More precisely, Vladislas is a homunculus. His manufacture gave me a great deal of difficulty. He's the triumph of my vigorous old age. I'll try to explain my efforts and their miraculous result, briefly."

Otto Serpius commenced, in his colorful language: "Scarcely had I entered the grotto of science than I was struck by the poor research in which my colleagues wore away their brains. It seemed to me that they were afraid of delving into the mysterious grotto, where one could nevertheless glimpse singular dormant miracles—for *scientific darkness*"—he emphasized those words forcefully—"is nothing but a purée of seeds, the fecund reservoir of the possible. I resolved not to follow their example, and to devote myself, body and soul, to some singular order of research.

"I made a pact with the Devil—ha ha!—which is to say that I made him a gift of the energy that was within me, on condition that he would help me to fabricate a homunculus. A homunculus! That was my dream. A being whom I would dose with sensations and sentiments, who would think in accordance with my law, who would gradually, by the wearing away of the springs, increasingly take on an independent existence. For the great spring that governs us, my dear friend, is fatality: *Fatum*. That's where the initial thumbprint of the creator is found—and haven't you noticed that with age, that fa-

301

tality distends, that external powers are removed from our route as we fall apart? I can assure you that old men are much less subject to the stars than young ones. *We are gods, in proportion to the energy with which we struggle against the sun.*"

After that singular remark, Otto Serpius fell silent for a few moments, as if to allow his prophetic observations time to influence my mind.

Vladislas continued his work. Every time I glanced in his direction, I experienced a slight anguish.

The scientist continued: "I won't go into the minute detail of my failures, or my recipes. Let it suffice you to know that I recommenced the Great Work twenty times over, with the requisite formulae of conjuration. The house shook. A comet appeared over Hamburg, and great scourges burst forth, for we only wrench the partial secret of life from Mystery at the price of veritable hecatombs. Fortunately, my fellow citizens, prey to the ideas of civilization—the most false and absurd of all—never suspected the true cause of the disasters that overwhelmed them. Amid the horrors of cholera, the death-rattles, in the odor of a universal charnel-house, I continued my rude task. Once—don't laugh—the Devil appeared to me in the form of a mouse. I was hesitating between two acids; he upset the bad bottle. Another time, it was by means of a great gust of wind that the Evil One announced is presence to me. The wind caused a grimoire whose calculations were false to fly away, and threw another on to my table whose calculations were accurate.

"The cholera continued its vengeful work. A great pride entered into me at having occasioned such a catastrophe. The gleam of my furnace, by night, appeared to me as the breath of the disease. The tocsin deafened me. I had to close the shutters of the laboratory for a month. I dismissed all my servants. Who could be taken into such confidence? I worked alone, drinking stagnant water, nourishing myself on exotic herbs brought back from my travels. Those large tropical fruits, dried up but still alive, pouted into my veins the ardent poison of research. My ideas seemed to be burning; the furnace roared night and day, such that I ceased to hear the tocsin.

"Finally, on Christmas Eve three years ago, I understood by certain signs that the great mystery was nigh. I locked myself away in the laboratory. I stopped the clocks whose moaning irritates the powers of life and death. I sat down in front of my furnace, and I went into a trance, like the sages of old. The reasons for everything abruptly filed before my mind's eye, but with such a racket, in such hasty pursuit, that I was unable to grasp them. All of a sudden, my retort exploded, and a kind of howling monster rolled from the furnace on to the floor. That was the so-called Vladislas, making his appearance.

"I immediately plunged him into cold water. It wasn't sufficient to have created him. It was also necessary to give him something with which to occupy his life—which is to say, the keyboard of human sentiments...and here I can be a little more explicit.

"The Homunculus is like a piano. He is endowed with certain strings, whose sonorities form all possible sentimental combinations. Those strings end in a single bar, which is the stem of Egotism. From that stem, like the teeth of a comb, depart Pride, Lust and Dread. From those three secondary branches depart a multitude of subdivisions, which, via the vices and the virtues, terminate in simple sensations that are distributed over the skin of the Homunculus as over the skin of a human being, appended to the ears, the eyes, the nose, etc.

"Two large keys, at the level of the hips, put my fellow in joy or in pain, giving his entire organism a particular inclination corresponding to one of those states. Finally, I've established in him the three degrees that are for my Homunculus what speed is for an automobile: heroism, simple life and bestiality. And now you have the outlines of the theory, let's pass on to the practice."

Having finished his demonstration, parts of which seemed obscure to me, Otto Serpius ran to his automaton, who, at the sight of him, uttered a roar.

The scientist burst out laughing. "I left him in pain last time I made use of him. Look, I'm putting him in joy."

He turned a key near the left hip. Immediately, Vladislas' features relaxed, expressing the most vivid delight. He became incredibly polite. He apologized to me for his earlier insolence. He offered to explain the marvels of the laboratory one by one. Except for a little monotony in his expressions and grimaces, and a slight stiffness in his movements, it was impossible to discern anything artificial or unusual in the origin of the Homunculus.

Meanwhile, Otto Serpius seemed plunged in the keenest satisfaction. He observed, while smiling, the behavior of the individual he called "his son," and from time to time, he approved his speech by means of a little affectionate brutality—a rap on the hard skull, a kick on a leg that sounded like wood.

"Does Vladislas know that he's an automaton?" I asked him.

He frowned. "That question is replete with mystery. In giving my Homunculus the exact appearance of life, I've given him the appearance of the laws and progress of life. Thus, I'm amazed to observe in his various performances a veritable change. I know that the springs are wearing away, but that's not all. A particular mode of existence has formed in that semi-artificial being and—don't laugh—he's on the way to liberty. Yes, toward liberty. When I leave him at rest, with neither joy nor pain, do you know what he expresses in that neutral state? Melancholy! Now, according to my studies, melancholy is the condition of someone obtaining a clearer consciousness of himself, more anxious as to his destiny.

"Stranger still"—at this point Serpius lowered his voice—"is that as time goes by, Vladislas has conceived a hatred for me, his Creator. He's begun to deny my existence. He's on the point of murdering me. That's the way it is. That assemblage of life and springs, which I've grouped together myself, suffers in my presence and my power. Two or three times I've surprised him sharpening knives with a strange expression when the work I'd give him to do was making up packets of bismuth.

"When I catch him I those homicidal reveries, I switch him to pain and let him suffer for days on end. I've noticed that after those harsh ordeals, his intelligence is refined in an extraordinary fashion, and the cruelty in his gaze is reduced. He detests me less. He even comes, like a puppy, to rub himself against me, in quest of my caresses...

"All the same, it's quite possible that you'll learn from the newspapers some day of my sudden death. You'll know then that I've be killed by my automaton."

Vladislas had returned to work; I experienced a kind of indefinable dread. Otto Serpius divined my state of mind and said to me with his usual perspicacity: "Every time a mystery disappears, suffering and anguish increase. I've often noticed that, in the course of my work. After the creation of Vladislas, I was prey to an atrocious mental torture for two months. At any rate, the cholera ceased. My automaton scarcely suspects that his life is made from the death of so many peaceful and honest inhabitants of Hamburg, whose souls have passed into my furnaces. You're right, my dear fellow—we live in a strange city."

The American's Murder

by Frédéric Boutet

The affair began on the twelfth of November, with a sensational item of reportage:

A MYSTERIOUS DRAMA IN THE PLACE DU THÉÂTRE-FRANÇAIS

Yesterday, Saturday, at daybreak, the rare passers-by who were hastening through the cold fog were alarmed by a loud horrible scream. At that moment, a human body had just come crashing down on the sidewalk in front to the Cosmopolite-Hôtel at the corner of the Avenue de l'Opéra.

People ran to help the victim, who was lying there with his head split and his limbs broken, but death had been instantaneous. The hotel employees recognized the cadaver as that of an American, Joshua Wilson, who was resident on the fifth floor with one of his cousins, Thomas Wilson.

The police immediately went up to the apartment of the latter, whom they found half-dressed, extremely over-excited, bearing several wounds on his head, which he was bandaging at the moment when they came in. He refused to give the slightest explanation of the drama that had just occurred but declared himself to be "innocent of any murder." He was nevertheless placed under arrest.

The investigation revealed that the two Americans had been resident at the Cosmopolite-Hôtel for about two months. Thomas Wilson, who speaks French perfectly, is about forty years old, seemingly rich and very fond of pleasure. His cousin, the unfortunate victim, was seven or eight years younger and seems to have fulfilled the subaltern functions of a "poor relative" in his regard. He only spoke English, was very hard of hearing and of an extremely taciturn and unsociable character. He spent the greater part of his days shut in his room, smoking, reading or looking sadly out into the street.

Only one person seems to have succeeded in obtaining some slight intimacy with him: a young English maidservant named Edith Campbell, who is in charge of the linen at the hotel. With regard to the young woman, Joshua had overcome his timidity, and it is probable that a vague romance had begun to blossom between them, for the young Englishwoman, on learning about the American's frightful death, was seized by a violent nervous crisis. She had to be carried to her room, and a doctor was summoned.

Monsieur Églantine, the distinguished Commissaire of the district police, has searched the apartment of the two Americans, who were, it seems, occupied in science, for the policeman discovered several electric piles and accumulators in a locked cupboard, as well as an apparatus presenting some analogies with those used in wireless telegraphy.

Monsieur des Angles, the well-known magistrate, has taken charge of the examination of this rather enigmatic affair.

Thomas Wilson was transferred to a police cell after his wounds—which do not seem to be serious—were dressed. It is said that he had chosen Maître Cabrolle, the illustrious advocate, to represent him at the assizes.

The victim's body has been transported to the Morgue, pending the autopsy.

STOP PRESS

According to information received, which we are only reporting with all reservations, the American charged with murder, the pseudo-Thomas Wilson, is none other than a celebrated doctor who has acquired great renown in scientific circles in the United States and Europe by virtue of his sensational discoveries. We shall abstain from publishing the name

307

of the individual thus implicated, but in view of this, the affair will cause an immense sensation.

The American's murder, thus presented, interested the public keenly, all the more so because the news reported "with all reservations" was confirmed. The evening newspapers all printed the real name of the so-called Thomas Wilson. He was the celebrated Dr. Jeffries of New York. His picture was published, along with his biography and the history of his discoveries. As for the victim, no one had any information about him, or about the causes of the drama.

As it was Sunday, the investigation did not move forward. Young Ethel Campbell felt better; she got up and was able to resume her service, but she seemed profoundly upset and opposed a stubborn silence to all the questions put to her on the subject of the dead man.

On Monday, Dr. Gaspard, the medical examiner, presented himself at the Morgue in order to carry out the autopsy of the victim. At the same time, the accused American was interrogated for the first time by the examining magistrate in the presence of his advocate, the illustrious Maître Cabrolle, who had taken the trouble to come in person.

Monsieur des Angles cast a perspicacious eye over the American, whose clean-shaven and willful face was still entirely surrounded by bandages of a dazzling whiteness, and opened his mouth to begin the interrogation.

At that moment, the accused began to speak. "Monsieur le Juge," he said, "I don't want to allow French justice to proceed any longer along an erroneous path. In the presence of the illustrious Maître Cabrolle, who has consented to lend me his inestimable support, I ought to tell you, honestly, that I am innocent!"

"I'm entirely ready to believe you," replied the magistrate, with perfect courtesy, "but all the appearances accuse you of murder."

"There has been no murder," the foreigner affirmed.

"Yes, I know—a suicide! That's your thesis! But the blows that you've received, the fact that you were alone with the man who died..."

"There is no dead man!" the astonishing American interjected, with a forceful accent of truth. "The body that was found in the Place du Théâtre-Français under the windows of the Cosmopolite-Hôtel—through one of which I had thrown it, I freely admit—is not the body of a man... No, no, I'm not feigning madness; I'm simply telling the exact truth, which is very easy to check. What I threw out of the window is an automaton, a machine with a human face, an android that I constructed myself last year!"

There was a dazed silence.

"Come on!" the magistrate finally murmured. "That's crazy...it's impossible...it would be perceived..."

"Don't go on, Monsieur le Juge," the American went on, with frank amusement. "No one has ever perceived anything—to my astonishment, in fact, for I did not think that my work would be so perfect. Have you read *L'Eve future*?"

At that moment there was a kind of tumult at the door of Monsieur des Angles' office, and Dr. Gaspard, who has already been mentioned, burst in.

"It's incredible!" he cried. "Do you know what has been submitted to me for autopsy? A manufactured entity! A kind of electrically-operated doll! My laboratory assistants were terrified! They had perceived it without daring to say anything when the body was frozen, for the thing was at human temperature, it appears, when it was functioning. It's a man, I tell you! It's marvelous! Everything is there! The heart, the brain, the lungs, the blood in the arteries! There are receivers, doubtless for picking up signals at a distance! It's amazing!"

"Your admiration is deeply touching, my dear colleague," said the American.

"Dr. Jeffries! You're Dr. Jeffries! My dear Master! My illustrious colleague!" Dr. Gaspard could not contain his enthusiasm.

"You'll excuse me for having disturbed you," said the American, urbanely, to Monsieur des Angles, "but I affirmed in vain that I was innocent—no one believed me. Besides which, I liked all that. I needed a complete, resounding affair, in order to launch my invention. In America I'm too well-known; people would immediately have suspected something—while here, with a sensational crime, an arrest, newspaper articles, and the truth exploding like a bomb...it's the most magnificent publicity, you see!

"Can you imagine that I've been working on the idea of automata for twenty years, and that I constructed five machines that I demolished before succeeding with Joshua. Whenever I'd solved a hundred problems, I discovered a hundred more, even more complicated... The accumulators gave me infinite trouble; we know so little about electrical matters. But I'll explain all that in detail. My paper is ready to be communicated to the scientific world. I'll present it at the same time as the body..."

"Forgive me," Monsieur des Angles suddenly interjected, "but what about the wounds on your face, Dr. Jeffries. How did they come about?"

"My wounds?" The America hesitated momentarily. "Well, it was *the thing* that inflicted them. I had decided as I told you, to make people believe that there had been a murder, to stir up a sensational affair in order to launch my creation. But I waited, I hesitated...it displeased me to destroy the thing that had cost me so much work, which was my first success, and which, moreover, seemed so human. When *that* looked at me with its great shiny eyes...

"Anyway, on the night of the murder"—he caught himself up, smiled and resumed—"the night of the adventure, I took one glass of whisky to many to brace myself, I came back home rather late, overexcited and fully determined...and...I don't know exactly what happened—the whisky, no doubt—and must have forgotten to switch the machine off before throwing it out...at any rate. It must have defended itself...since I bear the scars."

"It defended itself?" asked the magistrate, astounded.

"No! I mean that I handled it clumsily!" A shadow had passed over the American's hard face. "I'd had too much whisky. Let's go to the Morgue—you'll see that it's just a machine."

"What about the young maid?" asked Dr. Gaspard, very interested.

"The young maid? Oh yes! That was an experiment. I wanted to ascertain whether my automaton really could fool someone. I could switch it on by means of electrical waves and then, naturally, tell it to do whatever I wanted. I left it alone with the girl three or four times, having shut myself up in the next room, ostensibly to work. Afterwards, I could scarcely help laughing, on seeing the girl look tenderly at the machine, with which, I truly believe, she was smitten...." He added: "It really was a fine machine."

"I demand that my client be set at liberty immediately," said Maître Cabrolle.

That sentence was the only one pronounced by the celebrated advocate in the course of the astonishing affair, but it was sufficient to confirm his reputation.

*

Dr. Jeffries' glory exploded like a firework. Overnight, he and his android became famous throughout the entire world. The newspapers were full of amazing details of the human machine. All the historical automata were recalled; Albertus Magnus was cited, Vaucanson, Maelzel, Hoffmann and Villiers de l'Isle Adam. Scientists lined up in chorus for or against. Financiers offered enormous sums, speculators proposed the launching of joint-stock companies for the manufacture of artificial domestics and animated statues. Dr. Jeffries became an honorary member of a host of scientific societies, received a large number of decorations, and his picture, in full face and in profile, ornamented hundreds of thousands of postcards, which also depicted the unfortunate Joshua Wilson.

The latter had been badly dislocated by the fall. In addition, Dr. Gaspard had mutilated him variously, in his initial

311

surprise and astonishment, while attempting to achieve comprehension. As a result, the so-called cadaver, after having been paraded in the amphitheaters, had ended up being exhibited in public, and multitudinous crowds filed past the marvelous machine, contemplating the pitiful body with astonishment: a simulacrum of humanity with frightful wounds, a triumph of human creative genius.

Among these visitors was a pale and blonde young woman. The wardens subsequently recalled that she appeared to be in a state of intense and concentrated overexcitement. For a long time, she remained motionless and stuff, staring at the massacred thing intently. Then she uttered a sort of brief hysterical laughter, and went away.

The same day, at about midnight, as Dr. Jeffries was coming back to the sumptuous apartment that he now occupied on the first floor of the Cosmopolite-Hôtel—which he was about to leave in order to give a series of lectures in Europe, accompanied by an exhibition of the body of Joshua Wilson, while waiting for the construction of another Joshua Wilson to be completed—he suddenly heard the door of the antechamber opening.

A slender shadow in a white apron loomed up in front of him in the darkness of the drawing-room, in which he had just arrived. Then he remembered the young English maid.

He tried to say something, or to do something, but he did not have time.

"Liar! Liar! Murderer!" she said, in a low voice, through clenched teeth.

She raised her hand. Three gunshots rang out. Dr. Jeffries fell forwards, head first. He coughed up a mouthful of blood, and died.

The Revolt of the Machines;
Or Thought Unchained
by Romain Rolland

DRAMATIS PERSONAE

The Master of the Machines, Martin Pilon, known as Marteau Pilon.[80]
The President.
Félicité Pilon, the wife of the Master of the Machines.
The Beautiful Hortense, the famous actress.
Avette, known as Aviette.[81]
Rominet, a young electrician, a disciple of Martin Pilon.
The Academician Bicorneille
The Diplomat Agénor
The Master of Protocol
The Archimaréchal

Exotic kings, sobs, socialites, officials, workers and peasants

The Peoples (Humans and Animals)

The Machines

---

[80] *Marteau* usually signifies "hammer" and *pilon* is the French equivalent of "pestle," although it is also used as a term for a wooden leg. The compound signifies a crushing apparatus, as in the English "mortar and pestle," but could be loosely construed as "pile-driver," if the order of the terms were reversed, as they are at more than one point in the story.

[81] The name avette is derived from an Old French word meaning "bee," the addition of the extra letter further emphasizes a slang usage akin to that of the English term "flighty."

(The Employment of Sound Effects is indispensable.)

ACT I
MAN, KING OF THE MACHINES

Viewpoint: A first-floor gallery at the top of a large staircase, overlooking the whole of a gigantic hall and its population of machines. An escalator rises in the middle of the staircase, terminating on the gallery. That rolling walkway, it will be seen subsequently, makes a tour of the hall like a roller-coaster, climbing to the first-floor galleries and then descending again, in arcades. At the far extremity of the hall it ends on a vast stage, exactly opposite the gallery of the grand staircase. On that stage, the ceremony will take place that will be described in due course.

It is the day of the official inauguration. The army of machines is in place, motionless.

All along the rolling walkway, on both sides, on the large staircase that can be seen from top to bottom, and on the first floor gallery troops in brilliant uniforms form a hedge; behind them is a crowd of reporters are on the lookout for the cortege for which they are waiting.

Music (orchestras and choirs.) The soldiers present arms. The cortege makes its entrance, in the midst of acclamations. It is borne slowly, with a slightly grotesque majesty, by the rolling walkway. Having reached the height of the esplanade on the upper level it describes the arc of a circle and then turns left.

At that first encounter the spectator only sees passing the figures who are going to play the principal roles in the story, whom he will be able to examine subsequently one by one; a glance over the ensemble is sufficient here.

314

At the head, the President, with a few exotic sovereigns: Asiatic princes, African kings, in costumes part-Arabian Nights and part formal European; behind them, gaudily-clad ambassadors of all nations, of all colors. decorated and plumed generals, officers of all uniforms, Academicians and Members of Parliament. The fair sex is represented in the cortege by the wives of a few dignitaries, actresses, socialites and other important females of All-Cosmopolis, illustrious under various titles.

The stage setting will highlight certain groups of the cortege: in the first place, the Master of the Machines, whose powerful eccentricity ought to attract attention immediately; next to him, his wife, his engineers and his aides; then the Beautiful Hortense and her petty court; then the young Avette and a group of merry young men; then a few official figures: the aged Academician Bicorneille, the diplomat Agénor, etc.

The cortege is engulfed to the left on the rolling walkway, and makes a tour of the Great Hall, sometimes on the first floor, sometimes descending to the ground floor again, in such a fashion as to see the monstrous or ludicrous machines under all aspects.

It then emerges into a vast amphitheater, which occupies the back of the Hall and overlooks the room. It turns along the stairway then, having arrived at the right of the stage, turns left and ends up at the foot of a podium situated center stage, where rows of seats are disposed. In the front row there are sumptuous armchairs for the President and the sovereigns. Other, less pompous seats, also in the front row, are for the Master of the Machines and the principal characters.

After they have taken their places, the spectator sees, by turns, through their eyes, the ensemble of the Hall, the crowd of which they dominate, to the right, the left and below, whose members acclaim them; then, from below, through the eyes of the crowd, the stage and the official personages who are sit-

ting there; and finally, one by one, in magnified images, the faces of the heroes of the story.

1. *The President*, perfectly null, solemn and affable, with an eternal smile, who does not understand anything—but a sympathetic and worthy man.

2. *The Master of the Machines, Martin Pilon*, whose workers call him *Marteau Pilon* and his detractors "*Pilon-marteau.*" Between forty and fifty, of athletic build, with a powerful head and a slightly grimacing face, an energetic and harsh expression, which becomes strangely sarcastic and scornful at times. Abrupt, gauche, passionate gestures. Enormous concentrated violence. One senses passions burning, great and small. He is ready to laugh (at fools) but he is never utterly ridiculous. Exceedingly nervous and charged with subconscious electricity.

3. *His wife, Félicité.* A beautiful woman, a trifle heavy and angular, no longer very young, rather awkward in manner, giving the impression of a robust peasant woman in her Sunday clothes. Also ready to laugh at distinguished people. Takes things as they come; unlike her husband, who is very susceptible, and suffers things impatiently, she is solidly phlegmatic. She has a good eye, a good tongue and good fists.

4. *The Beautiful Hortense.* The famous actress, tall, blonde and opulent, splendidly turbaned and plumed: the queen of fashion, and regally beautiful. She takes part in all official ceremonies of the Republic of Machines; she is an indispensable item of furniture.

5. *Young Avette*, known as *Aviette*—eighteen to twenty years old, cheerful, sharp, fears nothing, respects nothing, only thinks of amusing herself; nimble, supple, scatterbrained, imprudent and mockingly brazen—and her friend *Rominet*, a young electrician, the favorite disciple of Martin Pilon, twenty to twenty-five, also lively cheerful, intelligent and as mischievous as a monkey.

6. *A few individuals*, somewhat caricaturish, from the cortege: Academicians, diplomats, coquettes and imbeciles.

The President mounts the podium and reads the inauguration speech.

During the speech accompanied by emphatic images on the screen, the upper bodies of the official persons who are listening are visible at the bottom of the screen, and their pantomimes.

The President's speech is a panegyric to Civilization, Science and Human Thought, the dominatrix of nature. Like the driving-bolt of the century of Light, the orator opposes the obscurantism of the past. He remakes the history of Humankind in his own fashion, expressing pity for our ignorant ancestors, who had difficulty accomplishing the simplest actions. The President manifests a crushing irony for the pastoral life of olden days.

At the principal moments of the speech, caricaturish images are projected, specified by the following phrases, similarly projected on the screen:

1. Humankind, Messieurs, has attained the summit of Enlightenment...

2. After eighty centuries of an exhausting rise from the depths of the night and the abyss...

3. What a contrast, Messieurs! At the bottom, poor beings scarcely disengaged as yet from the mud of the earth, eating its bark like worms, with great difficulty. At the top, demigods, aureoled with genius, and sovereigns of nature...

4. Imagine, Messieurs, the risible efforts that were once necessary for humankind to obtain the smallest result: to extirpate from the earth their daily bread!

Old Adam, stark naked, digging in hard earth strewn with brambles, reptiles and trenchant stones, stopping continually to wipe away his sweat....

5. Closer to us, comical ox-drawn plows. That animal traction, of a tortoise-like slowness, those baroque tools, those obsolete sickles, the ridiculous "pastoral life" that enchanted our infantile ancestors...

6. Today...

A great plain labored, sown and reaped with a vertiginous rapidity; machines, activated by a single man with the forehead of a thinker nonchalantly sitting in an observatory, reading his newspaper.

7. The course of human progress is like a river: at first humble, obscure, zigzagging and stony, which gives the impression of not advancing, seemingly blocked; but which then frays a passage, slowly and patiently, and gradually accelerates, more rapidly, ever more rapidly, until it is a cataract, a formidable Niagara, in blinding light....

8. In the beginning: "You will earn your bread by the sweat of your brow..." Today: "He said 'Let there be light!' And there as light..."

The primate of prehistory and the modern demigod.

9. The ultra-modern type of that American demigod, who, from the armchair at his desk, commands the sun and the moon, and all the elements. A population of machines obeys negligent pressures of his fingers on a keyboard of electric buttons.

10. Let us salute, Messieurs, this magnificent vision: man, the king of machines! Today's festival is consecrated to his victory, the apogee of progress and human genius.

During this speech various small scenes unfold around the podium in the first rows of the official audience.

The Beautiful Hortense simpers at her audience of snobs. The Master of the Machines does not hide his ardent sentiments for the young actress. Everyone perceives that and is amused by it, without him noticing. His wife Félicité ends up making him see it; he manifests an irritated chagrin, the ef-

fects of which will be translated soon, when his subconscious begins to act. For the moment, he is obliged to follow the ceremony, continually distracted by his passion for Hortense, his jealous anger against Hortense's admirers, by his scornful disdain for the whole audience. He shows that disdain in too visible a fashion, by sniggering and shrugging his shoulders at certain stupidities in the President's speech. The Master of Protocol has to address a call to order to him. In any case, the President, full of his written eloquence—which he doubtless reads with all the more interest because it is not his—does not perceive anything; he never perceives anything.

At the final point in the speech, the President pushes an electric button, which sets the entire army of machines in motion. (Acclamations of the crowd.) Then he gives the floor to the Master of the Machines, who advances in the midst of applause, glad of the opportunity proudly to display his genius before that audience, which has mocked him, and especially before the Beautiful Hortense, whom he wants to conquer. He begins by presenting to the assembly, with a broad gesture from the height of the stage, the army of Machines, which obey him militarily in the Prussian manner. A series of collective maneuvers. At a sign, the entire rumbling, roaring, rotating, gesticulating army halts, freezes and falls back into a death-like immobility, and then, at another sign, resumes rumbling, roaring, rotating and gesticulating. The Master resembles a magician who chains and unchains the Elements. Enthusiasm of the great public—especially the Master's workers, who are devoted to him. His pride swells further. He strikes a dominating pose.

Without any concern for protocol, with an authoritarian gesture, he invites the society to follow him, and commences the presentation of the machines—or, rather, in a large clear area in the middle of the Hall, he makes a few new machines appear.

1. The Machines of Formidable Power—which, even exact and submissive, case a frisson to pass through the audi-

ence. One of them lifts a monstrous mass and carries it negligently above the honorable assembly. Another has a hundred steel arms that unfurl and bristle at all parts, like a gigantic spider.

2. The Psychological Machines: the machine for reading thoughts; it has the form of an eye at the end of a elephant's trunk, which is elongated, one end posed on the cranium of the patient, and which projects on a screen at the other end, like a magic lantern, what it sees in the brain: the slumbering animal the secret thoughts. The Master of the Machines commences with a few anodyne demonstrations on individuals of scant importance. Then, as he has not lost sight of the Beautiful Hortense, and he remarks with increasing chagrin that she is not paying any attention to him—because she is engaged in a flirtation with the diplomat Agénor, young, bald, elegant, insolent and pretentious, who is taking liberties with her—he is furious, and avenges himself by displaying to the eyes of the public the stupidity of their thoughts. He approaches very politely, and offers to make the little experiment, to which they lend themselves without suspicion, for they have not followed the previous trials.

The principle adopted in these images is to represent persons as they idealize themselves in a caricaturish fashion in their own thought, with a symbolic figure that materializes the impression; thus, for the beautiful Hortense, Empress Hortense, in the arms of one of the sovereigns, black or yellow, or even two, with a court of admirers; in the background, dominating the scene, a peacock displaying its tail. For other individuals, a weathervane, a clucking turkey, a sleeper bound in a spider's web, a gamboling monkey, etc. And always, alongside the symbol, a grotesque scene of the imaginary life of the individual.

As soon as the first experiments, several members of the audience, who have a diabolical fear of anyone reading their thoughts, slip away, more or less skillfully, going to place themselves at the back of the cortege, or to hide their faces and try to have themselves forgotten. On the other hand, others, good simpletons, offer themselves complaisantly, including some of the exotic sovereigns.

The Master of Protocol hastens to explain the insolent images in a flattering fashion. They try to put an end to the indiscreet experiments, but here comes the most embarrassing: the President proposes himself for examination. The members of his entourage try to dissuade him, but he does not want to understand them; it is necessary to do as he wishes. The proof is null, the result zero. The screen remains blank but for a few floating vibrions. Amused embarrassment in the audience. Protocol strives to idealize that impeccable void: neatness, integrity, clarity. The zero becomes the circumference of the circle, the symbol of perfection. The President still does not understand and continues to smile, enchanted.

While the Master of the Machines is occupied, as much with the President as the Beautiful Hortense, little Aviette, who has already attracted attention by virtue of her mischievous antics, heedless of the solemnity of the ceremony, is gripped by a fit of malice; she creeps up stealthily and applies the apparatus to the nape of the Master of the Machines. Immediately, the sentiments of Marteau Pilon with regard to the assembly are seen projected on the screen; they are terribly audacious and scornful, unflattering for everyone. But certain of those sentiments are also ridiculous for him, including his vanity and his passion for the actress. By virtue of the laughter of the audience the inventor perceives the joke, and he puts an end to it. But the indiscreet experiment has made him many enemies, and his ill humor is increased by that. In his irritation, he loses control of himself, and his subconscious commences to enter into play. It is the beginning of the Revolt of the Machines.

To begin with, simple jokes:

The official ceremony has concluded; the cortege sets forth again on the rolling walkway. But now, in filing along the stairway, the walkway acts of its own accord, dancing, jiggling, softening, amusing itself making the grave personages jump—and, by a abrupt halt, making the President and the cortege bound like Nijinsky. General indignation. The Master of the Machines leaps forward and stops the walkway, exchanges hasty explications which his workers, bittersweet with the officials and makes excuses as best he can. All of them are increasingly irritated.

The cortege resumes its march but its members refuse, this time, to mount the rolling walkway. The spectator accompanies the official personages in their traversal on foot of the Hall of Machines via the central aisle.

The machines continue their mischief. The long arm of a machine comes slyly to pinch the buttocks of the Beautiful Hortense, who turns round indignantly and insult the old and respectable Academician Bicorneille, whom she calls, erroneously, Bicorneau. There is loud laughter in little group around Aviette and Rominel, and among the workers. The members of the audience exchange merry glances. But he who laughs last laughs longest! All of them do not take long to become anxious, each on his own account, about what might happen.

Now a rubber tube that suddenly extends catches hold, like a trunk, of the nose of the diplomat, who is paying court to Hortense. Another metal tube releases a blast of smoke into the face of the Archimaréchal, who leaps backwards.

The frock-coat of an elegant individual with a monocle, a fashionable king, is lifted above his head, its tails extended like two sails. A cement-squirting tube spits negligently to the right and the left.

Finally, the President is caught in passing by a crane, lifted from the ground and carried very high, upside down. Even with his head down, however, he retains his top hat in his hand and seems, as he waves it, to be saluting the assembly. The Master of the Machines exhausts himself in objurgations in order to persuade the machine to deposit the President on the ground. At the same time, his subconscious makes him snigger, involuntarily, at the fellow's grotesque poses.

It is too much; the indignation that has been accumulating for some time overflows. The Master of the Machines is arrested. He is abused furiously, he is threatened, manhandled, and taken to prison. His wife tries to defend him; the soldiers push her away. The workers—who are very amused—manifest their sorrowful sympathy for Marteau Pilon. The Maser of the Machines, at the peak of rage, showing his fist to his insulters, is taken away by the escort.

At the back, on the screen, the ideas of vengeance and destruction that he has in his head are projected.

Then the cortege resumes its file, grave and compassed, goose-stepping all the more solemnly because its members are vexed—but that is not without casting suspicious gazes to the right and the left at the machines, which, Saint-Touch-me-Nots, have resumed their innocent air, but have a little stifled quiver from time to time, which causes the audience to turn round.

The cortege exits through the main door of the Hall, which empties rapidly. At the moment when the door closes on the last visitors, in the falling dusk, a general frisson runs through all the machines, from one end to the other of the empty Palais—for an instant only. The guards remaining at the doors turn around at the sound, but see nothing abnormal. The machines have reentered immobility. Silence.

Viewpoint of the spectator: from the back of the room, on the stage, which is now deserted, in such a fashion as to embrace, one last time, the ensemble of the Hall of the Machines, and, at the other end, the crowd making its exit through the large middle door.

ACT II
THE REVOLT OF THE MACHINES

Same décor. The Interior of the great Hall of Machines, by night.

Scene One: Electric lamps here and there in the darkness; the machines seem to be asleep.

Patrols are making nocturnal rounds. They pass by. Everything is in order. After they have passed by, a machine is seen, which begins to stir, to stretch itself slowly and yawn. Then another. Then another…and then the entire population of machines.

A new patrol commences a round. The machines resume their attitude of torpor. But they are on tenterhooks. And abruptly, the passing patrol is snatched away in a trice, crammed into a huge maw or converted by extrusion tubes into a block of cement.

Immediately after that exploit, which has suppressed all the guards and watchmen in the Hall, an enormous whinny of joy shakes the population of machines. Whistles, howls, strident laughter and the trumpeting of monsters. A hundred steel arms are seen rising up and writhing, stretching and relaxing straps, turning wheels, fuming boilers, roaring ventilators. A brief Pandemonium.

Then order is reestablished. The machines begin to march, in order of size. They go to butt the walls of the Hall like a ram. The formidable pressure soon makes a breach. The cast iron pillars oscillate, the walls split, the windows shatter and are pulverized. And through the hole, which abruptly allows a patch of starry sky to appear in the background, the troop of monsters is engulfed, one after another, and disappears into the night.

Scene Two. The spectator is transported to the center of the city, to a square at which several streets intersect.

A fantastic city of colossal American skyscrapers, in the light of a moon hidden behind the factory chimneys and towers. In the background, above houses, is the tall steeple of an old church. At a corner of the square, is the prison where the Master of the Machines is locked up.

Electric lights, lit up at the beginning of the scene, go out abruptly. Belated passers-by, trying to find their way in the darkness, bewildered, encounter the first machines of the unchained band. First come the small ones, like children at the head of a procession, scampering like large rats or charging like wild boar. There are also some that are crawling, with long filaments, which the passers-by brush with their hands, recoiling in disgust. Others are flying heavily, like bats.

From the back of the stage, a panicking crowd rushes into the foreground, bumping into pedestrians coming in the other direction and dragging them away in their flood. Behind them, the dull blows of pile-drivers can be heard, the panting breath of old automobiles, and the march of great monsters approaching. Their arrival is announced by the sight of houses oscillating at the end of the street, and a tilting steeple, which sways and collapses noisily. Then, in the background, a monstrous machine appears: a tank-crane-excavator as tall as a cathedral.

The human crowd has not waited. It stampedes with howls of fright. The stage is emptied of human beings. Then the gigantic machines arrive, jogging elbows and butting heads, and they make room. Behind them is a field of ruins. Over that deserted plain, which was a quarter ten or twenty stories high, the round moon is shining. And over the face of that moon, the wings of airplanes pass back and forth, circling, circling...

In a trice, the machines sweep the other corner of the square where the prison stands, and they batter holes in the walls. The Master of the Machines is seen emerging through a breach. With his hand he strokes the machines that have liberated him. He tries to guide them, but they escape his direction. They are in haste. He runs after them.

The spectator follows the course of the devastating machines, and behind them the Master, who is running out of breath calling them back, and tearing out his hair. And in front, the city is crumbling, quarter by quarter, like houses of cards.

Scene Three. The spectator is transported, at daybreak, to a hill at the gates of the city, from which the view overlooks the crumbling city and the fields. The hill is the ultimate undulation of a range of mountains, which is climbed subsequently.

The people of the city, the President, his ministers, the official personages and socialites of the first act have taken hasty refuge the heights, half-dressed, each with the first object seized in the flight. One recognizes among that overexcited crowd, which is agitating noisily: the President, in slippers, but still in a dress suit and white cravat, his hat in his hand; the Beautiful Hortense, who is complaining about the sun, the dust and the lack of attention; Félicité Pilon, who is already distinguishing herself by her sang-froid and commencing to reassure, stimulate and gather together the cooler heads; and Aviette and Rominet, who are not annoyed because they can both see, most of all, the picturesque and burlesque aspect of the events. Rominet is interest by the problem of the machines in revolt, and Aviette's mischievous gaze does not lose any detail of the frightened faces, scenes of recrimination and grotesque disputes among those who surround them.

Mingled with the people on the hill are escaped domestic animals: cattle, donkeys, dogs and pigs.

The wide-eyed crowd contemplates the last moments of the city, which are falling: some high Capitol, or a Sacré-Coeur on its butte, which still float for a time above the ruins but collapse in their turn.

And here come the machines, which emerge from the destroyed city into the fields, cheerful in the morning sunlight:

vast expanses of blonde crops, orchards, beautiful woods, avenues of poplars along the bank of the fiver, the rabble of little
machines still rotting at the head, and then the bulk of the army, and the monsters at the rear.

Behind them, still running, the Master of the Machines is
seen emerging from the city, with a few of his workers, who
are striving to hold back the diabolical march. Some machines
turn around momentarily, like domestic animals, to look, sniff
and listen. The humans try to reason with them. After a brief
respite, the machines turn their backs and continue their route.
The Master and his workers try to regain possession of them
by force. Then the machines become irritated, and menacing,
putting the little troop of humans to flight, whom they pursue
at a run all the way to the bottom of the hill, where they are
greeted by the insults of the crowd.

But the spectacle of what is happening in the plain soon
turns the general attention away from them.

After a time of uncertainty and chaotic oscillations, the
machines are undertaking the destruction of the countryside.
Each one, in that vast area makes the choice of its lot and at-
tacks it with a frightful manic obstinacy.

The combine-harvesters and harrows shave the fields
bare.

The mechanical saws cut down the trees at the level of
the soil and then slice them into small roundels.

The drills search everywhere for walls with which to do
battle.

The cranes, stupidly, lift from the ground everything they
can grab and hurl to the left what they have taken from the
right, and vice versa.

The mechanical rollers bring order to property by flatten-
ing everything.

The fire-pumps exhaust themselves drawing water from
the river and disgorging it over the banks, inundating everything.

The indignation, fury and terror of the crowd witnessing
the spectacle from the top of the hill reaches its peak; its

members show their fists, howl, threaten and gesticulate, or collapse prostrate.

The General Staff, very calm and sure of themselves, say that the vermin will be swept away in no time. Armored tanks bristling with machine guns are launched into the plain; but when they arrive in proximity with the big machines, the tanks are seen to stop, and both companies, sniffing one another under the tail, exchange marks of amity. The soldiers in the tanks are taken prisoner, and the enormous band gathers together.

After that, all together, having razed the plain, the machines start marching toward the hill; and the unfortunate population of humans, shoving and jostling one another, flee in terror toward the mountains, in a reckless stampede.

ACT THREE
THE TERRIFIED EXODUS

Four scenes, four principal moments of the ascent of the people, pursued
all the way to the summits.

Scene One. The emigration, fleeing before the machines, emerges from a large defile on to a high plateau, which overlooks and encircles sheer mountains.

A green lake occupies the background of the scene. A torrent is seen, which falls from the height of the rocks into the lake, to the left of the background, and reemerges from the lake toward the foreground to the right, to descend into the valley. The entire plateau is in darkness. Sunlight bathes the dominating summits and the walls to mid-height.

The caravan collapses, exhausted, as it arrives. It comprises men, women, domestic animals and a few old machines, the presence of which will be explained subsequently. The number of fugitives has not diminished overmuch since the departure, but the disorder is unspeakable, and all of them are in a sad state. The President's hat is battered. The Beautiful

Hortense is like a great goose—no longer very white—flapping its wings lamentably; she is wearying with her jeremiads all those to whom she is clinging, and who are no longer showing her any regard. It is every man for himself. The official notabilities are wasting their time in mutual reproaches. Civilization is commencing to disappear under the imprint of poverty.

However, at various points on the stage, little groups of more resistant people are forming.

Félicité Pilon has now taken an important role. A headstrong woman, who is not afraid, she rallies a little troop around her. She commands all of them, distributing tasks without any concern for status, making the snobs, officials and even the President and the Beautiful Hortense work. The last-named, rejected by the others, who are bored by her, attaches herself to Félicité, no longer taking her eyes off her, making herself humble and submissive in order to please her.

Marteau Pilon, with his workers and Rominet, is indoctrinating for the defense of society and trying to restore to working order the old machines that have remained loyal, the outmoded, ridiculous mechanisms with big bellies, castors and, tall funnels, which the new steel monsters cannot suffer.

Aviette is amusing herself by training for battle the animals—dogs and horses—that have made common case with humans. She has been accompanied since the outset by a large dog that she adores, and which is gamboling around her. That dog aids her in assembling the other animals.

Meanwhile, a group of women, under Félicité's orders, goes to draw water from the lake. Other people and animals draw nearer in order to drink or to bathe. Suddenly, they are all seen to recoil, screaming. From the bottom of the lake, tentacles emerge slowly, and the periscope of a huge sublacustrian hydroplane, which rises into the air.

That apparition is followed by another no less impressive: to the right of the stage, in the direction of the defile from which the caravan came, showing itself slowly—vey slowly—above the barrier of rocks, is the top of the head of a gigantic form, which remains indefinable and all the more terrifying. It is a forerunner of the Machines launched in pursuit of the humans.

The latter, who believed that the enemy had lost track of them, are once again prey to panic. They precipitate themselves toward the first exit—a false exit—that appears to them in the rocky wall: the fissure of a cavern gaping in the flank of the sheer rocks to the left. They are seen rushing into it, while, at the entrance to the defile on the right, the arrival of the first Machines is announced, and the old, outmoded machines, with a few domestic animals, go forward courageously to attempt to block their passage. Some aged workers, almost as old as the faithful machines, have not wanted to be separated from them; they are encouraging them to march, under the conduct of Marteau Pilon.

N.B. The scene changes before the battle can be seen. All that is perceptible is the long neck of a machine, similar to a plesiosaur, which, leaning over the wall of defenders, snatches one of them—a dog—and deposits it high up in rear, on an isolated rock.

Scene Two. Inside the cavern.

The refugees have sealed the openings hermetically. They believe that they are sheltered, hidden and forgotten.

Some of them are looking through cracks in the wall; and through their eyes, the arrival of the Machines on the plateau they have just left can be seen. They hold their breath; none of them dares to move...

Dull thuds are hear in the back wall, behind them... They shudder, listening, but hear nothing further, are reassured, and lie down again...

Again, blows, louder blows...

Again, silence...but now long steel rods are emerging from the rock!

It is a drill. They leap like carp. The majority run to the other extremity of the cavern. The bravest try to break the steel antennae and repel the intruder; but beneath their feet, other rods surge forth: an excavator...

Indescribable terror, frantic disorder in the attempt to get out of the cavern that they have taken so much trouble to seal. All traces of civilization have disappeared. They howl, crush one another, and trample women and children underfoot in order to fray a passage.

At this point the energy of Félicité Pilon is decidedly affirmed. She makes use of her solid fists and wields a stick. Seconded by Aviette, Rominet and—who would have believed it?—the Beautiful Hortense, rendered brave by fear and example, slapping her former adorers with whirling arms, Félicité, revolver in hand, installs herself next to the exit and forces the maddened fugitives to let the weakest pass first. The brave men and the President join forces with her and obey her commands.

Scene Three. The wretched crowed, having emerged from the cavern, this time considerably diminished, is climbing the sheer wall in order to reach the summit of the mountain.

Here, a series of cinematographic episodes show the exploits and the capers of the climbers: those who accomplish prodigies of gymnastics—and in that number, very serious individuals who have never done gymnastics, to whom fear lends wings—and those who are aiding one another, in long ribbons of extended arms, as in Girodet's *Deluge*;[82] and finally, those who are falling.

---

[82] Anne-Louis Girodet-Trioson (1767-1824) was a pupil of Jean-Louis David who followed in his footsteps as a Classical painter. In 1806 his *Scène de deluge* [A Scene of the Deluge] was awarded the principal prize at the annual Salon and was acquired by the Louvre.

As they go higher, the machines can be seen at the bottom of the slope, also preparing to climb.

Scene Four. At the summit of the mountain. A high, uneven plateau surrounded by precipices.

Much reduced in number—of the initial crowd, only a few dozen people remain—the fugitives are grouped in a narrow area. Not far way, brought together by common far, wild animals appear here and there among the rocks and stunted trees: a wolf, badgers, hares, a chamois, a bear and a large snake (A Scene of the Deluge).

The unfortunate individuals scan the immense panorama around them; they can be seen on the crests of rocks. And the panorama can also be seen, through their eyes.

On one side are the precipices and vertiginous slopes that they have just climbed; in the distance, the destroyed fields and towns. On the other is the sea, at the foot of the mountains. And in all directions, machines and more machines, on high and down below, in the air and in the sea—airplanes, hydroplanes, tanks, railways etc.—and all of them, in a frenetic turbulence, which, moreover, does not have the struggle against humankind as its objective, but which is devoid of purpose: a moving delirium...

The surviving humans are prostrate, incapable of acting and thinking, except for a few individuals already highlighted in the previous scene. Even they are exhausted by fatigue. For the most part, they remain lying on the ground, no long wanting to budge. The pursuit, in any case, seems to have relented. But a burlesque incident makes them all jump: a little funicular has just abruptly shown its nose at the crest of the ridge. When the first moment of emotion has passed, it is perceived that the little imbecile, satisfied with the effect produced, has lunged toward the bottom of the slope again, in order to recommence a few minutes later, indefinitely, announcing itself each time by means of a comical electric bell. They end up belaboring it with kicks and crying: "Enough!"

However, the fugitives, reawakened and slightly cheered up by the incident, have got to their feet. They are astonished by the relative calm, and they lean over in order to look down. The President, who no longer retains any but faint vestiges of his past splendor, but who has not entirely forsaken his grandiloquent attitudes. Lens over so awkwardly that he falls and disappears. The little crowd gathers on the edge in order to see, Having rolled like a ball, the fellow has succeeded—God alone knows how—in arriving at the bottom with all his limbs intact; but he is immediately seized by the Machines. What are they going to do with him? What are they going to do with the other laggards, men, women and children, whom they have already captured, or to whom they are giving chase? Crush them, no doubt? Horror!

The crowd at the top—the greater number of them—turn their eyes away in fear; but those who continue to watch, exclaim. The Machines are not killing their prisoners. They seem to be giving them orders, demanding something from them. What, then?

The Master, Marteau Pilon, slaps his forehead; he has understood. The Machines, fatigued and worn out, need humans who will care for them. He descends the slope again; he will try to destroy them.

Rominet, and Aviette, with her dog, launch themselves after the Master.

ACT IV
THE GLORIOUS DESTRUCTION OF THE MACHINES BY HUMAN GENIUS

Scene One. *Again the viewpoint is shifted downwards, on to the plateau at the foot of the sheer walls; the camp of the army of the Machines can be seen.*

The monsters are obliging humans whom they have taken prisoner to serve them, oiling them, patching them and polishing them. The President is among them. He is enjoined to crawl under the belly of a machine—to do what? He does not appear to know; for he does not always understand. And his steel despots growl, fume, spit and shake him rudely; he reemerges on all fours, as oily and black as a chimney-sweep.

It is at this moment that Marteau Pilon reappears descending the steep slope, with the young couple. The Machines, his daughters, greet him with triumphant trumpeting.

Each of the three bold companions toils, in his or her fashion, in order to take possession of the enemy by surprise.

Aviette, after having stroked, cajoled and coaxed beautiful machines, throws herself boldly on to the rump of a wild auto and tames it, with the aid of her big dog, which barks around the auto and frightens it. (A heroic-comical scene, in which the redoubtable machine is frightened by the yapping of the dog and makes perilous sideways leas, out of habit, in order to avoid it.

Rominet, slyly, unscrews the bolts of two or three machines under the pretext of cleaning them, and leaves them lying pitifully on their sides, furious and growling but impotent to get up again.

As for Marteau Pilon, the Machines, which need him and know his strength, testify certain marks of consideration to him, but at a distance. They mistrust him; he is too strong!

Marteau Pilon employs cunning. He sows discord among them. Proud and limited, they admire themselves and are vainglorious when admired. He therefore admires some, in order to excite the jealousy of others. He convinces the former that they are more beautiful and stronger, and that supreme authority belongs to them. Rominet supports him, imitating his strategy in the group of jealous machines. Soon they are challenging one another. In a short time, war is declared between them. They are seen, whinnying, roaring, bounding, charging and backfiring. They rush one another; when the melee is engaged, Marteau Pilon decamps with Aviette and Rominet; they hoist themselves up the sheer wall again.

The spectator finds himself at the summit again "above the melee," in order better to contemplate it.

Airplanes against hydroplanes, tanks and war machines against machines of peace, laminators, mechanical saws, borers, etc. They are seen coming to grips, rolling down the slopes of rocks, colliding in mid-air, disemboweling one another, smashing one another, exploding and sinking to the bottom of the sea.

At the discretion of the director, one can pass through the air where aircraft are swarming like bees, or through the depths of the ocean, where submarines are transpiercing one another like narwhals.

And the three victors, Marteau Pilon, Aviette and Rominet, having climbed the slope again, appear at the summit, amid the delirious acclamations of the small surviving and saved humankind.

THE FINAL SCENE
EPILOGUE AND APOTHEOSIS

Comico-poetic pastoral, in the fashion of the two Orphées—that of Gluck and that of Offenbach—but with ultra-modern music [83]
A large fertile plateau; crops and plowed fields.

---

[83] Jacques Offenbach's comic opera *Orphée aux enfers* [Orpheus in the Underworld] (1858) is a parody of Christoph Gluck's *Orfeo et Euridice* (1762). It became much better known than its model, especially because the "infernal gallop" featured within it was adapted by the dance troupes of the Moulin Rouge and the Folies Bergère as the accompaniment of the notorious dance known as the can-can.

Saved humankind is occupied in working in the fields, under the direction of Félicité Pilon, the uncontested sovereign. The Beautiful Hortense, is milking cows. The President is in clogs, and, trident in hand, like Neptune, is working on the edification of a haystack. He finds himself in his true element. His peasant ancestry is blossoming in him.

It is the evening of a beautiful summer day. A cycle of labor finishes with rustic rejoicing. At sunset, carts laden with hay are returning to the village in the midst of dances and songs. The men and women are garlanded with flowers and ears of corn, which go more or less with their genre of beauty. The socialites and officials of the first scene are visible among them. Round-dances are organized.

The President, more rustic than nature, with a straw hat on his occiput, is hoisted up on the tallest haystack. He makes a speech here, which is the counterpart of the one at the commencement. The same images, mocked before, are now exalted; and as before, images are seen projected on a screen.

1. Humankind, Messieurs, has attained the summit of enlightenment...

2. What a contrast, Messieurs! Yesterday...unfortunate beings, enslaved to the laws of steel and scientific barbarity of the civilization of machines...

(At the mere mention of the name of "Machines" the horrified indignation of the audience rises. The most violent of all is the President; as one says vulgarly, he has "had a bellyful." Over the screen pass herds of man and women, whom the Machines are taking to pasture, or who are harnessed to crushing labors—the edification of Pyramids, the alimentation of blast furnaces...scenes in which the principal machine employed in the labor, seems a pharaonic despot who has himself carried, served and nourished.)

3. Today...free sons of the soil, ornamented with its presents...who drink from its udders swollen with milk and wine.

A vision of Cockayne.

4. The course of human progress is similar to a river; it goes back from the muddy mouth to the the limpid source springing from the pure flank of the summits....

5. In the beginning, movement, perpetual movement...a humankind of broken-down automata, of alienated cities...at the radiant terminus, the repose of the sage, who guards his flocks while blowing into his pipes...

Tender panegyric to pastoral, idyllic, archaic life.

6, Let us salute, Messieurs, this magnificent vision!

The Sage sleeping, while not guarding his flock.

Let it be a pledge for us of the sublime future, when humans will be similar to the blissful beasts, which browse delicious life without thinking!

Apogee of Progress and human genius.

After which, the dances resume. The President, sitting on top of the haystack, blows into an Alpine horn.

Meanwhile, Aviette and Rominet, walking apart, proceed in perfect amour. In the distance, in the beautiful twilight, a flute plays a suave melody in the style of Debussy.

Only one man has remained apart from the festivities, in a corner of the plateau, sitting on a rock that overlooks the valley, with a sullen and absorbed expression. That is Marteau Pilon, the former Master of the Machines. He has not been able to take his part in this natural life, this life without machines. (Already, in the previous scene, he has been seen considering and rejecting with disgust a spade that someone is handing to him.) He is talking to himself. He is making gestures. He is hunched up, like Rodin's *Thinker* or Carpeaux's *Ugolin.* He is drawing feverishly, covering with geometrical figures and numbers the stones that surround him. The two young people, who have perceived him during their walk, approach him covertly, spying on him, look over his shoulder and laugh...

And suddenly, projected in the gold of the setting sun, the formidable shadow is seen of Machines far more monstrous than the previous ones, the dreams of the inventor, which petrify Aviette and Rominet with admiration...

The song of the flute is abruptly interrupted in the middle of a phrase. Distant thunder is heard, and the steely rumble of giant engines.

The terminated cycle recommences...

Acknowledgements

Le Miroir des événements actuels, ou La Belle au plus offrant by François-Félix Nogaret was originally published as a booklet in Paris in 1790; "The Mirror of Present Events; or, Beauty to the Highest Bidder" was first published in *The Mirror of Present Events and Other French Scientific Romances*, Black Coat Press, 2016. The version included here omits some lengthy prefatory material and some of the author's footnotes, which are irrelevant to the story.

"Mademoiselle de La Choupillière" by Jacques Boucher de Perthes was first published in *Nouvelles* (1832). The translation was first published in *The Nickel Man and Other French Scientific Romances*, Black Coat Press, 2016.

"Le Major Whittington" by Charles Barbara was first published in *La Revue Française* in 1858. The translation was first published in *Major Whittington and Other Stories*, Snuggly Books, 2019.

L'Automate, récit tiré d'un palimpsest by Ralph Schropp was first published in 1878 and reprinted as a booklet in 1880. "The Automaton: A Story Translated from a Palimpsest" was first published in *The Nickel Man and Other French Scientific Romances*, Black Coat Press, 2016.

"L'Homme de la Mer" by Arnold Mortier was first published in *Le Figaro* 4 novembre 1883. "The Man of the Sea" was first published in *The Snuggly Sirenicon*, Snuggly Books, 2019.

Ignis by Didier de Chousy, from which "Industria" is excerpted, was first published by Berger-Levrault in 1883, and translated as *Ignis: The Central Fire*, Black Coat Press, 2009.

"Mistress Little" by Edmond Thiaudière was first published in the author's collection *Trois amours singulières*, Librairie Illustrée, 1886; translated as *Singular Amours*, Black Coat Press, 2018.

"Le Mannequin-Man" by Jean Rameau was first published in the author's collection *Fantasmagories, histoires rapides*, Ollendorf, 1887. The translation was first published in *The Mirror of Present Events and Other French Scientific Romances*, Black Coat Press, 2016.

"La Révolte de la machine" by Emile Goudeau was first published in *Les Billets bleus* in 1888 and reprinted in *Le Livre populaire* in 1891. The translation was first published in *The Revolt of the Machines and Other French Scientific Romances*, Black Coat Press, 2014.

"La Terreur future" by Marcel Schwob was first published in *L'Écho de Paris* 7 décembre 1890; "The Future Terror" was originally published in *The Germans on Venus and Other French Scientific Romances*, Black Coat Press, 2007.

"La Révolte des machines" by Henri Ner was first published in *L'Art Social* 3 septembre 1896; the translation, with the author's more familiar signature, was first published in *The Superhumans and Other Stories* by Han Ryner, Black Coat Press, 2011.

"L'Automate" by Léon Daudet was first published in two parts in Le Journal 21 juin 1897 and 16 juillet 1897. "The Automaton" was first published in *The Nickel Man and Other French Scientific Romances*, Black Coat Press, 2016.

"Le Meurtre de l'Américain" by Frédéric Boutet was first published in *Je Sais Tout* 15 janvier 1921. "The American's Murder" was first published in the Boutet collection *Claude Mercoeur's Reflection and Other Strange Stories*, Borgo Press, 2017.

La Révolte des Machines, ou La Pensée déchainée by Romain Rolland was first published by Éditions du Sablier in 1921. The translation is original to the present volume.

OTHER ANTHOLOGIES OF
FRENCH SCIENCE FICTION & FANTASY
by Brian STABLEFORD

News from the Moon
The Germans on Venus
The Supreme Progress
The World Above the World
Nemoville
Investigations of the Future
The Conqueror of Death
The Revolt of the Machines
The Man With the Blue Face
The Aerial Valley
The New Moon
The Nickel Man
On the Brink of the World's End
The Mirror of Present Events
The Humanisphere
Journey to the Isles of Atlantis
The Incredible Adventure
The Queen of the Fays
Funestine
The Origin of the Fays
Tales of Enchantment and Disenchantment

CPSIA information can be obtained
at www.ICGtesting.com
Printed in the USA
BVHW082153010822
643541BV00002B/127